# GANG
# LAND

Dubbed 'Queen of the Underworld', Jessie Keane is of Romany gypsy stock. She was born in the back of her gran's barrel top wagon and fled to London as a teenager, finding there a lifelong fascination with the criminal underworld and the teeming life of the city.

Twice divorced and living in a freezing council flat, she decided to pursue her childhood aim to become a writer. She sold her wedding dress to buy a typewriter and penned her first book, *Dirty Game*. This was followed by further acclaimed crime novels, all *Sunday Times* bestsellers. Jessie lives in Hampshire with her partner.

*By Jessie Keane*

### ANNIE CARTER NOVELS
Dirty Game
Black Widow
Scarlet Women
Playing Dead
Ruthless
Stay Dead
Never Go Back
Dead Heat

### RUBY DARKE NOVELS
Nameless
Lawless
The Edge

### OTHER NOVELS
Jail Bird
The Make
Dangerous
Fearless
The Knock
The Manor
Diamond

# JESSIE KEANE

# GANG LAND

HODDER &
STOUGHTON

First published in Great Britain in 2025 by Hodder & Stoughton Limited
An Hachette UK company

The authorised representative in the EEA is Hachette Ireland, 8 Castlecourt
Centre, Dublin 15, D15 XTP3, Ireland (email: info@hbgi.ie)

3

A CIP catalogue record for this title is available from the British Library

Hardback ISBN 978 1 399 72099 1
Trade Paperback ISBN 978 1 399 72100 4
ebook ISBN 978 1 399 72101 1

Typeset in Plantin Light by Manipal Technologies Limited

Printed and bound in Great Britain by Clays Ltd, Elcograf S.p.A.

Hodder & Stoughton policy is to use papers that are natural, renewable
and recyclable products and made from wood grown in sustainable forests.
The logging and manufacturing processes are expected to conform
to the environmental regulations of the country of origin.

Hodder & Stoughton Limited
Carmelite House
50 Victoria Embankment
London EC4Y 0DZ

www.hodder.co.uk

*To Cliff, who came along for the ride. . .*
*Love, as always*

# DARKE FAMILY TREE

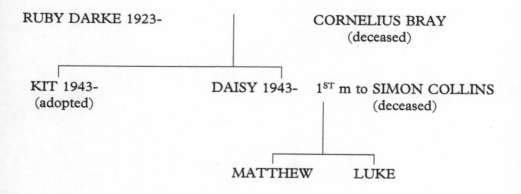

RUBY DARKE 1923-                    CORNELIUS BRAY
                                       (deceased)

KIT 1943-            DAISY 1943-   1ST m to SIMON COLLINS
(adopted)                                (deceased)

            MATTHEW        LUKE

        DAISY    2ND m 1980 to ROBERT HINTON
                        (deceased)

# PROLOGUE

## 1975

The man drove to his home deep in the pitch-dark Berkshire countryside, his mood lifting as he turned the BMW into the drive. He loved his house. It was big, white, impressive. His wife had hated it, called it 'The Mausoleum', said it was miles from anywhere and cold as the Arctic Tundra.

No matter. She was the past, anyway. Of course, he would like to meet someone new, someone who could be a *proper* mother to his kids, not like her. Some lovely docile woman who adored being at home, who would be there waiting for him at the end of the day with the house all warm and welcoming, a hot meal cooked, ready to listen to his woes; that was his dream.

As he pulled up outside the garage block he gave a sharp sigh, seeing the house in total darkness – there was no warm, accommodating woman waiting for him. He'd heat something up for himself, or maybe not bother, just grab a whisky and a sandwich. In the headlights' glare he could see that the damned gardener had left one of the garage doors open again; he had *told* the bloody man about that on more than one occasion. There were thieves out here, and some valuable stuff was stored in the garage. Why didn't the fool listen?

He switched off the engine and all was suddenly blackness and silence, but for the ticking of the engine as it started to cool. He got out, locked the car, stalked over to the open garage door, muttering in annoyance.

'Hey!' said a voice to his left.

He literally jumped. The shock of hearing someone in this place, in this dense, dark country silence, was immense. He whirled around, his heart in his mouth. Saw a shadowy shape, moving.

'Who the hell are you?' he demanded.

The fluorescent strip light that hung from the beams inside the garage flickered on. He saw two men inside, big burly men in black coats. One of them, older and taller than the other, had a long puckered purple knife scar running the length of his left cheek. It was hideous. The scarred one was pushing an old chair into the centre of the concrete floor. The other one . . .

The man felt his bowels grow loose as he saw what the other one was doing.

He turned to run.

The man on his left moved in, grabbed him; another came from the right. He started to resist, but to his shock one of them drew a gun and held the muzzle crushingly against his head.

'Shut up,' he said, and the man instantly stopped struggling.

'What's this about?' he panted out. 'If it's money—'

'It's not money,' said the one with the gun.

Between them they nudged him toward the garage, toward the scarred one with the chair – and the other one with the rope that he had thrown over one of the beams.

It was tied in a noose.

# I

# DAY ONE

**1982**

The explosion occurred at seven o'clock on a summer's evening, outside a large London house. It blew out every downstairs window in the building, scattering spine-sharp slivers of glass and metal shrapnel away from the central blast point. It was lucky no one was walking in the street, or they could easily have been killed. The police said that, afterwards, when they assembled to pick up the pieces – what little pieces remained, anyway.

It was a car that had blown up, a top of the range BMW. The force of the first explosion was so extreme that it lifted the entire thing into the air. And then the petrol tank blew. The noise was so massive that people immediately ran out of houses up and down the road to stare in horror at the flaming wreckage. Alarms on cars blared, rocked by the blast. Someone had the sense to go back indoors and phone the authorities, but most people just stood there, disbelieving.

This was *Hampstead*.

Things like this didn't happen here.

One mother ushered a small child away, averting her own gaze from what she had seen – because beyond the flames, beyond the mangled wreckage, there was a skull-like face behind what remained of the wheel of the car. Burned bones and a roaring inferno. It was *horrifying*. She had to turn away, had to go back indoors to safety, to normality, because this just couldn't be happening.

She knew – well, practically *everyone* knew – the man who'd just got into the BMW and started the engine on this sweet balmy summer's evening. He was one of her near neighbours. Always polite but reserved. A bit *scary*, actually, she'd always thought. Not someone you would easily pass the time of day with. You read about Thomas Knox sometimes in the papers. He was always squiring some glamorous young thing or other about town. One of those girls was now, apparently, his wife. Yes, Chloe. That was her name.

As the police and fire engine sirens came blaring ever closer, Chloe Knox came stumbling out of the door of the house, to where the car sat ablaze on the driveway; the double explosion had rocked the house, sent glass flying out from its shattered bay window. Her face was cut, and blood snaked down in rivulets from several small gashes, staining her pink T-shirt. She saw the car, scrapped and burning, saw black smoke pouring up into the sky. Saw the remains of Thomas – her husband – sitting behind the wheel of it.

Chloe fell to her knees.

Presently, she started to scream.

# 2

# DAY ONE

## 2 hours earlier . . .

Ruby Darke was sitting in the office behind her Soho burlesque club, Ruby's. She'd been toying for some time with
the idea of turning the upstairs stock room into a small
flat for herself. Some weekdays, she stopped overnight at
her son Kit's place rather than schlepp all the way back to
genteel Marlow, but the arrangement wasn't ideal. Kit had
women in sometimes, and it was embarrassing, bumping
into them in the kitchen in the mornings, most of them
wearing very close to fuck-all. At least she hadn't spotted
that copper among them, that DI Romilly Kane. That particular bout of madness appeared to be long over, and that
was, to Ruby, a huge relief.

Out in the main body of the club two of tonight's acts
were warming up. 'Hey! Big Spender' was shrieking out
through the speakers. Her office was barely quieter. The
door was open and she could see the stage from where
she sat. A woman dressed as a Bengal tiger was bouncing
around the front of the stage, cavorting with a man clothed
as an electric blue snake. Their choreographer was shouting
at them in agitation. Behind them was a copper bath, and

a girl dressed in a French maid's outfit was bending over the fake bubbles it contained, saucily testing the heat of the bath water and sending coquettish glances back at her 'audience' of cleaners, bar staff and arriving hostesses.

Ruby was reading the letter spread out before her, the envelope discarded. The letter had been hand delivered through the club's front door this morning, not sent through the mail. She read it once, twice, three times, poring over the words, letting them sink in.

> *I've been a damned fool. Can we try again?*
> *I miss you. Eight o'clock tonight? The usual place?*
> *I'll be waiting.*

With a sudden movement, Ruby crumpled the letter and threw it forcefully into the bin. Then she sat there, breathing hard for no good reason.

Thomas bloody Knox! She thought she'd seen the last of him and now here he was again, crawling into her head, forcing images of him to spring back to life when she had been convinced that all that was dead; finished. The straight, thick dark blond hair. The hard ice-blue eyes. The face, strongly chiselled; a real hard man's face. His tough, solid body, and – oh! – the feel of his skin beneath her fingers. Swimming naked with him in the indoor pool at his house. Making love with him.

But all that was supposed to be done with. Hadn't they agreed that? Yes. They had. Now he had a young wife, and the last Ruby knew there had been a baby on the way, which could almost have made her laugh if she hadn't felt so inclined to cry over it. A baby, and Thomas in his very late fifties. It would drive him nuts.

Still, he'd called it off with Ruby and said he wanted to make a go of it, properly, with – what the hell was her name? Big Tits, Ruby remembered that was what she'd always called her. Ah yes. *Chloe.* What she did recall, much more easily, was dinners with Thomas at the Savoy in the American bar. Then nights spent with him in a river-view suite. That was their place, hers and Thomas's. And he was going to be there at eight o'clock tonight, waiting for her.

She wasn't going to turn up, of course. She didn't want to be that sort of woman anymore; the mistress, the other woman, dancing to attendance whenever her married lover whistled, deceiving the poor bloody cow who was his wife, betraying the 'sisterhood'.

No. Of course not.

Didn't she have enough in her life to feel guilty about, after all? Her son Kit laundered dodgy cash through this very club and she let him. Once, she'd been a legitimate businesswoman. Now? Not so much. She had a minder – Brennan, who was outside the door of her office right now, idly watching the rehearsals – because Kit's way of life made that necessary; washing a little money was the least of it.

Although Kit didn't get into the real nasty stuff like drugs or trafficking, what he did do was run an extremely lucrative protection racket, taking money off traders all around his manor while using several legitimate businesses as cover for his illegal operations.

Sighing, Ruby got the letter out of the bin. Uncrumpled it. Read it again.

Not that she was going.

Not that she cared.

Of course not.

But . . . sod it. She knew she was already mentally trawling through her wardrobe, selecting just the right thing to wear. Thomas had always said that she moved like a jungle cat; he loved her trim body displayed in fire-engine red, loved the heat of it against her dark skin and thick black hair.

But she wasn't going.

No way.

Once again, she threw it in the bin. This time, she let it stop there.

# 3
# DAY ONE

The curtains were drawn, shutting out the remains of the bright summer daylight, plunging the cheaply furnished little room into gloom. Daisy Darke, Ruby's daughter, blinked, adjusting her eyes to the low light level, making out the shapes of the others seated around the table with her. A spasm of misgiving shot through her, but she breathed deeply, calmed herself. She wanted to do this. She *could* do this. She was, after all, not only the daughter of the famous Ruby Darke but also of big, blond and long-deceased Cornelius Bray, and she looked every inch his daughter. Daisy had the healthy complexion, golden-blonde hair, blue eyes and robust build of a Valkyrie – and she had the guts to go with it.

They had met, five of them, total strangers, in this tiny Bermondsey flat high up in a tower block, not far from the Rotherhithe Tunnel, overlooking the river. Mrs Chamberwell, the flat's elderly resident, had greeted them all at the door, given them wine and cakes.

Really, the woman seemed normal enough. She was exceptionally tall, her thin blonde hair scraped back into a purple net that matched her purple cardigan. She wore a white ruffled blouse, a cameo brooch at the throat. She looked like something maybe out of a Victorian painting. But she spoke in a low East End accent, its tone coarsened by a lifetime of cigarettes, and very quickly put them all at ease.

Most of them had arrived anxious, questions on their lips to which they had never been able to get answers. Now, wine and cakes despatched, they sat down in Mrs Chamberwell's miniscule front room at the circular table, and a hush fell.

'Sometimes, they don't come,' Mrs Chamberwell said. 'You mustn't worry about that. But no sudden movements please, no loud noises. Quiet now.'

Daisy was seated opposite Mrs Chamberwell. She saw the dim outline of the woman grow still. There was a moment's hush and then the woman held out her thin, long-fingered hands. 'Join with me please, everyone.'

They held hands. The very fat man beside Daisy had sweaty palms. The woman on her other side had a grip so cold that Daisy almost recoiled. But she wanted to do this. She *had* to do this. She'd lost Rob Hinton, her husband for far too brief a time, last year. She wanted to know he was okay.

She saw Mrs Chamberwell's head go back. The woman took several deep, shuddering breaths.

Daisy suppressed a shiver. Of course it wasn't growing colder in the room. She told herself that, very firmly. She was imagining it. Mrs Chamberwell's breathing grew louder, louder. It was all a bit stupid, theatrical, and she found herself having to suppress an uneasy laugh. Thank God that Daniel her minder – and Rob's younger brother – wasn't in here. He was waiting outside. He would have pooh-poohed the whole thing, scoffed at it, maybe even laughed out loud and offended the poor old dear.

'Is there . . . ?' she started.

There was silence all around the table.

'Is there anybody there?' she went on.

Silence.

They all held their breath.

Then Mrs Chamberwell shook her head, reached out to her left and turned on a rose-patterned standard lamp. It cast a faint creepy glow over the room.

'As I said, sometimes the spirits are reluctant to co-operate,' said Mrs Chamberwell. 'We'll try the board instead. All right?'

There was a murmur of approval. The black spirit-hunting Ouija board was already set out on the table, its neat lines of white letters and numbers clearly delineated, an upturned glass in its centre.

'Index fingers on the glass, please, everyone,' said Mrs Chamberwell.

Everyone obeyed.

'As I say, sometimes—' started Mrs Chamberwell, and then with a tiny jerk the glass started to move.

*Because Mrs Chamberwell is pushing it,* thought Daisy.

The glass juddered sideways, skimming over the surface of the board.

Someone gasped.

The glass settled on D.

'Quiet, everyone,' hissed Mrs Chamberwell.

It was moving again. It scudded across C, then B, and then it settled on A.

'Who's doing that?' asked the woman seated beside Daisy, a nervous laugh edging her voice.

'A spirit,' said Mrs Chamberwell, and took her own finger off the glass as if to prove it.

It *was* colder in here now. Daisy knew she wasn't imagining it. And the damned glass was off again. Now it *raced* over and landed on I. Daisy could feel her heart thudding in her chest like a brass band. Christ, this wasn't funny. Maybe the thing really *was* moving on its own accord.

It skittered across to S.

Then E.

'Daise,' said Mrs Chamberwell. 'Would that be Daisy? Is there a Daisy here? Is anyone trying to get in touch with a Daisy?'

Daisy had to swallow hard, work some spit into her mouth. She felt like all the blood had rushed out of her head and straight down to her feet. Finally, she managed to say. 'My name's Daisy.'

But the thing was off again. It was racing back through the alphabet, racing back . . .

'Whoever is doing this, it's *not funny*,' said the cold-handed woman sitting beside Daisy. She took her finger off the glass, scraped her chair back, stood up.

'Shhh,' said Mrs Chamberwell.

The thing was still moving.

It settled once again on D.

Then it raced away and skidded to a halt on O.

Slipped back and landed on N.

Then went to T.

There it stopped.

'What does it mean?' asked Daisy.

'I was hoping you might be able to tell me that. Is the message what you expected? Hoped for?'

If it was Rob, Rob who'd been shot and killed last year, what was he trying to say to her?

The thing had spelled out a simple message.

Was it *Rob* who'd done that, somehow reaching out to her from the other side? Or was it simply a trick, was it that Mrs Chamberwell had one of her stooges sitting here, shoving the glass about, making it spell out Daise. But she hadn't told Mrs Chamberwell her name – or any of the other attendees, either. She'd given a false name at the door, paid cash, there was *no way* any of them could know her true identity. And it had spelled out more than simply her name. It seemed to be a warning.

The glass had spelled out DAISE DON'T.

Don't *what*?

And there was the other thing, of course. The thing that made her shiver.

It was the fact that it was usually only ever Rob who called her 'Daise'.

And how the hell would anyone else here have known that – except her?

# 4
## DAY ONE

Kit Miller, son of Ruby Darke and in his mid-thirties, was the unlikely-looking twin brother of Daisy. Kit and Daisy were a rare phenomenon born out of Ruby's mixed-race heritage; Ruby's eggs had contained a mixture of gene coding for both black and white skin and – to her and everyone else's amazement – she'd given birth to blonde, blue-eyed Daisy – and at the same time to black-haired, dark-skinned but blue-eyed Kit.

It was a tough time for Ruby way back then. Kit did appreciate it, he understood it, although it had taken him a long, long time to come to terms with it all. She'd had no husband to support her. A career as a Windmill girl and then a reckless affair with Cornelius Bray had resulted in her pregnancy with himself and Daisy. Cornelius's barren wife Vanessa had snatched up Daisy, who was the dead spit of white, blue-eyed, blond-haired Cornelius – for a fee – while dark-skinned Kit had been left to kids' homes and then, later, he'd got lost on the mean streets of London.

Kit knew his mother's life had been a struggle. For years Ruby had been running the family store, expanding, turning it into a nationwide chain, losing all contact with her children. But she had regained that contact. Got them back, and not without difficulty. Kit had hated her for quite a long time, felt abandoned by her, forgotten. He'd suffered but he'd grown tough and eventually – slowly – he'd forgiven her. She'd been in a difficult situation; it hadn't been her fault. He could see that now.

Time did heal. But now there was this problem with Daisy. Kit was annoyed, frustrated about Daisy's inability to let go, to accept that Rob's untimely death last year was not his fault. Daisy was wasting her time, chewing over the past, and where the hell did that ever get you? Right now he knew she was in a Bermondsey flat, trying to get in touch with her dead husband Rob Hinton – who had also been Kit's best friend.

Kit was sitting in the office at the back of Sheila's restaurant in the heart of the city, idly watching the news on the TV. From Sheila's, Kit ran his thriving protection business that stretched its tendrils all around the east of the city and even extended up to the west. He had numerous shell companies on the go – clubs, car parks, car wash firms, all generating legal sources of income; their spare capacity was used to clean his illegal cash. Fats – skinny as a rake – was counting out monies from the various businesses that paid out to Kit, handing over bundles and thick wedges of cash. Young Ashok was lounging against the wall by the TV, cleaning out his fingernails with a penknife when there was a rap at the door. Ashok opened it and Daniel, Rob Hinton's younger brother, came in.

Kit looked up. 'Problems?'

'She's a fucking lunatic,' said Daniel. 'I got nothing else to say.'

'She went, did she? She see that woman over Bermondsey way?' asked Kit.

'She's up there now. Calling back for her in half an hour.'
Kit shrugged. 'If it helps . . .'

'How the fuck can it?' Daniel shook his head. 'Supposing
Rob appeared and said he was fine, what difference would
it make? The poor bastard's dead.'

Kit could understand Daniel's exasperation. After all,
Daniel was the one who'd been appointed – by Kit himself
– to look out for Daisy, to act as her chauffeur and minder,
keep her safe. And it wouldn't be an easy job, because
Daisy had a wild side and Rob's death seemed to have
somehow made that wildness even worse.

Daniel was pacing around in small, irritated circles. Kit
watched him, thinking that Daniel, despite his gripes, was
patient enough for the task in hand. He was a good, safe
pair of hands for crazy Daisy. Daniel might be immac-
ulately groomed in a Savile Row suit, tailored shirt and
Italian leather shoes, but he could cut up rough in an
instant whenever force should be required. Like his old
boss Michael Ward before him, Kit wouldn't allow scruffs
on his team and Daniel toed that particular line beautifully.
He had the super-clean and finely drawn looks of a perfect
specimen of manhood. His blond hair was tightly trimmed,
his khaki-green eyes – so like his brother Rob's – were
sharp as razors; his broad, solid body, shorter than Rob's,
squatter, was taut and ferociously fit.

'I think she still blames me,' said Kit. 'For Rob.'

'She'll come round,' said Daniel.

'Yeah? When?' Kit gave a wry smile.

'Listen,' said Ashok suddenly, indicating the TV.

It was then that they heard the news.

# 5
# DAY ONE

'Another glass of champagne Miss Darke?' asked the waiter, smiling.

Ruby looked up. 'No. Thank you, I'm fine.'

Thomas – the bastard – was late. She'd drained her drink and as the waiter withdrew she glanced at her watch *again*. Eight-thirty now. And here she was, waiting for him, wanting to see him. Kidding herself – oh, she was good at that – that she really didn't care one way or the other whether he actually showed up.

Thomas *fucking* Knox.

The American bar at the Savoy was full of happy chattering diners, and she was sitting here at *his* usual table, marooned in an ocean of silence, alone. Had he played her? Fed her a line, tried her out? Said, I want to see you, but not meant it? Or . . . had Thomas himself sent the note? Maybe he hadn't. Had his bitch wife imitated his hand writing, put it through the door of the club, and was now going to show up herself and say . . .

Well, say *what*?

Ruby stood up, feeling a fool.

She'd worn the red Chanel gown, the one he loved. And the fucker had *stood her up*.

Briskly she snatched up her gold clutch bag from the table and marched out of the restaurant, collected her coat. Then she turned around and to her surprise found her son Kit standing there.

'What . . . ?' she asked, surprised. She walked forward, kissed his cheek. 'You eating here tonight?'

'No.'

'I was supposed to be meeting someone. They didn't show up,' said Ruby.

'I know that. I went to the club to find you. I found the note in the bin. I thought that was over, you and Thomas?'

Ruby heaved a sigh. 'So, what are you doing here then? Is this an intervention? Are you here to save me from myself?' She smiled grimly. 'Too late. I am already saved. He's obviously had a rethink.'

'You'd better come over here and sit down,' said Kit, taking her arm, leading her across to a deep, comfy couch.

Ruby sat, feeling a stab of alarm. 'What is it?'

'It was on the news,' said Kit, sitting down beside her.

'What was?'

'I'm sorry,' said Kit.

'For what? Come on, you're scaring me now. What did you see on the news?'

'He's . . . there's been an accident. Well, not an accident. There was an explosion.'

'*What?*' Ruby stared at his face. 'You're talking about Thomas? Is he hurt? An *explosion*? For God's sake, you mean I've been sitting here cursing him and he *couldn't* come? What the hell are you talking about?'

'Mum.' Kit grasped her shoulders, stared into her eyes and at that point Ruby knew that this was going to be really, really bad. 'I'm sorry. I really am.'

'What . . . ?' Ruby's voice tailed away. She could see the answer in Kit's eyes. 'Oh . . . no,' she said weakly.

'I'm sorry as hell.'

'No . . .' Ruby felt the world sway around her. 'No, no . . .'

'Thomas is dead.'

# 6

# DAY ONE

It was a lovely evening in London. Summer celebrations in full swing. Rooftop shindigs in sky-high gardens. Parties at the V&A. Dances by the river. Champagne corks popping, everyone having fun. People lighting their barbeques in back gardens, music playing, the whole city glorying in the all-too-brief beauty of English summer days. And here was DI Romilly Kane, attending a scene of disaster. Of *murder*.

Romilly was a tall woman of thirty-two with a shock of wild dark curls tied back with black cord. Her eyes were brown and serious, set in a perfectly ordinary pale oval face. Her body was fit and well toned, because she worked hard to keep it that way.

'I hate this job,' she told Derek Potts the dapper bearded pathologist when he pitched up. She'd been at her parents' little celebration for their thirty-fifth wedding anniversary. And then the call had come and now she was here.

There was a big white tent covering the remains of the BMW, which had been literally blown up and had then burst into flames that had ignited the fuel tank. All around, there were scorch marks, broken windows, shards of glass being swept from the pavements now that SOCO had recorded the scene. There were plane trees with their leaves blown off, singed, ruined, standing stark as skeletons in the arc lights already set up by the police. Shadows moved, reporters smoked and crowded together, and there was Derek, with his neat goatee beard covered, his white coverall intact, stepping inside the tent and gesturing for Romilly, who was also wearing the required protective white suit, to join him.

'You hate it? Well I love it,' said Derek. 'How's your dad?'

'Getting very drunk at his anniversary party, which is where I should be, right now.' Romilly's dad had once worked with Derek; Dad had been a sergeant in the Met.

'Smell that?' Derek paused by the blackened bonnet of the car and inhaled deeply.

Romilly was trying very hard not to breathe at all. 'No, what?'

'Marzipan. First guess? I'd say Semtex.'

'Thought that was an Irish thing.'

'It was, some time ago. But now? In general use by every bastard who fancies blowing someone up. Originated in Czechoslovakia, you know.'

'No, I didn't know that.' Didn't *want* to, either.

Romilly was busy checking the scene inside the tent. The police photographer flipped the tent's side back and came in too and started clicking away, taking more photographs. DC Phillips and DC Paddick from her investigative team were right now working their way along the street doing door-to-door, finding out if anyone had seen or recorded anything on CCTV; anything suspicious going on, prior to the explosion. The house on the driveway of which the ruined BMW was parked was being left, for now. That was Romilly's job, telling the nearest and dearest that *their* nearest and dearest had been comprehensively fried to a crisp, and she would do it the instant she got her arse out of this bloody tent.

*I really hate this job,* she thought. And she realised that a year ago, such a thought wouldn't even have crossed her mind. But then – since then – a lot of things had changed.

'Just the one occupant?' she asked.

The 'occupant's' skull was grinning at her through the smoke-blackened, heat-crackled windscreen.

Derek pulled open the driver's side door and the occupant lurched at him like something out of a horror movie.

*Jesus,* thought Romilly, admiring the pathologist's cool. He pushed the corpse back upright and leaned in with a flashlight and took a really close look.

'Derek, would you mind if I . . . ?' asked Romilly, indicating the tent flap.

'No, you carry on. I thought this one might be Special Branch. Didn't expect you,' said Derek. 'But then your reputation precedes you, right?'

She knew that Derek was referring to the incident last year when she had successfully hunted down a rogue gunman and – just as a little side order – solved a years-old cold case that was connected to it.

'Yeah, but I don't think this is anything to do with national security,' she said. 'From what I hear, this chap was a crime kingpin.'

Derek nodded slowly. 'You hear much?'

'A lot. Enough to know that this is most likely gangs.'

'Speciality of yours, I guess.' Derek was bending over the corpse.

*Meaning what?* wondered Romilly. She was touchy on the subject, she knew it. But it was no use biting Derek's head off when he probably meant nothing at all.

Romilly went back outside and stripped off the protective suit. Then the news people were crowding around her.

'Keep back please, this is a crime scene,' said Romilly, and a girl with impossibly glossy brown hair and perfect make-up bustled forward, a soundman and a cameraman orbiting her like satellites around Venus.

'Are you the investigating officer for this case? What's your name? Can you say a few words to camera please?'

The red eye of the camera was shoved at her, very close.

'I'm Detective Inspector Kane. Sadly, there has been one fatality during this incident, and if anyone was a witness to it or has CCTV that can help then will they please come forward, we need to speak to them. Meanwhile, our investigations are ongoing. Thank you.'

'Do you have a name for this fatality?' asked the newsgirl.

'No. Not yet,' said Romilly, pushing through the three of them and away, up the drive to the house. She beckoned DC Phillips, who was standing on the front step of a property three doors away, talking to an elderly woman. Phillips quickly concluded her conversation and came over.

'Anything?' Romilly asked her.

'Not yet. Everyone's shaken up. Poor old girl I was talking to was in tears. Totally unexpected. Really shocking.'

Romilly rang the doorbell. The glass on the front door was crazed from the blast but had somehow – miraculously – stayed attached to the door. The bay window at the front of the house had fared less well; there was a tradesman already working there, nailing boards onto the window frames.

Someone came to the door; opened it.

'What the hell?' asked a thin brunette in a loud voice tinged with just a touch of Belfast. 'The poor cow's in bits

here, what d'you people want, to get all the fucking gruesome details off her? Leave her alone will you?'

Romilly pulled out her warrant card.

'I'm DI Romilly Kane, this is DC Phillips, may we come
in please?'

'Shit! Sorry,' said the woman, and led them inside.

# 7

# DAY ONE

'What's the matter with you?' asked Daisy from the back of the Mercedes.

'What?' Daniel snapped back to attention. After leaving Sheila's restaurant he'd picked her up from the Bermondsey flat and was now taking the road back to Marlow. He hadn't said a word.

'Why am I getting the silent treatment?'

'No reason.'

'Look. I've had a really strange evening.'

*You're not the only one,* he thought.

'Daniel?' Getting no reply, Daisy kicked the back of his seat.

'Hey! Don't.'

'Answer me then.'

'We've had some bad news.'

'Oh? What?'

'Maybe it's not my place to tell you.'

'Tell me what?' Daisy gave his seat another kick.

'I was with Kit and Ashok and Fats at Sheila's and we heard Tom Knox got done.'

Daisy was silent for a long time.

Then she said: 'Not – for God's sake – not *Mum's* . . . ?'

'That's the one.'

'Oh Christ. Does she know?'

'She was due to meet him at the Savoy, apparently. Kit went over there to break the news and now he's taken her home.'

'Oh God.'

'So you're not the only one who's had a bit of a night.' He flicked her a glance in the rear-view mirror. 'So what happened at the séance?'

'What? Oh! Something rather strange, actually.' Daisy was frowning. Thinking of Thomas. Of Ruby, too. It was awful.

'Like what?'

'Well . . .'

'Well, *what*?'

'Rob spoke to me.'

'The fuck he did.'

'He *did*, Daniel.'

'What, like actually *spoke*?'

'Well. Not directly. There was this Ouija board, and it spelled out my name.'

'Oh yeah?'

'Don't say it like that. It happened. It really did.'

'You sure it wasn't Leon?'

Daisy opened her mouth to speak and then stopped. 'That's low, even for you.'

Any mention of Rob and Daniel's missing brother Leon gave her the shudders. He *knew* that.

'All right. I'll give you that. So come on. Surprise me. What did "Rob" say?'

'He said, "Daise don't."'

'Don't what?'

'Only Rob called me Daise. It was Rob.'

'Right. Actually, no. Not right at all. Kit sometimes calls you Daise. I've done it once or twice myself. But don't what?'

'I don't know. And *don't* call me Daise, okay? It's over-familiar and I don't like it.'

'Oh, pardon me. I'll bear that in mind. Listen – it's all bullshit, Daisy. Total crap.'

'I knew you'd say that.'

There was nothing more to say. Resuming his silence, Daniel drove on until he turned the car into the driveway of Ruby Darke's Marlow home. The guy on the gate lifted a hand. Daniel nodded, thinking that he couldn't believe that two people born of the same woman could be so different. Not only in looks but in temperament too. Kit was controlled, cool, emotionally detached; Daisy was the exact opposite – fiery, impulsive, and – dammit – sexy as hell.

Truth was, Daniel had been obsessed with Daisy ever since he was a teenager and Rob had brought her home to meet the family. He knew it was ridiculous. He was mid-twenties now, she was a good ten years older. But the heart wants what the heart wants, right? And anyway – it was *never* going to happen.

Ruby's home was a Victorian detached villa, beautifully renovated by her and set in grounds of about an acre, with a separate garage block over which there were two staff flats, plus well-maintained gardens and a swimming pool.

'Look,' said Daisy, 'I know you think it's all crazy, this séance stuff—'

Daniel cut her off right there.

'Dead's dead, Daisy,' he said. 'Look at what's happened with Tom Knox. He's gone. And he won't be sending any bloody messages, either.'

The Merc crunched to a halt up by the house. Daniel switched off the engine and sat there, saying nothing more.

'Door,' said Daisy, and gave his seat another kick.

Daniel got out and opened the door for Daisy.

'Thanks,' she said, hurrying off toward the house.

'You're welcome,' said Daniel, and followed.

# 8

# DAY ONE

Before they could reach the front door it opened and out came Daisy's blond eight-year-old twins Matty and Luke. Instantly she was all smiles, catching Luke as he barrelled into her arms, while Matt pounded into Daniel, play-punching Daniel's stomach.

'When are you going to teach me some judo moves?' Matt burst out.

'When you learn some self-discipline, grasshopper,' said Daniel, catching Matt up and tipping him upside-down. Matt hollered in protest, grinning.

Daniel set Matt back on his feet.

'You been good?' asked Daniel.

'Good as anything,' Matt assured him. 'Luke wants a duck.'

'What you want a duck for, Luke?'

'That's what I said!' laughed Matt. 'They're squirty things, Dave the gardener told me. They shit all over the place.'

'Matt,' said Daisy.

'Well it's true. A rabbit would be better.'

'We'll see,' said Daisy, catching hold of the pair of them. 'I hope you've been good for Nanny Ruby? Only she's had some bad news and she needs lots of hugs.'

'We've been good,' Matt assured his mother. 'Nanny Vanessa brought us back but we're going back down to Brayfield tomorrow she said. We could have some ducks there on the lake, Luke,' he told his twin.

Daisy had to smile. Luke was always wanting some pet or other, something to cuddle. He was the tactile, sensitive one, whereas Matt blundered through life like a steam train. Both of the boys loved spending time at Brayfield House where Vanessa lived in pretty much splendid isolation except for her gardener/handyman, ex-army Ivan. Brayfield was an endlessly fascinating playground for the boys with its ancient boarded-up clock tower, its vast lake, its creepy family crypt with the inscription over the door – *hodi mihi, cras tibi*: Today me, tomorrow you. That inscription always made Daisy shudder. Particularly so, after the happenings of last year.

'Come on, let's get indoors and you can wash up and then we'll have tea, okay?' said Daisy, and they were off, thundering and screaming into the house.

Ruby appeared at the door. The kids streaked by her and tore up the stairs. Daisy went to Ruby and hugged her tight. 'You all right?' she asked her mother.

'I've had better weeks,' said Ruby sadly.

'Are the boys driving you crazy?' asked Daisy as Daniel got back in the car and drove it round the side of the house to the garage block at the back.

'No, they've cheered me up.'

'I'm so sorry about Thomas,' said Daisy. 'Daniel told me.'

Ruby's eyes filled with tears. 'I can't believe it,' she said.

'It must have been sudden. He couldn't have suffered,' said Daisy.

Ruby drew back, blinking, wiping at her eyes. 'Let's hope so,' she said. 'When Vanessa dropped the twins off here she said Bradley had called in on her earlier in the day.'

'Bradley . . . ?'

'Collins. Simon's father.'

'Oh!' As always, the mention of her ex-father-in-law provoked a little surge of guilt in Daisy. She'd never kept in touch with the Collins, Bradley and Susan, not after Simon her first husband's death. They'd never liked her much; and the feeling had been mutual.

'What did he want?' asked Daisy.

'Oh, it was just a social call. The twins were there at Brayfield and they're his grandchildren too, aren't they. He came over and saw them. Listened all about Luke and the ducks and the rabbits. He was great with them, apparently.'

Daisy put an arm around Ruby's shoulders. Night was drawing in and there was a chill in the air now. 'Come on. Let's get inside.'

# 9

# DAY ONE

Daisy led the way through to the little sitting room at the front of the house. Ruby sat down.

'I couldn't believe it when Daniel told me what happened,' said Daisy.

'I know,' said Ruby numbly. 'It's shocking.'

There was heavy thumping from upstairs as the twins shouted and jumped around, boisterous as puppies. Then Daniel appeared in the doorway. Ruby looked up at him. 'Will you lock up, Daniel? Then you can turn in for the night.'

Daniel lived in the biggest of the flats over the garage block, the one with the view of the garden, at the back of the house.

He nodded and turned away.

Ruby's attention turned back to Daisy. 'I was . . . we were going to meet up this evening. At the Savoy. Our usual place.'

'Mum . . .'

Ruby shook her head. 'I can't believe I'm never going to see him again.'

'I didn't know it was still going on. You and Thomas.'

'It wasn't. We'd agreed it wasn't. And then I got a note through the door at the club, saying that he'd be at the

Savoy at eight and I could come if I wanted to . . . my God. It was never going to happen, was it. Because now this.'

Daisy sat down beside Ruby and rubbed her mother's shoulder comfortingly. 'He couldn't have known a thing about it.'

Ruby turned a desperate gaze on her daughter. 'Do you think so?'

'I'm certain of it,' said Daisy.

'I wonder how she's feeling, right now.'

'Who . . . ?'

'Chloe. His wife.'

'Devastated, I should think. It's awful.'

'I suppose the police will be talking to everyone, asking if he had enemies. Which he did. Lots of them.'

'Mum . . .' Daisy didn't know what to say. Clearly her mother was in shock, sitting there in her favourite red dress and gold heels. She wasn't crying. She was seemingly reacting quite woodenly to the news that her one-time lover had died in such vicious circumstances.

There was a noise upstairs and Kit came down and stood in the open doorway. He looked at Daisy. 'Bad news,' he said.

'Terrible,' agreed Daisy.

'Whoever did this . . .' Ruby gulped. 'I want them found, Kit. You got that? I want them found and I want them punished.'

Kit nodded. 'You got it.' He looked around the room, focused on the window. The curtains were still pulled back, making the warm interior of the room visible from down the driveway. He saw the faint flare of a cigarette being lit, down by the gate; the gates were manned, night and day. He went over, pulled the curtains closed. 'Listen, keep out of this room when you can,' he told Ruby. 'It's too visible from the drive.'

Ruby looked up at him in surprise. 'What? You think someone might . . . ?'

'Best to be sure,' he said.

Daniel came to the door. 'All locked up. I'll go on over to the flat, okay?'

# 10

# DAY ONE

Fabio Danieri lived in Clerkenwell, which was known – because of the large number of Italian immigrants living around Clerkenwell Road or Farringdon or Rosebery Avenue – as 'Little Italy'. He was watching the late evening news in the kitchen of his house and he was smiling. A glum-faced but glamorously made-up newsgirl was speaking of the awful events surrounding an explosion in Hampstead. One fatality. A car bomb. A female police detective was solemnly answering questions.

Fabio flicked off the TV and stretched as luxuriously as a cat. And to think he'd been having a bad day! Suddenly things looked a whole lot brighter. He reassured himself. Preened himself. Yes – all in all, things were going well. Well, they would. Wouldn't they. Because *he* was in charge of the family these days.

*In charge!*

He hugged that phrase to himself like a lover.

Fabio didn't miss his dead brothers Tito and Vittore in the least. He was a Neopolitan, a member of the famed and frightful Camorra by birth. The Mafia? He would spit on them. To the Naples Camorra, the Mafia of Sicily were latecomers, lagging a hundred years behind the founding fathers of the true criminal fraternity.

Fabio was immensely proud of his heritage, of course, and obviously he wanted revenge on the one who had taken his brothers from him, but that was a matter of principal, not of feeling.

The truth was, he had *hated* Tito, his eldest brother, a sharp-suited blue-eyed greybeard who ordered the whole family about, Mama included, like they were his servants and duty bound to obey. When an unknown assassin had slipped a stiletto blade up between Tito's ribs one long-ago night outside a London Docklands development, of course it had been a shock; but really Fabio couldn't claim to be heartbroken – although he had acted the part superbly, of course.

And as for sluggish, squat Vittore, the middle brother – well, things had worked out just fine on that front too, some years back. That *schifosa* Kit Miller, with the backing of Thomas Knox, had turned the tables on poor Vittore during a kidnap handover and – well! – sad to say, Vittore had breathed his last.

A shame, yes?

Oh yes. How Fabio had wailed and cried at Vittore's funeral, just as he had at Tito's, holding up Mama (who had been getting a little frail and – not to put too fine a point on it – *vague* even then) and appearing so distraught that he himself had to be pulled away from Vittore's coffin by Pizza-Face Donato and several others, then helped back to a seat, patted on the shoulder, given water, because Fabio was just *so* upset.

Only, not really.

Not really at all.

Inside, he'd been triumphant.

*All hail King Fabio!*

The youngest of the three Danieri kids (he discounted his absent sister Bianca of course; she was only adopted anyway and she was just a girl, a nothing), Fabio had spent the better part of his young life as an also-ran. Yeah, almost a nothing like his sister. A whipping boy, a lackey for the two elder statesmen of the family.

But he had been cunning, carefully playing the long game. And finally – before Vittore could summon the wit to finally understand his younger brother fully and do the wise thing and kill him – he had been rid of the two in his way. His brothers were dead and he, Fabio, was boss at last!

Sometimes, life was good.

Now, for Fabio, it was very good indeed.

Everything that had been Tito's, everything that had been Vittore's, was now his. *Everything*. The whore houses and drug dens and clubs. The rackets that pulled in thousands every week from the Italian sections of the city. The snooker halls and restaurants and the pubs. He was a rich, rich man.

He still kept this house in Clerkenwell, where Mama still lived. And for quite a while he'd been dissatisfied with it. The place looked downright shabby, he thought, and he would like now, at this stage of his life, to have the place match his own rather more exuberantly baroque tastes. He'd decided on that, and so next week a decorating team were coming in to redo the hallway. Lots of golds, he envisaged. And reds. Dark blue-reds, the red of blood. He would – as a good son should – get a stairlift fitted, redo Mama Bella's upstairs suite to more ably suit her increasing frailty. Also, thinking about it, he was sure that there had once been a cellar here but now there was no sign of a door into it and a cellar would be handy – very handy indeed – for storage when things were being shipped. Drugs. Guns. People. He'd talk to the builders about it. See if they could maybe open it up.

Anyway – right now, he had other things occupying his mind too. He was Neopolitan, after all. He was *Camorra*. Business had to go on, to be conducted. Payments had to be received. Debts had to be settled.

And there was one that never had been.

Now that a satisfactorily large amount of time had elapsed, now that people had begun to relax, to forget that they had crossed the Camorra and would have a price to pay, it was time to settle up.

Oh yes.

Revenge was, after all, very sweet.

Ruby Darke and her family were going to find that out, the hard way. Starting *now*. He'd already done some of the groundwork. Patted a bereaved old soul on the back, sympathised, encouraged thoughts of reprisal. Set wheels in motion.

He paused in front of the hall mirror as he passed it by. Savile Row's finest adorned his trim body. His hair was dark, thick, gleaming. His eyes were a deceptively warm caramel-brown and very deep-set. Really, he was *extremely* attractive. *Terribly* handsome. The best-looking Danieri boy, no doubt about that. He looked up at the portrait of himself that hung at the top of the stairs; of him staring insolently into the distance, wearing a crisp white Gieves and Hawkes shirt, the cuffs turned back to display muscular forearms. And on his right hand, a gold knuckle-duster studded with emeralds. Women adored him. Sometimes he was cruel, cutting; but when he tried, he could be charming. Like his cousin. His cousin Luca would flatter, cajole, yes *charm,* exactly as Fabio directed.

'Where is Maria?' asked Mama Bella, her silver bun askew, her clothes dishevelled and food-stained as she wandered out of the kitchen.

Fabio kissed his mother's cheek, which had the texture of a softly collapsed balloon. Her cloudy old eyes held his, her gaze anxious. He gave her a squeeze.

'She'll be home soon,' said Fabio.

Maria – Vittore's wife – had been gone for years. But the fake news of her daughter-in-law's homecoming seemed to satisfy Bella.

'Any minute now,' said Fabio, and smiled.

'I'll cook something,' said Mama Bella. 'We can all eat together, yes? As a family.'

'You do that,' he said. Let the crazy old bat cook what she liked, who cared?

'I love to have all the family together.'

'Right.'

'What time is Vittore coming home?'

*Never.* 'Soon, Mama.'

'Oh, that's good. And Tito?'

*Also, never.* 'Very soon, Mama. You'll see,' said Fabio, and the doorbell rang.

'There they are now,' said Mama.

But it wasn't Fabio's long-dead brothers. It was his cousin Luca, and he was very much alive.

'You called?' said Luca.

Fabio embraced him warmly.

'A little job for you,' he said.

# I I
# DAY ONE

DI Romilly Kane was in the sitting room of a sprawling 1930s house in Hampstead, watching the blonde bloodstained woman seated opposite having a complete meltdown.

'They only got married a year ago,' the thin brunette was saying while patting the blonde's heaving back. 'This is awful. Can't you leave this? You can see the state she's in.'

'And you are?' asked Romilly.

'Her sister. Nieve. We were in for the evening, doing girly stuff. You know. Watching a weepie, eating popcorn, doing our nails.' She showed Romilly her nails. Bright fuchsia pink. The blonde's – Chloe's – were plum-red, like her fingertips had been dipped in blood. There was a sharp odour of acetone in the air of the room. That and the pungent stench of burning, which was drifting, like the sulphurous scent of hell, through the remnants of the shattered windows.

As Romilly watched, the workman outside placed another board, blocking off another section of the big bay alcove. She'd already asked the two women she was talking to if they wanted to go to hospital, but both had insisted they wouldn't.

'The blast,' she'd warned them. 'It can do unseen damage.'

'No,' they'd both told her firmly, both sitting there with tiny cuts, little rivulets of blood drying on their skins, staining their clothes.

'And Mr Knox . . . ?'

'He was going out. Business meeting, he said,' said Nieve.

'Could Mrs Knox answer, please?' asked Romilly.

'She's in no fit state,' said the brunette.

Chloe Knox was wailing and crying.

'She's had a very hard time of it. She lost a baby last year. And now . . .' the brunette's voice trailed away.

'Your full name?' asked Romilly.

'Nieve O'Malley.'

'Did you see Mr Knox leave, Ms O'Malley?'

'Well, I said goodbye to him, we both did, and then we heard him going out the front door. And then no more than a minute after that, there was this *explosion*. I've never heard anything like it. The windows blew in. We both screamed and I fell off the couch, it was *so loud*. Then when we pulled ourselves upright and looked at the window, straightaway we could see the car out there. We could see the flames. And . . . Thomas. Everything.'

'You didn't go out there.'

'No. We were . . . it was a shock. I didn't even think of phoning the police, someone else in the road must have done that.'

Chloe Knox was straightening herself up, her tears drying a little. She looked at Romilly with bloodshot eyes. One strip of false eyelashes hung down, ridiculously, on her right cheek, unnoticed. 'He's dead. Isn't he,' she said, gulping.

Romilly nodded.

'I'll make some tea,' said DC Phillips, and went off to find the kitchen.

'Mrs Knox, do you know where your husband was going tonight? Do you know anything about this business meeting?'

Chloe shook her head. 'No. I never asked about his business.'

'Has he received any threats?'

Another shake of the head. Nieve put an arm around Chloe's shoulders.

'Can't all this wait?' she asked irritably.

'Sadly no,' said Romilly.

'They have to ask,' said Chloe wearily. 'Just let them do their job for God's sake.' She swallowed hard and said: 'I'm the trophy wife, that's what they call me. When I'm out of earshot. And worse than that, I expect. I'm thirty and Thomas is almost sixty now. He has grown-up children. And Nieve's right, I've been through a bit of a hard time. I did lose a baby last year. And Thomas was playing around.'

'Playing around?' Romilly echoed.

'And now he's gone and I thought we could make things right but now we never will. The truth was, he didn't really want any more kids.' She shrugged. Tears trickled down her cheeks, diluting the bloodstains. 'I'm a young woman. I wanted children. I wanted *his* children. So he was going along with it. But I think he felt pressured. So he was having an affair. I knew about it. I warned her off, more than once. Told her to sling her hook.'

'Who was this woman he was having the affair with?' asked Romilly.

DC Phillips came back into the room with a tray laden with tea, sugar, milk, cups, biscuits.

'Ruby Darke. She runs a club. In Soho.' Her mouth twisted. 'The *whore*.'

'Yes, I've heard of her,' said Romilly, her face showing none of the emotions she felt at this revelation.

She knew damned well that Ruby Darke was Kit Miller's mother. And just last year Romilly herself had been having something of a fling – with Kit. A very bad boy. Red hot. *Smoking*. Also, deeply involved in gangland. She'd tried to resist, but in the end the fling had become a full-blown affair. And was it any wonder? Kit Miller was handsome, well-muscled, with skin the colour of café au lait. His face was as finely carved and nobly serene as an emperor's, his eyes not dark as expected but a fabulously bright icy blue.

Of course, she had seen sense eventually – been *forced* to – and had knocked all that on the head. Told him goodbye, that it was over, that it should never have begun. Then she had waited anxiously for him to get in touch with her superiors and finish her: tell them the whole unsavoury story and get her arse fired.

But he never had.

Slowly, she'd relaxed. Realised he wasn't going to exact revenge for her dumping him. Realised too that she had escaped a potentially disastrous situation by the skin of her teeth.

So – no more bad boys.

And for sure – no Kit Miller.

'So he had grown-up children, you say? Can you give me the name of Mr Knox's ex-wife? Her address?'

Chloe said nothing. DC Phillips poured the tea. At the window, the man finished the boarding-up, casting the room into blackness. Chloe reached out and switched on a cream-coloured table lamp with a marble Romanesque woman seated on its base. Nieve kept patting Chloe's shoulder.

'Have you somewhere else you can stay tonight? Are there other relatives we can contact for you?' asked Romilly.

Chloe shook her head.

'She can come back to my place, with me,' said Nieve.

'Thanks,' said Chloe weakly.

'What else are sisters for?' asked Nieve.

'Mrs Knox? The ex-wife, her details . . . ?' persisted Romilly.

Chloe sighed, reached out and opened a drawer on a low coffee table, took out a book, its cover bright with hyacinth macaws and jungle greenery. She gave Romilly a look.

'How long you got?' she asked.

'What?'

'There's a list of them.'

'Meaning . . . ?'

'There were four wives before me. And he had adult kids, as I told you. Declan's the oldest. There's Evie, and Olivia too. Oh and . . .' Chloe gave a grim smile . . . 'don't forget the mistress. Don't forget Ruby Darke. And you know what? Any one of those bitches could have wanted Thomas dead.'

# 12

# DAY TWO

Ruby woke up the morning after Thomas's death to the sound of someone knocking at the front door. Painfully she pulled herself from sleep, sat up, reached for her dressing gown – and then it hit her again, with a fresh sweep of horror.

*Thomas was dead.*

She'd been in love with him. She still *was* in love with him. Wasn't she?

Why else would she have shown up at the Savoy last night? Showing up there was the same as saying, yes, okay, we're on. She would have spent the night there with him. They would have made love. Then he would have gone home to Chloe his wife, and Ruby would have gone back to her kids Kit and Daisy, to her grandkids Matty and Luke – who were now, after the shocking events of yesterday, gone, staying the rest of the summer down at Granny Vanessa's place in Hampshire. Vanessa had collected them earlier, and the house already seemed deathly quiet without them. And Ruby herself? She supposed she'd go back to running the club, to normality. What else could she do?

Really, Thomas had had her dangling on a string. Everything *his* call, never hers.

She knew it. Hated it, really, and resented his power over her. But that was love. She'd been in love before – with Michael Ward, Kit's old boss. He'd been another powerful gang lord like Thomas. There was something just so *sexy* about that type of man, so alluring and so fucking *dangerous*. What else could you do but give in?

There came a knock at her bedroom door.

'Yes?' Ruby went to the door, opened it a crack.

It was Daisy.

'Mum, the police are here. They want to speak to you.'

*And so it begins,* thought Ruby.

'I'll be right down,' she said.

DI Kane was waiting in Ruby's sitting room at the front of the house, along with a large blonde female DS who was intently examining the large display of carefully lit China figurines in the wall unit. When Ruby entered, the blonde turned her attention to her. DI Kane rose to her feet.

'Ms Darke,' Romilly greeted Ruby. 'I'm DI Kane.'

'Yes – I remember you.'

Romilly indicated the blonde with her. 'This is DS Bev Appleton. You've heard the news? About Mr Knox?'

'I have. We were due to meet,' said Ruby. 'Last night.'

'Where?'

'The Savoy. At eight o'clock. But he didn't show.'

'What time was it when you realised he wasn't coming?'

'About eight-thirty I suppose. When Kit – my son, you know Kit? – he arrived and told me what had happened. Please, sit down.'

Yes, Romilly knew Kit.

They sat. DS Appleton started taking notes.

'This must be hard for you,' said Romilly. 'I'm sorry.'

Ruby shrugged, said nothing.

'I have to ask – what precisely was the nature of your relationship with Mr Knox?'

'I think you already know the answer to that.'

'Nevertheless . . . ?'

'We were lovers. I'm not particularly proud of that fact. I knew he was married.'

'I see.'

'But sometimes these things are not easy to extract yourself from,' said Ruby. 'I'd tried. And then I got a note from him yesterday, and we were back on. Stupid, or what?'

'Ms Darke, had you and Mr Knox argued recently? Fallen out?'

'No. Why do you ask that?'

Romilly shrugged. 'Maybe you were tired of being given the runaround by a married man and you snapped and decided to end it – finally – in a particularly violent way.'

A figure appeared in the doorway that led out into the hall. It was Kit.

'Okay in here?' he asked his mother. Then his eyes fell on Romilly. 'Detective. How are you?'

'I'm fine,' said Romilly.

'Would you like Daisy in here with you?' he asked his mother.

'No. It's okay, Kit. Really.'

Kit's gaze went back to Romilly. 'Detective,' he said again, and turned away, walking back along the hallway to the kitchen.

Aware that DS Appleton was looking at her, waiting for her to speak, Romilly cleared her throat and said: 'Ms Darke, can you give me any information at all about what's happened to Mr Knox?'

'No,' said Ruby. 'I can't. Now, if that's all . . . ?'

# 13
# DAY TWO

When the interview was at an end, DS Appleton went on out to the car. Romilly would have followed, but Kit stopped her with a hand on her arm. Fats passed them by in the hall and Kit turned to him briefly.

'Start the car, yeah?'

Fats nodded and, pushing past Romilly with a mocking smile, he went out onto the driveway.

'What the fuck are you playing at?' Kit asked her flatly.

'What do you mean?' asked Romilly, shaking her arm free of his grip.

'I *mean* treating her like a suspect.'

'Your mother? That's exactly what she could be.'

'You're kidding, right?'

'Until I know more about this case, that is precisely what I mean. I'm not kidding.'

Kit folded his arms and looked at her. 'She's upset.'

'So's Chloe Knox,' said Romilly, watching Fats going down the drive and shoving Bev Appleton aside as she waited by their car. He sauntered on, down to a long black A Class Merc which was parked near the gates. Its lights flashed as he pressed the key to unlock it.

'Chloe Knox? She's a piece of work,' said Kit. 'You seen her? All false tits and fake eyelashes.'

'Yes, I've seen her. What's your meaning?'

'She loved his money. Not him.'

'Just because she doesn't fit with your profile of an ideal woman, that doesn't make her a husband killer. You have any proof of these allegations?'

'Such a hard-nosed cop,' said Kit.

'That's what I am.'

'Not always.'

And it was all there, between them. The affair just last year. Ill-advised to say the least. A respected and accomplished Detective Inspector, rolling around in bed with mob royalty? No. She'd had to come to her senses, she'd had to see how stupid it was. Yes – ill-advised. So had come the break-up and the inevitable fallout. Romilly had saved her career by the skin of her teeth, stepping away from what could only ever be, for her, a disastrous situation. Ignoring his calls, ignoring *him*, and that hadn't been easy.

Seeing him today was a shock. She couldn't deny it. His physical impact on her appeared to be undiminished. It was the attraction of opposites, the lure of the dark side, and God how it tugged at her. She was squeaky clean, having worked her way up from the bottom of the force to a position very near the top and *he* – well, he was a mobster. He'd cut his teeth as a breaker – that was a breaker of bones – for the long-departed Michael Ward, then assumed control of Ward's manor, specialising in protection, security; strong-arm stuff. Not drugs, she knew. Not trafficking. Not prostitution either. Any of those and she would never have been able to forgive him, would – she hoped – have found the will never to have got involved with him in the first place. Now all that was *over*. Reluctantly, she'd discussed it with her dad, who'd been a copper himself – not with her mum, God forbid, because Mum's interests lay in her daughter finding a nice man, getting married, producing grand-children, and Romilly couldn't see that on her agenda, not now, not ever.

Dad had said for God's sake ditch him. Kick him *straight* to the kerb.

So she had. But there was no way she could pretend it had been easy.

'Goodbye, Mr Miller,' said Romilly, and turned away to join DS Appleton down by the car just as Fats got into the A Class Mercedes beyond it.

There was a sucking-in feeling, a sensation of air being pulled in like a vortex – and then the Mercedes exploded.

# 14
## DAY TWO

The world had gone deathly quiet, apart from this weird constant *humming* in Kit's ears. He looked – and he could *see* it; but he couldn't, not yet, believe his own eyes. Near the bottom of the drive, the Mercedes Fats had just started was a flaming wreckage. Bits of metal and glass were raining down, tinkling onto the driveway and thudding into the lawns and flowerbeds. Smoke was billowing up into the sky. Something hard had hit him in the ribs when the car exploded and there was pain there – Romilly Kane's elbow, maybe? She had been pushed by the force of the blast hard up against him. Now she pulled back, eyes closed, and fell against the house wall.

Having been much closer to the centre of the blast, DS Appleton was now sitting hunched on the gravel drive beside her car, blood pouring from her nose. He saw Romilly right herself, unsteady on her feet, put her hands to her ears, saw her eyes open wide in alarm and meet his.

Romilly's head turned to take in the scene on the drive. He saw her start to stumble down there to assist her colleague. Saw her fall onto her knees beside DS Appleton and shout something at her. Eyes shut, DS Appleton didn't respond. Then Romilly staggered to her feet and grabbed the car keys out of the fallen woman's hand. Shaking, she got the front passenger door open, reached in, said something he couldn't hear.

Then abruptly the world crashed back in. The humming stopped and sound was back, shockingly loud. The crackling of the fire. Ruby, coming charging out of the house, Daisy at her side, both of them asking *what the hell . . . ?* Grabbing at him. Asking him questions. Daniel came out, grabbed the pair of them and swept them back indoors.

'*Back-up! And an ambulance,*' Romilly was shouting. '*Officer down! Quick. Send help . . .*'

Romilly dropped the transmitter and sagged against the car seat. Kit shoved himself away from the house wall and when he got to her – himself unsteady, weaving on his feet, in a state of real shock – Romilly was half out of it, barely clinging on to consciousness.

Even at twenty feet away, Kit could feel the monstrous heat of the fire. The A Class was sizzling and popping, a pyromaniac's delight. He looked at what remained of Fats behind the wheel. He looked at the police car, which by good fortune hadn't been parked *too* close to the A Class, or it would probably have already gone up too. The Merc's diesel tank hadn't blown yet. Feeling the heat of the burning motor, he was anxious about the police car's proximity to the flames and the petrol in its tank. The guy who'd been manning the gate was standing there, open-mouthed.

'Get back,' shouted Kit, and he scuttled out into the road.

'We have to move her!' Kit then yelled in Romilly's face.

'We can't!' she yelled back. 'We could do her more damage . . .'

Both of them were struggling to make themselves heard above the noise of the flames.

'We have to! The tank could go up at any second. We're too close!'

Not waiting for her reply – argument or agreement, he didn't care – he grabbed Bev Appleton under the arm, ignoring the pain in his ribs, and hoisted her up.

Seeing this was going to happen whether she agreed or not, Romilly grabbed Bev on the other side and together she and Kit half-dragged, half-carried Bev away, up the drive to the house's porch.

The instant they reached it, the Merc's tank exploded.

They fell against the house wall in a tangle of arms and legs.

Seconds, later, overheated by this fresh blast, the police car went up with an ear-shattering *boom*.

Kit and Romilly clung to the wall. Bev lay on the ground beside them, eyes closed.

Then in the distance, coming ever closer, Kit heard the sirens.

For once in his life, he was damned glad to hear them.

# 15

# DAY TWO

After the explosion, the police swamped Ruby's place. Then the fire brigade arrived, and an ambulance followed swiftly, too. The medics scooped up DS Appleton and hurried her to the hospital, sirens roaring; they ferried her off on a stretcher and she'd been spark out, her face white and bloodied beneath an oxygen mask.

Now Kit was sitting in a corner near to a nurses' station at the hospital. There was a constant low-level hum of activity. His ribs hurt; actually, he thought it possible that one of them was broken, but he was alive. He'd spent a tedious couple of hours batting well-meaning medics away, assuring them that he was okay, really he was, and no he didn't want to slip into a cubicle and be examined, he was *fine*.

Before coming here, he'd talked to his boy on the gate of the house. The Merc had been sitting on the driveway all night, and it was clear that someone had got at it without attracting attention and placed an explosive device on it. And he was supposed to believe that his guy had seen *nothing*?

'Boss, I'm sorry,' he'd whined. 'I got to take a piss in the hedge sometimes, it must have happened then.'

'Somebody pay you?' Kit asked him.

'What, boss?'

'They pay you to look the other way? That what happened?'

'No, I would never—'

'You're sacked. Piss off out of it. If I ever see you again, you'll be sorry.'

He'd put a different man on the gates, one of his old boss Michael Ward's tough and dedicated old soldiers.

Now here was Romilly, walking toward him. She looked steadier. But she was still pale and her navy-blue trouser suit was dusty and torn at the knee from where she'd pitched down onto the gravel of Ruby's driveway. She slumped down in the chair beside him. Tipped her head back. Closed her eyes.

'How is she?' he asked.

'Okay. It was the force of the blast, she was so close to it. It shook her up, but they say there's no real damage. A couple of days' rest, she should be as good as new.'

'That's good to hear.'

'You?' asked Romilly.

'You stuck your elbow in my ribs, that's all.' He didn't add that the force of the blast had turned her arm into a hard projectile, hitting his mid-section like a piledriver. 'You?'

'Sorry. No, I'm fine. Have they checked you over?'

'No, they haven't, because I'm fine too. Have they checked *you*?'

'Yeah. No problems, they tell me. Shit! That was scary.'

'It was a shock.'

Romilly sat there, hands clasped on her knees. She dropped her head and stared at the floor. Then she said:

'This isn't good at all, is it. First Thomas Knox, now . . . what was his name?'

'We all called him Fats. Sort of a joke, because he was so skinny. His real name's Kevin Norton.'

'He works for you.'

'He did. Yeah.'

'For long?'

'For years.' Kit thought about that with regret. Fats had been an integral member of the team. A trusted friend and employee. And how the *fuck* was he going to tell Fats's mother about this? And there was more. Much more. 'The fact is, it should have been me in that car.'

'*What?*'

'If you hadn't arrived on the scene, it would have been. I was just going out to get in the car but then there you were, giving Ruby a hard time and I didn't even think about it, I just said to Fats—'

'I heard you. You told him to start the car.'

'Because I wanted to hang around indoors and hear what you were saying to her.'

'Kit Miller, the protective son,' said Romilly. 'That's a new one.'

'It's as much of a surprise to me as it is to you.'

'So *you* should have been the victim in the car.'

'Got it in one.' She'd saved his life, simply by being there. The irony of it. A cop was his own personal guardian angel. A cop who, incidentally, had up until the tail end of last year also been his lover.

'Jesus,' she said.

'Yeah.'

'Has something been going on between your lot and Thomas Knox?' asked Romilly.

'Such as . . . ?'

'I don't know. Territorial dispute maybe?'

'I've known and worked alongside Thomas Knox for a very long time. There is no dispute. There never has been.'

'His wife's in bits.'

'Of course she is.'

'She's in distress and it seems genuine.'

'Chloe Knox is perfectly capable of playing the bereaved widow.'

'That's harsh. She says he had other wives. Ones who hated him. I'll be speaking to them all, soonest.'

'What, hated him enough to do him over? I don't think so. And how would that tie in with what happened at Ruby's today?'

'Look, we've got ourselves something of a situation here.'

'We have.'

Romilly looked at him. 'I mean *us*. The force.'

'Well I mean us, as in you and me.'

'Shut up will you? This could be a pattern developing. I'd like to get to grips with whoever's doing all this before it goes any further.' Romilly stood up. 'And can I just make something else perfectly clear?'

'What?' Kit looked up at her.

'There is no you and me,' she said. 'I think you saved my life today. And Bev's. So thanks. But you just keep out of this.'

Kit watched her walk away, past the nurses' station, on down the corridor and out through the swing doors.

*That is one damned impressive woman,* he thought. Cold as fucking ice, too. He couldn't forget the way she'd told him it was over, that it had been a mistake and that it should never have begun. Maybe she'd been right about that. But

what they'd had between them had been hot, passionate –
and wildly addictive. Watching her now, he still felt the pull
of it. He wondered if *she* did, too.

He thought of how narrowly he'd cheated death today.
It wasn't the first time, either. He definitely wanted it to be
the last.

Now Fats was dead.

And Thomas too.

Keep out of it?

Fuck *that*, he thought.

# 16

# DAY THREE

Jean, Thomas Knox's very first ex-wife, opened the door to her house and found her adult son Declan standing there on the doorstep. He'd already broken the bad news to her about Thomas. Jean didn't have a TV and she never listened to music. She'd been in the garden, peacefully watering the geraniums in her greenhouse, when the call came through from Declan, telling her that his dad and her ex-husband Thomas – who had been married to her for fourteen years before that cow Ursula pitched up and ruined the party – was dead, killed in an explosion.

'Is it true then?' she asked her son.

Jean was an ordinary-looking woman in her early sixties, thin and not particularly tall, her faded hair tinged with grey, her unremarkable brown eyes peering at her son through thick rimless glasses. She was wearing an old brown pair of leisure trousers and a thin white top dotted with lavender sprigs. Her hands were worn, her fingernails cracked from hours working the soil.

*No wonder Dad left her,* thought Declan.

It was an uncharitable thought. Cruel and uncalled-for. He stepped forward and hugged her. Spoke against her hair. 'I'm sorry. It's true.'

'But who . . . ? Why?' she asked, her voice trembling, on the verge of tears.

'Don't know. The police don't either.'

'But what will they do? Is . . . is *she* going to see the body? Identify it?'

*She* was Chloe. The latest wife in a long line of them. Declan shook his head.

'They've asked me to do that,' he said. *Not that there would be much left*, he thought. But he didn't share that thought with his mother. He supposed she must still retain some affection for her long-departed ex, even if he *had* been a cheating bastard. He guessed – hoped, maybe – that his parents had been wildly in love, way back when. Hearing about Dad being blown to bits was hardly – bitterness at his betrayal notwithstanding – likely to delight his mother.

'Come in, come in,' she said, and led him through to the kitchen where a massive cream-coloured Aga pumped out remorseless heat, even on these hot summer days.

Declan took his jacket off, slung it over the back of a chair at the table. Loosened his tie. Sat down, pulled out a chair so that she could sit too. Jean did so. She stared at her son.

'I can't believe it,' she said weakly, and groped for a hankie up her sleeve and wiped at her eyes with it.

'Neither could I,' said Declan. 'Has to be one of the other gangs, don't you think?'

'That was your father,' sniffed Jean. 'Always getting into things he shouldn't.'

Declan glanced around the kitchen. Dad might have been a crook, but he'd certainly profited from his misdeeds and so had his 'families', the whole succession of them. This cottage was old. It was in an area of outstanding natural beauty. In all its thatched and beamed beauty, it was worth a fortune. When Thomas had run for the hills with that model-type whore Ursula he had at least done the decent thing and signed over this place in its entirety to his first wife Jean. For that, Declan supposed he should be grateful to his father. Not that he was. For as far back as he could remember – yeah, back to his fourteenth birthday when he had come home from school to find his mum crying on the stairs, abandoned by the man she loved – ever since then he had both admired and despised the old goat. But Declan was Thomas's only son, and so it was inevitable that he should be included in the business; he'd learned it from the ground up.

Declan knew that it would have broken his mother's heart to lose this house. To have been dumped was bad enough, but dumped *and* impoverished? That would have been the total pits. More than anything, his mother couldn't have stood losing the garden. She *lived* for that damned garden. Seemed not to care much about anything else, really. She spent every winter by the inglenook in the living room planning, poring over seed catalogues; then every spring she was out planting things; every summer was spent watering, tending to the tomato plants and the runner beans; and in the autumn she was sweeping up, making leaf mould from the oaks and beeches that surrounded the plot, bundling the leaves into plastic bags, stabbing holes in the bottom of them and watering them to make them rot down and create more compost for the garden.

'Mum,' said Declan. 'Dad's not the only one who's been killed.'

'What?' Her mouth dropped open in surprise. Once, his mother had been a strikingly good-looking woman. Now her skin looked like it needed an iron, and her hair, once a magnificent conker-brown mane, was scraggy, unkempt and mostly grey. Still, some hint of her former youthful beauty remained, tantalising, not there at times, at others very apparent – spoiled, though, by the seemingly permanent look of disapproval on her face.

'There's been another one of these car bombs out at Marlow. At Ruby Darke's place. Killed a bloke.'

Jean looked suitably gobsmacked. Then she said: 'Ruby Darke? But that's . . .'

'Dad's latest girlfriend. The one he's been cheating on Chloe with.'

Declan could see it in his mother's eyes – yes, she knew all about the scandalous Ruby Darke. Knew about Ruby's reputation as a high-flying businesswoman, the once-owner of the Darkes department stores, now a Soho club owner and with – apparently – ties to the underworld, never proved, always denied.

'Then this is . . .'

'I dunno what the fuck it is, Mum.' Declan puffed out his cheeks. 'But first Dad and then again at her place? Seems far too much of a coincidence, wouldn't you say?'

'My God. This is awful.'

Declan nodded. 'Yeah. It is. But I suppose this sort of shit can happen when you keep not only a posse of wives but also a stable of whores. Christ knows, *someone* is going to get pissed off with you.'

'Declan!'

Declan shrugged. 'You know it's the truth. You reckon Ursula's had a visit yet? Or Avril? Or Gilly?'

These were Thomas's *other* wives, the ones who had preceded Chloe.

'Have the police any idea . . . ?'

'I don't know. No doubt we'll find out.' Declan paused, his eyes speculative. 'You don't think it had started up again, do you? Him and Ruby Darke? Maybe *this* has something to do with *that*?'

'I don't know. How is . . . how is *she* taking it?'

*She* was Chloe. The fifth – the *final* – wife.

'She's a tough cookie,' said Declan. 'She'll cope.'

There was a knock at the door.

'Tell them to go away,' said Jean, clutching her forehead. 'Whoever it is. I can't cope with visitors right now.'

Declan went out into the hall, opened the front door.

A tall dark-haired woman in a navy trouser suit was standing there, a scruffy and corpulent middle-aged man at her side. She held out a card.

'I'm DI Kane,' she said. 'This is DS Jones. Can we have a word with Mrs Jean Knox?'

'She isn't called that anymore, not since my parents split. She uses her maiden name. Coyden. Jean Coyden.'

'It's important we speak to her.'

Declan nodded. 'We heard the news.'

'And you are . . . ?'

'Declan Knox. Thomas Knox's son.'

'I'm sorry for your loss, Mr Knox. Truly. If we can come in and talk to you and your mother . . . ?'

'Okay,' said Declan, and opened the door wide.

# 17

# DAY THREE

Daisy hadn't wanted to go out as she'd planned, not after yesterday, not after the day before that. Scary things were happening. Two explosions. And the weird stuff at the séance. She felt shaky in the extreme, thinking of Fats dead, Thomas dead, of her mother sitting there like a rock, unmoving. And the astral messages from Rob. A confidence trick, or the real deal?

Ruby was tough.

Much, much tougher than her daughter.

Daisy knew it. She knew that she herself was frivolous, sometimes careless. Knew that it was just her nature; there was nothing to be done about it.

'Go out,' Ruby had ordered her. 'Whoever's doing this, we're not going to let them win. Okay? Go out. Keep Daniel close but go out, live your life.'

So here was Daisy, in Annabel's, and the music was intoxicating, Bryan Ferry was smoochily crooning 'Jealous Guy' and she was swaying to the beat of it, trying to lose herself in the thunderous noise of it, trying to forget all that had happened, trying to . . .

'Hello?'

She opened her eyes and there was this extremely hand-some man standing in front of her. Dark hair, dark eyes. Well dressed. Quite tall.

He smiled. The strobes lit up his teeth; his smile was dazzling, like a toothpaste commercial.

'Hello,' she replied.

'Dance . . . ?' And he started swaying to the rhythm of the song, pulling her into his arms. She didn't object. It was wonderful, just drowning in the music and the admiration she could see in this dark stranger's eyes.

She didn't have to think about pain and loss. The anguish on Ruby's face. The explosions. Oh God . . .

'You all right?' he was asking her, leaning in close.

'Fine,' she said.

'Let me buy you a drink?'

She nodded. He was *gorgeous*. She followed him to the bar.

'What's your name?' she asked him.

'Luca,' he said with a smile. 'Luca Romano.'

Much later, Luca went to the Danieri house in Clerkenwell and reported that evening's happening's to Fabio.

'We're meeting again,' he told his cousin, his boss.

'She fell for it?'

'Oh yeah.' Luca flashed a confident smile. 'Did you ever doubt it?'

# 18

# DAY FOUR

Daniel was snapped rudely awake by someone tapping close by his ear. Jolted from sleep, he looked around in bewilderment. He'd fallen asleep in darkness and now it was daylight. The sun was shining. Morning was here. He was sitting behind the wheel of the car. His neck ached, and Daisy was glaring at him through the window. She tapped the glass again, hard. He let the window down and smelled booze and a musky whiff of marijuana wafting off her, like perfume.

'Why couldn't you have parked right outside? I couldn't find you,' she complained.

'There are these things called traffic wardens,' he said, yawning.

The square outside Annabel's had been teeming with life late last night. Having dropped Daisy off and seeing a uniformed warden stalking toward him, Daniel had parked in Hill Street, just around the corner from Berkeley Square. Then he'd fallen asleep, and now he had a kink in his neck, he wasn't in the best of moods and – yet again – the cheeky mare was having a go at him, having danced the night away while her mother Ruby was at home in bits.

'Traffic wardens are not my problem,' she rapped out in her cut-glass Home Counties accent. Then she stood there, staring at him. 'Door!' she said when he didn't move.

Daniel got out, opened the back passenger door for her. Daisy got in.

With exquisite patience, Daniel closed the door after her with a snap. Then he got back behind the wheel. Of course, fines only existed in a parallel universe to the one Daisy Bray – now *Darke*, he reminded himself – inhabited. As the late and not-much-lamented Lord Cornelius Bray's daughter, she'd been raised to always expect someone else to attend to the smaller details of life. He gave her a level stare in the rear-view mirror.

Daisy stared right back. '*Well?*' she asked, when he didn't start the engine.

Daniel turned the engine on and the radio blared into life. An incident on Blackfriars Bridge. Congestion on the North Circular. An upcoming interview with Geraldine Rees, who'd this year made history as the first female jockey to complete the Grand National. More guff about the royal baby. Then Dexy's Midnight Runners started telling Eileen to come on.

'Will you shut that thing off? I've got a headache,' said Daisy.

Daniel ignored that. He floored the accelerator and headed back to Marlow.

'I thought you might have wanted to stay with Ruby last night,' said Daniel. 'After what happened yesterday.'

He'd been very careful with this car, checking underneath, checking *everything*, before he took it out of the garage and ferried Daisy to her destination. He couldn't forget the sight of Fats going up in flames in the Merc on Ruby's driveway. He really didn't want to repeat that.

'She insisted I go out,' said Daisy. 'She had Kit with her, she was okay.'

After a pause, Daniel said: 'Going down to see the twins this weekend?'

'No, not this weekend. They're fine with Vanessa. She's looking after them and really that's for the best after . . . you know . . . Thomas and Fats and everything.'

'I think you should have stayed with Ruby last night,' said Daniel.

Daisy stared at him. 'Excuse me?'

'You heard.'

'She *insisted* I didn't change my plans.'

'And you didn't.'

'What are you implying?'

'Why are you such a selfish cow?' he asked.

'Look,' said Daisy, annoyed. 'You work for my family, don't forget that. I didn't ask for your opinion and I don't want it. Okay?'

'Gotcha,' said Daniel, and that was the last word they exchanged throughout the journey home to Ruby's place.

Daisy sat back, relaxing. All right, bad things, *terrible* things had happened. But right now? Not even Daniel bloody Hinton could ruin her good mood. She'd met a fabulous man in Annabel's last night and couldn't suppress a shiver of excitement about it. Luca Romano. Italian. *Gorgeous*. Tonight, she was seeing him again so she had to get home, rest up, select something stunning to wear, something that would blow his mind. She'd get Daniel to drop her off at London Bridge and then she'd walk over to Leadenhall Street, to the restaurant – one of a chain, apparently – that Luca's family owned.

She couldn't wait.

But . . .

*Terrible things . . .*

She thought of the explosion that had killed Thomas. The *second* explosion, that had killed Fats. Maybe she *should* have stayed home, with Ruby. But this man . . . oh, she'd liked him. Very much. No matter what anyone said, not even that tame gorilla behind the steering wheel.

She felt the first surge of untainted happiness she had felt in the whole low, grim time since Rob's death. Was it so bad, to want to be happy, to want to go on with life?

Tonight, she was meeting up with Luca again.

When they'd danced together, she'd not been thinking about Rob or that strange spiritual message of his or anything like that; she was just having pure clean *fun*. The Italian boy was so sexy. Very attractive, meltingly Latin. Charming. She rolled his name around on her tongue, silently. *Luca Romano*. Even his name, he'd told her, meant *charming*. And despite herself – yes – Daisy had been charmed.

# 19
# DAY FOUR

If you ever wanted info, Ashok was your boy; he'd been taught, and taught well, by Fats. A pang of real horror hit Kit's midriff when he thought of Fats, dead. His old mate. Comrade of a thousand dodgy deals and a ton of aggro. Up in a puff of smoke. *Gone*. Ruby's driveway was still scorched, still closed off. A police crime scene. Not, he thought, that the police would care all that much. Gangland stuff, Romilly's workmates would say. Sod them. Let them rot in hell. And after Romilly dumped him last year? Yeah, she'd say the same.

'He had five wives altogether,' Ashok told Kit while they sat in Ruby's kitchen at the back of the house. She was upstairs, taking a nap. Shattered, the poor cow. Ashok tossed a notebook to Kit. 'It's all in there, all the details.'

'What about the rest of the gangs? You think this could be one of them? Thomas had a lot of enemies.' Kit thumbed through the pages, pausing here and there. 'And me. Christ knows I've got a few.'

'We'll see,' said Ashok. 'Who knows yet. I got everyone out, ears to the ground. And you're right. This wasn't just a hit on Mr Knox, it was a hit on you too.' Ashok paused, thinking. 'The Francis mob weren't keen on him, were they? And he helped you out over that Danieri situation . . .'

'Come on, that was years ago. Six, seven years maybe.'

'You think the Camorra ever forget? Think on.'

'And these in here. His wives. What do you know about them? Give me a broad outline.'

'The first one's Jean. He lasted just a bit over fourteen years with her. Had a son with her, Declan.'

'Of course I know Declan.' Kit and Declan were of an age. They'd kicked arse around the town together as teenagers. 'He's sound. Always backed his father. Although he never seemed to like him very much.'

'Jean's reverted to her maiden name, Coyden. Lives in the country, Herefordshire. Declan remained a Knox. Could have changed it I suppose, but he didn't.'

'Right.'

'She calls the rest of the wives "the gang".'

'That don't sound complimentary.'

'It's not. Lots of bad feeling there. The second wife, I think of her as "The Beauty". Look, you see it? That's Ursula Grey. She took her maiden name back too.'

Kit looked and saw that rare thing, a perfect genetic sculpture; Ursula was stunning. Tall, black-haired, very thin and excessively beautiful.

'Mind you, that was taken a while ago when she was in her absolute prime. She was a model. Still is I think, though the work's thinning out. Story as old as time, isn't it? The first wife let herself go, Thomas met *this,* got felled by her like a bull calf by a hammer blow, and bingo. Her address is in there. Olympia, London. One kid, a girl, Evelyn, and then nothing.'

'Right.'

'Now we're onto wife number three.' Ashok paused. 'Jesus! Wouldn't it have been easier – and cheaper – to have affairs? What did he have to go and marry them all for?'

'S'pose he could afford it,' said Kit. 'Number three?'

'Number three is Avril Gulliver. She took her maiden name back too. Horsey type. Runs a stud down in Hampshire these days. Address is there. One child off Knox – a daughter, Olivia. Couple of pics of the both of them there too.'

Kit looked. One shot showed what was clearly a blonde mother and a bulky blonde daughter, both wearing jodhpurs and crossing a stable yard, the mother – pretty enough, but no Ursula – leading a beautiful grey horse with the distinctive dish face and arched tail of the pure desert Arabian.

'Number four?' asked Kit.

'Gilly Taylor-Black. Dad's an earl or something like it. She's a bit of posh. Very high maintenance. I can see the appeal, but really? That sort'd drive you mad after a bit, no matter how good they were between the sheets. Always zipping about the place on some rich bastard's jet, snorting coke and having ten holidays a year? Going with this or that mega-wealthy dude to his own island? They're just expensive tarts, that sort, no matter how upper crust they sound. My guess is she turned out to be a bit too rarified for Thomas Knox. Bit too rarified for *anyone* unless they were a billionaire, I reckon. Then he met Chloe, who was more on a social par with him. I guess he felt more comfortable with her. Understandable.'

'Chloe was a stripper, that right?'

'Yep. Always on the make. Tough as nails. Then she married Thomas and left all that behind her.' Ashok blew out his lips. 'Phew! You got to admire the bloke's staying power. Jean, the first one, she considers herself the true wife and despises the rest of them. They all got pretty decent divorce settlements off Thomas, trust funds for the kids. But they were always trying for more – once, apparently, they even pitched up together and tried to convince Jean that she really ought to sell the house that Thomas had given her, lock stock and barrel, when he moved out, having fallen for the sultry charms of Ursula – and downsize to split the proceeds with them.'

'Cheeky.'

*And then there was Ruby,* thought Kit. Thomas Knox had been his friend, his helper, but for Christ's sake *why* had Ruby got mixed up with him?

He thought about all these wives, bitching and circling and arguing about money. Thomas had had a way about him that made women fall at his feet. Those electric-blue eyes, the muddy blond hair, that crackling dynamism he always seemed to generate around him. Thomas was volatile – and he'd met a suitably volatile end. Nearly sixty or no, right up to his last gasp he'd kept his pulling power.

But now someone had killed him.

Someone, yes. But who?

Kit's main concern was, of course, for Ruby. She was very upset. There *were* such things as civilised divorces, but usually there were tears, recriminations, bitterness. Maybe even a need for revenge. There'd be, among all these abandoned exes and deserted kids, broken hearts and hatred. Bound to be. And he would have happily scrubbed his hands clean of the whole Thomas Knox thing, had it just been a case of Thomas and no more. But then – someone had tried to hit *him,* too. Tried, and failed. Got poor bloody Fats instead. There was no way he could let that go.

Somewhere there had to be a clue as to what the hell had been going on to make Thomas wind up dead and himself to cheat death by the narrowest of margins. Somehow, someone had got past the guard on Ruby's gates and planted that bomb. Yes, he'd sacked the silly bastard right away because there was no way he could be trusted anymore; and he'd grilled him first – roughly – in case he'd planted the thing himself. He hadn't. Kit was completely sure of that. But if *he* hadn't, then he'd been dossing off when he should have been on alert – so he'd *had* to go.

Now Kit thought of those *other* gangs. The London mobs he knew so well. He had his manor, his patch of the London underworld, and there were many others too, some he trusted, some he never would.

He thought of all those wives.

'Have any of these women threatened Thomas at all? At any time in the past?' he asked.

'Funny you should say,' said Ashok. 'Wife number three, Avril Gulliver. Her and Thomas had a bit of a domestic one Christmas.'

'Define domestic.'

'Declan told me she cracked Thomas over the head with a full bottle of Bushmills. Could have killed the poor cunt.'

Kit absorbed this information with interest. Whatever DI Romilly Kane might say with that stick up her arse, he was going to get to the bottom of this and find out who'd killed his old ally – and one of his closest friends.

Which reminded him.

The police would already have done this, but it was his duty to pay a visit, too. He had to go and see Fats's mother. And then he'd pay a call on Declan. He'd talk face-to-face to the only son of Thomas and his first wife, Jean.

# 20

# DAY FOUR

Fats's mother was devastated.

'We'll look after you,' Kit told her, Ashok standing silent at his side as she sat in a chair, howling with grief. Fats had been her only son, unmarried, devoted to his mother. 'Financially, you'll have no worries. I'll get an account set up. And one of the boys is going to call in every week, make sure you've got everything you need, all right?'

She nodded.

'But nothing's going to make up for this, is it? He was my boy.'

And she was off again, crying. Kit felt a surge of impotent rage at seeing this gentle old woman so reduced. And she was right. How could money ever compensate for the loss of a loved one? Kit couldn't tear his eyes away from the mantelpiece in her little sitting room. There were stacks of framed photos on there, mother and son smiling, waving, wearing dopy Kiss Me Quick hats at Margate and Southend, eating candy floss and jellied eels. Memories of happier days.

'Anything you want,' Kit said. 'Anything at all, you tell us and it'll be sorted. You understand?'

'All I want is for you to find whoever did this.'

'We will,' said Kit, and left her there, still sobbing her heart out.

They crossed the river to Battersea. Declan had a place there in a long row of terrace houses. It was nowhere near as grand as his father's gaff in Hampstead, but it was neat, freshly painted, clearly cared for. When Kit knocked on the door, leaving Ashok out in the car, there was a long pause. Maybe Declan was out? But after a while he came to the door in shirtsleeves and slacks and opened it.

'Kit!'

Kit held out a hand. Declan clasped it in his.

'Bloody hell, mate,' said Kit. 'Sad times.'

'Yeah. Come in.'

Declan led Kit through to a neat, uncluttered little lounge. 'Get you something? Tea? Coffee?' he offered. 'Something stronger?'

'Whisky.'

Declan went to a cabinet on the far side of the room and poured out the drinks. Kit noticed two more glasses on a small occasional table in front of the couch – both empty but one marked with lipstick on the rim. Declan came back, handed over the drink, clinked his glass against Kit's.

'To Thomas Knox. A hell of a guy,' said Kit.

'Yeah.'

They drank. There was a pause. 'What a fucking shock,' said Kit.

'You had a shock yourself, I heard,' said Declan. 'At your mum's place.'

'One of my boys got it. Fats. You knew him?'

Declan nodded.

'I just called on his mother.'

'Rough.'

'It was. It wasn't meant for him, though. It was meant for me.'

'Christ.' Declan downed another amber mouthful. 'You tightening up then?'

'In spades.'

'And you want me to do what?'

'Help out if you can. You hear anything on the grapevine?'

'Nothing useful, yet. But sure I'll help out. The old man . . .' Declan paused, blinked hard. 'He was a bastard with the ladies, but he was sound in all other departments, wasn't he? I can't believe he's gone.'

'Me neither,' said Kit, thinking of Ruby out there in Marlow, shot to pieces by the loss of her lover, sunk deep in grief. He drained his drink. 'You keep in touch, yeah?'

'Sure. Yeah,' said Declan, and they shook hands again. Kit left.

# 21

# DAY FOUR

The Italian restaurant in Leadenhall Street was lovely: Daisy liked it instantly. It was a bit naff and it was, without a single solitary doubt, pure Italian cliché with its vivid checked red-and-white table cloths, empty Mateus Rosé bottles stuffed with melting and warmly flickering candles, piped mandolin music.

'This is nice,' said Daisy.

She was fully aware that Kit hated Italians – any Italian – since his brush with the Danieri clan. So she was aware that she could not, under any circumstances, tell Daniel or Ruby or *anyone* that she was meeting up here with Luca Romano tonight, even though he'd had absolutely nothing to do with any of *that*.

But it hadn't been easy. Daniel had probed. Who was she meeting? What time? What time for the pick-up, and why over the other side of the bridge? She'd told him she was meeting a girlfriend.

'Who?' he'd asked, and she'd dredged from her memory a random school friend, reminding herself that she would have to phone her and be sure her story was backed up.

Irritated beyond belief, feeling like a wild bird locked inside a cage, she told Daniel she didn't want a pick-up, she was going to get a cab and maybe stay at her club tonight if she didn't go back to Ruby's.

'No way,' said Daniel. 'No bloody way, Daisy. It's not on.'

And so it was agreed that he would pick her up. Fuck him. She sometimes wondered just who worked for who in this relationship? He seemed to be the boss of her and she hated that.

'This is the best table. They keep it for me,' said Luca.

'It's great,' said Daisy.

'You look terrific,' said Luca.

'You too,' Daisy smiled.

She'd made a huge effort tonight. She was wearing a shimmering tasselled silver Chanel mini dress that hugged all her curves. Her long corn-gold hair was swept up in a chignon, her lips were tinted crimson and her huge cornflower-blue eyes outlined with deepest black mascara.

For a while, trotting over the bridge in her beautiful but ridiculously high Manolos, her mood blackened by her departed minder's incessant carping, she'd wondered if the whole damned thing was worth the effort. And she did have a creeping uneasy feeling that Daniel did have a point. Maybe she *should* be spending more time with Ruby, supporting her. She'd phoned the twins before she'd come out tonight. Luke was still going on – and on – about having a pet, and Daisy had promised him she'd see.

But now she was here, and she put the troubles at home aside for a while. Luca was every bit as intriguing and enticing a dinner companion as she had expected him to be.

They ate scallops on black pudding for starter, then pasta puttanesca for their mains, and finished the meal with crème brûlée and some deep, hearty Italian wine.

'Have you told your family about me? About "us"?' he asked, smiling.

'No. There's been some trouble. Everyone's a bit . . . you know . . . strung out.'

'Fair enough. Later, yes?'

*If ever,* thought Daisy.

She didn't think that Kit or Ruby would ever soften their stance against Italians in general, however blameless. And that was unfortunate, because she found Luca extremely fanciable. So charming. She loved his richly accented voice, it was supremely sexy. He called her 'cara' in those lovely melting Italian tones. She loved that. It thrilled her. So it was simple, really: she was going to have to keep her family in the dark about the whole thing.

Whenever possible, she was going to give Daniel the slip.

And so Kit would *never* know.

She thought then of the medium, of that weird thing in the darkened Bermondsey flat with the Ouija board, the glass gliding, then juddering, settling on one letter and then another.

*Daise don't.*

A shudder coursed through her.

*Don't what?* she wondered.

Don't do this? Don't meet up with this gorgeous Italian?

Oh, but she'd been so miserable for so long. Mourning Rob and the horror of his death. Feeling so penned in, so bereft, her family guarding her, corralling her within their control. Strong, cool, dictatorial Kit, calling all the shots. Ruby, the matriarch, laying down the law. Daniel, watching her, coldly questioning every move she made. Checking up on her. It drove her *mad.*

Somehow, in the midst of it all, she had carved out a space for herself. Found a bit of freedom, and by doing that she had met Luca and it was wonderful to feel desired again, *wanted* again.

It would be okay.

She would *make* it okay.

'I want to see you again,' he said, and picked up her hand and – thrillingly – brought it to his lips and kissed each finger, lingeringly, one after the other. 'I think I'm already a little in love with you, cara. Do you feel the same maybe?'

'Not yet,' said Daisy, smiling. God, he was sweet. 'Soon though, I think.'

*Very* soon.

# 22

# DAY FIVE

Kit and Ashok drove to Marlow to see Ruby. The front drive was still scorched black from the car bomb's blast, crime scene tapes were still strung up in a neat square around it.

Ruby was up, in her sitting room, reading the day's paper, dressed in a simple black shift. Kit glimpsed a shot of President Reagan, riding alongside the Queen at Windsor Castle, saw pictures of panicking people and the headline 'Israel invades Lebanon'.

'Where's Daisy?' asked Kit. He'd seen the Mercedes that Daniel usually drove Daisy in, parked at the side of the property.

'Still in bed.' Ruby folded up her paper and laid it aside. 'She was out last night.'

'How are you?' Kit sat down.

'Fucking awful,' said Ruby with an unsteady smile. 'I keep turning it over and over in my mind and I still can't seem to take it in that he's gone. I wake up and it's there, staring me in the face. A nightmare. And that awful thing with Fats. Is this the start of something?'

'Meaning?'

'Meaning war. Is someone pushing into your manor? If you know of anything, I should know too.'

'There's been no sign of anything. Only this business with Thomas and the hit on Fats.'

'Which wasn't meant for Fats at all. We've got to be very careful. *You* have to be, in particular.'

'I'm always careful. I've been talking to Declan, Thomas's boy, about the situation. Did you know there's a lot of bad blood among Thomas's ex-wives?'

'I never discussed any of that with him,' said Ruby.

'Well, it made for an interesting conversation. There's Jean – the first wife and Declan's mum – then Ursula, who gave him a daughter called Evelyn, then Avril who gave him *another* daughter, this one called Olivia, and then Gilly.'

'And then Chloe,' said Ruby.

'Then Chloe, yes.'

'He would have divorced her in the end too, I suppose. There are men like that you know – they're endlessly searching for some perfect domestic set-up but never finding it. Some of them get off on the arguments. Makes them feel alive I suppose. They prefer it to the resounding silence of singledom. And then I suppose you think he'd have proposed to me?'

'Wouldn't he?'

Ruby managed another thin smile, but it had a bitter tinge to it. 'No, I don't think so. Even if he *had*, what would I have needed with a husband?'

Kit had to smile at that. His mother had been a feminist since before feminism was even thought of. A risqué Windmill girl back in the forties, she'd had him and Daisy by Cornelius Bray and built her father Ted's modest corner shop into a nationwide chain – all without the help of a man. 'These wives. They fight like cats in a bag, apparently.'

'Oh?'

'None of Thomas's break-ups was peaceful. Sounds like he was pretty fair with them; they got alimony, child maintenance, but they always wanted more. Three of them went to the first wife's – Jean's – place and said she ought to downsize and share out the proceeds among the rest of them.'

'Which she didn't, I'm guessing. Did she tell them to piss off out of it? I would.'

'She did. But what if one of them – maybe even Jean herself, the first and original betrayed wife – decided to hire in help to polish Thomas off?'

'That doesn't explain why someone was also trying to hit *you*.'

'No. It doesn't. You're right. And that sort of hit? Explosives? Seems unlikely.'

'But not impossible. Anyway, leaving that to one side, there is something I ought to tell you.' Ruby looked uneasy.

'Oh? What?'

She hesitated.

'What is it?' asked Kit.

Then she said: 'I don't think this was the first time an attempt was made on Thomas's life.'

# 23
# DAY FIVE

Kit stared at his mother. 'Oh? You've never said. You mean *recently*?'

'Yes. Months ago. Before Christmas, I think. We were coming out of the Dorchester.'

'And why the fuck didn't you tell me at the time?'

'Because Thomas was convinced it was accidental. Now? I don't think it was.'

'Did he report it to the police?'

'You're joking. Thomas? Come on.'

'So what happened?'

'We came out, said goodnight to the doorman and then this car came up, engine roaring, right over the pavement. It was travelling very fast and the headlights were on full beam. It was coming straight at us and we jumped back. Thomas pushed me out of the way, up the steps. But *he* was the target, he was the one it was aiming for, not me, I felt sure of that at the time.'

'Was he hit?'

Ruby shook her head. 'The front wing brushed up against him and he tore his coat on the wing mirror. You know how he loved that vicuna overcoat; he was furious. Then as soon as the car had appeared, it was gone. We didn't get the registration number or even the make. It was just a big dark car. Dark windows too. There and gone. Quite shocking. The doorman fussed over us, asking if we were all right. Which we were. Thomas sort of laughed it off. Said some drunken fool at the wheel had obviously lost control of the car and nearly knocked us both over. No harm done. We went on to the Langham and had a couple of toffee vodkas to steady ourselves. In fact, he was so blasé about what had happened that he convinced me it was nothing. A drunk driver, he thought. Or some fool reaching for the glove compartment when he should have had both hands on the wheel – or trying to insert a cassette tape into the player. Something like that. A pure accident, he told me. And he said no wonder the driver didn't stop, he or she would have looked such a berk. But you know what? Looking back? With all that's happened since then? I don't think it was nothing.'

'What do you think it was?' asked Kit.

Ruby stared straight into her son's eyes. Her expression was deadly serious.

'I think it was a first attempt,' she said. 'And having failed, they tried again, this time boobytrapping his car. And this time, they succeeded.'

# 24

# DAY FIVE

Kit went to visit Ursula Grey. She was like one of those exotic birds he'd seen on TV jungle programmes, building nests with bright stones and leaves picked up here and there. Ursula's Olympia apartment was a decorative backdrop, lavishly decked out in mauves, rich dark blues, vivid sea-greens and stacks of peacock feathers, all to reflect the beauty of its owner. And it had to be said, Ursula was *extremely* beautiful – so beautiful that it was almost beyond belief. Her long thick black hair, glossed to a mirror shine, tumbled down over her shoulders. Her face was a sculpture, the lines of it so pure, the cheekbones so high, the lips pillowy cushions, the nose utter perfection. Her eyes were perfect ovals, startlingly blue. She was so tall that she had that almost stretched look about her that was so common in models. Blown-up photos of Ursula in her prime were plastered all around the walls of the hallway as Kit entered. He was confronted by Ursula smiling, frowning, full length, close-up, pouting at the camera, swirling priceless gowns around her.

'Bailey took that one,' she said, languidly indicating the photo over the hall table. Kit admired it as instructed, noticing that on the hall table in a gold dish were many invitations to stylish fashion events – and also red bills and brown envelopes, a stack of them. Ursula led him through to the living room and he stood in front of the fireplace, gazing up at a fantastic shot of a much younger Ursula above it. This time her angelic profile was wreathed in clouds.

The only jarring note in the room was a sulky-looking girl draped across a huge purple velvet sofa in jeans and T-shirt, looking bored but displaying her mother's etiolated build, her eyes, the same black hair. Another beauty in the making, Kit thought.

'She tells everyone that,' said the girl. 'About Bailey.'

Ursula shot her a sour look. 'Evie, don't you have course-work or something?'

'No,' said Evie. 'She *also* tells everyone that I'm fourteen. I've been fourteen for four years, because it makes *her* look younger.'

Ursula gave her daughter a catty smile and turned her attention to Kit. 'Ignore her. Now – you're a friend of Thomas's, you say? And you wanted to talk about this ter-rible business? Well, I don't see why. Or how I can help. It's so awful to hear that he's died. And that way. So *violent*. Dreadful.'

'Oh don't cry, you'll smudge your make-up,' said Evie. 'Or worse, cause wrinkles and then how will you clear those bills?' Evie looked at Kit. 'I don't think she's the least bit sorry Dad's dead. In fact, I think she's glad.'

'Evie! That's a horrible thing to say,' said Ursula.

Evie shrugged. 'You heard of the word narcissistic, Ursula? Well, that's you. You hated him because he got sick of you forever gawping at your own reflection. It's all a bit one-dimensional, you know. A bit *tedious*. So he ran off with Avril when he met her at Cheltenham races and knocked her up with Olivia. That's the truth.'

'Shut up. Look, a lot of water's flown under the bridge since then,' said Ursula, sending Kit a desperate glance. 'It's true that Thomas and I parted acrimoniously. But I wouldn't have wished this on anyone, not even him.'

Evie ignored that. She looked at Kit. 'Olivia's not bad, actually. Better to have a half-sister than no sister at all I suppose. I'm going out,' she said, and sprang lithely upright on long coltish legs and strode off into the hallway.

'Kids,' said Ursula with a weak smile.

'I guess divorce upsets them,' said Kit as the front door slammed.

'Yes. Although Thomas was pretty okay about it. Kept in touch with Evie. Gave her gifts. Trips. Never chipped in on the school fees though, he drew the line at that.'

'Well . . . that's good.' But cash was no substitute for proper parenting, as Kit himself knew only too well.

How old was Ursula, he wondered? He guessed mid-forties, but she was so fabulously beautiful and so faultlessly well maintained that she could have been ten years either side of that. From experience with his own mother and sister, he identified the long swirling dress she wore, in broad bands of royal blue and emerald green, as vintage Missoni. Her face was perfectly made up, her hair artfully dyed to conceal any hint of impending grey. Her fingernails were perfect pink shells, her toenails, peeping out from thin gold leather sandals, the same.

'You know, I think Thomas mentioned you. Once or twice,' she said.

Thomas hadn't mentioned this glamorous creature. Or indeed *any* of his collection of women and children.

Thomas was all about the business. Private life? That was *private*. 'There are quite a few of you,' said Kit. 'Ex-wives, I mean.'

'Yes, that's true.'

'And you get on okay? I mean, you have kids, all of you, so for the sake of them I suppose . . . ?'

'We get along fine,' said Ursula.

'Only I heard that you and Avril and Gilly called on Jean and tried to intimidate her into selling up, downsizing and sharing the proceeds from her very expensive house with the rest of you.'

Ursula's mouth dropped open.

'Which she refused to do,' added Kit coolly.

'Who told you that? Was it that bolshy little prick Declan?'

Kit gave a dry smile. 'I never reveal my sources.'

'I *bet* it was. We just suggested it, that's all. It crossed our minds and—'

'Whose mind?'

'What?'

'Who thought of it first? You?'

'No. It wasn't me, it was Avril.'

'That's the same Avril who I hear knocked Thomas over the head with a bottle of whisky? She seems to have a bit of a temper.'

'What?'

'Didn't you know about that? I suppose that was just about the final straw for him. After that, he met Gilly Taylor-Black and called an end to his marriage to Avril. Right?'

Ursula gave a bitter little smile. 'I did know about it, yes. It happened at Jean's place one Christmas. I was there. We all were. Three-line whip, you know.'

'What?'

'Jean insisted. Thomas was very hot on ending marriages,' she said. 'Not very hot on keeping it in his pants though, I'm afraid.'

'Someone's been pretty hot on ending Thomas,' Kit remarked.

'What, you . . .' Ursula let out a bark of startled laughter. 'You don't actually think one of *us* could have been behind any of this?'

'You all seem to have hated him. He had some very dodgy connections. Surely you know that. Maybe through your association with Thomas you had some dodgy connections of your own.'

'So you come here pointing the finger at me? That's crazy. It could have been *anyone*,' she protested.

'I'm just asking around,' said Kit.

'Well, don't. In fact,' said Ursula, drawing herself up to her full magnificent height, 'get *out*.'

# 25
# DAY FIVE

Kit was just leaving Ursula's place when he bumped into DI Kane.

'What the fuck?' said Romilly.

'Detective,' said Kit cordially.

'Mr Miller.'

'The name's still Kit.'

'What?'

'I know we're not an item anymore. You cooled it and that's fine. But the name's still Kit and you can still use it.'

'Right.'

'You ought to know it by now, after all. I think you even screamed it, once or twice.'

Romilly stared at him without expression. 'I'll stick with Mr Miller,' she said.

'How's your DS doing?'

'She's much better. Taking a couple of days out, resting up at home.'

'Good.'

'What are you doing here?' asked Romilly.

'Visiting Ursula,' said Kit.

'Why?'

'Just a social call. You know. As you do, after a family bereavement.'

'I told you. I want you to keep clear of all this. Don't get involved.'

'I'm already involved. Thomas Knox was very close to my mother and to me. Someone killed him. Someone also killed a good friend of mine. And let's not forget, someone tried to kill me too.'

'Are you listening to me?' Romilly asked, rattled by the sight of him but determined not to let any sympathy for him touch her.

Yes, he'd been through the mill. He'd lost his best mate last year and now two more of his friends had gone. She knew that he could hurt, could suffer, just like anyone else: but that wouldn't be – *mustn't* be – her concern.

'I'm trying not to listen to you,' said Kit.

Romilly looked over to where Ashok was waiting patiently beside a long black car. 'Got your minder with you, I see.'

'Pays to be careful.'

'Yes it does. Keep your nose out, Mr Miller. And don't get in my way.'

# 26

# DAY FIVE

While Kit had been speaking to Romilly, he was aware of Evie loitering not ten feet away from her mother's doorstep, chatting to another girl who was as fair and bulky as Evie was dark and thin. As Kit approached, the other girl peeled away and was gone, into the crowds.

'Hi again,' he said to Evie.

She said nothing.

'Walk with me,' said Kit, and set off toward Kensington High Street. Once they got there, he turned into Church Street and Evie followed him into Maggie Jones's restaurant near the rear entrance to Kensington Palace.

They got settled into one of the tight booths and Evie started telling Kit about Princess Margaret sneaking out of the Palace long ago to meet her hoodlum boyfriend John Bindon.

'She liked crooks. Found them attractive. Risky, I suppose. A bit thrilling,' said Evie.

She was staring at Ashok, who had settled himself at a table nearby and was watching Kit and everything that was going on around him. 'What is he? Your bodyguard or something?' she asked as a waitress approached. 'Can I get a vodka and Coke?' she asked the girl.

'Don't worry about him. He's not your concern. You can get a Coke,' said Kit, and ordered.

'I'm over eighteen,' Evie objected.

'Let's not take any chances on that. Tell me about your mum and the other wives. Do they get on?'

Evie let out a loud honk of laughter. 'Hardly,' she said. 'What, you haven't met the others yet? Boy are you in for a *treat*.'

The waitress came back with their drinks. Evie fell on hers and started slurping it up through a straw. Maybe, he thought, she really *was* fourteen?

'Tell me about Avril,' said Kit.

'What, wife number three? Nothing very exciting about her. Stinks of horses all the time. Number four's *much* more interesting. Gilly's Daddy's an earl and she's a smackhead. Dissolved her septum, did you know that? Stuffing all those Class A drugs up it. That's the bit in the centre of your nostrils you know. She'll have to get it remade. Going to cost her a small fortune I'm guessing. Jean and Mum and Avril have all been laughing their tits off about it. Not to Gilly's *face*, of course. God no. It's all tea and sympathy on the surface, but the minute Gilly's out of earshot, they're in fits.'

'Is it true that Avril hit your dad over the head with a bottle of whisky?'

'You heard about that? Mummy told you I suppose. Yeah, she did. What a temper!'

'And all the abandoned wives applauded when Avril hit him?'

'They did. Ursula – I don't call her Mummy, you know, and it drives her absolutely batshit crazy . . .'

'That why you do it? To get her attention?'

'You're pretty sharp, aren't you? Jean and Ursula and Avril and Gilly were all singing from the same hymn sheet when it came to Dad. They all hated him. Well maybe not Jean. But the rest, oh yes, they did.'

'Did *you* hate him?'

Evie looked at Kit sharply. 'You're one of his gangster pals. Shady lot, aren't you. What is this, you all closing ranks now that one of your own has gone to the big gang-land in the sky?'

'Only you don't seem that upset about all this. Your dad's dead. I would have thought you should be devastated.'

Evie looked at the remains of her drink. 'You could put a voddy in that,' she said. 'Easily. To comfort me in the extremity of my grief. If you're so interested in what I've got to say.'

'No,' said Kit.

She tilted her head and stared at him. 'You've got a dangerous sort of look in your eye.'

'It's been said.'

'Fancy a date?'

'No. And no vodka. Maybe another Coke.'

She gave a shrug, let it go. Then she grimaced. 'There were always arguments. Tons of them. I got used to it. So did Olivia, Avril's girl.'

'Was that her?' asked Kit.

'Hmm?'

'The girl I saw you with round the corner. The one who vanished the minute I turned up.'

'Yeah, that's Olivia. Ollie I call her. She doesn't mix much. She's like a cat. Solitary. But we get on okay. It makes you sort of *detach*, when your parents split, do you know what I mean? You move away from it, if not physically then mentally for sure. You pull down the blinds and say, "not listening to any of that". You put on your fave tracks and you chill, or you try to. Christmases were always the worst. Absolute *murder*. I suppose that's a tradition that Jean will still want to carry on.'

'Will she? What *is* the Christmas tradition?'

'Bloody great dry turkeys, indigestible Christmas puddings, charades, church, the Queen's speech every damned year. It was always the same because Jean insisted and what could the rest do but fall in line? She loves yanking all their chains, does Jean. And there's always the faint suggestion that if they do that, year in, year out, she might – just *might* – decide to liquidate a few assets – i.e. the house that's worth a sodding fortune – and fling a few breadcrumbs their way. Which – of course – she never did. And never has any intention of doing, either.'

'Go on.'

'Dad would always try and ingratiate himself to us kids. We used to compare the presents he gave us. Huge, lavish gifts. Cars and ponies, stuff like that. Olivia took up sailing and he went and bought her a twenty-four-foot yacht of all damned things. All guilt money, of course. And Jean – his first wife, plain old cow – she would always play mother hen, invite the whole crowd of us over to hers even though she couldn't stand the sight of us. Even that bloody tart Chloe, and who the fuck wanted her there? None of us, that's who. Then one of the gang would start crying or shrieking or lobbing insults at one of the others and – yes – it's true. During one of those Christmases, someone *did* throw a bottle at Dad's head. I don't think I could blame them, not really. It was like being in a pressure cooker over at Jean's for Christmas. It was hot, stifling. Horrible.

Dad didn't mind it. It seemed to amuse him, somehow. He created chaos wherever he went, my dad. Sometimes I think he actually *enjoyed* the rucks. I don't think I am *ever* going to get married. No way.'

Evie drained her drink, making a noise with the final dregs as she sucked it up.

'More?' asked Kit, feeling sorry for her. He'd had a rough childhood himself, and he could see the signs. He'd been scarred by his. She'd been scarred by hers.

'Nah.' She stood up. 'I have to go,' she said.

Kit pulled out a card with his number on it. 'Get in touch if you think of anything you want to tell me.'

'Oh! Okay,' she said, and left.

# 27

# DAY FIVE

Ashok drove Kit back down to Ruby's house. Kit felt he had to go there, even though what he *really* wanted was to get home to his own place, have a shower and a meal, try and relax for the evening. When they arrived, there was – depressingly – the same mess on Ruby's front drive, reminding him all over again of the terrible end Fats had come to. The police tapes had been removed and now there were two of Kit's senior boys keeping watch by the gate. They waved Ashok and Kit in.

'Everything okay?' asked Ashok, pausing there.

'Fine,' they assured him, and he eased past the scorched patch of driveway and took the car around the side of the house to the garage block.

Kit noticed that Daniel's car wasn't there, but Daisy's bone-rattling little old Mini Cooper with its Union Jack top was. He let himself in the back door and Ashok stayed in the kitchen making coffee while Kit walked on through the house to find his mother.

'The police have been back then?' he said, finding her in the sitting room at the front of the house with the curtains open. No TV on, no music. She was just sitting there, staring into the fire. It was a summer's evening, but Ruby had always felt the cold. Exotic blood in her, not too distant from the plains of Africa. Now her appearance startled him. She looked shrunken, grey – not herself.

'Yeah. And I suppose they will be back again, soon. They're going to clean up the driveway, they said, and not to worry,' she told him.

Kit stared at his mother. They'd been estranged once, for a long, long time. Out of touch with each other. So it was fairly new and odd, the concern he felt for her. He went over to the curtains and closed them.

'I've told you. It's safest at the back of the house. If you're going to sit in here, at least keep the ruddy curtains closed,' he said sharply.

He switched on a table lamp and a warm glow lit the room.

'You know, don't you, that I'll get them? Whoever they are?' he asked.

Ruby just returned his stare.

'Listen. Whoever tried for me but killed Fats by mistake, whoever killed Thomas. They're dead already. Dead and buried. They just don't know it yet.'

Ruby's eyes were resting on her son's face. Slowly, she nodded.

'You didn't know, did you?' asked Kit.

'About . . . ?'

'About all the wives.'

'What?'

Kit outlined Thomas's marital adventures, described the women involved. Ruby looked at him in shock when he finished speaking.

'No. I didn't know about any of that,' she said at last. 'Thomas rarely discussed his past. I only knew about Chloe.

I don't suppose he ever thought it was a relevant thing to tell me. That he'd been married . . .' she paused. '*How* many times?'

'Five.'

'Good God.' She shook her head. 'Oh! Someone telephoned, asking for you,' she told him.

'Who was that?' Kit asked, flopping down into an armchair, wondering if she was reassured by his words or even more alarmed than she had been before.

'A priest. Father Riley. He said he wanted to speak to you as a matter of urgency.'

'A *priest*?' Kit had never been overfond of the church – or of religion in general, come to that.

'He's phoned three times at the club. Said it was really urgent. They passed me his details and I said I'd pass it on to you. The number's on the pad there.'

Kit reached out, looked at the numbers. London. He picked up Ruby's phone and dialled. It rang and rang. He was about to replace the receiver when it was picked up.

'Hello?' said a thick Irish brogue.

'Father Riley?'

'This is he.'

'I'm Kit Miller. You contacted my mother, asking to speak to me . . . ?'

'Ah! Yes. At last. I thought you'd not reply in time.'

'In time for what?'

'I am sorry to tell you, your friend is sinking fast Mr Miller.'

Kit stiffened. 'What? Who are you talking about?' Hadn't he had enough death and disaster? 'What friend is this?'

'It's a Mr Gabriel Ward, he was in the Crisis shelter and now he's been transferred to hospital; but I am afraid he won't last the night and he's agitated, he says he wants to speak to you. He says he has a message for you.'

The mention of that name – Gabriel Ward – was like a cold hand brushing over the back of Kit's neck. Years ago, Kit had been head breaker for Michael, Gabriel's father. It was Michael who had taken Kit off the street, saved his life really, taught him the ins and outs of the protection business, made him almost into a son. When Michael was murdered, Kit had been decimated by grief. And Michael's waster of a son Gabriel – Gabe, most people called him – had been a druggie, a disgrace to the Ward name. Hearing that he'd been in a homeless shelter and was now on his last legs in hospital came as no surprise to Kit – he'd always felt that Gabe would wind up that way one day – but it was rotten news, all the same. Who would wish an end like that on anyone, even useless, feckless Gabe?

'I can't think of a single good reason why he'd want to talk to me,' said Kit. He didn't want to get involved in this. It was none of his business. 'Whatever he's told you, we've never been friends. His father was good to me. Like a second father he was, really, a *proper* one. And Gabe and his dad were estranged. We rarely communicated. Never wanted to.'

'I've heard his confession,' the priest persisted. 'He's had a hard life, Mr Miller. And now he's asking for you and I think it would be the Christian thing to do if you could spare him the time to talk. And he *does* have a message for you, he says. A message from his father.'

This sounded like pure bullshit to Kit. Michael was long dead. He'd despised his son for his weakness and had more or less, so far as Kit knew, cut all ties with him.

'Look,' he said. 'Can we do this over the phone?'

'Sadly, Mr Ward is too weak for that. If you could come in . . . ?'

*Shit.*

'Father, I'm very busy.'

'I appreciate that. But this would be a kind act. He seems troubled by the news he wishes to impart. And it would be good of you to put his mind at rest.'

'And he hasn't told you what this message is in relation to . . . ?'

'No. He says he wants to speak to you. And, as I say, it is urgent. Will you come?'

*Shit, shit, shit.*

'I'll come,' Kit said.

# 28
# DAY FIVE

It was nearly midnight when Kit entered the hospital, Ashok plodding doggedly along at his side. As was always the case, the place was brightly lit, full of hurrying people – nurses, doctors, relatives of the sick and the injured – and somehow or other Kit and Ashok found their way to Father Riley's little chapel room. The priest was a short wide man, barrel-chested, grey haired, blue eyed, about fifty years of age. He was sitting there alone, looking up at a big wooden cross on the wall when Kit and Ashok entered. He came to his feet.

'I'm Kit Miller,' said Kit, and the priest shook his hand.

'Thank you for coming. I was beginning to doubt that you would,' he said.

'Well, I don't know what I can do for Gabe at this stage,' said Kit.

'Just let him talk and pass on this message he has for you from his father. That's all.' The priest picked up a tan-coloured Bible from a chair. 'He's close to the end, as I said. Please come with me.'

Kit and Ashok followed the priest out into the corridor and up a flight of stairs. Another corridor, then the priest turned left into a small ward. Three men were laid out, apparently sleeping, in metal beds; and a fourth was concealed behind drawn curtains. It was quiet up here; peaceful. Father Riley stepped in behind the curtains around the fourth bed, the furthest from the doorway, and Kit followed, leaving Ashok outside.

Seeing Gabriel Ward after all these years was a shock. He was of a similar age to Kit, but he looked twenty years older. The skin on his face had the distinctive network of broken veins that denoted the heavy drinker and dedicated drug taker. His nose was bulbous, mottled. His father Michael had been a handsome man and he had passed on those looks to Gabe, but Gabe had long since lost any pretence of beauty. He wore a thin hospital gown and he looked scrawny, like he didn't have an ounce of muscle left but was all loose skin and desiccated bone. His eyes were closed, his lips as cracked as a dry riverbed. An oxygen mask was over his nose and mouth, moisture beading the inside of it with every low breath he took.

'Gabriel? Can you hear me?' asked Father Riley. The priest touched Gabe's arm gently. 'It's me, Father Riley. You remember?'

Gabe's eyes flickered open. The whites were yellowish, the pupils mere pinpricks, the irises a milky old-man blue. His gaze went to the priest's face, then slid slowly over and came to rest on Kit's.

'Y . . .' Gabe started, then he coughed, a horrible bone-deep rattle.

Father Riley hastily poured water into a cup on the bedside table, lifted the oxygen mask, held Gabe's head up a little, let him sip some water. Then Gabe sank back, smacking his lips. The priest put his mask back in place. All throughout this, never once did Gabe's eyes leave Kit's face.

'You,' he managed to get out this time. 'Jesus, it's been *years* . . .'

'You wanted to see me. Father Riley said so.'

'Didn't think you'd really show up,' said Gabe, and coughed again.

'More water?' offered the priest.

Gabe shook his head, still looking at Kit.

'You inherited the earth, didn't you,' said Gabe. 'I was the son, but it was you he loved, wasn't it. Always you.'

The priest shot Kit a questioning look.

'He's talking about my old guv'nor,' said Kit. 'Michael Ward.'

The last time he'd been anywhere near Gabriel Ward, he'd been at Gabe's flat in Bermondsey. A shit-hole, basically. Even then Gabe had been on the product, living in filth, sour over the bad blood between him and his father, unable to wrench himself away from the wrong side of the tracks, tormented by something, Michael had always said, in his far-distant past, although Michael would never say what that 'something' might be.

'They didn't get on,' said Kit to the priest.

'Don't understate the situation,' said Gabe, almost pouting, making a sorry joke of it. 'My dad hated my guts.'

'Maybe he was hopeful that you'd pull yourself round. Give up the drugs and the booze. But seeing you here, today? Looks like he wished in vain, don't it,' said Kit.

'Do you think he wished for that?' Gabe gave a gruesome smile. His teeth were brown and uneven. 'I don't. I think he could feel superior, the big boss . . .' Gabe coughed again. 'While I was a wreck, he could do that. He never had any time for me.'

'Maybe you wore him out,' suggested Kit.

'Maybe I did. Kids need some understanding, don't they. Help when they're in the shit. Pardon, Father.'

The priest shrugged. It was okay.

'God, I'm tired,' said Gabe, and coughed again.

'Would you like me to leave the two of you together here?' asked the priest.

'He'd probably choke me to death if you did that,' said Gabe. 'And that's going to happen soon enough anyway, without his help.'

The priest looked awkwardly between the two men.

'Look, say what you've got to say, will you?' said Kit. 'You asked me to come and here I am. The father said you had a message for me from Michael. So say it and then I can fuck off, okay?'

Gabe shook his head tiredly. 'You think you're so smart.'

'Just spit it out, will you?'

'All right. I will. You think you're clever but you're not.'

'And the message . . . ?' prompted Kit.

A thin smile twisted Gabe's mouth beneath the mask.

*Christ, what was this?* wondered Kit. He had a prickling feeling of unease.

'Did you have something to do with the car bombs?' he asked sharply. Because if this little druggie tick *had*, then Kit was going to beat him about the head, whether the priest cared for it or not. Fats had died. Thomas had died. And if he thought they had done so because of some warped vengeance wreaked by this sorry excuse for a man, then Gabe Ward was going to suffer for it.

'Me?' Gabe's eyes widened. 'Nah, you're going to have to look *much* closer to home for whoever did that. Although I did hear about it. And I was glad.'

Kit took a step nearer to the bed, his eyes murderous.

'Perhaps I had better . . .' said Father Riley anxiously.

Kit pulled the mask off Gabe's face. Put a hand to his throat, pressing. Gage gagged, his face contorting.

'That's it! Enough! I'm calling security,' said the priest, and bustled away, elbowing his way out through the curtains around the bed and pushing past Ashok, who had come closer on hearing raised voices.

'Let him go,' said Kit to Ashok. Then he turned his attention back to Gabe. 'They won't get here fast enough to save you,' Kit told Gabe. 'So say what you've got to say and then we can *both* be on our way.'

'Bastard,' moaned Gabe, choking.

Kit let Gabe go. 'What the fuck's going on here?' he asked.

Gabe drew in a long whistling breath. Fumbling with the oxygen mask with trembling fingers, he got it back over his nose and mouth. Dragged in a long, blissful breath. There was something in Gabe's eyes that Kit couldn't understand. What was that – triumph? And a message from Michael? That was the one thing – the *only* thing – that could have persuaded Kit to come here today. And it had worked.

Kit stared at Gabe's face. 'You haven't got anything to tell me, have you? There is no message from Michael. You rotten little runt, what's going on?'

'I don't know . . .'

'Yes you fucking do. You got me here because that means I'm not somewhere else. I'm missing something. Missing *what*, arsehole?'

Gabe was grinning.

'Or I'm here as a target?' Kit wrenched back the bedside curtains, looked around at the other three men occupying this ward. Had he been set up? But they were still in their beds, all three of them. Just dozing. 'What the fuck?'

Yeah, there was triumph in Gabe's eyes. Something had worked out for him.

Kit felt an icy shiver ripple down his spine.

'You're too late,' said Gabe, and coughed long and hard. He drew in a whistling breath and lay back on the pillows. 'You're too late. It's already being done.'

'*What is?*' Kit was dragging the mask off Gabe's face once more.

But then security showed up in the shape of two burly men and they grabbed him and Ashok and hustled them both outside.

# 29

# DAY SIX

Ashok drove Kit straight back to Ruby's place after they'd been tossed out the door of the hospital.

'Get Daniel up,' he told Ashok when they got there, having already checked with the men on the gate that nothing had – so far – happened here this evening.

Ashok drove the car round the side of the house to the garages while Kit let himself into the house at the front. The downstairs alarm started to beep and he tapped in the code that deactivated it. Then he called up the stairs.

'Mum! Get up.'

*It's already being done. You're too late.*

That last line of Gabe's kept playing and replaying through Kit's aching brain. His biggest fear had been that he would pitch up here and find Ruby and Daisy missing or dead. But after a couple of beats he saw the light on the upstairs landing come on, heard hurrying feet, heard Daisy say: 'What's going on?'

Then Ruby was hurrying down the stairs, fastening her robe as she came.

'Kit?' Her eyes were panicky. 'What is it?'

Kit went into the kitchen at the back of the house, where they would be less visible, less *vulnerable,* from the road.

Daniel was letting himself in the back door and looking around, taking in Kit, Ruby, Daisy. Ashok followed close behind him.

'What's up boss?' Daniel asked Kit.

'Anything happened here tonight? Anything at all?' Kit asked them.

They all shook their heads.

'What's this about?' asked Ruby, pulling out a chair at the table, sitting down.

'You know that call we had from Gabe Ward? The priest?'

She nodded.

'He said something was already happening. That we were too late. He wouldn't say what. I was just about to beat it out of him when security arrived and hauled us out of there, but the bastard was pleased about something.'

'But nothing's happened,' said Daisy.

'That we know of,' said Kit. 'I've got a bad feeling about this.'

'It's this terrible business with Thomas and Fats,' said Ruby. 'Of course you're worried. But maybe that's all there is to it. You're jumping at shadows. Just getting spooked.'

Kit shook his head and slumped down in a chair.

'I spoke to one of Thomas's wives yesterday. Ursula, the second one, and her daughter Evie.'

'And?' asked Daisy. 'What are you saying?'

'You know, I was thinking at first that this was one of the other gangs, looking for a takeover. But maybe that's wrong. Maybe this is altogether more personal. Gabe was saying about looking closer to home. Whose though? Mine? I don't think so. Thomas's, then?'

'What – the wives? That's absurd,' said Daisy.

'Is it though?' asked Kit. He was thinking in particular of Chloe, who Ruby had crossed over the matter of an extra-marital affair with her husband Thomas.

'What – Semtex, they thought, didn't they? Well, where the hell would one of them get Semtex from? And even if they got it, they wouldn't know what to do with it,' scoffed Daisy.

'Yeah, but you can hire people who know *exactly* what to do with it,' said Daniel, who was leaning against the back door in a stance that was typical of him. Legs spread, head thrown back, arms crossed. Solid as a brick wall.

'What, from the London gangs? Who'd do that? There's peace at the moment, why would anyone want a war?' asked Ruby.

'But maybe that's what this is, just beginning,' said Kit.

'You could be right,' said Ashok.

There was a gloomy silence. Finally, Kit said: 'I want a sit-down with the other guys. I want to thrash this out.'

'You want me to do that? Get it arranged?' asked Daniel.

'No. Ashok, you do that. Dan, you stick close to Daisy and Ruby. Move into the house, would you? I don't want you out over the garage flat, not right now. I want you in here, close.'

'Sure.'

'The twins are with Vanessa and Ivan, yes?'

'I told you,' Daisy said. 'I already *told* you this. Yes, they're with Vanessa and Ivan. They're safe. I've spoken to them on the phone. They're fine.'

'Thank Christ for that.' Kit considered. Vanessa might be a well-meaning Tory flake, but Ivan was sound: a wiry little ex-army officer, sharp as a whip and bullishly protective of Vanessa and her grandkids.

'Who's going to be taking over from Tom Knox?' asked Daniel.

'Declan of course,' said Kit, thinking about that. So far as he knew, Thomas had got on pretty much okay with his son. But was that the true picture? Was there resentment there, were there secrets?

'Ashok, get someone out there keeping an eye on Declan's movements, okay?' said Kit. 'Anything fishy going on, I want to know about it.'

'Such as?' asked Ashok.

'I dunno. Anything at all. Who's he seeing, who's he talking to? Anything that smells wrong.'

'Can we get back to bed now?' asked Ruby wearily. It was gone two in the morning.

'Yeah. Okay if I stay here tonight?' asked Kit.

'You know it is. Always. No need to ask.'

# 30
# DAY SIX

Half an hour later, Daisy was out on the landing saying goodnight to Ruby.

'You okay?' she asked, hugging her mother.

'Right now, I don't feel that I'll ever be okay again.' Ruby managed a thin smile, but her eyes were full of tears. 'I've always thought of myself as tough. Hell, I *am*. But this! God, it's horrible. Losing Thomas. And all right, I *know* he wasn't mine to lose, but still. And Fats! His poor mother, I just can't imagine what she's going through.'

There was nothing to say, no words of comfort were going to help. Daisy kissed her mother's cheek and then, as the bedroom door closed behind Ruby, she turned and was confronted by Daniel, who had collected clean clothes and his washbag from the flat over the garage and was about to go into the spare room.

'G'night,' she said.

'Hang on,' said Daniel.

'I'm tired, Daniel. What is it?'

'I'm just wondering when you're going to tell Kit who you've been meeting.'

Daisy stared at him in surprise. '*What?*'

'I followed you over the bridge. Right up to the door of the Italian restaurant. I saw you in there with that fucker, looking very cosy.'

'What are you talking about? And just who the *hell* do you think you are, following me, making my life an utter bloody misery?'

'Oh come on. I couldn't believe it when I saw it. You and a Danieri, doing that whole Lady and the Tramp thing over the pasta? You have got to be *kidding* me.'

Daisy froze, her eyes locked on his face. He looked furious. She had never before seen Daniel lose his rag. Rob had, lots of times, but Daniel was altogether different. Calmer. Steadier. Or so she'd thought, anyway. Now this sudden rush of rage from him was like a long-dormant volcano, exploding in her face. Something Rob had once said to her floated into her brain then: 'Dan's the quiet one, but for fuck's sake don't be deceived. Never upset him. It's like a bomb going off.'

'I don't know what you're talking about,' she said blankly.

Daniel's khaki-green eyes – so disturbingly like Rob's – were boring into hers. 'What, Daisy? Are you going to ask me not to tell Kit about this? Because I can't do that. For Christ's sake – a Danieri? Really? If you'd picked on *anyone*, it wouldn't be so bad. But one of those bastards? How long has it been going on?'

'Going on? For God's sake! What are you talking about? Nothing's "going on". I've only just met the guy and I've no idea what you mean when you keep saying Danieri. He's *not* a—'

'Daisy!' snapped Daniel. 'He *is* a Danieri. Luca Romano's one of the cousins.' Daniel stared at her shocked face. 'Christ!

You mean you really didn't know? Is that who you were with at Annabel's?'

Daisy crossed her arms over her middle and glared at him. 'Fuck you, Daniel.'

'It was, wasn't it.'

'I'm going to bed.'

'Not before I've said what I've got to say. You've been like this ever since Rob died,' said Daniel. 'Going bloody crazy. And you've got the kids to think about. Luke's having nightmares and wetting the bed, you know he is, he's anxious since Rob went. And Matt's trying to tough it out, being the big man, but he needs you and where the hell are you? Oh yeah. Out. Having fun. It's not on, Daisy. Particularly not now, with the shit hitting the fan like it is. You've got to toe the line.'

That stung, but Daisy knew there was more than a hint of truth in Daniel's words. Daniel *knew* her, maybe better than anyone else. Now there were horrible embarrassing images crowding into her brain. Him getting her some coke soon after Rob's death, because she'd asked him to, pleaded with him to do it; him dragging her half-conscious and naked out of Ruby's swimming pool. She knew she owed him, hugely. He was her protector, the one person who was always there, right at her shoulder. But right now, she hated him. Because the truth did hurt, and he was right. She *had* lost herself since Rob's death. She was still trying to find her feet and – yes – drinking too much, partying too hard, trying to lose herself in mysticism and pleasure but never, ever succeeding because her brain couldn't seem to take it in – that Rob was gone forever. She'd loved him. And now all she had was this lost feeling, this awful lack of direction. Luca Romano was a distraction. And maybe he would have grown to be much, much more. But this! It was a shock. He was inextricably linked to the Danieri clan, and they were the blood enemies of Ruby's family.

'Have you been sleeping with him?' Daniel asked, stony-faced. 'Literally *sleeping with the enemy*?'

'None of your *bloody* business,' snapped Daisy. She hadn't. Not yet. But it was on the cards. And she wasn't about to tell Daniel anything about that. 'Look, all that with the Danieri clan, that happened *years* ago.'

'Have you forgotten what they did to Ruby?'

'That was the other ones. That was Fabio's brothers, wasn't it? Vittore and Tito.'

'Those bastards are the lowest of the low. They're vicious and treacherous. What the *fuck* can you see in him?'

Daisy shook her head. Luca was exotic-looking, Italian, handsome as a god, charming as could be. And she'd been trying to find something different, something exciting, something . . .

*something to take her mind off losing Rob.*

Was she succeeding? No, she didn't think she was. And now Daniel's interrogation was offending her, wounding her. Shocking her.

'He doesn't bore the arse off me,' she threw out. 'Not like you. Christ, you're so sanctimonious, so fucking *right* all the time, aren't you? It gets on my bloody nerves. *You* get on my nerves.'

Daniel was quiet for a beat, staring at her face, and then he said, very low: 'You tell Kit about this, or I do.'

Now she wanted to apologise, to take back those cutting words she'd just uttered. He wasn't boring. And the rest of it? Well, he was just doing his job. Of course he was. And doing it well, she knew that. That had been a cruel and stupid thing to say. She wanted to take it all back, but, dammit, her pride wouldn't let her. He *did* drive her mad. He was just always on her case, always *there*, blocking her every move, stopping her having fun, *irritating* her to death.

'Daniel—' she started.

'No!' Daniel rapped out. 'This is it, Daisy. I'm drawing the line right here. Now I'm going to bed.'

# 31
# DAY SEVEN

The sit-down of the gangs took place the next day in a bar that looked out onto Berwick Street market. All the big names were in attendance including the newish Albanian contingent, Mr Chang from the Triads in nearby China-town, Welsh Joe Williams who arrived swaggering about the place like the prick he was, singing out a mucky rhyme at the top of his voice: 'Never mind her cries of passion, whup it up her doggy fashion!'

Then he grinned broadly and looked around at them all.

'Well damn me the gang's all here! Hiya, boyos! Anyone want a free rub and tug, my girls are available night or day!'

Welsh Joe ran hundreds of strip joints and massage par-lours and bingo halls and he had a thriving blue movie business going on. He looked like a huge bull elephant seal; he had a pendulous nose, a vast square chin, bulging eyes. He was – everyone said it – ugly as sin, with a curly mop of white hair topping off his massive frame.

The Italian boys were of course a no-show – no sur-prises there, they were well known to hate the Darkes for their involvement in the past deaths of the two Danieri family members – and the mad red Irish scrap-metal kings the Delaneys from over Battersea way were a dim and not-much-lamented memory. But Max Carter, who was deeply into legitimate VIP protection these days, had arrived promptly, sleek and expensive-looking as always and fiendishly handsome as he approached his fifties, wearing a sharp black suit and flashing a gold pinky ring set with a block of royal-blue lapis lazuli. A massive bald-headed minder with a gold crucifix in each cauliflower ear stood solidly at his side, eyeing everyone with extreme suspicion.

Kit knew that there was only one rule with Max and that was that you *never* mentioned his wife Annie or their on/ off marital arrangements. Kit had seen Annie often around town, and – for God's sake! – she was an absolute stunner who flashed super-intelligent looks at you with amazing dark green eyes, looks that said she knew you, she understood you, and she would happily slit your throat if you dared cross her.

Kit couldn't help but contrast the thought of Annie Carter with what he'd seen of Ursula Grey; both were beautiful, but Annie was so obviously a different breed: she had the brains and the drive to go with that, she was streets ahead of what had always been a very dirty game. Once – when Max had gone missing in foreign parts, presumed dead – Kit knew that she'd crossed the pond and married a Mafia don called Constantine Barolli, and he also knew that the Mafia connection had endured, passing down to Constantine's son Alberto who was apparently still a reliable ally to the Carter family.

Max patted Kit's shoulder and said: 'Sorry to hear about Thomas. He was a mate for a lot of years. It's sad news.'

'And to me,' said Kit.

'Anything I can do . . . ?' asked Max. 'How's Ruby taking it?'

Everyone around town seemed to know about Thomas and Ruby. 'She's taking it badly. But she'll be okay.'

'Maxy my boy, you all right?' said Joe, patting Max matily on the shoulder.

'Fine,' said Max.

'And the lovely Annie?' Joe beamed. 'How's the missus?'

Kit knew that Joe didn't have a lick of sense, and here was fresh evidence of that fact. Didn't the fool *see* the rise of the scorpion's tail, the stiffening of Max's body, the hard stare from his eyes? Clearly not.

'She's fine,' said Max and took a seat at the already crowded table.

Looking in on the scene, anyone would think this was a board meeting of a large and thriving corporation. Silver coffee pots were placed in the centre of the table, bone China laid out, milk in jugs, hot rolls and pastries with butter and jam.

Declan arrived and everyone rose, pumped his hand, slapped him on the back, commiserated, offered help. He'd lost his dad, after all.

Kit watched Declan circulate, then finally Declan arrived at his side. 'Take a seat,' said Kit, and the waiting staff departed, closing the kitchen door behind them. The bartender went, too. With the place empty of listening ears, the meeting began. Kit rose to his feet and said: 'Thanks for coming—'

He was interrupted immediately by Welsh Joe.

'Can I interject here?' asked the big man, leaning back in his chair, dusting pastry crumbs off his chubby fingers.

'All comments welcome,' said Kit.

'It's just the way things were going, I'm not surprised someone offed Declan's dad.'

There was a pause, then: 'You fucking *what*?' asked Declan. Joe wasn't known for his finesse, but for God's sake! Talk about putting your foot straight in your fat bloody mouth.

Joe held up his shovel-sized hands. 'No offence, no offence. But my money's on the Francis lot. They been pushing at Thomas's boundaries for a long time and now here we are, he's blowed up on his own bloody doorstep. I say you ought to go in and go in hard on them bastards.'

Kit narrowed his eyes. 'What, start up a fucking war with no proof whatsoever?' he asked.

'Seconded,' said Max. 'Why pile in when you can't be sure of the facts?'

'The fact *is*,' said Declan, 'we've had peace on all fronts for a long while. We don't want that to change. Business is brisk and all the arrangements we have between ourselves – even with the Francis mob who were invited to come here today but haven't shown up – they're funny buggers, we all know that – are running smoothly. Why go steaming in and live to regret it?'

'But steaming in's the best option,' persisted Welsh Joe. 'Catch the cunts unawares. And can I just point out? Pat Francis always hated Thomas's guts, we all know it.'

'That proves nothing,' said Mr Chang. 'That was just territory issues. Long since resolved.'

'Yeah, if this *is* down to them, fair enough,' said Declan. 'If not? You've started something big, and you're bang in the frame as another target. Not cool. Not clever.'

Kit was deep in thought. He couldn't seem to shake from his brain all that stuff about the wives Thomas had gone through, over the years. He was still considering all that Ashok had passed on to him about them – including

Jean, Declan's own dowdy housewife mother, who seemed always to be peacefully and happily pottering away in her country garden, but then – appearances could be deceptive. Was she plotting? Was that possible, the meek little woman Ashok had shown him pictures of, who he'd already discounted as any type of threat? And if she *was*, then plotting *what*? Maybe nothing. Or maybe the murder of the husband who had abandoned her years ago for a succession of flashier, livelier women. With Thomas out of the way, the path was clear for her son Declan to take over. And was Declan up to it? Or was dowdy little Jean feeding the bullets in and waiting for Declan to fire them?

And what about Chloe, who Thomas had been married to at the time of his death. Ruby *hated* Chloe. Maybe with some justification. But, boot on the other foot? Chloe certainly had reason enough to hate Ruby right back. Ruby had been sleeping with Chloe's husband, and Chloe knew all about it and had already tried to warn Ruby off, quite forcibly, barging into her office behind the burlesque club last year and – according to Ruby – waving a knife around. So was this a double strike? Hit her cheating husband and hit Ruby's close family too? Double bubble, right? Of course Kit – and Declan, and everyone else around here – would think *gangland*. One of the crews that occupied the streets around them, breaking out, pushing boundaries, eager for more turf. They wouldn't think of glam young Chloe, the grieving widow, wouldn't put her together with explosives. Why would they?

'Whatever we come up with here today,' said Kit to Declan, 'we have to take this as a clear warning of more to come. Tighten up all around. Agreed?'

'Too right,' said Max.

'I agree,' said Mr Chang.

'Not my plan,' said Welsh Joe, shaking his head. 'And don't forget I said so. All right? But if that's the general view, fair enough I suppose.'

'We watch our backs,' said Declan. 'And we watch each other's, too.'

And it was then, right at that very moment, that it happened.

# 32
# DAY SEVEN

'What the *fuck*?' bellowed Chris, Max's minder, as the massive *boom* reverberated through their bones. The ground seemed to shift beneath them. The cups on the table rattled and a cafetiere fell, spilling black scalding coffee onto the pristine white napiery, drenching the remains of the pastries.

Then Ashok raced in through the door from the street, eyes wild.

'It's the club,' he said.

'What the . . . ?' Declan reeled. They had all heard the explosion but they had *felt* it too, trembling up through the floor of the building. Suddenly they were all on their feet. Somewhere, car alarms were sounding. There was distant shouting and people were running past the front of the bar.

'It's Ruby's place in Old Compton Street,' said Ashok, and Kit was out of the front door in an instant, running. It wasn't far but it felt like ten miles. He knew Ruby wasn't in at work today. But others were, weren't they? Staff setting up for the evening's rush? People rehearsing their acts?

He rounded the corner and came to a screeching halt. He was *seeing* it, but somehow his brain refused to take it in. He couldn't move. Couldn't feel his feet.

'Christ in a sidecar,' he muttered, looking onto a scene that could have come straight out of the Blitz. The entire frontage of Ruby's club was blown out. There were flames, leaping up. Cars parked in front of the club were ablaze. Alarms were shrieking. *People* shrieked too, and staggered, and held their hands up to bloody dust-smeared faces. Some just stood around, open-mouthed with shock. A mother with a small kid was clutching her child to her breast, smoothing the screaming child's head to comfort him. A waitress from the café opposite the club ran out onto the pavement, took one look and fainted dead away. A police car, it's siren dying to a muted howl, pulled into the other end of the street and within moments Kit could hear other sirens, coming closer.

He stood there and stared, disbelieving, aghast, at Ruby's pride and joy.

The club was destroyed. The big windows, where massive photographs of the club's star performers had been on display, had been blown out onto the pavement. The huge *Ruby's* signage that had once been above the windows was gone. The upper storey of the club had collapsed down into the main body of it, leaving what looked like a blackened crater where once had stood tables and chairs. The bar had vanished completely.

'What the *fuck*?' Declan said at his shoulder.

Kit looked around at Declan's face, which was white with shock. He'd lost his father just days ago with something like this. Now here it was, again. An explosion.

'Could be gas,' said Kit.

'You don't believe that.'

'I don't know *what* the fuck I believe, right now.'

Two burly policemen got out of their patrol car and were approaching the building, one of them talking into a radio. Then the first of the fire engines came hurtling round the corner and pulled in, its siren blasting away the lesser shriek of the car alarms and the cries and screams of panicked pedestrians.

Kit walked forward and one of the policemen said: 'Keep back sir, it could be dangerous.'

'This is my mother's club,' said Kit.

'Was she in there, sir? When the explosion took place?'

'No. She wasn't. But other people might be. I'm not sure.'

'Just stay back. Don't try to go in there. Wait here, will you? We may need to speak to you again.'

# 33
# DAY SEVEN

There was nothing else Kit could do but follow the police's orders. Flames still flickered further back in the partially collapsed building and the firemen started unwinding their hoses, connecting them to the water supply, then the first jets of water were pouring into the ruined shell of what had once been Ruby's.

Kit turned to speak to Declan, but he was already gone. None of the other gang leaders had followed, either, although each of them would soon know the full details of what had happened here. This fresh disaster would shoot around the network of London watchers and listeners like a virus. Only Ashok was nearby, as ever, watching Kit's back.

Kit's stomach was clenched so hard he felt sick. He ran to a call box and dialled the Marlow house number, just to be sure. What if Ruby had changed her plans? What if she *had* been in there when the place went up? And – good Christ – what about Daisy? She called in at the club sometimes. What if she'd abandoned Chelsea and her regular rich-girl haunts for once and had instead come downmarket to Soho? It was possible.

'Hello?' It was Ruby's voice. 'Kit? That you?'

Kit felt a sharp spasm of relief. He'd been holding his breath, dreading what he might hear. 'Is Daisy with you? Is she there?'

'Yes. Of course she is. Why? What's the matter?'

'The club's just blown up.'

'*What?*'

'I was in a meeting just round the corner. We heard it go, a big blast. It's . . .' he hesitated, unsure of his words. This place meant a lot to her. But pulling punches would do no good. Sooner or later, she was going to see how bad it was. 'It's been gutted. The fire brigade are here. The police too.'

'Oh God.' She was quiet for a moment, then she said: 'I'll come up.'

'No,' said Kit flatly. 'Don't do that. Stay there. Put Daniel on, would you?'

While Ruby fetched Daniel, Kit stood numbly watching the flurry of activity going on around the bombed-out building. Finally, Daniel picked up.

'Kit?'

'Put two on,' said Kit. It was a simple order but it meant that security around Ruby and Daisy would be doubled immediately.

There was a moment's silence and then Daniel said: 'What's happened?'

'Club's just got done. Blown to fuck.'

'I'll do it right away.'

'Pity Leon took off like he did, we could use him right now.'

'We have plenty,' Daniel reassured his boss.

'Doesn't he ever get in touch?'

'No. He doesn't. As I say, we're fine without him. No worries.'

'Do it then. Tell Ruby I'm going down to Hampshire today. I'll catch up with her later.'

'It's done.'

Kit rang off and stood there, watching the firemen, the police, the shattered members of the public being wrapped in silver blankets and led away to ambulances.

First Thomas, he thought.

Then Fats.

Now – who else? Some innocent barmaid, bottling up? A cleaner, hoovering and dreaming of other, better things? Maybe a drayman, filling the club cellars with booze and meeting his end in this gruesome way?

Three explosions. And one link. Just one.

The link was Ruby Darke.

The link was his mother.

And then Gabe Ward's words echoed in his head.

*You're too late. It's already happening.*

Well maybe it was. But if he had anything to do with it, he was going to put a stop to all this shit.

'What now, boss?' Ashok asked behind him, through the stink of brick dust and smoke and the cries of the shocked and the wounded.

'Got to pay a visit,' said Kit.

# 34

# DAY SEVEN

At the Marlow house, Daniel put the phone down and said to Ruby: 'We're doubling up on security.'

She said nothing in reply. Over these past few days she really hadn't been herself; she'd seemed dazed, out of it. Too many knocks, too much grief. He could understand that. So he turned and went out of the sitting room into the hall, closing the door behind him, leaving her in peace.

But there was no peace for *him,* because Daisy was just coming down the stairs. Daisy with her cornflower-blue eyes, her long tumbling corn-gold hair, her magnificent breasts and shockingly long legs. She was wearing a pink dress and long rust-coloured suede boots and she looked – as always – a knockout. She didn't even have to open her mouth to disturb him. She never had. Even when he'd been a teenager, even when she'd been with Rob, even when she'd been dating Rob, engaged to Rob, *married* to Rob – oh so briefly – Daniel had, irritatingly, only to see her to feel that *need* wash over him, drenching him with lust. He was ashamed of it – Christ, his brother's wife! His brother's *widow!* – but he couldn't seem to stop it happening, every time. As a boy, he'd wanted her. As a man, he still did. And it was totally out of the question. He knew that.

'What's going on?' she asked.

'Kit's just phoned. The club's been done. We're doubling up. I've got some calls to make, so if you'll excuse me . . . ?'

'Hang on.' She caught hold of his arm as he made to pass her, heading for the kitchen. 'What d'you mean, done? Done *what*?'

'There's been another explosion. At the club. Kit's there, he's fine, but he's just called and he says we're to double up.'

Daisy dropped her hand. 'I don't know what you mean. Explosion? For God's sake, how many more? Is anybody hurt?'

'We don't know that yet.'

'And what do you mean, double up?'

'Two stay with you, two with Ruby, wherever you go.'

'*What?*' This didn't sound good to Daisy's ears. She was already sick of Daniel trailing after her like a lost sheep, rapping out orders, being *bloody* annoying, so was this going to mean even more of an intrusion into her private time than before?

'Look,' said Daniel. 'When you go out, one of the experienced drivers takes you. And I come too. He waits with the car, I go with you. To restaurants, to clubs, shopping, whatever. I don't just drop you off like we did before. *He* drops us both off, and I stay with you. Clear?'

Daisy bristled. 'No. Absolutely not.'

'Why? Because you're still planning on meeting that arsehole Romano and you still haven't told Kit about it and you don't want me listening in to the pair of you cooing love words in each other's ear?'

'You are such a prick! I'm saying no, Daniel. And I mean it.'

'Well Kit says yes, and he means it too. And he's the boss, so what Kit says, goes. All right?'

'But—'

'He just asked me about Leon.'

She froze, staring at his face. 'What?'

'He said it was a shame he took off like he did.' Daniel's eyes were sharp as they rested on her face. 'We've both got secrets to keep, haven't we Daisy. So don't be bloody difficult. Just take orders and keep safe.'

Daniel started to make for the kitchen. Conversation over.

'So – you won't tell him that I've been seeing Luca then? You'll let me do it?' said Daisy behind him.

Daniel stopped, turned. 'I told you. I won't say a word so long as you tell him first. And that's putting my neck on the line, which I'm not happy about. You tell him and you tell him soon. I'll give you this week. No longer.'

'Look! I never *intended* to meet the damned man in the first place and I didn't have a clue about his connection to the Danieri family. He never told me. And I told you, I won't be seeing him again. Why would I, after what that family did to Mum and to Kit.'

'And to your first husband. That poor sod Simon. You forgotten him?'

Daisy gritted her teeth. 'Of *course* I haven't done that. Yes, Simon too.'

'Good. Then we understand one another.'

'Yes. We do. Now will you kindly *shut* the fuck *up*?'

# 35

# DAY SEVEN

By the time Kit and Ashok got down to Hampshire it was late afternoon, so they found a B & B for the night. Once there, Kit made three calls. One to Ruby to see if she'd had any fresh news about the club – she hadn't. The next was to Avril Gulliver to say that he would be calling in the morning.

'What for? I don't know you, do I?' She sounded instantly on guard.

'My name's Kit Miller. I've got an Arab mare I want covered,' lied Kit. 'Your stud was recommended to me by a friend, but I'd like to have a look around your facilities before I commit.'

The distant jingling of a possible payoff reassured her. She warmed considerably then, gave him helpful directions, said she was looking forward to seeing him tomorrow.

Then Kit made the third call. It was picked up on the second ring.

'Hello?' she asked.

'Romilly? It's me. You know anything about what happened at Ruby's club this morning?'

She was silent for a moment and then she said: 'Do *you* know anything?'

'I was around the corner in a meeting. Heard the blast and ran round. Didn't see much except a lot of people screaming and a bloody great hole in the place.' Kit paused. 'Was anyone inside?'

Romilly let out a whoosh of breath. 'Luckily no. Nobody. Another half an hour and it would have been a different story. We've been all over it, and the bomb squad will be doing their thing tomorrow morning at around ten. Any more questions?'

'Nope. Well yeah. One maybe.'

'Okay, shoot.'

'When are you going to stop playing hard to get?'

Another *whoosh* of breath. She did that whenever she was agitated. He knew that. He thought it was cute.

'I'm not playing at anything. I'm serious.'

'You know you're going to give in, in the end,' said Kit.

'*My arse.* If that's all?'

'Please don't go mentioning your arse to me, or this is going to turn into phone sex very quickly. It's a very nice arse after all. Like a little peach.'

'Mr Miller—'

'Kit. The name's Kit. You know it is.'

'I'm hanging up now,' she said.

The line clicked. Dial tone.

Kit was almost smiling. He suspected she was, too.

# 36
# DAY EIGHT

Next morning the sun was shining brightly. It was going to be another hot one. Ashok drove the car round to the front of the B & B while Kit settled the bill, and they proceeded down to the Martingale Stud Farm, which was a series of long, low barn-like buildings, wooden clad and stained dark brown, seeming to blend into the fields and dales all around it. MARTINGALE ARABIAN STUD was picked out in black on a big white metal hoop set over the high wide entrance, big enough to accommodate horse boxes, and Ashok drove straight through and parked up close to the front of the building by a tatty-looking door with a badly painted sign that said RECEPTION.

Kit thought the whole place could do with a clean-up. There were weeds in the driveway, some of the fencing was crumbling away to nothing, and there were tiles missing here and there off the moss-blackened roofs of the buildings.

Kit said to stay with the car and Ashok nodded, going to lean on the bonnet, slipping off his jacket and loosening his tie. Kit went over to reception and poked his head inside. Nobody there. He stepped in, wondering whether to take a peek at the chaotic papers heaped on the reception desk, then decided against and stepped out again. He could hear movement and a loud constant whickering coming from the larger barn next door and he could see a big concrete yard over to his right. Several equine heads of various colours, each displaying the large eyes and dish face of Arabians, poked out curiously over half-doored stables, ears twitching.

'Hello?' said a female voice behind him.

He turned. A chubby, surly-faced blonde girl of about sixteen wearing a tightly buttoned white shirt, straining jodhpurs and well-worn riding boots was staring at him with hostile eyes.

'I'm looking for Avril Gulliver? I told her I was calling this morning to see over the place? I'm Kit Miller.'

'Oh yes.' The expression in the eyes thawed, just a bit. 'That's my mum. I'm Olivia. She mentioned you called. She's in the breeding shed.' She paused. 'You look familiar. Have you been here before?'

'No, but we have crossed paths. I saw you with Evie Grey in London.'

'Oh! Oh yeah. Well – follow me.'

Olivia led the way ten feet along the building's length and opened a door heavily festooned with rusting horseshoes. They stepped into a cool high space thickly hung with massive A beams and rafters. The atmosphere inside was dense with the cosy smell of horses and hay. At one corner stood two stable girls, one holding a pail of water, the other not, next to a tall blonde woman holding onto the head of a chestnut Arabian. The woman looked across when Olivia led Kit inside the barn and she smiled. 'Mr Miller?'

'Yeah. Avril Gulliver?'

'You couldn't have timed that better. Gay Day Abu Dhabi is about to do the business. This mare's a seasoned pro, she's had three foals off him so far, all champions.'

Kit was staring at the mare's nose. It seemed to be tied up in a knot. It looked painful.

'This is a twitch,' explained Avril, seeing the direction of his eyes. 'It doesn't hurt her. Just keeps her still and calm while she's being served, that's all.' She turned to her daughter. 'See how she's lifting her tail? All ready, Ollie. Let him in.'

Olivia went over to another door and, standing swiftly back, opened it. Kit was a bit stunned by what followed. A huge glossy black beast of an Arabian, with an arched neck, a magnificent plumed tail and a massively engorged prick came storming into the barn. He galloped straight over to the tethered mare and was up on her back in an instant.

Kit had never seen anything so shockingly sexual in his entire life. Snorting and battering at the mare, the stallion pushed and shoved while the mare stood there immobile, laying her ears back. Suddenly the stallion dropped down onto his feet. One of the girls, grinning, unceremoniously chucked the pail of water onto Gay Day's wilting dick. The other grabbed the stallion's halter and slowly walked him back out of the barn.

Avril Gulliver unfastened the mare's twitch and the mare wandered off, seemingly unconcerned, in search of a hay bale.

'Come outside, we'll have a talk and I'll show you around,' said Avril, and led the way out into the sunshine.

# 37

# DAY EIGHT

'We have great facilities here,' Avril said, busily giving him the sales patter as she strode out across the stable yard. Kit saw her clock the high-end car and its driver, saw her adding up sums and coming to a cheery conclusion. 'Seven loose boxes, four foaling boxes, twenty-three acres of prime grazing, but of course our most prized asset is Gay Day himself, who's marvellously fertile and—'

'Miss Gulliver?' Kit came to a halt. They were just ten feet from the car, Ashok now sitting patiently behind the wheel.

Avril stopped walking. 'Yes?'

'I'm not interested in getting a mare served, Miss Gulliver. I'm interested in talking about a friend of mine who's recently died. Thomas Knox. Your ex-husband.'

Avril's whole face changed. From animated and keen to share, it shut down completely. 'I don't understand,' she said.

'You know that Thomas died,' said Kit. Of course she did. *Everyone* knew. You couldn't miss it.

'So all this is just a blind?' Now she looked as hostile as her daughter. The warm, encouraging sales chat was gone, forgotten. Her face was hard – and Kit couldn't help thinking about that story of her braining Thomas with that full bottle of Bushmills. 'You mean you're here under false pretences?'

'If I'd said over the phone why I wanted to speak to you face to face, would you have been willing to see me today?'

She was silent, staring at the ground. Then she said: 'We're long over anyway, Thomas and me. The minute he started messing around with that high-class tart Gilly, I was out of there.'

'Gilly? That was his next wife after you, wasn't it. Gilly Taylor-Black?'

She gave a sour smile. 'Someone's been doing their homework.'

'Pays to,' said Kit.

'I'm sure it does.' She heaved a sigh. 'What's your interest in Thomas's death then?'

'Thomas was a friend. In particular a friend of my mother's—'

'Oh!' she gave a snort of laughter. 'Not another one.'

'Meaning?'

'Oh come on. He had a pattern, did Thomas. He got a wife and within a few years he was being unfaithful to her. He started an affair with Ursula when he was with Jean – although who can blame him, Jean's dull as ditch water. Then he started with me while he was still with Ursula. You remember that Carly Simon song, 'You're So Vain' – that could have been written for Ursula, suits her to a T. I'm a country girl and by that time I suppose he'd had enough of artifice, enough of Ursula. He got interested in racing and we met. I barely look in the mirror at all, most days I slob around in riding gear and maybe he found that a refreshing contrast to all the skin treatments and designer gear and shit that Ursula went in for – and still does. Who knows? And who cares, really. The shine wore off pretty quickly anyway. For a while we were quite happy together and then I think he got bored because I spent all day in the yard and he was still looking for the perfect wife, still not finding her. Maybe Jean was the perfect one, the home-body he was looking for? Maybe he should have stuck with her and got a mistress on the side. Might have suited him better. Cheaper, for sure.'

'So he took up with Gilly while he was still married to you?'

'Of course. You see the picture? You get the pattern that emerges?'

'Tell me about Gilly,' said Kit.

Avril sent him a steady look. 'Or what?' Her eyes nar-rowed. 'You're like him in a way. Got that air about you. In the same dodgy business I suppose?'

Kit said nothing.

'Well, Gilly. What can I say? She's high maintenance, bitchy, great fun. She's from old money and she spends all her time having holidays at the expense of very rich men.'

Olivia came out from the stable door, stood for a moment gazing over at Kit and Avril, then went back inside.

'So that's your daughter? Thomas's daughter?' he asked.

She nodded. 'That's Olivia.'

'Must be hard on her. Losing her father. And like that, too.'

'They weren't particularly close.'

'So Gilly's wealthy? So, why'd she join in the witch hunt over Jean's place?'

'Gilly isn't wealthy.' Avril let out a croak of laughter. 'Daddy cut her off years ago, wasn't very impressed with the high-octane lifestyle and was even *less* impressed when she took up with Thomas. Ten holidays a year and never a damned day of work, all paid for by rich men. Those pics you see of celebs on yachts in the Med, lounging around with a boatload of topless girls? Well, one of those girls would always be Gilly Taylor-Black and boy did she love that style of life. But you get to your middle years and then the gloss sort of wears off, don't you think? The offers from men dried up and suddenly she was in difficulties just like the rest of us. So yes, she went with us to see Jean. And no, we couldn't get the old bitch to budge and sell up. And then along came Chloe, and Thomas was off again. So your mother – was she next in line for the much-prized but rarely achieved "try to hold onto Thomas Knox" award?'

'Maybe,' said Kit, thinking of the pile of unpaid bills he'd seen in Ursula's flat. He wondered about Gilly, who had been set aside for Chloe. Was she too up against it, money-wise?

'Let me tell you something about the great Thomas Knox,' said Avril.

'Go on then.'

'He was a cheating piece of *scum*. And I'm glad he's dead.'

# 38
# DAY EIGHT

'And . . . ?' prompted Kit, wanting more.

'Thomas wasn't that great a prize, I can tell you,' Avril scoffed. 'You're probably realising that Thomas catapulted from one type of woman to another like a demented pinball. Always searching for the right one. And never finding her. And now he never will.' She sighed and looked around at the soft rolling countryside. Over in a large paddock, mares and foals were grazing and dozing in the shade of a large oak. This place, although shabby and obviously in need of attention, was idyllic.

'Can I tell you something, Mr Miller – is that in fact your real name?' she asked.

'It is.'

'Looks lovely here, doesn't it? But it costs a bloody fortune to run and the truth is, I've been struggling. Your cash for a successful mating with your mare would have been very welcome but it wouldn't really have made a lot of difference. Gay Day does fine, but my other stallion standing at stud, it turns out, despite a previously blameless record, has now got a bit too long in the tooth and has been firing blanks for the past year and I've been getting it in the neck from my clients, so that means he's only fit for hacking out or dog meat and my reputation as a rock-solid breeder has suffered. Word travels fast in the equine world. If there's no foal then people don't pay, no matter how good a reputation the sire has had in the past. Still, I keep up the advertising and keep passing the word around in horse circles that we're still in operation, that there's still Gay Day and he's terrific, a fantastic bloodline. But the truth is I do need to buy another top-line stallion and really – I can't afford to.'

'I heard that Thomas gave you – each of you, his divorced wives – fair settlements when he walked away.'

Her smile was bitter. 'Oh, you heard that, did you? From the saintly and long-abandoned Jean, I suppose.' Gilly shrugged. 'Well it was worth a try,' she said. 'We even tried tapping up Thomas for a bit more, but he had his hands full with Chloe, in more ways than one.'

'In what ways do you mean?'

'Well, we could all see the signs. Chloe and Thomas were arguing and so Chloe was obviously going to be abandoned. For your mother, I presume. I'll bet she's the exact polar opposite of Chloe.'

Kit considered this. Yes, his mother was a mile apart from loud, overdone Chloe. Ruby was elegant, contained, accustomed to running her own businesses, very much her own woman – yes, Chloe's total opposite.

'And so he'd have been on to the next one. Fact is, you could never please Thomas. It was always the thrill of the chase with him. Something *different*. That just about summed him up. If someone hadn't killed him, his own temperament would have eventually done the job. He'd have worn himself out.'

'But someone did kill him,' Kit pointed out.

'Yep. I suppose Jean's upset. You know something really sad? I don't think poor Jean ever got over him.'

'Jean calls you all – Ursula, Gilly, you and Chloe – the "gang", did you know that?'

'No, I didn't know that. The gang, huh? That's low. But no, I'm not upset that he's gone. Not me. Not Ursula either, I shouldn't think. And Gilly Taylor-Black? That bitch hasn't the emotional bandwidth to care for a cat.'

Kit stared at the ground, thinking it through.

'About Chloe . . .' he said.

'What a cow,' said Avril.

'In what way?'

'Well she's a match for Thomas, I'll say that for her.'

'Again – in what way?'

'You mean you don't know?' She was smiling, like this gave her some secret pleasure. 'Listen – Chloe didn't wait for him to trade her in.'

'Meaning?'

A fiendish little smile. 'That would be telling.'

'Yes it would. So why not? . . . Well if you change your mind—' he said.

'I won't,' she said, and walked away.

Kit got back in the car beside Ashok.

'You'll never guess,' said Ashok. 'Daniel just phoned. Had a visit from one of the guys.'

'About what?'

'About Declan. Said he's been knocking off Chloe, Thomas's missus.'

# 39

# DAY EIGHT

The CID police team were assembled in the main office – DI Romilly Kane, her now-recovered DS big blonde Bev Appleton, and DS Barry Jones, who was a large flabby man. In his beige cardigan, loose fawn trousers and ill-fitting shirts he looked like a cosy house husband, which was deceptive; Barry in fact had a very sharp brain. The DC's assigned to the case were there too: young Tony Gutteridge, the sharp yet winsome Fiona Batesy, and the grim and permanently unamused Camille Porter.

'The three incidents are almost certain to be linked,' Romilly was telling the team. 'First explosion on day one in Hampstead, Semtex used to kill Thomas Knox, who was the lover of Ruby Darke. Then Semtex again in Marlow, this time to pick off Kit Miller – Ruby Darke's son – who by chance didn't get in the car. His friend Kevin Norton did and died. And finally, Ruby Darke's burlesque club blown up, *also* with Semtex.'

'The Irish love that stuff,' said Barry.

'Yes, but it's also used quite commonly right up to this day in demolition, things like that,' said Bev.

They paused, looking at the pictures pasted up on the white wall. A burned-out car smouldering on a driveway with something fresh out of a nightmare perched grinning behind the steering wheel. Another car ablaze, the doors blown off, skeletal remains sitting there in the driver's seat. And then the club. The Ruby's signage shattered and half down, the dust-choked gaping maw of the place that had once held tables, chairs, nightlife, happy paying customers. Now – nothing.

'So – suspects?' asked Romilly.

'Where would you start?' Barry scoffed.

'Meaning?' asked Bev.

'Meaning, Tom Knox was a villain. Fingers in all sorts of nasty pies. And Ruby Darke? Mistress of Tom, mother to Kit, I mean, you wouldn't have to look very far with that bunch, now would you?'

'Their enemies, then.'

'Too many to count.'

'Nevertheless,' said Romilly, 'count them we will. Bev, you take the Marlow end, dig around there. Barry, Tom Knox. I'll do the club. We want to know everything about these people and who had the motivation to commit these crimes against them.' She saw Barry smirk. 'Bad 'uns or not, the law's the law and whether they involve villains or upright pillars of the community, the fact remains the same: we uphold it. Right?'

'Right, Chief,' they all echoed.

'Okay, let's crack on,' said Romilly.

# 40

# DAY EIGHT

Tarrant the bomb disposal man had a coldly crisp army manner and an air of deep dissatisfaction at finding a female in charge of the investigation surrounding the destroyed burlesque club. He was inside the police tapes poking around in the wreckage of it when DI Romilly Kane met up with him.

'Hell of a mess,' he said, barely glancing up at her face but giving her tits a thorough once-over.

Romilly had to agree with his diagnosis. Underfoot there were shards of glass, shreds of photographic paper depicting smiling artistes, three jagged metres of fractured pink South African quartzite that had once been the bar. The overwhelming stench of brick dust was mixing with booze from the shattered optics – whisky, vodka, brandy. You could get drunk if you just breathed in too hard, she thought. The firemen had shut off the water, and the electricity and the gas main – intact – had both been turned off.

'At least no one was in here when it blew,' said Romilly. 'The barmaid was late opening up thank God.'

'Hmm.'

'Any clues as to the—?'

'Semtex. Behind the bar, that's the flash point. Tucked in behind one of the fridges there. The blast blew up and out to the front of the club. Strong old building, this one, but they'll have to check out those on both sides, make sure they're still safe and sound. Which I think is likely. Old Victorian stock, this. Built to last. We've discounted ether, by the way.'

'Ether—?'

'Also butane, propane, bottled gas.'

Romilly was beginning to get annoyed at his offhand manner. And she hadn't cared for the tit inspection, either. 'Explain about the ether.'

'It can be used for making cocaine.'

'This is a working club. I actually know the owner. Nobody was making drugs on these premises. For one thing, there wouldn't have been the space to facilitate that, and for another, the owner wouldn't be so bloody dense as to do it.'

He looked at her. Directly in the eyes this time. *Yeah, buster. My eyes are up here, okay?* 'People do,' he said.

'Not these people.' She wasn't going to explain about Ruby Darke and her son Kit, both of whom were already far too close to other dealings in the dark belly of the underworld to risk growing weed on their own premises.

Tarrant was staring at her doubtfully, a flicker of amusement in his eyes now. Just as if, in fact, she was some soft-headed twerp who didn't know her own arse from a hole in the ground. Infuriating. 'You're sure?' he asked.

'Positive.'

'Don't go into the back office. Unsafe in there. We'll get in RSJ's and it'll be shored up by tomorrow. I'll get the report written up,' he said, and strode off, crunching through the debris.

'Arsehole,' said Romilly loudly. She didn't like the major, but she'd had plenty of brushes with him in the past and he certainly knew his job. If he said this was Semtex, then it was Semtex. And it was Semtex that had killed Thomas Knox and Fats.

'Who is an arsehole?' asked DS Bev Appleton, delicately picking her way over to where Romilly stood amid the rubble, looking none the worse for all her troubles.

'The sergeant-at-arms there. I think he'd like to drill me. And not in a good way.'

Bev grinned. 'You've chewed up and spat out tougher than that. What's his opinion then?'

'Semtex.'

'Same as the other two.'

'The same.'

Inwardly, Romilly was groaning. She was going to have to talk to Kit Miller again.

# 41
## DAY EIGHT

Kit got home late and let Ashok and himself into his Knightsbridge place, hoping for nothing more than something that passed for instant and edible in the freezer, followed by a hot shower and then bed.

'It's a damned good motive to kill someone, don't you think?' he asked Ashok. 'Thomas abandoned Declan's mother for a horde of women, and now we hear Declan's up to all sorts with his father's widow?'

'It's a very damned good motive,' agreed Ashok. One of his watchers had put some photos through the letterbox and he was now going through them. Declan and Chloe arm in arm, shopping in St James's. Chloe and Declan going through the front door at his house, Chloe's face marked with scratches from the flying glass of the explosion that had killed her husband. Lots of eye contact there with her and Declan.

The answering machine was blinking, so Kit picked up. One message from Ruby, asking him to phone. And another from Max Carter. He called Max first.

'Max? What's up?'

'You're not going to like this.'

'What?'

'Welsh Joe's boys have got hold of the youngest Francis kid and they're beating the crap out of him over at the arches.'

*Shit.*

'For what?' asked Kit.

'Trying to make him confess to the Francis mob knocking off Thomas, I reckon. Joe's got shit for brains. No doubt he thinks this'll get him in good with you – and Ruby, too.'

Kit stared at the phone. 'Hold on. You're not telling me that ugly great son of a bitch thinks he's got a chance there? With Ruby?'

'She's a handsome woman,' said Max.

'She'd eat him alive,' said Kit. 'Talk about punching, the stupid fucker.'

'Well, if anything could start a war, *this* could. The Francis lot won't like this. All they'll see is Joe's connection to you.'

'There *is* no connection.'

'Joe thinks there is. And by the time he's through fucking everything up, they will too.'

That was Kit's peaceful night done for. 'Thanks Max. I owe you.'

'Yeah. You do.'

He was going to have to run. But Ruby. He paused. Quickly called her back. 'Mum? Can we hurry this up?'

'Why? What's happening?'

He told her about the action over in the arches.

'It's just that Father Riley phoned,' said Ruby. 'Nothing to hold you up I suppose but sad news anyway – Gabe Ward passed an hour ago.'

Not so much 'sad' as hotly anticipated, thought Kit.

'How d'you feel about that?' he asked.

'Relieved, I think. Michael never liked him and I always thought it was a shame, but there you go. He's in a better place.'

Kit kept replaying his hospital conversation with Gabe over and over in his brain.

*You're too late. It's already happening . . .*

'Go to go,' he said, and hung up and practically ran out of the house, Ashok tight on his heels.

# 42

# DAY EIGHT

It was all kicking off over at the arches. When Ashok stopped the car they could hear it straight away – someone in there was screaming the place down.

'Stay here,' Kit told Ashok. 'Keep the motor running.'

Then he got out, went to the boot, snatched out what he needed and strode off in the direction of the noise.

One of Welsh Joe's boys, mean-eyed, squat and wide as a tank, stood in Kit's way.

'Mr Miller?' He put a restraining hand flat to Kit's chest, but Kit was already swinging the baseball bat round. It connected with the man's head with a noise like a cracked walnut and he keeled over. Kit strode on past the fallen man and there was Welsh Joe in the centre of one of the arches, the place coldly lit up with harsh fluorescents, with the skinny, bloody and beaten Francis kid, not even seventeen years old yet, tied to a chair, his big brown eyes bulging with terror.

Welsh Joe, standing to one side, looked up in astonishment as Kit came in.

'What the fuck? Kit?' he had time to say, starting to smile, before Kit came at him swinging. The bat *whopped* against Joe's head and he staggered back and collapsed to the floor like a sack of shit. Blood started seeping from a cut on his massive brow.

Two of his boys stepped up.

Kit turned on them.

'*Oh yeah? Really? You want some too?*' he yelled in their faces.

They stopped, uncertain.

'Untie the kid you arseholes,' he snapped.

They stood looking to their fallen boss, not knowing which way to jump.

'I *said,* untie the poor little bastard. Right now,' Kit said flatly.

Joe, on the floor and clutching at his head, looked up at his men and nodded.

They stepped forward, untied the boy. The Francis kid staggered to his feet and lurched, bent double, past Kit, heading for the door.

'The car's outside. Asian guy at the wheel. Get in it,' Kit told him, and the boy ran on, weaving like a drunk, skirting the man at the door who was now sitting up, clutching his head.

Then Kit turned to Welsh Joe, pointed the bat at him. 'Not clever, Joe. Not clever at all.'

Joe's two cronies started pulling their boss back to his feet.

'Fuck's sake, I was helping you out,' shouted Joe.

'*Really?*' Kit stepped forward, wielding the bat. The three of them shrank back. Kit Miller in a fuming temper wasn't pretty. 'Well don't help anymore, Joe. Or I'll help *you* into a fucking wooden overcoat. I mean it.'

Kit turned, walked past the man on the door and out to the car. The Francis kid was in the back, shivering with shock.

'Let's tidy this cunt up and get him home to his mother,' said Kit. He looked at the kid. 'And you. Listen. You keep it buttoned, all right? You don't know who attacked you. You didn't see a thing. That's the only way we're going to keep this from blowing up into outright war.'

# 43
## DAY EIGHT

At midnight, Kit's doorbell rang and he and Ashok – they hadn't bothered going to bed, they knew this night's excitements were nowhere near their end – shot each other a look that said *here we go then*.

They had delivered the Francis kid back home to Pat Francis's place in Northdown Street, just along the road from the Prince of Wales pub, which the Francis gang owned, along with just about every other business around that area.

Mrs Francis had opened the door, seen her bleeding, bedraggled son, opened her arms and let out a wail of maternal outrage. She all but dragged the boy in through the door. With the kid inside, Kit stood there and waited for Pat to show himself, a big, fat bald-headed bruiser of a man. He came to the door in vest and braces with a face like a bulldog on the attack, his two huge sons – the kid's older brothers – behind him. None of them looked pleased at this turn of events.

'*Who?*' roared out Pat Francis.

'No ideas about that Pat. But we found your kid down Bermondsey way,' was all that Kit would say. 'He's okay. Shaken up. A bit hurt. He'll be all right.'

Pat stared at Kit hard.

'G'night,' said Kit and turned away.

He only realised he was sweating when he heard the door close quietly behind him. He walked back to the car, listening for hurried footsteps at his back. Ashok was at the wheel. Kit got in the car and that was that. Ashok drove them back to the Knightsbridge house and they sat in the lounge, waiting. Hoping for nothing, hoping that when it passed around two o'clock they could get off to bed, get some sleep.

Then, the doorbell rang.

Kit and Ashok went out into the hall. The camera over the front door porch told them that their visitor was Welsh Joe with a huge blood-stained bandage wrapped around his massive head. Nobody was standing behind him. A car, engine running, headlights blaring, was stationary out in the road; that was all.

Kit went back into the lounge and looked around. Damn, he really liked this wallpaper. Osborne and Little. Very nice and extremely expensive. Quality.

He opened a drawer, closed it, then nodded to Ashok, who went out into the hall and pressed the intercom.

'Where the fuck are you, Miller?' yelled Welsh Joe from outside.

Kit took a seat as Ashok opened the front door. Joe bustled in down the hall and barrelled into the lounge at ninety miles an hour, shoving his vast bulk into the centre of the room. He planted himself there and pulled out a machete from beneath his coat and stood over Kit.

'What the fuck d'you—?' he started.

Kit shot him.

# 44
# DAY EIGHT

The *bang* of the gun going off reverberated in the enclosed space like a sonic boom. No plaster flew from the walls, no blood spatter marked the pricey wallpaper. Even so, Welsh Joe dropped the machete and went flying back onto the floor as if the hand of God had struck him. He lay there gasping, staring up at the ceiling.

Ashok left the room, closing the door quietly behind him. Kit stood up, kicked the machete out of harm's way. Waited. Slipped the gun back into his jacket pocket. Waited some more.

'What the fucking hell?' asked Joe presently.

He sat up shakily.

Kit prodded him with his toe. 'You all right there, Joe?'

'You fucking shot me!'

'So I did.'

'For fuck's sake!'

'Yeah. Only – Joe – I've got to have a word with you about all this.'

'What?'

Kit hunkered down beside Joe and said, very gently: 'Joe. You're a mate, right? So listen – just between us – as a mate, I'm saying this to you. You keep away from my mother, she don't want your attention. There's no vacancy to be filled there. Don't fool yourself. Don't be a cunt. Also – keep your nose the fuck out of my business, Joe. I mean it. You go charging in like that where you're not wanted just one more time and that's it, there's going to be trouble. I delivered the Francis kid back home to his mother, and Pat Francis looked at me like he'd like to tear my guts out and throttle me with them. I wasn't sure he was going to let me go, but luckily enough he did. So it's done and we're all square. Everything's fine. Now all that remains is for you to take what I'm telling you on board, Joe, or I'm telling you, there'll be a fight.'

'You fucking shot me,' Joe gasped again, shock plain on his face. He patted his stomach.

'Oh shut up you tart. I aimed for the vest.'

Kit knew – in fact *everyone* knew – that Welsh Joe was always in girlish fear of assassination and so wore a bulky Kevlar construction around his oversized gut. But Kit had lied. He hadn't been going to aim for the vest, he'd intended to aim for Joe's left upper arm. A wound there would hurt like a bastard but wouldn't do much damage – except to Kit's pricey wallpaper. The sight of the machete in Joe's hand, however, had changed Kit's mind at the last minute, so he'd hit Joe square in the middle, right in the vest, to knock all the wind out of him.

'You got me, Joe? You understand what I'm saying? Let's put this to bed right now, okay?' said Kit.

Joe was nodding his big head.

'We understand each other?' asked Kit, holding out a hand.

Joe nodded again. He took the offered hand and was hoisted back to his feet.

'Now listen. You listening, Joe? I don't want to have to talk about this, ever again,' said Kit. 'Are we clear?'

Joe nodded – and left.

# 45

# DAY NINE

Next day, Kit went to Ruby's place and to his surprise found his mother up, dressed in her pin-striped business skirt suit, her hair in a neat chignon, her make-up faultless. It was over a week now since Thomas Knox had bought it. And a week since Fats had bought it too, sitting on a bomb that had been intended for her own son. Kit expected Ruby still to be sloping around in her dressing gown, shedding tears. But then – this was Ruby Darke. And Ruby Darke might sometimes be beaten, but she was *never* down and out.

'Going somewhere?' he asked.

'Got to sort out the insurance on the club. And see where we go from here. Can it be rebuilt? Do I *want* it rebuilt? We'll see. Lots to do, none of it very enjoyable. But it has to be done.'

'You up to it? Can't Daisy help?'

'I'm going to,' said Daisy, coming into the sitting room also suited and booted. 'Ready, Mum?'

'We waiting for Daniel?' asked Ruby.

'Yes. You are,' said Kit. 'And a driver, too. Safety in numbers.'

*

Later that morning, DI Romilly Kane called in at Ruby's once again to find that Ruby and Daisy were gone but Kit was there. Ruby was, he explained, conducting the tedious but necessary business of tidying up the club's affairs.

'I heard there was a bit of a scuffle last night out Bermondsey way,' she said.

'You heard that did you? What happened?' asked Kit.

'Someone seems to have been assaulted.'

'Oh?'

'With a baseball bat, was what happened. Apparently.'

'All sorts kicking off these days.'

'You weren't anywhere near there, I suppose?'

'Me? Nah.'

Romilly eyed him steadily. 'Okay,' she said.

Joe had been an expanding problem for months now and Kit knew where the Welshman was coming from. Having had big problems on his own patch, Joe had been looking at Kit's well-ordered streets with envy and casting covetous glances at Ruby, determined to make himself look the big man to impress her – particularly now that Thomas Knox was off the scene.

Hell, maybe *Joe* was behind Thomas's death, who knew?

Stranger things had happened.

And then, Kit pondered, had Welsh Joe – with Thomas out of the way, Thomas who was now sitting on a cloud somewhere twanging his harp alongside that loser Gabe Ward – had Joe then thought, *hey, get* Kit *out the way too and I can take over the whole shebang*? Take Kit's protection rackets, his clubs, his streets, his everything, and even get a crack at his glamorous mother. Was that what was going on here?

Now Kit was wishing that he had hit Joe's head much sooner – and harder.

Right now he felt weighed down with troubles. He missed Fats around the place, a calm and reassuring presence. And while his brain spun, Romilly, businesslike as ever, was checking and rechecking the statement he'd made to her the other day, letting him make any minor alterations, getting him to sign it. Again.

'If that's all . . . ?' Kit asked, exasperated, wanting to get on.

'I was at your mum's club yesterday,' said Romilly. 'Hell of a mess.'

'Yeah. A bastard,' agreed Kit.

'Seems like someone's got it in for your family,' she said.

'Don't it just.'

'But bearing in mind the people you deal with . . .' she said, shrugging.

'It's not surprising? No. I suppose not. If there's nothing else . . . ?'

'There isn't,' she said, and left.

# 46
# DAY NINE

As DS Bev Appleton drove her back to the office, Romilly sat beside her and chewed it all over. She didn't like to think about *any* of it, but having just seen Kit, she couldn't avoid it. He was the catalyst and now her brain was charging along, debating, saying *well it was for the best* while of course her stupid heart wasn't saying the same thing, not at all.

'You okay there?' asked Bev, mid-journey.

'Fine,' said Romilly, and offered nothing more.

*Kit.*

Just last year.

Oh shit, just last year.

They'd had a hot, *hot* affair. Meeting each other in secret, tearing the clothes off each other, hungry for the sort of mind-numbing lust-driven sex that she'd never experienced before. He was a great, great lover and she'd been happy. Truly happy. Whistling on her way into work, cheerful as hell. Knowing it was all mad, all completely crazy, but what could you do?

And then she had gone over to her parents' house one Sunday evening, the usual visit to the folks, to see Mum who was forever wondering out loud when her daughter was going to settle down, and her father, who had once been a copper like Romilly and was on this particular visit curiously quiet, taking his daughter to one side and saying he wanted a word, all right?

'About what?' she'd asked him. She had never seen him look so solemn.

'I hope it's nothing,' he said, and led the way out into the garden and said: 'But look – I heard something.'

'What are you talking about?' asked Romilly, admiring the roses, cheerfully ignorant of the fact that her world was about to come crashing down around her ears.

'Something about you.' Her dad hesitated, then charged on: 'About you and that bloody mobster Kit Miller.'

Romilly froze. 'What?' She could feel her face reddening, could feel her mouth settling into a false, bewildered smile. Couldn't seem to help it.

'You know we meet up, me and some of the boys from the old brigade,' he went on. 'Sometimes I would walk into a room and have the feeling they'd been talking about me, you know? Conversations sort of tailing away, sideways glances. Nothing you could put your finger on, not really. Brian Cross, my oldest friend, you know Brian?'

Romilly nodded. She had to force some spit into her mouth to be able to speak. They'd been discreet, hadn't they? *More* than discreet.

*But these are cops,* she thought.

'I know Brian,' she managed to get out.

'Well, you know him; he always calls a spade a shit-shovel. No pussyfooting around the place with him, is there.'

'Right.'

'And he told me there are rumours – *strong* rumours that there is something going on and that you'd better put a stop to it because you could find yourself in trouble. At best you'll be back on the beat, at worst you'll be sacked, disgraced. He said I ought to have a word with you. So that's what I'm doing.'

'Dad . . .' She didn't know what to say. She felt unable to respond in any coherent fashion.

'I know these things can be . . . well, overwhelming,' he went on. 'I *know* that. Being older and being married don't mean you forget what it's like to feel passion. God knows I got into a few scrapes myself in the past. But . . .' He stopped speaking, shook his head, stared hard at his daughter's guilty-as-fuck face. 'God's sake, Romilly. God's *sake*. Kit Miller? You know what he is. You know the rackets he's into. Are you kidding me?'

So, there it was. Dad knew. All his mates knew. Which meant others on the force must know too.

Next day she phoned Kit, arranged a meeting.

Told him it was all over.

He'd taken it well, she thought.

She'd gone home, locked the door and cried.

But it was a clean break. Not painless, but complete. Done, dusted, *over*.

She knew she'd done the right thing.

Then she got into work a week later and her boss, DCI James Barrow, who was a highly respected copper with faded ginger hair and thick spectacles, called her into his office, told her to sit down and promptly proceeded to tear the arse off her.

'Are you fucking deluded?' he roared.

He ranted for a good ten minutes and then flopped down in his seat behind the desk. He flung his glasses down onto the desktop and shook his head.

'You bloody fool,' he said more quietly.

'It's over,' said Romilly.

And it was. Of *course* it was. It had to be.

'I ought to take this further,' he said.

'Yes,' said Romilly.

He was silent, staring at her.

'You're one of the brightest and best on the force,' he said.

Romilly said nothing. Waited for the axe to fall.

'I'm not going to take it any further,' said DCI Barrow.

Romilly stared at him in blank surprise. 'Sir . . . ?'

'It's done. It's over. That's the truth? It better bloody be.'

She nodded. Heart broken, head reeling. 'I swear.'

'Then get the fuck on back to work and don't let me hear another word about this. All right? If I do, your arse will be out that door faster than you can turn around, you got that?'

'Got it, sir.'

She'd been as good as her word. Got on with her job, solved cases, led her team, ignored the longing, the crushing, *crucifying* longing for him.

Now this case had brought her into contact with him again.

But she could be strong. She knew that.

Christ, she *had* to be.

She closed her eyes and tried to doze as Bev drove on. And she tried not to think about Kit Miller.

# 47

# DAY NINE

At lunchtime, Kit was in the Ivy – and there waiting for him was the fourth wife, the one before Chloe took over the outfit: Gilly Taylor-Black. Gilly was seated on a bar stool, smiling a glitteringly white smile, all dolled up in a flashy sequinned designer trouser suit.

Just one of those women would have exhausted and exasperated him, Kit knew it. Drab little Jean – who after quite a long stay as Thomas's wife had then been supplanted by the beautiful but tediously vain Ursula. Then one daughter from that union – the maybe-fourteen-year-old-or-maybe-not Evie – and then on to the next when Thomas's fancies turned to the horse world and he tripped over Avril Gulliver at Cheltenham and another daughter emerged – Olivia. Now here was Gilly. She hadn't kept the Knox name either, he noted. As soon as the ink was dry on the divorce papers, she'd taken back her own surname.

'Mr Miller?' she asked, giving him the once-over. 'I'm Gilly Taylor-Black.'

She had an upper-crust accent that reminded him of his twin Daisy. Cultured and low. Gave a person a big advantage in life, he knew that. His own voice was pure East End hardman. Which also, come to think of it, had its advantages.

*Her daddy's an Earl,* Ashok had told him.

'You're very handsome,' she said.

'So are you,' said Kit, taking a seat beside her and ordering a martini. She was a good-looking woman, exquisitely made up, her glossy auburn rich-girl hair hanging in loose luxuriant curls around her shoulders, tinted with paler strawberry blonde streaks around her face to pimp her up like a lighting movie master. The only flaw he could find in her was some strange business going on under the tip of her nose.

'Are you loaded then, dahling? You have the look,' she said archly. 'Yes, I think you're loaded. Where are you from? Somewhere exotic, I bet.'

She reached out, emptied her glass of some yellow liquid and nodded for a refill. It crossed Kit's mind that it was barely twelve-thirty and she was already well on her way to being drunk.

'Yeah. Very exotic,' he said, not wanting to get into that.

He wondered – not for the first time – if the accident of his and Daisy's birth could have given a very different result. He'd suffered indifferent kids' homes and then a wild life fending for himself on the streets, while Daisy had been swept off to Brayfield House, pony clubs and private schools. What if it had happened the other way round? What if he'd been the golden boy and Daisy the unacceptable one? Useless to speculate. It was what it was. How Ruby had produced twins that were totally different in skin tone – and what all that had meant for them – he had no intention of *ever* discussing it. It stung, even now, the way he'd been treated because he'd been dark while Daisy had been fair, even after all the years that had passed, all the reunions and partings and fights and make-ups; ridiculously, it *still* could hurt.

'Do you know what my father told me when I was very, very young?' Gilly asked him.

He sipped his martini. 'No. What?'

'He said don't go to places where there are poor people. Never hang around public houses and working men's clubs and snooker halls. Things like that. Don't do it. As if I ever would.'

'I'd say that's useful advice,' said Kit. 'My mum told me that you never meet a nice girl down the pub.'

'Quite. Of course, he said don't *marry* only for money and make yourself miserable if you have no feelings for the fellow involved. But you must go to where money *is*. Places like this. And follow the season, of course.'

'The season?' Kit squinted at her.

'Cheltenham. Wimbledon. Ascot. The Regatta at Henley. Things like that.'

'Lots of monied people in here,' Kit said, looking around.

'Yes there are,' she agreed, still smiling that shiny-white smile. 'You see him over there?'

Kit looked. She was pointing out a tall silver-haired man at one of the far tables, huddled with a group of people in a cosy banquette. He had the unmistakable gloss of riches and he looked familiar. Kit knew he'd seen him somewhere. Maybe on TV?

'He's a football manager. See that woman with him, isn't she pretty? Much younger than him, and so polished don't you think? Well she has to be. That's his mistress. He's married of course. And that particular mistress has been around for a while. Long-term for a mistress – around two years – is always bad news. These men are high achievers and they get bored very quickly. He's bored right now, I can tell. The mistress will be abandoned.'

'Which leaves a vacancy. Do you think you'll fill it?' asked Kit.

She widened her eyes at him and let out a peal of laughter. 'You're audacious! Are you gay? You don't look it.'

'I'm not gay.'

'Well – let me tell you – a football manager is very much a prize. Pots of money. A girl could always be sure of turning left on commercial aircraft if she was with a man like that. Or better still, private jet. That's the way they often travel, you know. And it's very, very nice, I can tell you. Or if there's no football manager – or footballer – available, how about a company CEO? That's a good one. I had a Crown prince once, briefly. Attention span of a *gnat*. Over in six months. But so much fun. Yachts in the med. Monte Carlo. Cap d'Antibes, Cannes. Forget turning left in commercial aeroplanes with that one, it's strictly private all the way. Those jets fly at forty thousand feet, you know, not thirtyish like the commercial airliners, so all that horrid turbulence is avoided. *Really* comfortable, just *luscious*. He had money in – where is that place? – the Caymans. And Monaco of course. They all bank abroad, these men. And don't believe for one moment what the politicians tell you about cracking down on 'non-doms'. They've no intention of doing that. They wouldn't – *couldn't* – do it. What, and have all their friends send them to Coventry? Or – worse – cut themselves out of all the best deals? No way.'

'You heard about Thomas?' Kit chipped in.

That sobered her, but only slightly.

She nodded.

'Yes. Of course. So sad.' Then she summoned the bartender, gestured for a refill, and she was straight off the subject of Thomas and back onto her favourite one: herself.

'My father cut me off, you know. Just cut me off without a single penny, when I married Thomas. Daddy said he was a dreadful low-life Cockney wideboy and he wouldn't lower himself by associating with such a creature.' She pouted. 'Well Thomas *was* all of that. He was my "bit of rough" I suppose. He was edgy and forceful and – well – *rich* too, and that was, all in all, a very attractive package.'

'Who would want to kill him, do you suppose?' Kit asked.

The bartender brought the drinks and she gulped down a mouthful, reeling a bit on her bar stool.

'Steady,' said Kit, reaching out a hand to stop her falling.

'I'm okay,' she said. 'You just startled me. Saying that.'

'Any ideas?' asked Kit.

'Well, we all hated him in the end. Maybe not Jean, but the rest of us? He treated us very meanly.'

That wasn't what Kit had heard. Apparently, Thomas had been fair to the women. Incapable of fidelity, of course, but he'd seen all these women – and the kids – more or less okay when he'd moved on.

'Jean calls you all "the gang". Did you know that? She was offended when you all showed up and asked her to sell the place Thomas had left her.'

Gilly sniffed, took out a handkerchief. Dabbed at her nose. Saw Kit watching her and looked almost embarrassed.

'Don't stare,' she said.

'I'm not.'

'I'm getting it fixed.'

'What?'

'It was inhaling the powder, you know. It sort of dissolved the inside bit, right there. Stupid. You should never over-use that stuff.'

Cocaine. She was talking about cocaine. So Gilly not only had expensive tastes, she had expensive habits, too. He thought of 'the gang'. One a rich man chaser and drug user, one with a horse-breeding business going to the bad, another with a very costly appearance to upkeep.

'Want my number?' she asked, and for a moment he could see it all quite clearly, her sitting here day after day, patient as a black widow spider, waiting for the next rich patsy to fall into her web and be trapped, sucked dry and spat out – and the wealth of the men diminishing slowly, in direct relation to her fading looks, as the years passed by. It was fucking tragic.

'Yeah, sure,' he said. She handed him a card.

'Thanks,' he said, and left.

\*

When he got home, the answerphone was blinking. It was Father Riley asking him to call back.

'I just wanted to let you know that poor Gabriel Ward's funeral is scheduled for tomorrow.'

He gave Kit the details.

'I doubt there'll be much attendance, so your presence would be appreciated.'

'By who?' asked Kit.

'By God, Mr Miller,' said the priest. 'By God.'

# 48

# DAY TEN

Gabriel Ward's cremation was not a high church affair. No weeping women, no thunderingly sad organ music. There were just a lot of empty seats and a whimsical taped melody being played in the background when Kit arrived. Gabe's coffin was already on the dais and the priest, a big, grey-bearded man, was ready to do what he could to send Gabe on his way to wherever his soul was destined to go.

Father Riley was there, in his dog-collar and black robes, and when he saw Kit walking up the aisle he stepped out from his seat and held out a hand. Kit shook it.

'You came!' said Father Riley.

'Seems like it,' said Kit, and they took their seats.

Kit looked around. The funeral bearers had gathered at the back of the crematorium, black-suited and visibly bored. Then the door opened and in came a woman, a grey little hen in a feathered black hat and a black dress. She was carrying a large, square black handbag and wearing matching highly polished shoes. She took a seat several rows back from where Kit and Father Riley were sitting.

Kit recognised her easily from the photos Ashok had shown him. It was Jean, Thomas Knox's first wife.

The service began. As it did, the door opened again and Fabio Danieri came in all dressed in black and clutching an enormous wreath of red roses. He went to the front, placed his offering on the steps leading up to the dais, and went and sat at the back, passing close by Kit as he did so and giving him an insolent smile.

The service began. Kit thought the priest painted a deceptively rosy picture of Gabe and his life. All his own experience of Gabriel Ward had portrayed quite another image, nowhere near as flattering. Gabe had been a druggie, a waster, mixing in with a bad crowd – particularly the Danieri mob, as was proved by Fabio Danieri pitching up here today – and had driven his mother Sheila and his father Michael to the brink of despair.

Michael, though dead and gone, would forever be a hero to Kit. Michael Ward had been magnificent; but his son Gabe had been a grasping loser. Kit knew that. The situation had got so bad in the Ward family that Michael had totally rejected his son. Instead, he had favoured Kit, who he'd dragged in off the mean streets where he'd been drifting, rootless and starving after coming out of a kid's home.

Kit remembered those days all too well. He'd slept on park benches, stuffing newspapers down his clothes to try to keep warm. He knew he'd been on the brink of going under, not surviving. So when Michael had taken him in, seen something in him, Kit had been eager to repay his debt. He'd learned the game and swiftly climbed the ranks. He'd become both polished and deadly and ended up as Michael Ward's chief breaker. Michael had given Kit everything – including, much to Gabe's fury, the inheritance that would otherwise have passed to *him*.

Not that any of it mattered now. As the ceremony came to a conclusion, Kit watched dispassionately as Gabe's mortal remains disappeared behind the curtains. He wasn't really listening anymore to the priest as the man wound up

176 *Jessie Keane*

the ceremony. His attention was fixed on Jean Knox – now Coyden – who had left her seat and was heading for the door. Without saying goodbye to Father Riley and noting that Fabio Danieri had already gone, leaving his ostentatious wreath leaning against the steps up to the dais, Kit hurried after her and caught up with her outside the crematorium's entrance.

'Jean? Miss Coyden?' he called out, because she had gone down the steps and was looking around the car park as if expecting someone.

She turned, looked at him blankly.

'Kit,' he said. 'I'm Kit Miller.'

'Oh! Oh, yes.' She looked irritated by his showing up here. 'I'm waiting for Declan, he said he'd pick me up at one.'

'And he's not here?'

'No. He never could get *anywhere* on time.'

'I wasn't aware that you knew Gabe,' said Kit.

'Not that it's any business of yours, but yes, I do. *Did*,' she corrected herself. 'It's a very sad day,' she added primly.

'Yeah,' said Kit, thinking of Gabe lying in that hospital bed saying it was too late, it was done, and laughing. *Laughing.*

Thomas dying.

Fats, dying.

Ruby's club, going up in smoke.

'While you're waiting for Declan, can we talk?' he asked.

Her eyes were still combing the – practically empty – car park. Even the hearse was gone. Ashok was sitting in the car, forever patient, watchful, waiting. It was a hot summer's day, but the wind gusted then and Kit felt a shiver go through him.

'All right,' she said.

# 49

## DAY TEN

'So what's your connection to Gabe Ward?' asked Kit.

Jean gave him a stony look.

'*Not* that it's any concern of yours,' she huffed, 'but Gabriel and my boy Declan grew up together. Played together as little kids. Of course, as they got older they drifted apart, went on to different things, *very* different things.'

'Like drugs, in Gabe's case,' said Kit.

'He was a troubled boy.' Her eyes were resting on Kit's face, and they were not approving. 'His father as good as abandoned him, which broke Sheila his mother's heart and I think it broke Gabe's too. Of course, everyone knows that Michael favoured you over his own son. Which I think was unforgivable.'

Kit took this on board. Then he said: 'Michael tried with Gabe. I know that. But he seemed to be determined to go bad. And he did.'

She shrugged. 'And I dare say that suited you very well, didn't it?'

'In what way?'

'Well I heard that Michael left everything he had to you. Are you telling me I've got that wrong? The restaurant – Sheila's, it was called, after Michael's wife – and the snooker

halls and the clubs and all the other bits of business he liked
to be involved in. You got the lot, didn't you? Snatched
Gabe's inheritance out from under him, the poor boy.'

Kit stared at her levelly. 'I didn't "snatch" anything.
Michael fell out with Gabe long before I came on the scene.
I had no hand in that.' A sleek red car was pulling into the
park. Declan, at last. Jean visibly relaxed.

'If they were boyhood friends, why didn't Declan attend
the service?' asked Kit.

'He hates funerals,' said Jean.

'Will he show up for Thomas's?' Kit had been wondering
about that. A bit fucking cheeky, when you consider Declan
had been boffing Thomas's latest wife.

'I don't see that's any of your business,' she said frostily.
'Will *you*?'

Jean tucked her chin in and primly straightened her handbag. 'Again – not your business,' she said, and went down
the steps, got into the front passenger seat of Declan's car,
and was away.

'Well that's me told,' murmured Kit, and then he became
aware suddenly of movement in his peripheral vision. He
thought: *Fabio.* He felt his heartbeat accelerate and he spun
around fast, ready to lash out.

He stopped dead.

It was DI Kane.

# 50

## DAY TEN

'Jesus!' yelped Romilly, flinching back.

Kit took a breath. Shit, he'd nearly punched her lights out.

'You know, if you go sneaking around like that, you are very likely to get your teeth back in an ashtray,' he said. His heart was pounding. He'd been jumpier than he'd thought. The upheavals of the last week or so had got to him. He didn't like that.

'And hello to you too,' she said, coming to the edge of the steps and watching Declan's car spin out of the drive with a chirp of rubber, then out into the road and away. 'That's Tom Knox's son, isn't it? And the woman, wasn't that . . . ?'

'Tom's first wife,' said Kit. 'Jean.'

'She doesn't like you.'

'Oh, you heard?'

'A bit. Enough.'

'Can't be Mr Popularity all the time,' he shrugged.

'She thinks you shafted Gabriel Ward. Michael Ward's son.'

'She does. Actually, I didn't.' *Or maybe he's shafted me.*

'I'm surprised to see you here. You were hardly pals.'

'Father Riley appealed to my better nature.'

'Wasn't aware you had one.'

'Neither was I. Yet here I am.'

'And you visited him in hospital, too.'

Kit widened his eyes. 'Detective, you've been keeping tabs on me. Yes, I did.'

'Why?' she asked.

'Because the priest asked me to.'

'Storing up points for heaven?'

'Maybe. I like to hedge my bets.' For Christ's sake, had he actually been *scared* just now, for a split-second? He didn't know the meaning of fear, not usually. But seeing Fabio Danieri here today had rattled him. He had a hidden enemy skulking about, under the radar – and now he had made a *new* one in Welsh Joe, which had been unavoidable but unfortunate. He'd had to lay down a marker, to say to Joe firmly, *enough.* He didn't like any of this, and felt the need, the *urgent* need, for movement. He went down the steps, heading for the car, where Ashok was waiting. To his annoyance, Romilly followed.

'Hey. Don't rush off,' she said.

Kit stopped, turned, eyes narrowed. 'You didn't say that last year. You said – oh let me see – oh yeah. You said *fuck off out of my life,* those were your exact words.'

Romilly stopped too. Crossed her arms. Tilted her head and looked hard at him.

'*What?*' asked Kit, exasperated.

'Nothing. I'm just surprised you remembered the *exact words,* that's all. It's as if they meant something to you.'

'If there's nothing else . . . ?' said Kit.

'There's plenty else. I'm investigating two murders and the destruction of your mother's club, so if there's anything you know about any of that, you tell me.'

'Right. I'll bear that in mind.' He turned away.

'And don't get snippy with me. I assume you want a result on all this just as much as I do. More, probably.'

Kit turned back. He stepped toward her, his eyes half-laughing, half-threatening, as they met hers.

'Don't get *what*? *Snippy?*' He let out a bark of laughter. 'What is this, the fucking school yard?'

Romilly said nothing.

'Look, Detective . . .' said Kit, squaring up to her.

'It's Detective Inspector. As you fucking well know.'

'Only what I heard—'

'What?' Romilly snapped.

'I heard you nearly found yourself back on the beat. Some arsehole on the force thought there was something going on between us and so—'

'Mr Miller.'

'And so I was dumped. That's what happened, isn't it?'

'Mr *Miller.*'

'No need to be so formal. The name's Kit. I told you.'

The trouble was, Romilly thought, he was too damned clever. Not having spoken to him at any length in months, she had forgotten – she had *chosen* to forget – how quickly Kit Miller's mind worked, how deftly he could dominate a conversation and turn things to his own advantage.

*And* he was so damned good looking. In a white shirt, black suit and tie, he looked nothing short of fabulous. Romilly felt a pain in her chest, a pain that was pure loss. Into her mind then, unwelcome and unbidden, came a vision; the two of them tangled on a bed, laughing, kissing, making love. All gone. She'd abandoned *that* and saved what she had once strived her whole life for: her career on the force.

But the trouble was, she found it hard after the event to justify that decision. She *had* told him to fuck off out of her life. Her boss had been mad at her, her father furious. Her mum disappointed, embarrassed. It had seemed that her entire life was suddenly a highly visible wreckage, up to and including her useless ex-husband Hugh, who had actually – cruelly – *laughed* at her over it.

'Boffing criminals? God's sake Romilly – *really?*' he'd mocked her.

Her mother had told him about it. Her mother still *loved* Hugh and thought Romilly was a fool to have walked out on marriage to him.

And at the bottom of it all was her undoing – Kit Miller, the dodgy bastard, who had somehow – *how?* – overcome her strict work ethic, her principles, her firm moral code. She didn't know how any of it had happened. Had she been on the rebound after the divorce from Hugh? Possibly. Or had she just been lonely? Had she been isolated by the pressures of her job, needing to find some sort of release?

Well, whatever: she'd found it. She'd lived a secret and exciting life full-pelt for a while, convincing herself that she could keep the two halves of her being separate, that *his* ways were not hers but nevertheless she had fallen in love with him and had stupidly hoped that maybe – eventually – it would all somehow work out.

Then the whole thing had imploded. Her job was – *had been* – everything to her. She had lived and breathed the force, and she was in serious danger of losing that. So Kit Miller had to go.

He'd gone.

It sounded so easy. She'd told him to go and he had.

But he'd left a gaping hole in her life. She'd toughed it out, drank too much, cried herself to sleep on the odd maudlin occasion. She'd buried herself in the work, but the truth was it didn't fulfil her the way it had before. She solved cases but felt none of that fierce, scorching after-burner pleasure she'd felt on previous cases. She felt *numb*.

Get back on the horse, she told herself. That's the fastest way to really get over it. So she had. She'd gone on a date with another copper. What a bloody disaster *that* had been. When he'd moved in for a kiss, she'd nearly thrown up and then she'd run in the opposite direction as fast as her legs would carry her.

Now Kit Miller was standing inches away from her. Kit Miller, the object of her moral ruination, nearly the ruin-ation of her entire *life*, and she was thinking, *Oh Christ, I don't know what I'm doing any more.*

He was gazing up, above the crem's rooftop. Her eyes followed the direction of his. Thick grey smoke was waft-ing up from the chimney, spiralling up into the bright blue summer sky. Despite herself, she shuddered.

'Well, there goes Gabe,' said Kit, and in that moment Romilly knew that she was going to have to be very, very careful. Yes, she was going to use Kit Miller's information, his gangland contacts, and *at the same time* she was going to have to keep him at arm's length.

That was all she had to do.

He turned to her and smiled.

'By the way,' he said, 'do you know Declan Knox is shafting his dad's widow Chloe?'

# 51
# DAY TEN

After Gabe's cremation, Kit went down to Ruby's in Marlow. He'd been thinking about her talking about turning the club's stockroom into a flat for her to use when she was up in town. If she'd *done* that, stayed over there, she'd be dead. He was aware of things moving way beyond his control, and he didn't like the feeling. And his chance meeting with Romilly at the crem had disturbed him more than he cared to admit.

*He* was usually the dumper, not the dumpee. And she'd kicked his arse to the kerb so suddenly, so unexpectedly late last year, that he'd smarted over it for months. There had been other women, of course.

Into his mind flashed *Gilda*.

Oh yes. He'd been flat-out utterly in love with Gilda. But she'd been Tito Danieri's property and the fact that Kit had forgotten about that – ignored the fact of it – had meant her death and his torture. He had the scars to prove it.

It had taken a long, long while before he'd got so involved again. And then it had been another mistake. Bianca, the sister of the Danieri boys. She'd vanished off the scene and then he was alone again. Alone didn't bother him, usually. But then Rob had died last year. Rob, his best mate, Daisy's then brand-new husband – and into his life had come Romilly Kane, sharp-eyed detective, challenging him not only physically but mentally too. She was smart. She was pretty. She was *irresistible*.

Then – too soon – she was gone.

Seeing her today? Yes, it had troubled him.

He went into Ruby's place and found his mother and sister in the sitting room at the front of the house, the curtains flung back, their security compromised. Straight away, he was irritated.

'I told you about this. Sit in the back, keep out of this room for now. It's too close to the drive, don't be so bloody *stupid*.'

Both Ruby and Daisy looked at him in flat astonishment.

'Who the *fuck*,' said Ruby, 'do you think you're talking to?'

'That goes from me too,' said Daisy. 'Who died and made you king of the world?'

Kit toned it down. 'It's not safe, that's all I'm saying. I'm thinking of you. This isn't a power play.' He drew the curtains closed, switched on a lamp.

Ruby and Daisy exchanged a look. 'So what's put you in this mood?' Ruby asked him.

'Just come from Gabe Ward's cremation,' said Kit, flopping down onto the couch. He didn't mention seeing Fabio there. *Or* Romilly.

'How did it go?' asked Daisy.

'How do you think? The place was damned near empty and nobody shed a single tear.'

'It's sad, isn't it,' said Ruby. 'Michael dying before they could be reconciled.'

'Anyway. It's done,' said Kit.

Daniel moved into the open doorway, and something passed between him and Daisy. A look from him, a sudden flicker of unease from her.

'What?' asked Kit.

'Daisy's got something to tell you,' said Daniel.

'Oh – that,' she said tiredly.

'Like what?' asked Kit.

'What's this about?' asked Ruby.

'You're not going to like it,' said Daniel.

Daisy jumped to her feet and rounded on Daniel. 'Will you shut up? I said I would tell him and I will. This is me, telling him. Okay?'

'Telling me what?' asked Kit.

'I started seeing someone,' said Daisy. 'Recently.'

'All right. Who?'

Daniel opened his eyes wide at Daisy and crossed his arms over his chest.

'Luca Romano,' said Daisy.

'Luca . . . the Danieri cousin?' asked Kit.

Daisy nodded. 'And before you start, listen – I didn't know he was anything to do with that mob. If I *had*, I wouldn't have gone near him.'

'Fuck's sake! What are you playing at, Daise? It has to stop,' said Kit.

'It already has,' said Daisy.

Kit shot Daniel a look. 'You've been party to this?'

'When I found out who she was meeting, I told her that she had to tell you. Or *I* would tell you.'

'Yes, such an *obedient* little puppy-dog, aren't you?' sneered Daisy.

'Don't have a go at Daniel,' said Ruby angrily. 'He only ever wants to keep you safe. You know that.'

'It stops now,' said Kit, getting to his feet. 'You been sleeping with him?'

'That's none of your damned business.'

'It's very much my business. You *know* what he is.'

'I didn't know a damned thing about his Danieri connections before Daniel started following me all around the town and saw us together.'

'You *know* what they put Ruby through, that crowd of wasters. And for fuck's sake! Have you forgotten what happened to Simon? You remember that poor sap, your first husband? The Danieri clan strung him up, killed him. You want any more instances of why this is a bad idea?'

'I *know* all that! God's sake, there's no point even talking to you,' Daisy said, and jumped to her feet and left the room.

# 52
# DAY TEN

Kit found Daisy out by the pool in the back garden, sitting on the big double swing. He sat down beside her and neither of them, for quite a while, said a thing.

'It's just that I miss him, you know,' said Daisy.

He didn't have to ask who. Not Simon her first husband and the father of the twins Matthew and Luke, for sure. Simon Collins had been a burly little bully made rich by his family's aggregate business – and he'd been too free with his fists. She was talking about Rob of course. Rob who had been first her bodyguard, then her lover, then her fiancé and for too brief a time, her husband. Rob who had been Kit's best friend for years, climbing the ladder beside him in Michael Ward's old crew. He'd been through everything with Rob and had never, ever imagined a day when Rob wouldn't be right there beside him.

'I know you miss him. I do too,' said Kit.

'I'm entitled to a private life,' she said, frowning. 'But I didn't know. About the link to the Danieris. He never said.'

'He's been worming his way in with you. Angling for something, who knows what? Of course he never said.'

'Shit.' She was silent for a while, then she said: 'I wasn't in love with him or anything. Nothing like that. We've barely just met.' Daisy sighed and leaned her head back upon the seat. 'I've been feeling sort of numb. You know. Since Rob. I was just . . . I think I was just trying so hard to forget Rob. To convince myself that another man – a *different* type of man – could fill that void, you know?'

Kit nodded. He knew.

She sighed. 'I won't see him anymore.'

'Okay. And this business with the séances . . .'

Daisy's head turned sharply. 'Oh, Daniel's told you that too, has he?'

'It's bollocks. You must know that.'

'It sort of comforts me. That's all.'

'He said that Rob said something to you during the last one. Or the woman who held the séance did.'

'It was Rob. He said "Daise, don't."'

'Don't what? Couldn't be "don't get tied up with the Danieri mob", could it?'

'That's why I'm going again. To find out.'

'That's definitely the sort of advice Rob would give you.'

'Don't take the piss,' she said, and gently thumped his arm.

'Go if you want to,' sighed Kit. 'But remember: always, always keep Daniel close.'

'I'll remember.'

Kit stood up, feeling relieved. She was going to dump Romano, that was the main thing. He thought again of Fabio Danieri at Gabe's funeral, giving him that glinting, sly smile. What the hell was he up to? And the rest of it? All that bullshit with the séances? Daisy would get over it. She'd see, eventually, that it was all nothing but smoke and mirrors. But when he went back indoors, he drew Ashok and Daniel aside and told them to get someone staking out Fabio's place, see what the fuck he was getting up to these days.

# 53
## DAY TEN

'Hey! *Hey!* You can't afford these goods my friend, so don't handle 'em!'

After his chat with Daniel and Ashok, Kit walked back through the kitchen and found himself following a shrieking female voice down the hall to the open front door. There Cole, one of Kit's boys who was six and a half feet tall and lean as a whippet, was restraining a struggling dark-haired girl in his arms.

*Fuck's sake*, thought Kit. He was tired. He wanted to forget all that had happened over the past week or so, to get some bloody peace for a change. And now – this.

Ruby came out from the sitting room, looked at the girl, at Cole, at Kit.

'It's okay,' said Kit. 'I know her. You can let her go.'

'Who the hell is she?' asked Ruby.

'Evie. Thomas's daughter.'

Ruby eyed the girl frostily. 'Check her over first,' she snapped at Cole.

Cole did so. His thorough pat-down of the girl's body was accompanied by a barrage of swear-words from the furious girl.

'You kiss your mother with that mouth?' Kit asked Evie, amused despite himself.

Cole shoved the girl away from him. 'She's clean,' he said, and caught the girl's hand as it swung round, aiming for his head. 'Don't,' he told her.

'Arsehole!' she spat.

'Enough,' said Kit, and grabbed Evie's flailing arms and steered her down the hall, into the kitchen. He tossed her against the worktop where she stood, glaring at him.

Daisy came in the back door. 'Who's this?' she asked.

'This is Evie. Thomas's daughter by his second marriage to Ursula Grey,' said Kit. He turned back to Evie. 'How'd you get here? More important, how'd you know about this place? And more important than *that*, how'd you get past the guys on the gate?'

Ruby followed them out to the kitchen. Now Daniel appeared too, a solid block of muscle, and Evie suddenly didn't look so self-assured.

'Answer me,' said Kit when she gulped and hesitated.

'I drove here,' she said. 'And parked along the lane.'

'Go on.' *So, not fourteen then,* he thought.

'Getting past the gate was easy. Jesus, was that where it happened, the car blowing up, right there inside the gates? There's a mark. Lots of black stuff. I saw it.'

The police had tried their best, but sooty stains remained down there at the bottom of the drive. A horrible reminder of Fats' rotten end.

'Shut up, Evie. Stick to the point,' said Kit, annoyed. Christ, this wouldn't do at all, people wandering in at will. He wanted this place locked down. Buttoned up *tight*.

'I jumped over the wall about a hundred yards down the lane, it was easy.'

'And then you came up to the house and Cole grabbed you. How'd you know I'd be here? How'd you know about this place at all?'

Evie was regaining some of her uppity self-confidence.

'Oh, that was easy too,' she said. 'When Ollie—'

'Who's Ollie?' interrupted Ruby, frowning.

'Olivia,' said Kit. 'That's who you mean?' he asked Evie. Evie nodded.

'Olivia is the daughter of Thomas's third wife, Avril Gulliver,' he explained to Ruby.

'Yeah, so when Avril was suspecting dear old Dad of playing the field she got a private detective onto him and one of the places Dad was visiting pretty regularly was this one, which the dick said was Ruby Darke's house, and she's your mother. So when I couldn't find you in London I reckoned you might be here. And I was right. Right?'

'She's precocious,' said Daisy, eyeing up Evie dispassionately. 'For her age.'

'She's older than she looks,' said Kit. 'And craftier. Evie – what's my London address?'

'Oh, I know that too. The private dick again. Sometimes your mother stays overnight at your place in Knightsbridge, doesn't she.' Evie reeled off the details. 'But you weren't there today, so I came here.'

'For what?' asked Daniel.

'To talk, of course.' She looked at Kit. 'To tell you something important.'

'Which is . . . ?'

Evie's eyes wandered around the room. Went to Daisy, to Ruby, to Cole and to Daniel.

'I want to tell you who murdered my dad. It's his fifth bitch of a wife of course,' said Evie with sudden passion. 'It's Chloe.'

'What about her?' asked Kit. Chloe again. Chloe who was busy fucking Declan, Thomas's son.

'Her dad was a bomber. With the IRA. I'm telling you, it's her. *She* did it.'

# 54
## DAY TEN

'Do you think she actually has anything to back that up?' Kit asked the room when Evie had departed.

Everyone was silent.

'It's a guess, right?' sighed Kit. 'Because she hates Chloe. But it's interesting, what she said about Chloe's dad being IRA. I had no clue about that.'

'I'm going out,' said Daisy, and left the room. Daniel followed. Ashok snatched up the day's newspaper from the worktop. He took it out into the hall and sat down and started thumbing through the pages. Left alone with Ruby, Kit kicked the kitchen door shut.

'Well?' he said.

'Well,' said Ruby after a moment's deliberation. 'What I think is this. We'll work our way through it and we'll get the answers. And you're not going to keep me out of this one Kit. Don't even try.'

'I don't think—' started Kit.

'I *said*, don't. I'll tackle the "gang', as wife number one Jean calls them. I'll tackle Jean too. She's not in the clear. Not yet.'

Kit was silent for a moment. Then he said: 'You still got that gun? You used to keep it in your drawer in the office at the club . . .'

'I have it here. In the sitting room, locked away.'

'Carry it with you. And if you sense the need, trust your gut: don't ignore that. Use it.'

'And meanwhile you'll be sifting through the *other* gangs, yes? Like Welsh Joe. And the Francis mob. And the Danieris.'

Kit gave that some thought.

'The Francis lot have never cared for me, that much is true – and I guess they like me even less now that Joe roughed up their kid. Got out of *that* one by the skin of my teeth, I can tell you.'

'Joe has shit for brains,' sighed Ruby.

'I'm not sure that Welsh Joe's an ally anymore – not after I told him to stop poking his ugly fat face into our affairs.'

Ruby almost smiled at that. 'Did you warn him off me, too?'

'I told him he was punching.'

Ruby winced. 'He won't forget that.'

'He can fucking well lump it.' Kit gave a grin. He thought of Joe limping back out into the street last night, throwing curses around him like confetti at a wedding.

'Who'll take over Thomas's affairs, I wonder? Declan I suppose. Look, Kit,' said Ruby and her eyes were like flint. 'Someone killed Thomas. I *loved* Thomas. Then someone killed Fats, who's been a friend to this family for years. Their true target was *you*. And now, my club. My bloody *club*, Kit. I'm seriously pissed off. And I am *not* going to stand still for this and let you do all the donkey work. Okay?'

He shrugged. 'Okay. But you keep Brennan with you, yes? And one of the other boys too for a driver.'

'Yes. Of course.' She liked Brennan. He was one of Kit's newer recruits, and he was short and solid. A bundle of quick-moving muscle, shoulders big as a truck.

And you *always* carry that gun.'

'That too.'

'Good job you hadn't left it at the club. Old Bill would have had a field day with that if they'd found it there. Look – I'm bloody sorry about Thomas. I liked the guy. He was a rogue, and a terror with the girls, but he had something about him, didn't he.'

Ruby nodded and her eyes softened. 'He certainly did,' she said.

'I'll never forget the way he backed us over the Danieri affair. He didn't have to do it, but he was there when it mattered.'

'I know.'

'Fabio Danieri was at Gabe's funeral,' Kit told her.

Ruby looked thoughtful. 'Michael always said that Gabe was in Tito Danieri's pocket.'

'He was.' Kit looked at his mother in concern. 'You going to cry?' he said, worried as all tough men are at the prospect of female tears.

'Nope,' said Ruby. 'I'll cry when this is over. For now? I'm too fucking mad to do that.'

# 55

# DAY TEN

Welsh Joe was *exceedingly* annoyed. Here he'd been, doing a favour for that smooth bastard, bringing trouble to himself from the Francis crew maybe, all to be helpful to Kit fucking Miller, and what did he get in return?

Smacked in the head with a baseball bat was what.

Yeah! Smacked in the head in front of his own crew. Made to look like a complete fucking *idiot*, and he hated that. And were the bastards laughing at him? Would they *dare*? He suspected they were, spinning the story around down the snooker halls and the pubs and the whore houses, that big strong-man, ex-army, ex-boxer Welsh Joe had been bested by a bloke half his size and half his age. If he heard a single damned word of it then he would cut their mouthy heads right off their shoulders. His own head ached for days after the assault but far worse than the pain of that was the pain of his wounded ego. Fuck's sake, was that any way to treat a pal, someone who was only trying to help out in a crisis?

It was not.

And Kit's crack about Ruby. All right, he'd been quite keen to have a go at her, she was hot stuff, a looker, and he would have gone down the traditional route for that.

She was not a woman to be rushed, she was intelligent, she was *tasty*. He would have sent flowers. Wined her. Dined her. A steak dinner, the best. Then into bed, when she was good and ready.

Now Kit Miller had told him *no fucking way*.

That hurt.

All right, Joe admitted it to himself. A major part of his motivation to help Kit had been the prospect of bedding Kit's mother. But now the whole damned thing had gone to the dogs. He'd been made to look a fool. He'd been hurt – his head was fucking *killing* him – by the very man he was trying to help out. Added to that, Pat Francis had been round issuing threats, asking had he been involved in Davey's night of terror, which of course he'd denied.

But a crack at Ruby?

He was bitter about it. He was *mad* about it. He went out into his backyard gym and hit fuck out of the punchbag there to let off some of the steam that was building up in his poor bloody head. Oh, it ached. Ached like a bastard.

Really, Kit Miller was to blame for this whole sorry situation.

Kit fucking Miller.

He punched the bag some more.

By the time he'd finished punching this time, his head was clearer and his path was laid out for him.

He'd get Miller for this. Call in a few favours. He'd see the bastard buried and then Ruby'd be crying on *his* shoulder over her late lamented son.

Yes *sir*, she would.

# 56

# DAY ELEVEN

Nieve O'Malley opened the door of her basement flat to Ruby Darke next day and stood there gazing at her expectantly. 'Yes?' she asked. Behind Ruby stood a short, broad dark-haired man, suited up like a bailiff.

'Can I speak to Chloe Knox?' Ruby asked.

'No. Sorry. Trouble in the family.'

Nieve was starting to close the door. Ruby put her foot in the gap so Nieve couldn't complete the movement. Brennan reached one arm over Ruby's shoulder and placed a hand the size of a shovel up against the door to press the point home.

'I'm Ruby Darke,' she said. 'I was a friend of her husband's. It's important I speak to her.'

'Who is it?' came a female voice from within the flat.

'Someone called Ruby Darke.' Nieve opened the door wider and Ruby, uninvited, stepped into a spacious kitchen all done out in creams and golds. Chloe was sitting at a massive table hewn out of a solid plank of oak. She was wearing a pale pink dressing gown, no make-up, and her hair was scraped back into a ragged bun. Her face was scratched; Kit had said she'd been hurt in the explosion.

'Can I have a word?' asked Ruby.

'Sure you can. In fact, you can have two. The first begins with an F, and the second with an O.' Chloe gave Ruby a bitter look then she raised the crystal glass containing some sort of dark liquid and took a slurp. 'You've got a fucking nerve,' she said. 'Coming here.'

Ruby approached the table, pulled out a chair and sat down. She looked at Chloe.

'Thomas was due to meet me on the evening he died,' she told her.

At that, Chloe surged to her feet, leaned in, and spat: 'Get *out*, you cow!'

'Not until we've talked,' said Ruby calmly.

'There's nothing I want to say to you,' said Chloe, sinking back into her chair. She dropped her head into her hands. 'Oh for Christ's sake. Just fuck off, will you? What the hell d'you want with me?'

Nieve came and stood behind Chloe's chair, placing a consoling hand on Chloe's shoulder.

'She's really not up to this,' said Nieve coldly. She glared at Brennan as he stationed himself against a worktop near to where Ruby was sitting.

'I'm okay,' said Chloe.

She's drunk, thought Ruby, at ten in the morning. Well, she certainly had cause.

'Do you know,' said Ruby, 'that Evie Grey's going around saying that you killed Thomas?'

Chloe's bloodshot eyes opened wide at that. 'You *what?*'

'She knows some very interesting things about you,' said Ruby.

'Like what?'

'Like your father was a bomb-maker for the IRA and that you sat at his knee in his workshop as a little girl and

learned all about how to use Semtex. Is that right? Funny
thing, I'd never noticed the Irish accent before, but it's
there, isn't it?'

Chloe stared at her. 'You *what?*' she echoed faintly.

'I always thought you were an East End girl, but you're
not, are you? So – is it true?'

'Of course it's not true.'

'Your father wasn't Terry O'Malley? Banged up for
gun-running for the provos in Ireland?'

'Yes, but—'

'And this is your sister, yes? Nieve's a very Irish name.'

'But—'

'You were there, were you? On the night it happened?
Thomas's car blowing up? I can see you've still got the
damage to show for it.'

'Yes,' Nieve answered for her sister. 'She was there. So
was I. The damned thing blew up on the driveway not ten
feet away from the house and we were in the front room.
We were *right there.* All the windows blew in, the shock was
awful. We could easily have been killed. And you think Chloe
would actually be dumb enough to do that? Sit right next to
a bloody bomb she'd set, knowing it was going to go off?'

Ruby considered. Chloe was no brain of Britain, but
Nieve did have a point. Would she seriously risk her own
life to get rid of her husband? And why would she want
to be rid of him? Granted, Thomas was, as Kit put it, 'a
devil with the girls'. He'd been deep in an affair with Ruby
herself while he was married to Chloe – not something she
was proud of. And Chloe had more than once tried to warn
Ruby off.

But there was something else to think about. If Chloe's
dad had passed on his knowledge to his daughter, could

Chloe have judged how close she could safely sit to an explosion? And wouldn't that give her a perfect alibi, clearing her of any guilt? She'd been right there, on the spot; nothing more, it would seem, than an injured party.

Or was she?

'Did you argue with Thomas over me? Over his *relationship* with me?'

'Piss off,' snapped Chloe.

'Did you?' Ruby waited for a beat. Then she said, very low: 'Chloe. Listen up.' She nodded toward Brennan. 'He isn't just for decoration, you know. Bad things can happen.'

'Oh Christ as if anything worse can happen after all of this.' Chloe gulped and got out a hankie and loudly blew her nose. 'It's not ten minutes since I've had the police in here asking the same questions. They don't know about our dad yet. But I suppose they soon will. Who told you?'

'I told you. Evie, Ursula's daughter.'

'That little cow. How did she even *know*?'

'Evie's curious,' said Ruby. 'Your dad was quite a celebrity in the IRA. Any fool can do the research and find the answers. And Avril hired in a P.I., according to Evie, to dig around for the dirt when she suspected that Thomas was playing around again. The IRA stuff was unearthed by him. And I warn you – she's probably talking to the police as we speak.'

'So that makes me number one suspect, yes?' Chloe gave a watery smile. Then she patted Nieve's hand, which was still resting upon her shoulder. 'And Nieve too? That's such bollocks. Just because Dad knew explosives doesn't mean that I do too. *Or* Nieve.'

'Your dad still alive?'

'No. He's not. Yes, all right – Thomas and me, we argued. And yes, we were well on our way to the divorce courts. I suppose you would have been wife number six.'

Ruby shook her head. 'Not a chance. Thomas was great but me and a serial womaniser? I think I'm worth more than that.'

'Yeah? Well that's bollocks too. You know it and I know it. He had a way of sucking a person in, I can tell you. You might *think* you can resist, but when he lays on the charm, it's usually a done deal.'

'Not with me,' said Ruby, although she did wonder.

*Would* she have succumbed, eventually, to Thomas? Joined the line-up of abandoned wives? But she was different to the rest of them, wasn't she? She had her own fortune. She had never needed or wanted so much as a penny from Thomas; and she wasn't young. She was of a similar age to him; he could relax with her. Be himself. Talk to her.

Damn, she'd loved him.

She had *thought* he'd loved her. Fooling herself, maybe. No, *definitely*.

Ah, what the fuck. It hurt, but so what? It was done now. Done and over. Irritably she shoved her chair back and stood up. 'I'll be keeping my eye on the pair of you. So watch out.'

The phone was ringing. Chloe gave Ruby one long hate-filled look and then snatched it up.

'Yeah?' she said.

Ruby picked up her handbag and then something in Chloe's face made her pause. Chloe had gone pale. Alerted to the changed atmosphere in the room, Brennan shoved himself away from the worktop and moved in closer to Ruby. Nieve was tapping Chloe's shoulder, mouthing *what . . . ?*

Chloe paid none of them any attention.

'All right,' she said into the phone. 'Thanks.'

She hung up, replacing the phone carefully on the table. Her hand was shaking.

'Who was it?' asked Nieve.

Chloe looked around herself vaguely, as if this was a dream that she would soon wake from. 'It was the police.'

'And . . . ?'

'They're releasing Thomas's body for burial.'

There was silence in the room.

Ruby finally broke it: 'So soon?'

'It's been nearly two weeks,' said Chloe. The hatred flared in her eyes again as she stared up at Ruby. 'Nearly two weeks since I lost my husband. Now I've got to bury him. And if I see you anywhere near that funeral, you bitch, you are *dead*.'

# 57
# DAY ELEVEN

Mama Bella kept wandering out from the kitchen and down the stairs and into the hall, stepping in the dust and the dirt, her face a picture of confusion. Really, Fabio was getting annoyed that he had even thought of the idea of redoing her suite upstairs and of knocking down what turned out to be a stud wall and accessing the cellar that must surely be there, off the hallway, just as he was sure he remembered it. Stupid Vittore had blanked it off; he, Fabio, would never have done that.

He already had plans for the cellar. Storage. All sorts of things. Drugs of course. People. It would be very, very useful.

'What are they doing?' asked Mama Bella, over and over. 'Vittore, what's happening?'

Fabio grabbed hold of the nurse, who was meandering down the stairs and looking like she had not a care in the world. 'Hey! You're supposed to be keeping an eye on her. Take her upstairs.'

'Are you Maria?' asked Mama Bella, blinking at the nurse.

'No she's not Maria, Mama. Go on, go upstairs.'

'What are these men doing here, Vittore?'

'I'm not Vittore, I am Fabio. And they're doing a little building work for me, that's all.'

'So . . . is Vittore coming home soon?'

They'd had this exact conversation *so* many times. 'Soon, yes,' he told her.

'And Maria?'

'Yes, Mama. Soon.'

The nurse took Mama Bella upstairs.

There was a builder hammering at the plaster on the wall, chunks of it falling onto the dust sheet on the floor.

'Hurry it up will you?' Fabio barked out, and went into the kitchen, slamming the door behind him.

A couple were parked along the road in a very old and very nondescript car. They'd been there for some time. Occasionally they kissed, caressed. Mostly, however, they followed their orders from Kit Miller's people: keep a tight eye on whatever Fabio Danieri might be up to. Which was, so far as they could see, nothing very much.

'Skip delivery,' said the woman, stroking her companion's hair and watching the lorry offload the large-sized skip onto the driveway. Then the driver pulled back into the road and was gone. Presently the door of the house opened and a man in overalls started throwing chunks of debris into the skip. There were bags of cement, a mixer, stacks of bricks and a couple of doors, all propped up against the front wall of the house.

'Not the most exciting day I've ever had,' complained the woman in the car mildly.

'Pay's good,' her companion pointed out.

'Time to check in?'

'Yeah, let's,' said the man, and started the engine.

At Sheila's restaurant they met up with Ashok. 'Anything?' he asked.

'He's got the builders in, doing something. Doors and bricks and stuff going in there, debris coming out,' said the woman.

'Okay,' said Ashok, and paid them.

He reported their info to Kit. It was nothing very much. But Kit felt uneasy. All that rubbish from Gabe. *It's already happening.* Losing Thomas. Losing Fats. Fabio, turning up at Gabe's funeral . . .

'Can you get one of our own in there, with the builders?' he asked.

'Boss, this is Camorra. They won't go for it.'

'Then one of theirs with a grievance, ready to turn. Offer a new I.D. and an obscene amount of cash.'

'I'll do my best,' said Ashok, and left. He was back within the hour.

'Nothing. And it's bloody dangerous, getting in amongst that lot.'

'I have faith in you,' said Kit. 'Go again.'

This time took longer. Ashok was back.

'Think I've found a weak link,' he said. 'He treats his crew like dirt. And some of 'em don't like it. I'll try pressing this one, see if he gives.'

Ashok left. Then he was back. Again.

'Done?' asked Kit. 'Only I've got a creeping feeling about all this. Who knows what that arsehole's plotting.'

'No worries,' said Ashok. 'I got one.'

# 58

## DAY ELEVEN

'Where next?' Brennan asked Ruby when they were back in the car.

Ruby glanced at her watch. 'Number four wife. Gilly Taylor-Black.'

'And she is where?'

'At this time? According to Kit, she'll probably be in The Ivy and that's where we'll find her.'

Gilly wasn't at The Ivy. But Kit had got one of the telecoms boys on the payroll to trace the number she'd given him to a rented address off Berkeley Square. Ruby stepped up to the door and rang the bell, Brennan standing close behind her. A very upper-class female voice came scratchily over the intercom: 'Yes?'

'I'm Ruby Darke. I'd like a word.'

'What? Who?'

'Kit Miller's mum?'

A murmur of voices.

'It's not very convenient.'

'Tough.'

'What do you *want*, anyway?'

'Just a word. That's all.'

'Oh for Christ's sake . . .'

The door clicked open. Ruby and Brennan stepped into a chic tiled hallway and the door shut behind them. A dishevelled red-haired woman was tying a mint-green silk robe around her as she came barefoot down the stairs. She was very pretty, but there was something odd going on with her nose. She reached the bottom step and at the top of the stairs a grey-haired man appeared, stuffing his shirt into his trousers. He looked familiar and for a moment Ruby trawled the info bank in her mind, searching. Then she had it. Football manager. He quickly stepped back, out of sight.

'Look, this had better be important,' said Gilly, hustling Ruby and her minder through a door to their left. It was a sitting room, tastefully furnished. Gilly shut the door carefully behind her. Ruby could hear someone coming down the stairs. Then the front door opened and closed. 'If Kit Miller wanted to get in touch, I *told* him to phone first . . .'

'Kit doesn't want to get in touch,' said Ruby.

'Well look this is really *very* inconvenient.'

'It won't take long.'

'What won't? Look, I've just had some upsetting news. My ex-husband's body has been released for burial.'

'Who told you? Chloe?'

'Yes. She just phoned. She's phoning round all the wives.'

'Ex-wives.'

Gilly sat down on a couch but didn't offer her visitors a seat. She stared up at Ruby. 'So *you're* the famous Ruby Darke.' She raised a hand self-consciously to her nose. 'Don't stare. I'm getting it fixed.'

'What?'

'My nose.'

'Inhaling product is never a good idea,' said Ruby. 'Doesn't it put off the bloke we've just heard leaving?'

'As my dear old Papa always said, one doesn't look at the roof when one is stoking the fire. And I'm getting it fixed, I told you. I told Kit too. So thanks for the lecture, but in future you can keep your opinions to yourself.' Irritation coloured Gilly's cheeks. 'Anyway, he's not that great. I'm going to dump him tomorrow. He likes the rough stuff too much. I've got someone much, much better lined up. Someone who absolutely *adores* me. So what do you want?'

Brennan stirred restlessly. Ruby shook her head, just a fraction.

'To talk, that's all,' she said.

Gilly was staring at her speculatively.

'You know what?'

'No. What?' said Ruby.

'You would have been next, wouldn't you. Big cheese, weren't you, back in the day. Had a retail concern didn't you. What, you run out of money now? Is that why you're getting so aerated about Thomas's passing? That you missed out on the boat carrying all that lovely cash?'

'I don't want Thomas's money,' said Ruby. 'You been seeing much of him since you divorced?'

'As little as possible. Not that it's any of your business.'

'I'm making it my business.'

'Well, don't.'

'Can't avoid it I'm afraid,' said Ruby. 'Brennan?'

Brennan straightened, watching Ruby's face.

'You see that nose? Break it, will you?'

Gilly was on her feet the instant Brennan started moving toward her. She darted behind the couch and held out a placatory hand.

'Now whoa! Wait! There's no need for any rough stuff.'
Brennan stopped moving. He looked at Ruby.

'Then you keep a civil tongue in your head,' said Ruby
flatly.

'I got you,' panted Gilly. 'No need for that. I got you.'

'Good. Now sit down and answer my questions. Okay?'

'Sure. No problem. Why didn't you say that in the *first*
place?'

# 59

# DAY ELEVEN

Pizza-Face Donato's cousin Dante didn't like Fabio. He never had, not since Fabio had stubbed out cigarettes on his big cousin's face way back in the day. You didn't forget a thing like that, or forgive it. Donato was soft, letting Fabio treat him any way he chose, acting almost as if he *deserved* such treatment; Dante was not such a soft touch. And when Kit Miller's crew offered him, yes, an *obscene* amount of money to inform on Fabio, plus the promise of a new identity somewhere safe abroad, he'd jumped at the chance.

So he was helping out with the building work. Getting covered in dust and dirt, doing dogsbody stuff that he hated, but he was actually keeping an eye on Fabio, seeing what went on, and reporting anything of interest back to Miller's lot. Not that there was anything of interest, yet. Maybe there never would be. But he was here, on the spot, a trusted member of the ancient Camorra; spying on his boss. Risking his neck in doing so, he knew that. It was all rather exciting, actually. He was like James Bond. Working undercover.

Bloody brick dust got everywhere, though.

# 60

## DAY ELEVEN

The Lyceum was rammed to the hilt and everyone was dancing wildly. The strobes were spinning and Daisy was out on the floor while the massive pounding beat and Tina Turner's fantastic vocals on 'River Deep Mountain High' swirled around at a deafening level.

Daisy loved to dance. She particularly was enjoying dancing tonight because Daniel was over there by the bar, sipping what was no doubt a lemonade or something equally damned boring because he never drank on duty, and he was on duty, watching her. Watching her *disapprovingly,* in fact, which amused her no end and made her throw a few extra-wild shapes just to annoy the bastard. And then . . .

'Hello!' someone was shouting in her ear.

She turned, smiling . . . and oh fuck it was him. Luca Romano.

'Hi,' she said, and danced on, moving away from him.

He followed. 'What, not talking?' he asked.

This was awkward. 'Having too much fun,' she said airily, moving away again.

*Again,* he followed. Granted, he looked hot. White shirt, tan cord jacket, tight faded jeans. Black hair that flashed midnight blue in the light of the strobes, black eyes. A hawkish face, all sharp angles. *Tasty.*

But off limits. Of course he was. The Danieri link was the clincher.

'Come on, what's up?' he said, and caught hold of her flailing wrist.

'Nothing's *up*,' returned Daisy. 'Just . . .'

'Just what?'

'You never told me you were related to the Danieri family.'

He was silent for a beat. The music bellowed at them, the lights whirled and flashed and Daisy, quite suddenly, wanted to go home. His hand on her wrist was hard. Not crushing, but *hard.*

'*Should* I have?' he asked.

'My family don't care for the Danieris,' said Daisy.

'*Don't care?*' His eyes were coldly amused.

'That's what I said.' Her heart was thumping. He didn't look *hot* now. He looked menacing.

Abruptly, she jerked her wrist free of his hold. Damn, she'd been enjoying herself. Winding Daniel up, dancing, being free; now the Italian boy had gone and ruined the whole evening.

'Bye,' she said, and turned and weaved her way between the thrashing, gyrating couples back over to the bar. She wasn't going to come in here again, not if *he* was going to show up. She'd just avoid the places where they'd met before. That was why she'd come here tonight and ditched Annabel's, her usual haunt. But here he was, again. Shit – was he watching her? *Following* her?

'What, packing it in already?' said Daniel, draining his drink.

'Not in the mood,' said Daisy. So he hadn't seen what had just happened on the dance floor. Her wrist throbbed. There would be a bruise. No, she wouldn't come in here again. She wouldn't go to *any* of the places where she was likely to meet up with the Italian boy, including that lovely little restaurant his family owned a share of, where he'd wined and dined her so sweetly and hadn't seemed *at all* threatening.

She felt sad all of a sudden. Another dazzling possibility had been stripped away. After Rob died, she'd tried – quite desperately – to regain her *chutzpa*, the over-brimming life force that was usually such an integral part of her outgoing, chirpy personality. She'd felt she was getting it back and she knew that her attraction to Luca Romano had been a part of that.

Her heart – even though she didn't want it to, sometimes couldn't *bear* it to – was mending.

Rob was fading into the background and life was going on, just as everyone had told her it would. She hadn't believed it could be possible; but they were right.

She *hated* that they were right.

It was crazy and it was somehow *despicable* too, that her strong healthy body carried on wanting, feeling, needing. She hated herself for that. Despised herself.

Sometimes all she wanted was for the pain to go away. And the twins were a comfort – her beautiful boys. But she knew she was forever letting them down, not being the mother they deserved, palming them off on Ruby or Vanessa too often, feeling relieved when either of the grandmothers took the weight of them off her.

*She* ought to be taking them out, treating them, in the summer holidays, to theme parks, abroad. Anywhere they wanted to go. Luke had said he'd like a pet – ducks, wasn't it? Or a dog maybe, he'd even mentioned pygmy goats, and would it have really been so much trouble to sort that out for him?

But she hadn't.

Their paternal grandfather Sir Bradley Collins had offered, through Vanessa, to get Luke his little goats, but Daisy hadn't yet said yes to that. She rarely saw Bradley or his wife Susan, had never cared very much for either of them – and felt guilty about it.

*Oh, to hell with it.*

She knew that she would have slept with Luca, if only as an experiment, to see if that erased all the memories, the ones that tormented her, that jolted her awake hot and restless in the night with Rob's name on her lips.

As they went out to the car where Cyril, another of Kit's crew, was waiting behind the wheel, Daniel turned to her and – shockingly – said: 'Who was that? The dark-haired bloke on the dance floor? That wasn't—?'

The floor had been so crowded that Daisy was sure he hadn't seen. But – oh God – he had.

'It was nobody,' said Daisy.

Daniel opened the rear passenger door for her. 'It wasn't nobody, Daisy. It was Luca fucking Romano. He looked very . . . *intent,* is that the word?'

Daisy shrugged. 'Intent? Goodness, what a vast vocabulary you've got all of a sudden, Daniel.'

'Don't be a cow,' he said.

'Look! I told you. I've only met him once or twice before. And I won't be meeting him again,' she said positively. 'Now let it go, for the love of God, will you?'

'It *was* him. Wasn't it. The Danieri cousin. Well fuck *that.*'

He didn't even give her time to answer. To Cyril, sitting behind the wheel, he said: 'Wait here.'

Then he slammed Daisy's door closed and was off, back into the club.

# 61

# DAY ELEVEN

Daniel found Luca Romano standing unzipped at one of the urinals in the capacious men's loo. Another man followed him in while the hard thrumming jungle beat flowed all around them, and Daniel turned to him in the doorway and said: 'This is a private conversation, mate. Fuck off will you?'

It was said without force, but one look in Daniel's eyes was enough to make the man turn around then and there. It was only a little quieter in the toilets, and as Daniel approached Luca he saw the Italian spot him in the mirrors over the long row of sinks. Luca moved quickly, attempting to rezip his fly, but he wasn't quick enough to avoid Daniel coming up close and slamming his head into the white-tiled wall in front of him. His forehead smacked up against it. He let out a grunt of surprise and pissed all over his Italian leather shoes and cashmere socks.

'Luca Romano,' said Daniel by his ear.

'What the f—' started Luca.

Daniel pushed Luca's head hard up against the wall, mashing his nose against the cold tile. Then harder, so that his teeth connected agonisingly with the icy porcelain.

'That's not me,' said Luca.

'The fuck it isn't. Listen.' Someone else shoved the door to the gents open, and Daniel turned and roared: '*OUT!*' and the man quickly reversed, letting the door close behind him.

'Listen, arsehole. You better take the hint, right now. Daisy Darke is off limits to you, you got that? You don't come near her, you don't speak to her, you don't show your face anywhere around her. Understood? Because if I see you within a mile of her just once more, I won't be talking to you nice and polite like this, you got me? I will be booting your sorry arse around the floor and the next thing you'll know is a long stay in hospital and having your dinners through a straw. You understand me?'

'All right, all *right*,' said Luca, his head getting mangled against the wall, his dick still hanging limp in his hand. 'Who are you, her fucking *mother*?'

Daniel gave the tiles another *smack* with Luca's bruised head. 'I'm your worst nightmare pal, that's who I am,' he told him. 'You want to go on with this? I could do it all day.'

Daniel pulled Luca's head back once again. Blood was starting to trickle down from a cut on the Italian's forehead, and from his mouth.

'No! That's enough,' said Luca.

'Good. That's good. Sensible,' Daniel congratulated him. 'Now, remember this. No kidding. Everything I've said to you, you take it to heart. And if you ever, *ever*, see Daisy Darke again, you walk the other way. Or *I* come after *you*. Got it?'

'I've got it,' said Luca.

'Good,' said Daniel, and he let him go and left the club.

# 62

# DAY ELEVEN

Kit should have known, really, that the Francis mob were not going to so easily let the thing drop. When he'd walked away from their gaff a few nights back, the kid delivered intact, he'd felt their eyes on him and he had thought, seriously, this is it. He'd been sure they were going to follow, Pat in his vest and braces and those two strapping older Francis boys with him. He had fully anticipated that they were going to grab him by his arsehole and rip him a brand new one to match.

But – they hadn't.

And for a few days, it had seemed like they wouldn't, either.

Just a few days.

Then he walked out of one of the Soho clubs late and there was no Ashok waiting behind the wheel of the car. He had time to notice that and only that, before he was coshed behind the ear and dragged, stunned, around the corner into an alley.

*Well this is fucking tedious*, he thought.

Someone kicked him hard behind the knee and he went down on the rain-greasy cobbles face first. His nose started to bleed. Someone kicked him hard in the ribs. He curled into a ball, the best – the only – way to protect himself as they piled in hard.

Then, about a century later when they were done, someone waved a pudgy finger in front of his eyes and spat out: 'That's for Davey!'

Davey was the young Francis kid's name.

*Joe, you arsehole, thank you very much,* thought Kit as the Francis crew walked away. Seconds passed. They stretched into minutes. Or possibly hours. Someone came out of the back of one of the restaurants, saw him lying there, and went back inside.

*Cheers,* thought Kit.

After about another century had gone by, Ashok came stumbling around the corner from the main road, supporting himself against the wall. He limped over to Kit.

'Boss?'

'Here,' said Kit after a while. He felt like a ten-ton truck had been driven into his spleen.

'You OK?' asked Ashok.

'Peachy.'

'There were too many.'

'I know.'

'Can you get up?'

'Give me a hand and I can probably do it.'

Ashok reached out his hand. Hauled Kit staggering and gasping and wincing back to his feet.

'Shit,' said Kit. Everything hurt.

Ashok got his arm around Kit's waist and helped him back to the car, got him into the passenger seat. Didn't even check under or around it. An explosive, right now, would have been a merciful release, thought Kit. Go out in a blaze of glory and to fuck with it all.

But Ashok drove him home, and got him indoors, and sprawled him out still bleeding and groaning on the couch.

'Need the doc, you think?' Ashok asked.

'No. You?'

'No.'

'Just leave me here for a bit.' Kit pulled out a handkerchief and held it to his nose. Not broken. Hey, bonus! 'Bring me a whisky. You have one too if you want.'

'Don't drink, Boss. You know that,' said Ashok and he fetched Kit a drink, placing it on the coffee table beside him along with some painkillers. Then he poured himself a mineral water, grabbed another handful of pills, went over to a recliner and sat down, hiked the thing up until he was lying out flat.

'Think that's all of it?' asked Ashok.

'Yeah, they've said their piece,' said Kit, dabbing at his nose. The bleeding had nearly stopped. His whole midriff ached and he felt weary to his bones.

'Ashok?' he said.

But all that came was gentle snoring. Ashok was asleep. Wincing, aching, Kit did his best to do the same.

Finally, as dawn approached, he did.

# 63
# DAY TWELVE

Next day, Luca went to Fabio's place in Clerkenwell. Pizza-Face Donato opened the door to him and ushered him inside. Donato's cousin Dante was there in overalls with another of their crew, dust-covered, knee-deep in debris in the hall. It was utter bloody chaos here. You had to fight your way past all the shit out on the drive and when you got indoors the place looked like a wrecking ball had been taken to it. Mama Bella, stirring a pot of something in the kitchen, looked at him with a trembling smile and said: 'Vittore?'

Fabio came into the kitchen, glanced at Luca and then away.

'No, Mama,' he said. 'Vittore will be along later. Remember? I told you.'

Fabio looked back at Luca. At his mangled face.

'What the fuck happened to you?' he asked.

'One of Miller's,' said Luca. He went to the mirror over the sink and prodded at one of his upper front teeth. 'Christ's sake, I think he's knocked the damned thing loose. That bastard.'

'Bad language, Vittore,' scolded Mama Bella.

Fabio was irritated. He'd given Luca a simple brief, yes? Seduce the Darke girl. Shouldn't have been at all difficult, she was nothing better than a whore anyway, ready to fall into bed with anyone. Why not with Luca?

Actually, he was *more* than irritated. He was a neat man and he liked his surroundings neat too. But here were the boys, that surly little fucker Dante among them, treading dirt all through the house and now he really did regret his decision to open up the cellar that he was sure had once been there. But it would be useful. He had to keep telling himself that. And the phone was always ringing off the hook with that *other* little matter concerning him right now. Everywhere he looked there seemed to be trouble.

The phone was ringing again.

He patted Luca's shoulder and Luca flinched.

'We're going to sort all this out,' Fabio promised him. 'Just wait and see.'

And he went through to the sitting room to take the call, to pour oil on troubled waters all over again.

# 64
## DAY TWELVE

Romilly was in a meeting with Major Tarrant form the bomb disposal squad and her boss DCI Barrow. They were discussing the use of Semtex in the three explosions that had occurred, and Major Tarrant was making expansive use of his greater knowledge of the subject to beat the two police personnel over the head with.

'Of course I would expect the force to be aware of the nature of these powerful plastic explosives. Semtex contains RDX and PETN. It's like C-4 you know, malleable, and it remains plastic between -40 and +60 degrees. It's waterproof. And while C-4 is white, Semtex is usually red or orange.'

'So how much would have been needed to blow up those two cars? Or Ruby Darke's burlesque club?' asked Romilly. She didn't need a breakdown on the ins and outs of explosives; she just wanted some basic facts surrounding the incidents that had happened on her watch.

'The club?' He blew out his lips. 'Six ounces would do it. The cars? Maybe three per piece.'

'Six *ounces*? That's an unbelievably small amount.'

'Nevertheless. It's used all around the world, you know. Comes from Czechoslovakia originally. Fourteen tons of it went to Vietnam during the war with the Vietcong, seven

hundred tons to Libya between 1975 and last year. Islamic
militants in the Middle East favour it, as do the provisional
Irish Republican Army and the Irish National Liberation
Army in Northern Ireland.'

'There's a possible link there isn't there. Romilly?' said
DCI Barrow.

'Yes, Chloe Knox. Thomas Knox's widow – her father
was involved with the IRA. We're following that line of
inquiry closely.'

The Major nodded, his eyes – as usual – on Romilly's
chest. She could have laughed, if it didn't piss her off so
much. The Major could clearly still not believe that he
wasn't talking to some butch hairy-arsed male police detective about this. Sometimes the Major had a look in his eyes
of almost puzzlement when she spoke – as if a chair or a
seat cushion had suddenly started spouting opinions.

*Well soak it up, arsehole,* she thought. *There's no chance*
this *girl's going back to the kitchen sink anytime soon.*

'Sales of explosives are becoming more regulated now.
It shouldn't be *that* easy to get hold of,' said Tarrant. He
looked at DCI Barrow almost accusingly. 'We would like a
result on this, soonest. I need to file a comprehensive report
to my superiors. The Army takes matters like this very seriously indeed.'

'So do the police,' said Romilly.

'Yes. I'm sure.'

The Major stood up.

'Thank you for your time,' he said to DCI Barrow, who
nodded.

Romilly gathered up her notes and followed the Major
out of the door. Once in the corridor, he stopped walking
and turned to her.

'Drink? Dinner?' he snapped out, like this was a military parade.

*And they say romance is dead,* she thought.

'Thanks. That's kind of you. But no. Czechoslovakia, you said? What's the plant called?'

'Explosia. It's in the file. And the Semtex itself is named after a suburb of Pardubice called Semtín.'

'Right.'

He nodded, spun around and walked away toward the front of the station.

Romilly went in the other direction, thinking of nasty deaths and the events of tomorrow, when she would be in reluctant – but very necessary – attendance at the funeral of the late Thomas Knox.

# 65

# DAY THIRTEEN

They might have been burying a popular head of state. The church was rammed with mourners. Everywhere there were flowers in vast lavish arrangements lining the aisle, perched in every broad windowsill beneath the stained-glass windows and mounded upon the huge mahogany coffin which lay on the dais at the front of the church. The choir were singing the beautiful Mozart's 'Requiem' and the church organ rumbled out an accompaniment so loud and powerful that it shook the floor. You felt it in your chest, your lungs, your *heart*.

Contrasting this elaborate shindig to the sorry little spectacle he had witnessed at Gabe's cremation, Kit couldn't help but feel a pang of faint regret as the vicar climbed into the pulpit and started on his funereal speech.

Kit felt low in general. His body ached from the pounding the Francis boys had given him, and now they stood across the aisle from him, all dressed up in their Sunday suits, little Davey the arches' victim among them, apparently models of good behaviour. And there was that moron Joe near the back, bellowing out the hymns in a fine Welsh tenor, a large plaster on his stupid head. Kit could also see Max and Annie Carter, DI Romilly Kane, the Richardsons – no Declan – and a selection of women seated together up in the front pews that he recognised as Thomas's ex-wives – Jean Coyden, Ursula Grey, Avril Gulliver, Gilly Taylor-Black. Ursula's daughter Evie was there too, dressed in shocking pink, not black, and Gilly's daughter Olivia was beside her. And there just in front of them, alone but for her sister Nieve, sat Chloe, Thomas's widow.

It was a long service, full church, high church, designed to send the soul on its way on wings of angels. Whether or not Thomas Knox was headed up or down, Kit didn't pay that much attention. He was standing beside Ruby, and Daisy was on her other side. Beyond Daisy, who was clutching two small bouquets, one of red roses, another of peach blooms, was Daniel. Behind Ruby was Brennan, and behind Kit was Ashok, who looked just about as fit for action as Kit did himself. But then, who expected action at a funeral?

Nobody.

When the coffin had been removed by the pall bearers at the end of the service and the bulk of the congregation had already gone outside into the summer sunshine, there was an altercation from the front of the church, raised voices, and then – shockingly – Chloe Knox stepped forward and slapped little Jean Coyden, Thomas's first wife, right across the face.

'*What* did you say?' Chloe shrieked.

'Oh come on . . .' said Ursula, looking supremely beautiful and rather bored in black Dior and a huge matching cartwheel hat.

'No! You heard what she said?' demanded Nieve.

'Ladies—' started the vicar in alarm.

'She said I'd be copping the lot, did you hear that? She said that was all I wanted anyway, Thomas's money,' spat out Chloe.

'You know what Jean's like,' said Avril while Evie and Olivia were practically hopping with unconcealed glee at this turn of events. 'Doesn't think before she speaks. Sorry Jean but it's true.' She turned to the little woman in the black feathered hat. 'You say the most Godawful things and then you expect people not to be offended. Or maybe you do it deliberately. See how far you can push your luck. Is that it? Making remarks about Ollie being fat. I've heard you. And saying her hair's thin.'

'She *hit* me,' said Jean, clutching her cheek.

'You asked for it,' said Gilly blandly, unconcerned.

'Thank you,' said Chloe, then paused and added: 'not that I give a stuff for your opinion.'

'I'll press charges,' said Jean.

Romilly came up the aisle, alerted by the noise. 'What's going on?' she asked and flashed her warrant card. 'Ladies? Can we all calm down here? This is a solemn occasion, please behave.'

'She said I was only with Thomas for the money,' said Chloe.

'Well that's true enough,' snapped Jean right back. 'And now he's dead and gone, you scoop the whole pot up, don't you.'

'Jean!' said Avril.

'Ladies!' snapped Romilly.

'That isn't true,' said Nieve, clutching at Chloe, who was in tears.

'Of course it is,' said Gilly. 'But it hardly needed saying, Jean. Not today of all days.'

'She's right,' drawled Ursula, taking out a gold powder compact to check her reflection.

'And anyway, it doesn't matter. It isn't true. It isn't true *at all*. Because Thomas and I decided to divorce at Christmas last year,' wept Chloe. 'And you know what I got in the post on the day after Thomas died? The fucking irony of it! I got the decree absolute. So yeah – yack it up, you cows. The marriage was *finished*.'

# 66

# DAY THIRTEEN

The silence in the church was resounding. Most of the mourners were already outside, but a few stragglers remained at the back, fascinated, listening. Waiting for the punchline. There surely had to be one.

*Chloe and Thomas had been divorced at the time of his death.*

As one, all of the women in the front pews turned and stared at Ruby Darke.

'My God,' said Gilly. 'Is that true? So what happens to his money?'

'He hasn't married her in secret, has he?' said Avril, picturing Ruby getting the lot while her stud farm crumbled into dust.

'What? You mean Thomas and *her*?' said Gilly, looking daggers at Ruby.

Ruby stepped forward. 'I can put all your minds to rest about that,' she said flatly. 'Thomas and I were not married. Not in public. Not in secret. Not in *anything*, thank you very much.'

'She doesn't need the money anyway,' said Ursula, tossing her ebony hair back over her shoulder. 'She's loaded.'

'So who benefits from Thomas's death?' asked Avril, her eyes greedy.

'It's obvious,' said Gilly. 'Declan does. Maybe Thomas will leave something for Evie and Olivia, but Declan inherits the earth, you can be sure of that.'

'As Chloe can attest,' said Ursula, casting a bitter slit-eyed look at Chloe. 'Darling, we all know you've been knocking Declan off. Don't look so surprised.'

'This is all a bit bloody undignified, don't you think?' asked Ruby, disgusted with the lot of them. She might be 'the mistress', the 'other woman', but she hoped she could behave with a bit more dignity than this crowd of bitches. 'Come on,' she said to Daisy and Kit and their minders. She led them all out of the church and into the sunshine, away from the gang of women who seemed not so much devastated at Thomas's loss as by the prospect of not getting a share of his money.

'What a floor show,' said Daisy as the Darke party rejoined the rest of the mourners at the graveside, where they were lowering Thomas's coffin into the soil.

The vicar emerged, red-faced with fury, and took his place at the graveside and, composing himself, went on with the final part of the service. Slowly, one by one, the exes came out of the church and joined all the others. First Chloe and then the ex-wives took a handful of earth from the offered box and tossed it down onto the coffin lid. Each handful made a nasty *thud* as it struck the highly polished wood.

'Ashes to ashes, dust to dust,' droned the vicar.

'Amen,' the watchers said.

# 67

# DAY THIRTEEN

'Come on,' said Daisy quietly to Daniel, and they peeled off from the group around the graveside. Daisy led the way across the tussocky grass to the far side of the church yard, well away from the cluster of mourners. She found the grey granite headstone she knew, the one she always came to. It read:

*Robert Hinton*
*Dear son and beloved friend*
*Husband of Daisy*
*Much missed, much loved*

It was Rob's grave; she'd married him in February of last year and mourned him ever since then. Wilting pink roses were in a vase in front of the stone; Eunice, Rob and Daniel's mother, always laid pink roses here. Kneeling down, Daisy removed the pink flowers, tossed the rancid water aside. Daniel took the stone vase over to the nearby tap. He filled it with fresh water and came back. Daisy knelt and placed the red roses she'd brought with her in the vase, adjusted them, placed a kiss on the headstone and stood up.

'I wonder, I really do, what he's trying to tell me,' she said, gazing at the gold lettering on the headstone, remembering Rob's beloved face.

Daniel was silent for a moment. Then he said: 'I told you. It's bollocks.'

'I'm going again.'

'If you say so.'

'I do. And can I just say? You didn't have to plough in like that with Luca the other night. I'd already told him I'm not interested.'

'Humour me,' said Daniel. 'I just wanted to reinforce the message, okay?'

'Let's . . .' said Daisy, irritated, and moved away from Rob's grave, heading for a cluster of newer black headstones and a mound of earth on one freshly dug grave with a metal tag set in the dirt which read 'H153'. These graves were all set close to the boundary wall of the graveyard.

Daisy halted at a particularly elaborate headstone, the resting place of her first husband Simon Collins. Live red carnations on this one. She wondered who'd put them there. Probably Lady Susan, his mother. Daisy remembered Simon, bursting with life force, an aggressive bundle of red-haired dynamism. Sometimes she saw clear echoes of Simon in the personalities of her eight-year-old twins – more in Matthew than in Luke. Matthew was the go-getter, the one who set the pace. Put him down anywhere and he'd be absolutely fine. Luke was quieter, shyer, sweeter. He would find life harder, she thought. Much harder. She would phone them tonight; talk about the goats Luke wanted.

Not wanting to move the red blooms, feeling that it would be disrespectful, Daisy placed the peach roses in with them, tapped the headstone, and stood up.

\*

*No kiss this time,* thought Daniel. *Oh, and have you noticed? She's had two husbands. Two! And both of them are dead.*

Over by Thomas Knox's graveside, people were moving away, going to their cars. Daniel saw Kit there with Ashok – and wasn't that the policewoman, the Kane woman, stopping Kit with a hand on his arm? And Ruby was there by the car, talking to Declan. The funeral was over. All that remained was for the automated digger to come and fill the grave in, bid Thomas Knox goodbye once and for all. As for who killed him?

Well, who knew?

Maybe, thought Daniel, they would *never* know.

# 68

# DAY THIRTEEN

'Hey, what's up with you?' asked Romilly, catching up with Kit by the lychgate and touching his arm. To her surprise, he flinched.

*I shouldn't be asking,* she thought. I shouldn't bloody care. But he looked sort of *grey,* as if he was ill. And so did his minder, who was waiting patiently – as always – in the car.

'Nothing,' said Kit.

'You look like death warmed over.'

'And you care why?' he asked.

Romilly held up her hands in a *peace* gesture. 'You look ill,' she pointed out.

*So would you if the Francis crew had been using your ribs as a football,* thought Kit. 'I'm fine,' he said.

'Okay. Good. So look, I need a word.'

'Right. Go on then.'

'Who in the London gangs would be known for using Semtex? Can you think of anyone?'

Kit gave her a wide-eyed look. 'And if I *did,* and I told you, what would that make me? Piss off.'

'Thomas Knox was your friend.'

'He wouldn't grass anyone up. And he wouldn't expect me to do that either.'

'There could be more incidents like his death, and your friend's death, and your mother's club being blown to bits. This might not be the end of it. And if it's not, how would you feel about that? Knowing you had a chance to help and didn't.'

Kit stared at her. She was right. 'Chloe's dad was IRA,' he said.

'I know that. We've questioned Chloe and her sister intensively – nothing. We've already turned the Hampstead house over, and her sister Nieve's flat, inside and out. Had the sniffer dogs in there. Nothing. Not a whiff of explosives, not Semtex or any other sort, anywhere. Her father lived in Belfast, but he died several years ago. The Garda have turned his widow's house over at our request, but nothing. We've traced a brother in Dublin and the Garda are getting thoroughly pissed off with us because they're hitting a dead end there too. So now I'm talking to you – as an expert in the underworld – to see what I can dig up.'

'What about your narks? They're on the street, they see things, hear things.'

'Nothing yet. Kit.' Romilly looked him dead in the eye. 'I could use some help here. I don't want to be standing in a week's time, in another graveyard, seeing someone else getting buried.'

'Not even if it's a bad 'un?' Kit almost smiled.

'I don't show favouritism and I don't discriminate. That's not my job.'

'Christ, don't you ever go off duty?'

'Rarely. You know that.'

'Too bloody right I do.' Now his tone was bitter and he wasn't smiling at all. 'If that's all, Detective? I have a wake to get to.'

He turned away.

'Kit.' She touched his back. He flinched again. Romilly looked at him sharp-eyed. 'What is it? You *are* hurt, aren't you?'

'Fell down the stairs.'

'Oh for God's . . . that's not true, is it. Is it?'

He shrugged.

'Look,' said Romilly bluntly. 'This all seems to be centred around your mother, wouldn't you say? Her lover, dead. Her son – you – escaping being another victim by the merest chance, so your mate Fats bought it instead. Am I right? And then Ruby's club, flattened. What's she done, Kit? Who's she crossed?'

'That's something we'd all like an answer to,' said Kit.

'And Gabriel Ward.'

'What about him?'

'Who's he been seeing? What's he been up to? Why did he summon you to his hospital bed, and why did he say it was too late, that it had already happened?'

Kit stiffened. 'How *did* you know about that?'

'Oh for fuck's sake. Work it out.'

'Father Riley?'

'Nurses see everything, you know. And they have big ears.'

'But if we're comparing notes,' said Kit, half-smiling now. 'In a purely business-like way, that is . . .'

'Then bring on the notes, Mr Miller. I need info to solve cases. And you're more close-mouthed than the grave. Which irritates me.'

'Oh, I irritate you?' Kit stared at her face. 'Right back at you.'

'So . . . have you anything you should be telling me? Anything at all?'

Kit had a think about that. Then he said: 'Boy Ankara. He drinks in the Lamb and Flag and he used to be, back in the day, the go-to man for plastic explosives.'

'Used to be?'

'Oh, he was a great expert safe man. Cracked more safes than you had hot dinners. Used to explain to us lads at length how you could make a blast go up or down or out. Bragged about his expertise with gelignite and – yeah – with Semtex. It was fascinating, really.'

'And . . . ?'

'He lost both legs in an explosion.'

Romilly stared at Kit's face. 'You . . . you're having a bloody laugh, right?'

'Splendid irony, yeah? No, I'm not joking. He really did blow his own legs off.'

'So not so much of an expert.'

'These days? No. But if anyone can tell you where to get hold of an under-the-counter batch of Semtex, he can.'

'Right.' Romilly glanced over to her car, where Bev Appleton was waiting. 'Will he talk to me?'

'Not a chance.'

'I'll rephrase. Will he talk to you, while I'm there?'

'If I give the word you're sound.'

'And will you? Give it?'

'Why not?'

# 69

# DAY THIRTEEN

'Ms Darke? Can I have a word?' asked Declan.

Ruby was about to get into a car. Cyril was behind the steering wheel, waiting.

Brennan pushed himself away from the car bonnet, looking a question at Ruby.

'It's all right,' Ruby told him. She turned to Declan. 'Yes. You can have a word.'

'Can we . . . ?' he said, indicating along the lane. He walked and Ruby fell into step beside him. It was the weirdest sensation for her, because he was so damned like his father. If she'd ever had a type, then Thomas Knox was it. But Declan was like Thomas thirty years ago. Fit. Young. Strong. And with the same dirty-blond hair and sharp blue eyes of his father. It was unnerving, being this near to Declan – particularly today, with all this fresh sadness welling up in her, the whole sorry devastating business of losing Thomas eating at her, making her choke back tears.

She was disturbed by Declan. And more than that, she was disgusted with him, because he had been having a fling with Chloe and in Kit's estimation that was why his dad's marriage had foundered. Maybe Thomas had discovered Chloe's infidelity, or maybe she had simply confessed it.

Or maybe Declan had bragged about it. Who knew? And who the hell was she, anyway, to take the moral high ground? She herself had done Chloe wrong. She knew she didn't come out of any of this looking good. All those bitter, grasping ex-wives were right.

'You okay?' he asked her.

'I'm fine,' she said flatly.

'I heard all that going on,' he said. 'Right load of harpies aren't they. Ripping you to shreds in there.'

Ruby gave him a tight smile. 'I'm a big girl. I can take it.'

Declan eyed her speculatively. 'Yeah, I think you can. One thing about my Dad, he had pretty damned fine taste in women.'

Ruby stopped walking. She turned and faced him. 'Meaning what?' she asked.

'I should think that was fairly obvious,' said Declan.

'Kit told me all about you and Chloe.'

'Ah. Did he.'

'Yes, he did.'

'Ouch.'

'So please don't try flattery on me, Declan. I'm old enough to be your mother, and I'm wise enough to know bullshit when I hear it.'

'Nevertheless . . .' said Declan, smiling.

'What, is this a pattern with you? He marries them, you follow on knocking them off one by one? You done this with Ursula, have you? With Gilly? With Avril too?'

'Listen, I—'

'Shut your face Declan. It's a sad day and it wouldn't take much to upset me, right now.'

'I can see what Dad saw in you,' said Declan. 'And listen. For the record. Chloe came on to me, not the other way round. And it's over between us; it barely even started, really.'

'What, you dropped her when it looked like you might get implicated in your dad's murder? I can understand that.'

'You want the truth? It felt like treachery. It was treachery. And I couldn't go on with it, particularly after what happened to him. And no – I haven't been near the others.'

'Well done.'

'It's interesting, you know, looking back on my father's escapades with women. My mum the solid one, the domestic. Then Ursula the goddess and Avril the horse-mad one, and then Gilly who really ought to leave the coke alone, and Chloe who's not terribly bright – and then you. You, Ms Darke, are something truly special. Something *different*.'

'And you – Mr Knox – are full of shit.'

Declan's eyes were smiling into hers. So like Thomas's. And it would be so easy, so dreadfully easy, to fall into something stupid right now.

When Declan spoke again, his voice was low, intimate.

'Anytime, Ms Darke. All you have to do is say the word.'

Fuck's sake! On the day of his father's funeral, he was actually coming on to her. Because dear old daddy had had her? Yes. It was probably that. It had to be that. She felt a shiver go through her – an appalling mix of horror and excitement. She ignored it.

'Fuck off, Declan,' she said, and walked away, back to Brennan and Cyril and the car.

# 70

## DAY THIRTEEN

Fabio Danieri did a lot of shoulder-patting. Reassuring people. Gabe Ward, for instance. And work colleagues, fellow board members on various companies. He could console, he could assure people that everything would work out well. He was doing that now, with this big *doink* Welsh Joe, who had come to Fabio's house, which was pretty much a war zone. Dust and crap all over the place, Mama wandering around, the nurse dossing off and he was going to fire *her* arse, soonest. The builder making a hell of a noise, useless Donato's equally useless cousin Dante ineffectively sweeping up muck while the builder pounded away upstairs in Mama Bella's suite and downstairs at the wall into the cellar. Fabio no longer cared whether the cellar was there or not. He just wanted all this mess and disorder *gone*.

'Bastard belittled me,' Joe was telling Fabio, while standing there amid the debris.

*Thump* went the sledgehammer, bashing through the wall.

'He did? Oh for fuck's—' Fabio's attention had been captivated, ever since Joe had come to the house, by the massive bandage attached to Joe's equally massive head. It looked *funny*. He was trying – very hard – not to laugh. Also, not to shriek in annoyance at all this bloody noise and disorder. 'So what would you like me to do? How can I help?' he asked.

*Boom!*

Joe told him.

'Of course,' said Fabio, sighing a little as he looked around him.

'What you having done here?' asked Joe.

*Boom!*

'Making a bit more space,' said Fabio, sighing. 'Now, if you'll excuse me . . . ?'

He ushered Welsh Joe out of the front door. The driveway looked like an earthquake had hit it.

*Boom!*

*That's it,* thought Fabio, *I am going to take that* fucking *sledgehammer and . . .*

Suddenly, there was silence.

At last!

Fabio stepped back inside the front door, closing it, crunching over the debris which lay inches thick on the dust sheet. He turned and there was Dante, Donato's cousin, covered in all sorts of shit, gasping like a fish.

'Boss!' he said.

'Yeah? What is it, Dante?'

The builder came stumbling out of the hole he'd just knocked in the hallway wall. Swirls of dust followed him. It was like Carter, Fabio thought, bursting through into Tut's tomb. A musty, ancient smell came up with the builder. *Finally,* they'd unearthed the cellar.

Dante's mouth was opening and closing, no sound coming out.

Mama was wandering down the stairs again. No nurse in attendance.

'Is Vittore home yet?' she asked.

'You got it, then? It's there, the cellar, like I thought?' Fabio said to the builder.

*He* didn't seem able to speak, either.

'What, you found something down there? What is it?'

No answer. The builder just stared. So did Dante.

'Something wrong down there?' said Fabio. 'Come on! What's up?'

'You better come and look,' the builder managed at last.

# 71
# DAY THIRTEEN

Fabio had never, as a child, gone anywhere near the cellar. He supposed that his older brothers Tito and Vittore had made use of it. He never had. Now he stepped through the jagged opening from the hallway and found that the cellar was a big box some twenty feet square, illuminated by a single light bulb in its centre. He took a step down the concrete flight of stairs, thinking *wow yeah, this would be useful,* and then he looked down and all further thought seemed to freeze in his head.

He stared toward the bottom of the stairs.

'Have you seen Maria?' he could hear Mama Bella asking, up there in the hallway.

Down here in the musty silence, the world above, the normal human world, was muted. He was alone here with – *oh shit* – nothing for company but what appeared to be a *corpse.*

# 72

# DAY THIRTEEN

The curtains were drawn again, closing out the warm summer daylight, cloaking the little room in gloom. They were all here, all the regulars including Daisy, at the flat high up in the Bermondsey tower block.

Candles were lit in an elaborate silver sconce on a side table, and this time the Ouija board was set out at the ready, the upturned glass beside it, while they all took their seat and tall, thin Mrs Chamberwell, dressed all in pale mint-green this time, with her sparse grey hair pulled back into a matching hairnet, told them all to hold hands.

'You mustn't break the circle once it's formed. There could be consequences,' she said.

*Like what?* wondered Daisy.

Daniel was standing across the room, watching the proceedings. Mrs Chamberwell had said he ought to go outside, but Daniel had refused to. Actually, Daniel's more cynical view of all this had slightly affected Daisy's own take on it. Now she was wondering if this actually *was* all bollocks. She was wondering if she was wasting her time and her money on what was no more than a clever confidence trick, a nice little earner for a woman who didn't have much in the way of worldly goods.

*But what if it really was Rob, trying to speak to her? What if he had something important to say?*

What had he said last time? Yes. *Daise don't.*

But don't *what?*

Ever since she'd been here – and oh God, was it really a fortnight ago, with the rotten horrible things that had happened since? Yes, it was. Ever since she'd last been here, she'd been turning it all over in her mind, wondering, puzzling. Maybe here, tonight, she would at last get some answers.

'Now is everybody ready?' asked Mrs Chamberwell.

They were holding hands. The man to the left of Daisy still had horrible sweaty palms. The woman to her right still had ice-cold fingers. They all nodded affirmation, and Mrs Chamberwell leaned over and blew out the candles on the side table, one by one.

*Darkness.*

Daisy was aware of Daniel, standing not five paces behind where she sat; silent, watching, having refused to wait outside the door. Slowly her eyes adjusted to the half-light that spilled through the thin curtains up at the window. She could hear the faint traffic noise out there clearly. Breathing in here. The sweaty palms man again. Asthmatic? Maybe.

'We seek entry into the spirit world,' said Mrs Chamberwell slowly. 'Is there anybody there to guide us?'

Silence.

'Sometimes they're reluctant to talk,' said Mrs Chamberwell to her assembled clientele. 'We'll try the board,' she said. 'Everyone? Place one index finger on the top of the glass please. Let's see who is there to speak to us.'

Everyone placed one finger on the glass.

Nothing.

'A slow day in the spirit world,' said Mrs Chamberwell with a little laugh. 'Come, is there anyone there to speak to us this evening?'

The glass moved. The woman to the right of Daisy gave a startled gasp.

'Hector . . . ?' she half-moaned.

'Hush now,' said Mrs Chamberwell.

The glass was moving.

'Who's pushing that?' asked someone across the table.

'Hush.'

The glass raced across the board and landed on *D*.

Then it moved back and landed on *A*.

Daisy felt her stomach flip over.

*I.*

*S.*

*Y.*

'Daisy?' said Mrs Chamberwell. Daisy could see the woman, dimly, across the table. 'Aren't *you* Daisy?'

Daisy had to swallow hard before she could speak. 'Yes. I'm Daisy.'

'He – that is Rob, your late husband, he tried to contact you last time you were here, didn't he.'

'Yes. He did.'

'He said—'

'He said "Daise don't."'

'He is obviously trying to prevent you from doing something? Trying to protect you from it? Have you any idea what this something could be?'

Daisy thought of Luca. 'There was a man. Someone with bad connections. I think maybe he was trying to warn me about him,' said Daisy.

'Oh!' Daisy could see that Mrs Chamberwell was faintly smiling there in the gloom. 'Isn't it comforting, knowing that he's still there, still watching over you. Oh, look . . .'

The glass was moving again, racing over the letters.

*D.*

*O.*

*N.*

*T.*

*G.*

*O.*

*T.*

*H.*

*E.*

*R.*

*E.*

Then, as suddenly as it had started to move, it was still.

Everyone held their breath.

'He's gone,' said Mrs Chamberwell at last. She struck a match and relit the candles and looked disapprovingly at Daniel, who was now standing behind Daisy's chair. 'I don't think the presence of a doubter right here in the room with us particularly helps the spirits to come through. I did *say* that, at the start of this séance.'

Daisy was chewing her lip, wondering. There? Don't go there? But where . . . ?

'Where does he mean? Where is it I'm not supposed to go?' asked Daisy.

She found herself looking up into the gloom near the ceiling, thinking that he was *here*, he was really here and he was trying to tell her something important.

'Rob?' she said, her voice shaking.

They all sat silent.

Daisy's finger trembled on the glass. The glass didn't move.

'Rob?' asked Daisy plaintively. 'Please . . .'

No movement.

'I'm sorry my dear, but he's gone,' said Mrs Chamberwell. 'Now – who else do we have, was it Hector you wanted to speak to my dear . . . ?' she asked the cold-fingered woman beside Daisy.

'No!' Daisy burst out.

'Look, dear, he's gone, I told you.' Her eyes flicked to Daniel. 'And I did warn you this might happen, didn't I.'

And the whole thing moved on, Daisy's question left unanswered.

Daisy sat there, fury bubbling away in her guts. Yes, the woman had warned her. Daniel should have been outside, not in the room with them. It was *his* fault that Rob had broken off communication with her. It was *always* his fault, everything, following her around, dogging her footsteps. She *hated* him. And she'd made her mind up. Tomorrow – somehow – she was going to give him the slip. She was going to *change* this stifling situation.

# 73

# DAY THIRTEEN

The thing was, not to panic. Cringing with distaste – he was not an insensitive blockhead like his brother Vittore had been, nor a complete monster like Tito – Fabio picked his way down the cellar steps and *looked.*

It *had* been a corpse. Once. Now it was just a sad collection of bones. Shards of desiccated flesh still clung on to it, here and there, brown as tobacco leaves. There was long hair – *dark* hair – clinging to the scalp, and the finger and toenails had carried on growing after death, twisted into long talons.

He shuddered. *Horrific.*

But what struck him most forcibly was the clothes the corpse – the *skeleton* – wore. A little cheesecloth top, very mouldy and dirty now but still visibly cream-coloured, covering the top half of the skeleton. The lower half was covered by a ragged pink skirt.

He *remembered* that skirt.

Maria, Vittore's wife, had worn it often. He could actually remember ripping the thing off her in a fit of passion on one of their many afternoon hotel romps. Yes, he'd been screwing his older brother's wife, and enjoying the fun of it immensely – until he'd suspected that Vittore might be aware of what was going on, and then Fabio hadn't been able to back-pedal fast enough. He'd called off the affair. Maria had wailed and objected, but he had stood firm. Vittore terrified him. And now? Looking at this sad jumble of bones, all that was left of Maria, Vittore's wife? You could see why.

'I won't wash after this evening,' he remembered her saying. 'I'm going to leave your scent all over me.'

And no doubt she had. Also, no doubt, she had left evidence of his possession of her inside her body. Could the police – was it possible? – trace his semen on her, when all that remained of her was bones? No. Surely not. He *hoped* not. But Maria had been mad for him, worryingly so. There had been a gold locket she wore and she said she had a lock of his hair in it.

'But I never gave you a lock of my hair,' he'd protested at the time, half-smiling, half apprehensive because she was getting far too serious about all this and he was starting to worry that the silly bitch might actually *tell* Vittore what was going on, and if she did that, he was dead.

'I cut it off – just a tiny bit – while you were asleep,' she had said, smiling.

*Shit! And where was that locket now?*

Overcoming his revulsion, he stepped down, closer. He mustn't panic. He peered more intently at the skeletal skull. There was a large indentation in the back of it. A killing blow, and who but Vittore could have made it? Which meant that Vittore *had* known of Maria's treachery and had exacted his revenge. Fortunately, Vittore had run out of time to exact a similar punishment on Fabio.

'Boss?' asked a voice close behind him.

Fabio nearly shrieked. He turned, heart thumping. '*What?*' he spat out.

'What we going to . . . ?' asked the builder. One of his own boys, just like Dante was, so all that was good. He was safe.

'Fetch some big storage boxes. Three ought to do it,' said Fabio. 'Get the sledgehammer. Get Dante standing guard, don't let anyone else down here. We'll break the thing up and ship it out.'

'Dante's gone home.'

'*What?*'

'Said he felt sick, sort of dizzy, seeing that.'

*Shit, shit, shit.*

But no matter. Fabio would make a call, get reinforcements in here. And now, leaning over the skeleton, he could see it: the locket which had that tell-tale treacherous clipping of his hair inside. He reached down to take the thing off, nearly ripping Maria's skull from her bony spine.

The builder, watching, crossed himself.

Fabio pocketed the locket.

First chance he got, he'd throw the damned thing in the Thames.

# 74

# DAY FOURTEEN

DI Romilly Kane was called into her DCI's office where she endured – as expected – an eye-watering bollocking.

'Two bloody weeks,' he said when he'd finished tearing into her. 'Two weeks and nothing? Come the fuck on, Romilly! Not good. Not good *at all*.'

Romilly had little to say in her defence. She had narks out everywhere, watching the gangs all around London; she had Bev turning over the Marlow end, Barry looking into every possible nook and cranny involving Thomas Knox; officers were watching the deceased's ex-wives; she'd dug around in Chloe's Irish past and – great excitement! – had actually found a real, living brother who still resided in Dublin, and at her request the Irish Garda had obligingly turned his house, his garage, his sheds inside out, making themselves exceedingly unpopular, and found nothing at all.

Now she told her DCI that she was turning her attention more closely to the ex-wives; to Chloe – who had clearly been involved with Declan, Thomas's son – to Gilly, to Avril, Ursula and Jean. She suspected – but didn't tell her DCI – that Kit Miller was doing exactly the same. She had bored people on stake-out duty, sitting in cars for hours on end and seeing probably nothing of very much interest at all. It was all costing time and money, neither of which the force could spare.

Having covered all this with the DCI and reiterated – again – her commitment to solving this case with all speed, she spent an hour with her team in the main office, going over and over the ghastly facts and the even more ghastly photographs on the wall, checking tiny details, shuffling bits of paper, sifting through anything that referred to this case, which had been labelled Operation Game right at the outset by Romilly and should, she thought, have been named *no* game, as in no game and no bloody results either.

After that, Romilly left the station and went around the corner to the Lamb and Flag, where a sign bearing a morose-looking sheep wrapped in a Union Jack greeted all those who entered. A set of stained-glass doors led into the main body of the bar.

Inside, the lighting was subdued and behind the bar, above the optics, was a line of pottery flasks in a multitude of colours. Blinking in the gloom, Romilly looked around. Punters were sipping halves at circular tables. An elderly pair of men were playing dominoes. And Kit Miller was leaning on the bar talking to a bloke who was sitting in a wheelchair, a tartan rug over his lap and an empty space where his legs ought to be.

Kit saw Romilly enter and came over. Earlier in the day, he told her, he'd had an over-excited visit from Dante. You wouldn't believe what we found at the Danieri place, he'd told Kit. In the cellar. A skeleton. A woman's skeleton.

'Who is she?' asked Romilly.

'Dante thinks it's Maria Danieri. Wife of Vittore. She went missing a long time ago. Dante reckons Fabio's going to ship the remains out to Epping tomorrow, bury them under cover of darkness.'

'That's useful,' said Romilly. 'Thanks.'

'Come and meet Boy.' He led the way over to the bar. 'Boy, this is DI Kane,' said Kit. 'Romilly – meet Boy Ankara. You want a drink?'

'Orange juice.'

Kit ordered from a brassy-looking barmaid with a massive frontage.

'Boy?'

Romilly thought that the poor chap in the blanket-wrapped chair could hardly have had a more ironic name. He was so old that he could barely be described as a man at all. He was hunched up, wearing a loud red-checked shirt with a fraying collar over what was little more than flesh and bone, but his grey greasy hair was surprisingly thick and lush. His face was long and designed for misery. His eyes, pale blue, were watery but alert.

'Pint of London Pride,' said Boy. Then he looked up at Romilly. 'Filth, eh? You don't look like filth. Too pretty.'

'Don't be taken in,' said Kit, ordering another pint for himself. 'She's deadly.'

'Kit says you're extremely bright,' said Boy.

'That's good of him,' said Romilly, not without sarcasm. 'Has he told you what we're here for?'

'You want the inside track on some plastic,' said Boy, taking his pint down off the bar and slurping back most of it in one go.

'Semtex. The bomb squad's identified it as Semtex,' corrected Romilly. 'There can't be much of that floating around loose, can there?'

'You might be surprised.'

'That's the point, right there. I don't *want* to be surprised. I want to know where it is and who's got it.'

Boy looked at Kit. 'Sharp, ain't she. Straight to the point.'

'You can say that again.'

'I'm sure that it's sometimes used for legitimate purposes . . . ?'

Boy drained his pint.

'Another?' asked Kit.

'Not for me or I'll be spark out all afternoon,' said Boy. He looked at Romilly. 'There are commercial applications of course. Blasting for the mining industry, but demolition's the most common I would think.'

'Like bringing down old power plant chimneys with a controlled amount of explosives, that sort of thing?' Romilly sipped her juice.

'That's it, yeah. Very specialised, steeplejack work. Have to be acutely aware of what's around the site, you've got to bring it down just so. Skilled stuff.'

'But this stuff would be stored very carefully, surely? All stocks noted and accounted for. Temperature controlled?'

'Of course. But accidents happen. Human error. Plus, you might have a bad egg in the basket, know what I mean?'

'Explain.'

'It's worth a lot of money to some very dubious people, that stuff. Maybe someone's got money troubles – a gambling habit, say – and they work in stores, what do they do? Fuckin' obvious, I'd say.'

'Don't they have tight checks on stores though? They have dogs that can sniff out this stuff. How the hell would you get it out without discovery?'

'Ah, there's always ways and means,' said Boy. 'It's a wicked world, right enough.'

Romilly considered this. They were going to have to recheck all the demolition companies in the area, see if anything had gone missing, even a small amount. Six ounces of the stuff, according to Major Tarrant of the bomb squad, could do incredible damage. And six ounces was *tiny*.

Boy started telling wartime stories of his days in bomb disposal. 'They use rats now,' he told them gloomily. 'Trained rats 'cos they're light enough to sniff out explosives like land mines and not get blown to buggery. And robots. *Robots*, I ask you. It ain't the same.'

*But safer*, thought Romilly, pointedly not looking in the direction of Boy's missing legs.

Kit persuaded Boy to have another pint and after half an hour more they left him there, thanking him. Kit slipped him a wedge of cash and asked him to get in touch if he thought of anything else that might be of use.

'I'll ask around. Discreetly, like,' said Boy.

They stepped back out into the sunshine.

'Poor old bastard,' said Romilly.

'Makes you think,' said Kit.

'Think what, exactly?'

But he didn't get time to answer.

# 75
## DAY FOURTEEN

After it happened, all Kit or Romilly could say was that it was a long, dark metallic grey car. There wasn't time for anything else. It mounted the pavement outside the Lamb and Flag, coming right at Romilly, who was walking out of the pub in front of Kit.

She froze in shock.

Kit grabbed her arm and yanked her back, into the pub doorway. They fell heavily backward into the little entrance section, crashing through the double doors there, shattering the pastoral scenes on the stained-glass windows.

The car engine roared and then it was off, away; Kit was scrabbling back to his feet and staggering out to the pavement. Ashok was running from the car, which had been parked nearby, saying what the fuck?

The grey car was gone.

'You get the reg number?' Kit snapped out.

'No. Too quick,' said Ashok. 'Didn't catch the plates.'

Kit went back inside.

'What's going on?' demanded the barmaid, while Romilly got to her knees and then to her feet, crunching shards of shattered glass around her.

'He was coming straight at me,' she said, breathing hard.

'Did you see the reg number?' he asked.

'No. Wasn't time.'

'You okay?'

'Yeah. Bit shaken up, that's all. Thanks.'

'She all right, is she?' Boy called over from the bar. Everyone in the pub was staring, astonished.

'She's fine,' said Kit, and took Romilly's arm and led her outside once more.

To Ashok he said: 'Take the car on down to Ruby's.' Then he raised a hand to summon a black cab with its yellow light ablaze. He gave the driver his address, shoved Romilly in the back and followed her in.

Romilly seemed finally to be aware of what was going on around her.

'I can't,' she said. 'I've got work—'

'Fuck the work,' said Kit sharply.

They said no more. He paid the driver when they got to his place and ushered Romilly inside, sat her down and put a glass of brandy in her hand. Then he poured one for himself and threw it back in one swallow.

'You could have been killed,' he said.

'I know that.' She was watching Kit pace back and forth on a massive Aubusson rug in tones of red and orange and wondering why he looked so bloody furious. But she thought she knew. He was thinking – and she was thinking it too – that life was short, horrifyingly so, and you had to grab on to anything that was precious, unrepeatable, and hold it tight. Because it could – so easily, so quickly – be snatched away and then there would only be regrets. He was right. She *could* have been killed.

As if she needed that spelling out for her though. She had lived on regrets these past few months. She'd wished that she'd never got involved with him at all because then she would never have known how good it could be. After the desert of marriage to Hugh, the blast-furnace heat of her affair with Kit had come as a massive shock. She hadn't been able to get enough of him. She – oh Christ – she'd adored him. And she couldn't afford to. Her career. She loved her career too. One more slip – just one – and she could lose it. No going back. No second chances. Finished.

Dazedly she stood up. Yes, she was in shock. A car coming right at her. Him yanking her back. Nightmare. She'd been numb ever since that moment, putting one foot in front of the other, barely aware, but now she had to get back to the job, she had to stop this.

'I have to go . . .' she said, looking around for somewhere to put the empty brandy glass. She shook her head. Nothing was making any sense.

This mustn't happen, she thought, and he was standing there, not pacing anymore but standing right in front of her. As if making a decision, he took the glass out of her hand and tossed it into the empty grate, where it shattered loudly. He grabbed her arms. Yanked her against him. Eye to eye they stood there. She was as tall as him, could stare him straight in the eye and she did so, frozen, wondering what was going to happen next.

Then he kissed her so hard and so long that it actually *hurt*.

'Kit, we mustn't . . .' she managed to get out at last.

'Shut up,' said Kit against her mouth. 'Christ, I've missed you.'

'I can't.'

He was kissing her again and her mind was spinning. She wanted this. But she could not, dare not, have it.

Kit won the argument by putting his right foot between her ankles and flipping her onto her back so that she fell beneath him, onto the soft wool of the Aubusson rug.

'You bastard,' Romilly complained, winded, but Kit was already wrenching off her navy jacket, pulling at the buttons of her white blouse, getting them undone, pushing the silky fabric aside so that he could reach in and unfasten her bra and with a grunt of triumph take her naked breasts into his hands.

He was kissing her again and there was nothing, nothing she could do because she didn't want to, she couldn't bear to stop this, not after this awful dry time without him.

Now he was tugging at her slacks, yanking them down, taking off her shoes, and disposing of her strictly service-able and very unsexy pants until she lay there utterly nude while he was still fully clothed.

'I bloody hate you,' she said.

'Shut up,' he said, grinning, and kissed her, their teeth clashing, his tongue invading her mouth, moans of despair and desire escaping her as his hands roamed over her exposed skin.

She was hot for him, liquid, open, drenched with desire. When he knelt between her legs she knew that all resistance was gone, it was useless. She put her hands above her head, feeling the rug scratchy but soft and so very sensual under her skin. She watched him, languorous, hungry for him as he unzipped and freed his cock and put it where she wanted it. As he entered her she sighed and lay back, surrendering, utterly undone.

Soon, she would have to think, to consider the disaster her life had so suddenly become, all over again. But for now, he was inside her, big, powerful, moving, groaning out his need of her – and she couldn't think at all.

# 76

# DAY FIFTEEN

Daisy went out very early in her little Mini with the Union Jack on the roof. The curtains up in the spare room where Daniel was sleeping were pulled tight shut, and that was good. He was used to her getting up late and had adapted to her daily pattern. Also good. She was careful not to slam the door as she got in, started the engine, drove slowly and gently down the long driveway. The two guys on the gate looked at her, but she zipped out onto the road before they could stop her, question her, and then she was away, free, for a day's retail therapy in St James's.

The day passed happily; she bought clothes, make-up, gifts for the boys which she would tell them all about when she phoned them this evening. She did have a twinge of concern that this might be a worry for Ruby so she called her when she stopped for a coffee and croissant at one of the posh eateries she liked to frequent.

'Where the hell are you?' asked Ruby.

'Jermyn Street right now. I've had a lovely day.'

'Are you all right?'

'I'm fine. Really.'

'I suppose you realise that Kit's going apeshit?'

'Fuck him.'

Ruby let out an exasperated breath. 'So long as you're all right. Look, isn't it time you came home? I know you think all this fuss is unnecessary, but it isn't. It really isn't. Please come home now.'

So Daisy polished off the last crumbs of croissant, swilled back the excellent coffee, picked up her bags and headed for the multi-storey where she'd parked the car up on the top floor. She'd made her point. Fair enough. Now she'd go home and having made it perfectly clear that no one was the boss of her, she would apologise for her lateness, act surprised that she had worried the entire household, play the dutiful daughter.

Feeling tired now, she walked through to the multi-storey and stepped into the lift, thinking of how thrilled the boys were going to be with what she'd bought them.

Just as the doors were about to close, a hand reached in and stopped them.

The man who pushed the doors open and stepped inside was *hideous*.

He was dark, skinny, dressed in a black suit. His face was pock-marked here and there with what looked – but couldn't be – the scarred remnants of cigarette burns. He was grinning at her.

Daisy felt her bowels churn uneasily at the sight of him.

'Miss Darke, yes? Daisy Darke?'

His voice was accented. Italian, she thought.

Oh Christ.

*Italian.*

He made a disgusting kissing motion with his fingertips against his lips. '*Bella.*'

Daisy said nothing. She flattened herself against the far wall of the lift, as far away from him as she could get.

'I am Donato. They call me Pizza-Face, do you know why?'

Daisy just stared. Couldn't even seem to shake her head. This was a *nightmare*.

'Once, I brought bad news to the Danieri family. A tragedy, and I told them what had happened and of course they were angry. Fabio burned me. Stubbed out many cigarettes on my face, which I think was fair. I would have done the same, had anyone given me such news.'

He turned, pressed the button. 'Top floor, yes?'

*So he knew her car.*

Daisy felt her whole body break out in a cold sweat.

'So what have you been buying, Miss Darke?' he asked as the lift started to rise.

She couldn't answer. Couldn't somehow get her dry tongue to work in her mouth. He moved toward her and she cowered back. He reached into one of her bags, peered inside.

'Ah! For the boys, yes?' said Donato.

*He knew about her kids.*

Daisy didn't dare move, didn't even *breathe*. But then he stepped back, away from her. The lift doors opened and Donato indicated that she should go first with a courtly wave of his hand.

'Someone wants a word with you,' he said, and drew level with her, took her arm in a steely grip. 'Fabio Danieri. My boss.' Pizza-Face Donato leaned in, so close that she could smell his breath, which was foul. He indicated his scarred face. 'He did this to me,' he whispered. 'So who knows what he's going to do to you, huh?'

# 77
## DAY FIFTEEN

They were there waiting for her, clustered around her Mini, dark men, hard men. Not many cars up here on the top floor of the multi-storey now, everyone was going home and those few that remained were being very careful not to get involved, not to look and see that she was in trouble.

But there would be CCTV up here, wouldn't there? The Danieri mob wouldn't *dare* do anything to her, because it would all be recorded on camera. She looked around, looked up: yes, there were cameras. But she saw with a stab of real despair that those nearest to her Mini, those crucial ones, were covered in blue paint, blinded.

Whatever was going to happen now, no one was going to see it. But would security come and check? See their blank screens and investigate?

They would.

*Surely* they would.

But when? How long would it take them to act? Would it be soon enough?

Fabio was at the centre of his pack of wolfish men, leaning casually against the bonnet of her Mini. *Fabio Danieri.* She had come across him face to face just once before and had hoped, fervently, that she would never do that again.

*Long ago and far away . . .*

Her mind flashed back to that day. She had been standing in the road clutching a bouquet of flowers, an offering that she intended to leave at the mouth of the driveway leading into what had once been the Berkshire home of her and her first husband, Simon.

Simon had, it appeared, killed himself. Hanged himself in the garage block near the house. He'd left a suicide note. But it *hadn't* been suicide. The Danieri clan had forced him to write the note, and then they had strung him up, killed him. So long ago now, but the memory of it was horrible: terrifying.

On that day she had been transfixed with horror, scared out of her wits. Now she felt the same.

'Miss Darke!' Fabio said warmly.

Daisy gulped in a breath. 'What the hell do you want?' she managed to get out.

There were three of them. Fabio and Pizza-Face Donato and – for fuck's sake! – there was Luca Romano too, his handsome face still bearing the marks of Daniel's attack on him.

'She's asking what we want!' Fabio echoed, looking at his companions. Then his eyes flicked back to Daisy. 'What we *want,* Miss Darke, is you. I mean, look what you did, look what that *schifosa* who was guarding you did to my poor sweet cousin here, my sweet Luca who never did a single soul any harm at all, isn't that right, Luca?'

'That's right,' Luca agreed, eyeing Daisy greedily.

'It's okay,' said Fabio, patting his cousin's cheek. 'No worries, huh? Because I'll let you have first turn at her, how is that? Yeah?'

Daisy's blood froze in her veins.

'And then,' he went on, 'it's my turn. I'll bet she's *sweet* after all this time as a widow, don't you think? We'll be doing her a favour, huh?' He reached out and patted Daisy's cheek. She flinched back and he frowned.

'*Basta,*' he hissed. 'But we'll tame you, yes? Oh yes – we will. And then Donato, you go, after we've had our fun.'

'You touch me,' she said coldly, 'and I warn you – you die.'

This sent all three of them off into peals of laughter.

'She jokes with us!' said Fabio admiringly, his laughter fading. Suddenly his face was totally serious and his dark eyes were searing into Daisy's with lethal intent. 'You think you can frighten me? *You* are the one in trouble here, Miss Darke. And it's time you realised it.'

Donato snatched her bags away from her, walked over to the edge of the multi-storey, held them up over the drop to the street below. Stood there, grinning back at her.

'Give those—' started Daisy, and Donato opened his fingers and dropped the bags. They fluttered down, away. Her gifts for the boys. Her own *stupid* impulse purchases. The expensive scent for Ruby, the costly aftershave for Kit. All of it, gone.

'What you have to realise, Miss Darke, is that you are in serious trouble here,' said Fabio. No laughter now. No joking. They were closing in on her and they were going to hurt her. She felt her back touch the Mini as they crowded in around her. Nowhere left to go. Nowhere to run. There was nobody about except someone – one person – who was now coming at them very fast, running toward them through the vast echoing building.

It was *Daniel.*

# 78

# DAY FIFTEEN

Daniel dropped to his knees as he came hurtling toward their little group. He slid in and the effect was like skittles: he took Luca's feet from under him, knocked Donato to one side, shoved Fabio back so that he fell right across the bonnet of the car. Daisy, at the centre of it all, lost her footing and fell down. Above her, she saw Donato right himself and come at Daniel, who kicked out hard. She heard a distinct *crack* as Donato's leg broke. Donato let out a shriek of pain. Then Daniel was on him, shoving him back, away from Daisy.

Luca piled in, throwing himself at Daniel's back, but Daniel was already turning, punching hard. His fist connected with the side of Luca's head and Luca collapsed to the hard concrete floor.

Donato was trying to get up, dragging his damaged leg, trying to get back to grips with Daniel. Fabio was standing aside, watching. Donato gave a yell and launched himself at Daniel, who fell back but quickly righted himself and grabbed the front of Donato's suit jacket and shoved him hard so that his legs hit the edge of the multi-storey's concrete barrier.

For a frozen moment, they stood there.

Donato teetered, snatching at the edge of the barrier.

Then – suddenly – with a wail of despair, he went over, and was gone: vanished from sight.

# 79
# DAY FIFTEEN

'Get away from the fucking car,' said Daniel to Fabio.

Down below, out in the road, they could hear people running, shocked cries.

Fabio was staring open-mouthed at the empty space where Donato had just been standing. Luca was on the floor, dazedly trying to get back to his feet. His face set hard, Fabio stepped away from the Mini.

'Keys,' snapped Daniel to Daisy.

With shaking hands Daisy somehow got her purse out of her bag, found the keys, handed them to Daniel, clambered back onto her feet. Found that her legs were shaking so much she could barely stand. She looked at Fabio as Daniel opened the driver's-side door and got in.

'This isn't over,' hissed Fabio.

Daisy flung open the passenger-side door, scrambled in and shoved the door lock down hard. Daniel started the engine, flung the Mini in reverse, skidded it backward and then forward, and they were out and away.

Not a word passed between them for a long time, and then Daisy said: 'How did you . . . ?'

'How did I know where to find you?' Daniel spat out.

Daisy nodded. It really felt like too much effort to speak. To think. She couldn't believe that she was still in one piece, unhurt, not raped, not defiled, not beaten.

'Thank Christ you phoned Ruby,' he said. 'I was already in town looking for you. She told me Jermyn Street and this was the nearest multi-storey so I had to hope you'd be parked here. I looked on every fucking floor. Didn't think I was going to find you, but then I got right up to the top and there was the Mini. And Fabio *fucking* Danieri and his pals were there, waiting for you.'

'There's no chance he'll be alive, is there?' Daisy asked, thinking of that ugly bastard Donato stumbling against the balcony edge and tumbling over, into oblivion.

'None at all. And thank Christ they sorted out a problem for us, didn't they. Blanked out the security cameras in that quarter of the floor, did you notice that?'

Daisy nodded. She had.

'So no record of what happened. Which is good.'

'Daniel . . .' She ought to say thank you. She'd come up here, unescorted, to spite him, to teach him a lesson. But actually, he'd taught *her* one. She'd behaved like a fool and despite that he had saved her.

'Shut up, Daisy,' he said. 'And there's no need to worry your mother with any of the fine details about the Italian lot being there today, okay?'

She nodded. *Wanted* to apologise. *Ought* to apologise. To thank him.

'Daniel—'

'What we are going to say to her is this. I came up to town and I found you, safe and sound. Ruby don't need any more of your shit right now.'

'Daniel . . . they were going to . . .' She couldn't finish it. Couldn't bear to even *think* of it.

'What the hell else would you expect them to do?'

She sat there, shuddering, thinking that she'd had a very narrow escape. That she owed him. That she ought to *say* something. A thank you would be a good place to start. But she couldn't form the words. Couldn't yet emerge from the nightmare playing over and over in her head. Donato cornering her in the lift. Tossing her lovely gifts for the boys away. Falling from the car park onto the street below. And the greasy, sneering satisfaction in his and Fabio's and Luca's eyes when they thought they were going to have her. They would have torn her to bits between them, like rabid dogs.

'Daniel—' she started again.

'Shut the fuck up, Daisy.'

She shut up.

# 80

# DAY FIFTEEN

Ruby had already talked to Chloe – wife number five – and Gilly – number four – now Alan, a short, ginger-haired old boy of Kit's was driving her, along with Brennan riding shotgun, down to the Arabian stud that Avril, wife number three – owned and ran, apparently with the assistance of her young daughter Olivia, who was, according to Kit, friendly with Evie, daughter of wife number two.

*Christ, Thomas, you serious?* she thought as Alan steered the car in through the moss-covered entrance and up a long gravel drive. To the left and right were paddocks, mares grazing, foals at foot. Up ahead, a mouldering sign said RECEPTION.

Kit was right, the place looked tired. Tiles gone off the roof, fences rotting. And yet, hadn't Kit also said that Thomas had been fair with his settlements to the ex-wives and their children? Yet, they wanted more. Well, maybe they *needed* more, to be fair. A place this size would cost vast amounts of money to run and that would be a stretch unless Avril had acquired a new partner – which, according to Ashok, she had not.

'Wait here, both of you,' said Ruby, and she went to the reception and looked inside. Nobody there. She went over to the door of the main house, which needed a good clean up and a lick of paint, and rang the bell. Nobody answered.

Glancing back at her two minders, she motioned for them to wait and walked on around the side of a couple of long barns. She could hear a cracking noise in the distance and she followed the sound. Around the back of the building was a big sand-covered area and in the centre of it a woman with a blonde ponytail, wearing jodhpurs and a cream shirt, was lunging a chestnut horse on a rope so that it cantered around in a tight circle. The woman was cracking a long whip behind it so that it didn't slow down.

'Hello,' said Ruby loudly.

Avril turned and stared. The horse slowed to a trot.

'Remember me? Ruby Darke?'

Avril didn't speak for a beat or two. The horse slowed to a walk and then stood, snorting. Avril went to its head, unclipped the long rope from the halter, and the horse meandered off. Looping the rope over her shoulder, Avril walked over to where Ruby stood. She came through the gate, closed it behind her.

'Yeah, I remember you. How could I forget? The mistress who had the brass neck to turn up at the funeral.'

'It was a hell of a do,' said Ruby.

'At least you didn't have the cheek to turn up at the wake too.'

The wake had – of course – been held at Jean's place.

'I thought about it. Reckoned I wouldn't be welcome.'

'You got *that* right. What do you want?' Avril stepped past Ruby, heading for the back door of the house, over cobbles that were green with moss, slippery; past old stone pots caked in lichen after years standing in deep shade. Someone had put a few plants, some geraniums and a few scant patches of annual lobelia in there, but they were long dead. The paint was peeling on all the windows and doors back here, it was worse than the front of the building. Ruby's eyes wandered further. In the far distance, a grey-haired man was standing under a leafless oak. He drew back, moved some twenty feet away. There was a muffled *bang* and slowly the old dead tree canted to one side and then with increasing acceleration hit the ground. There was another *whumph* of sound, much heavier than the first, as it struck the earth.

'What's he doing?' asked Ruby, pointing.

'What, Timothy?' Avril shrugged. 'Blasting out an old tree, that's all. It was getting dangerous, had to come down.'

Ruby stiffened. *Blasting?* She thought of Thomas, blown to smithereens. Fats, the same. And her club, eviscerated.

'I didn't know people still did that,' she said. 'Years ago, maybe. I think I've heard of it. What does he use to do that?'

'Oh – black powder, I think.'

'And he works for you?'

'Yeah, he's been at the stud on and off since he was a teenager. Worked elsewhere for a while but came back here in the end.'

'Can he get his hands on anything else?'

Avril's attention sharpened on Ruby's face. 'What are you getting at?'

'He's using black powder. How about plastic explosives?'

'What? Now you're just being fucking ridiculous,' snapped Avril.

'Is it true that you once hit Thomas over the head with a full bottle of Bushmills?' asked Ruby.

Avril stopped walking. 'He asked for that,' she said.

'Did he? How?'

'He was fucking that whore Gilly when he was married to me. I found out about it.'

'Seems like there was a pattern there with him,' said Ruby.

'Yeah. And then there was Chloe and then there was *you*. Christ you're bloody nosy. You know, it's time someone taught you a lesson. It really is.'

'About what? Keeping my hands off some other woman's man? But Thomas never belonged to *any* woman, did he. I think I always knew that. A pity you and the others didn't.'

'You think you're so smart,' said Avril, her face set with anger.

'Smarter than you, for sure. I knew the deal. You didn't.'

'Bitch!' Avril snapped and lashed out with the whip.

Shocked, Ruby jumped back and fell against the side of the house, grazing her suit jacket on the dirty green brickwork. *That's one* hell *of a temper,* she had time to think before Avril cracked the whip again. It came close – dangerously close – and if it hit you, Ruby thought, it would sting, it would hurt; and if it caught bare flesh, it would certainly *cut*.

Ruby backed away. If that thing hit her head or arms, it could do damage.

Avril let rip again.

*Crack!*

There was real danger here. That whip could twine around her neck and throttle the life out of her. And Avril was so furious that she wouldn't hesitate to do that, she could kill before she even had the sense to know she'd done it. Ruby cowered back, but Avril followed, her eyes unfocused, rage in every movement.

'*Mum!*'

The voice seemed to cut through the fog of Avril's fury.

She stopped moving toward Ruby and let the whip hang loose in her hand.

Ruby's rescuer was a short blonde girl. Olivia ran at her mother and snatched the whip away from her. 'What the hell is this? What's going on?'

'Just get her out of here,' said Avril faintly. Then she turned and went into the house, closing the door behind her.

Ruby sagged back against the wall, feeling weak and not caring whether it marked her clothes or not. That had been bloody frightening. She wondered what would have happened if Olivia hadn't shown up at that precise moment. She didn't have the gun with her and Brennan and Alan were out of earshot at the front of the building. Her eyes wandered over to the man in the far field, still there beside the corpse of the fallen oak. She'd had a mad woman here and an explosives expert, and no visible back-up.

*Black powder.*

*Explosives on Avril's property, and Avril with that damned awful temper of hers. Could she have got mad enough to kill Thomas? Kill Ruby's son? Kill* her?

Aware that her heart was thundering in her chest like an express train, that her skin was moist with the sweat of fear, Ruby pushed herself away from the wall.

'Sorry,' said Olivia, looking embarrassed. 'Look, you'd better go.'

Ruby needed no second telling.

She went.

Arriving back at the Marlow house they found Ashok just turning Kit's car into the drive ahead of them.

'Where's Kit?' asked Ruby, wanting to talk to him, to tell him about what had happened.

'Left him in town like he asked,' said Ashok.

'What's he doing?'

'No idea,' said Ashok.

# 81
## DAY FIFTEEN

'Oh for God's sake,' said Romilly, groaning into one of Kit's thousand thread count Egyptian cotton pillows. Hers were nylon. Serviceable but far from comfy. His were lush. Luxurious.

'What?' Kit rolled over, stared into her eyes.

They were both naked and they had been in this bed for the best part of two hours and she felt as though if she didn't get out of it very soon, she never would. She would just stay here, making love, protesting occasionally – feebly – but making absolutely no attempt to get up and get on with business.

'This,' she said drowsily, 'must not happen, ever again.'

'I think you said that last time it happened,' Kit pointed out. 'Last year, wasn't it. When you told me to fuck off out of your life.'

'Did I? Well, I meant it. I have to get up now.'

Kit nuzzled his lips into her neck. 'Off you go then, Detective.'

'It's Detective Inspector. As you bloody well know.' She touched the rainbow bruises on his middle. Kit flinched, slightly. 'I *knew* there was something wrong with you. Who did this to you?' she asked.

'Nobody. Fell down the stairs. Didn't I tell you?'

'How about the truth?'

'All right. I upset somebody. All sorted now. And when that bomb blew up on Ruby's drive and killed Fats, it turned you into a one-woman missile. That can happen with blasts. All the objects around it plume outward and the effects can be bad. Did you know that?' He paused. 'Time for you to go, yeah?'

'What, are you kicking me out now?'

'You said you wanted to go.' His lips nibbled at her ear. His hands smoothed over her torso, found her breasts, moved over them, teasing, caressing. His mouth placed butterfly kisses all the way down over her collarbone and then fastened on each nipple in turn, sucking until they were almost unbearably hard.

Romilly moaned. 'I have to go. And I want you to understand, there will be no more *incidents* like this. Okay?'

'Off you go then,' he murmured against her skin. 'I love your nipples,' he said.

'Don't, you'll make them sore.'

'All right. Oh, they're hard. *So* hard. Do they feel sore then?'

He was driving her crazy. Her whole skin – *all* of it – felt unbearably sensitised. She should *never* have let him do this. But oh, this was bad, this was a disaster. Because this wasn't just sex. She wished it was, but it wasn't. This was a need so overpowering that it swept her away, every time. And of course this was the end, for her, if she allowed it to be. Career, gone. Life, torn apart.

'Go on then. Off you go.'

'In a while. Maybe.'

'It's getting late. You could stay here. I'll cook you dinner.'

'You can cook?'

'I have a housekeeper.'

'Sure you do.'

'I do. And then you could stay the night. What's the rush?'

'What's the *rush*? For God's sake, you know what the rush is. The rush is my work, and *that* is why I'm getting up right now.'

Romilly tore herself away from him and sat up. She was expecting Kit to pull her back down, and she was very afraid that she would let him, too, and be glad of it – but then the phone rang on the bedside table.

'Fuck that thing,' said Kit, and picked it up. 'Yes?' he snapped.

'Kit? It's me.'

'Mum? What's up?'

'I've just had a very interesting conversation with Avril.'

He put the phone on speaker and Ruby told him about Timothy blasting out the old oak and the black powder he had used – and probably should not under any circumstances have been in possession of – to fell it. Romilly sat there, taking it all in.

'And that woman's bloody demented,' Ruby finished up. 'I was asking her some questions and she took offence. She came at me with a whip.'

'She *what*?'

'She did. Her daughter stepped in, stopped her. Just as well, really. She meant it, Kit. She's *very* violent.'

'But wasn't Brennan with you? And Alan?'

'I went round the back to find Avril and told them to stay put. My fault, not theirs.'

'Not clever.'

'No.'

'Isn't she the one who hired the private detective?'

'That's right. She did. And what are you up to?'

Kit raised his eyebrows at Romilly, sitting there naked on the edge of the bed, listening.

'Nothing much,' he said. Romilly threw a pillow at him.

'You coming down tomorrow?'

Romilly was now retrieving her bra and pants, disappearing inside the strict no-nonsense navy-blue trouser suit and white blouse that was her standard police service uniform. She was yanking back her unruly mound of long curling dark hair, securing it with its usual plain black shoelace. Kit watched her, smiling.

'Yeah, I'll be coming,' he said.

'Good. See you,' said Ruby, and Kit put the phone down as he reached out an arm and yanked Romilly back down onto the bed. 'Half an hour more?' he asked.

'No! Not a single second.' She tore herself free of his grip. Why did he have to look and feel so damned good? He'd brought her to orgasm three times since carrying her and her belongings up the stairs – like a leopard hauling its kill up into a tree, she'd thought on the way up here to the bedroom. Three orgasms in two hours? It was enough to drive any woman insane. She didn't feel her usual no-nonsense self at all. She felt deeply relaxed and yes – sated. Utterly sexually fulfilled. This man was *dangerous*. But then – hadn't she already known that? So how the *hell* had she wound up here, again?

'Look,' she said, averting her eyes because she so wanted – *desperately* wanted – to touch his body again, to feel him – once again – on her and inside her. 'I have things to do, places to go.' She switched to business mode. *Had* to.

'That was interesting, don't you think? What your mother said about Avril? And explosives on the premises? Maybe we got our lead at last.'

'Maybe,' Kit said. 'Come on, Romilly. You know you want to. Five minutes? Less? Okay. I promise I'll be done in two.'

'Nope.' She gathered up her bag, thinking that she *did* want to, but she certainly wasn't going to. This had been craziness, a mad impulse on both their parts. But now it was done. They'd revisited the thing, and this was an end to it. She slipped on her shoes. 'Now I'm not fucking about. *Never* again, you got me?'

'You're a very hard woman.' He gestured down his body. 'And I, sadly, am an *extremely* hard man. So what now?'

'Now?' Romilly took a calming breath and got her mind back to where it should be. She'd weakened, but that wouldn't happen again. 'Now,' she said firmly, 'I am getting back to work. First, I am going to check for any viable CCTV outside the Lamb and Flag. Then I'm getting a warrant so I can turn that stud farm inside out.'

'And then?'

'Then I'm going to pull Avril and this "Timothy" person in and find out where he got black powder from. Because maybe if he could get that, he could get Semtex too. And then we'll have our killer, bang to rights.'

# 82
# DAY FIFTEEN

The thing *definitely* was, not to panic. But – okay – Fabio did panic a little when Luca went over to Dante's flat and found that he wasn't there.

'What do you mean, he wasn't there?' Fabio demanded. 'What, is he out down the shops? Buying bread? What? He isn't working here, and he's supposed to be sick. Now you tell me he's out? What the fuck's going on?'

'Fab,' said Luca. 'Listen. The place is empty. The landlord grabbed me and asked if I was a relative of the little cunt and he said he was due two months' rent. I told him I wasn't and he showed me the flat. Stains on the carpets, mould up the bathroom walls where the twat never opened the windows, he reckons it's going to cost him a small fortune to get the place put right. And Dante? Boss, he's *gone.* He's legged it somewhere.'

Dante had clearly not wanted to find himself involved with the finding of a dead body. That *schifosa!* He had forgotten the Camorra creed and run. Well, Fabio, on whose property the corpse had shown up, didn't have the luxury of doing that. He had to sort this small matter out, and tonight him and his crew were going to do it.

\*

They hacked the skeleton into pieces and packed it into three big house-moving boxes. Once it was full dark, they stowed the boxes into the back of the car and set out for Epping.

Once in the forest, Fabio and Luca and one of the other guys grabbed the tools they'd packed in the boot. They trudged through the greenery until they found a suitable site for the first box. The second they'd bury fifty feet away. The third another fifty.

'You going to say a few words, boss?' asked Luca.

'Yeah, I'm going to say go to hell and damnation, Maria,' snapped Fabio, glaring at the first of the boxes. 'That cunt never caused me anything but trouble and here she is, dead in three boxes, and she is *still* a pain in my arse.'

So saying, Fabio started digging.

'Come on, you two, get busy with those damned shovels, we don't want to be here all night!' he hissed at them.

They got busy. The first box was duly interred. They moved on, buried the second. Then again, and the third hole was dug out and they were all three of them sweating and cursing and wishing they were somewhere – *anywhere* – else, when a voice came out of the darkness at them.

'*Police!* Stop right there.'

Torches beamed on, dazzling them. Not pausing to make conversation, Fabio fled. Unable to see where he was going, he simply *ran*, brambles tearing at his expensive clothes, ripping his skin, tree branches striking his head. He neither cared nor felt pain. He wasn't being caught, because how the hell could he possibly explain? That the crime had to have been his brother Vittore's, and not his?

He still had the damned locket in his jacket pocket.

He still thought that he would be caught by the lethal methods the police had at their disposal, that something on her skeleton would somehow match him to this crime and he would be put away.

*Fuck you, Maria,* was his final thought, before they grabbed him and wrestled him to the ground.

# 83
## DAY SIXTEEN

Avril was furious to be called in for questioning by the police. Her helper Timothy Copnor, a large and very fat man in his fifties with poppy grey eyes and a face like a full moon, was simply scared, because he *had* stored illicit black powder in one of the disused stables on the stud farm – and detonators.

'I would never use the stuff for any bad purpose,' he protested to Barry Jones while sitting in interview room A. 'Do I need a lawyer? All I keep it for is—'

'Miss Gulliver mentioned that you used to work in the nearby quarry,' interrupted Barry.

'That's right. I did.'

'So this stuff, this black powder and the detonators – you must have pinched these things from your place of work? Stolen them? Is that correct?'

'No, I—'

'Is that correct?'

'It was old stock, they were clearing it out; I didn't mean to do any harm . . .'

'And you thought it would be useful.'

'I did. Yes. I just used it now and again to blow out old trees that are hazardous. Cheaper by far than getting in tree surgeons. Avril never wanted to do that.'

'And at the quarry, did you handle plastic explosives of any sort?'

'Plastic? No, never.'

'Like PETN or RDX? You know? Semtex?'

'No. Never. I swear.'

Meanwhile, in interview room B, Romilly was questioning Avril. She'd gone straight from Kit's place to the magistrates', got the warrant, presented Avril with it, ushered in the troops to turn the stud over top to bottom, and now she was sitting across the table from the bolshy blonde asking her all about what had been going on.

'So you knew that Timothy Copnor was experienced in handling explosives?' asked Romilly.

'I knew it, of course I did. I didn't *condone* it. Look, how much longer is this going to take?'

'As long as I want it to,' returned Romilly. 'This is a murder investigation. Did you ask him to remove the tree using black powder? The tree that Ruby Darke saw him fell when she was at your yard yesterday?'

'I told him to sort it out, get rid of it. Branches were coming off, it was a hazard. I knew he had the stuff tucked away, but I didn't specify how he should get rid of the tree.'

'So he knew you were cutting corners? Not wanting to hire in expensive tree surgeons?'

'I'm always trying to trim expenses, that's true,' said Avril, shaking her head in exasperation. 'Christ, do you know how much that place costs to run every year? If that tree had fallen and injured somebody, I'd be liable, wouldn't I? So it had to go, and I knew Tim could see to it.'

'With stolen black powder from the quarry he used to work at.'

'Look, *I don't know* where he got it from. I never inquired. That was his business.'

'Did he ever talk to you about these explosives?'

'No, not really.'

'How about plastic explosives?'

'I don't know what you mean.'

'Like Semtex, for instance.'

'I haven't the faintest idea what you mean. Semtex? What is that?'

'It's the explosive that was used to kill Thomas Knox. Your ex-husband. You know? The one you once hit over the head?'

'Oh that? That happened *years* ago.'

'You've got quite a temper. I heard that just yesterday you threatened someone with a whip.'

'I don't know—'

'Ruby Darke, it was. A *hell* of a temper, yes? And you hired a private detective to follow Mr Knox when you were married to him, because you believed he was having an affair with Gilly Taylor-Black.'

'I was right about that,' said Avril, folding her arms over her middle. 'Wasn't I? Do I need a lawyer here?'

'What was the name of this private detective? Where did he practise?'

Avril told Romilly the name and address of the man she'd hired. 'But it's yonks back, I'm telling you. He might not even be in business anymore. Look – *do* I need a lawyer?'

Romilly stared at Avril. *Could* she have done it? Offed her husband, then tried for Kit to spite Ruby and hit Fats instead, and then – finding out about it and hating the fact that Ruby and Thomas were back on – had she got her pet helper Timothy to blow up Ruby's club?

It was possible. And the more she spoke to this 'gang' of women, the more acrimonious the whole mess seemed. They were bound together by their history but hated each other. Purred over each other like pals and then delightedly, gleefully, stuck the knife in when one or other of them was out of earshot.

Romilly could imagine them cooing in sympathy to Avril if she had to sell off her stud farm, saying oh what a pity, you poor thing – and then laughing behind her back, saying, did you hear about poor Avril? Now you must never repeat this because if you do, I will know where it's come from, all right? And on and on, each of them passing on the information, revelling in Avril's misfortune.

Jean, Ursula, Avril, Gilly, Chloe – they were not Romilly's idea of the sisterhood, not at all. They were bitches clamouring for the prize – Thomas's money. Only Jean had come out of the whole multi-marriage debacle with any dignity intact; the others were endlessly grasping, forever trying to outdo each other. They were not friends; they were, in fact, sworn enemies.

'Hey!' Avril thumped the table when Romilly didn't answer. '*Hey!* Do I need a lawyer in here?'

Probably not, thought Romilly. Which was a shame. She would love to have nailed Avril's stroppy arse.

'No,' she said. 'You know, when you hit Thomas with that bottle?'

'Oh for God's . . . that was just the heat of the moment.'

'Why did you hit him?'

'Oh, who knows? It's in the past.'

'Well, Jean – who was there at the time, having invited you and the rest of Thomas's ex-wives over to her house for Christmas – says that it was about money. That you wanted a larger allowance from Thomas. That you weren't happy with the divorce settlement.'

'Jean's a cow,' Avril said sharply. 'And I had good reason to kick off. Thomas's meanness has left me in dire financial straits. I struggle all the time to maintain the stud and to look after Olivia, and she's his daughter for fuck's sake. I know he gave her presents, but it's cash that's really needed. You'd think he could have spared a bit more, if only for her. Talk to Ursula. Talk to Chloe. We're all in the same bloody boat. Only Jean – that cow – is sitting pretty.'

'But striking him on the head with a full bottle of whisky? That could have killed him.'

'It didn't though – did it?' said Avril tartly.

'No. But now someone's finished the job, haven't they.' Romilly stood up. 'Interview terminated at . . .'

Romilly walked out to the front of the station to get some air. Something about the whisky bottle and Avril wasn't quite adding up.

On the way outside she passed three handcuffed men with Italian accents who were being hauled into the station by one of her contemporaries DI Turnbull, along with three large boxes wrapped in evidence bags. The men were protesting their innocence. The desk sergeant gave her a laughing glance.

'You believe this?' he asked her. 'That's one of the Danieri lot. They were out at Epping, burying a skeleton. It's in those boxes. Silly bastards.'

'I'm innocent I tell you!' one of the Italians was screaming.

'Yeah, yeah. Tell it to the Marines,' said DI Turnbull, ushering the lot of them toward the cells.

# 84
# DAY SIXTEEN

Later, Romilly, DS Appleton and DS Barry Jones were assembled at the station, once again examining evidence, chewing the whole things over.

'The gangs,' said Bev. 'We know the gangs. We know the *patterns* of the gangs, and up to this point not one of them's been using plastic, not the Brindells, not the Fretts, nobody. The Welsh man, didn't he used to be in the heavy game?'

'He did,' said Bev. 'Joe Williams did a ten stretch for the job outside Gatwick. But these days? Armed robbery's too damned risky now that the banks have tightened up their acts. People shy away, don't they. Drugs are easier. More profitable. Safer.'

'What about the CCTV outside the Lamb and Flag?' asked Barry. 'Any news on the car's plates?'

'There *were* no plates,' said Romilly, who had checked this personally, guiltily, rather than let any of her team see her coming out of a pub with Kit Miller and draw the wrong conclusions – or, worse, the right ones.

'You what?'

'That's right. No front plate, anyway. The back wasn't visible. And the windows were tinted so it was impossible to see who was driving.'

Barry tilted his chair back and folded his arms comfortably over his middle. 'All right. Leaving that aside for the moment. Back to the explosions. This isn't about profit, is it? This is a hit. Vengeful. Well, *several* hits. First Thomas Knox. Then Kit Miller targeted but missed so that one of his boys got a one-way ticket to hell instead of him. Then the Darke club. The one thing that pulls all those things together is Ruby Darke. She's Kit's mother. She owns the club. She was the mistress of Thomas. Someone's got it in for her.'

'So maybe not the gangs at all?' Romilly chewed her lip and turned to the board where their pictures were; all the ex-wives. 'Maybe that *other* gang? One of them? I swear Avril's hiding something. God knows what.'

'Maybe,' said Bev. 'The female of the species and all that.'

'Is deadlier than the male. Wasn't there an old song? Scott Walker?' suggested Barry.

Romilly levered herself to her feet and stabbed a finger at the oldest – and plainest – woman on display. 'Well, Jean. What about her? She seems like the mother figure but she's cold, manipulative. An odd character. Has them all over for Christmas every year, who the hell would do that? Or maybe she just enjoys seeing them tearing at each other's throats. Maybe it's all about control.'

'Jean was a starter wife,' said Barry.

'Meaning?' asked Romilly.

'Okay at twenty, had one kid – Declan – and it was finished after that. Let herself go. Put the kid first, lots of women do that and it's death to a marriage. She was deadly dull by the time she hit forty, I bet. So Thomas shipped out.'

'Yeah, to Ursula.' Romilly pointed out the model. Tall, cool, her dark hair cascading around her angular shoulders. Staring meltingly at the camera with her impossibly beautiful dark eyes. 'You can see the attraction.'

'I wouldn't kick her out of bed,' said Barry.

'She'd never get in it,' said Bev.

'A fella can dream,' said Barry, unoffended.

'Big contrast between her and Jean,' agreed Bev. 'Talk about beauty and the beast.'

'And so Thomas was smitten,' said Romilly. 'Liked the look of the thing, yes? But maybe a little too cool? She had just the one kid off him – Evie – and I'm guessing she didn't like the way motherhood impeded her modelling career. Maybe – this was my impression – a little dim and a lot self-centred? And little Evie's not too keen on her dear old mum. Cheeks her all the time. Mocks her vanity. Gets digs in about her age.'

'Yeah, you could be right there,' said Bev. 'I think if a bloke came near Ursula she'd want him to be wearing Marigolds. Very much a "touch-me-not" type. Gorgeous to look at – but stone-cold.'

'What about Avril?' asked Barry.

'Another kid there from Thomas. Olivia. After her birth it seems Avril proceeded to pester Thomas for more and more money. Avril's quite the firecracker,' said Romilly, who had spent the better part of the day interviewing the amazingly aggressive stud owner and her shit-scared worker. 'And here we start in on some really interesting stuff. Timothy Copnor's clearly terrified now that his collar's been felt. He's pleading innocence of the car bombs and the club bombing and I believe him. But could there be something else going on here? Avril's stronger personality influencing this poor sap? So she has a worker on the premises who understands – and has been using – explosives. Not plastic, but still. He'd worked in the Therex quarry and he'd had access to these things.'

'Motive, means, opportunity,' said Bev thoughtfully.

'Motive? Avril hates Ruby Darke because Ruby's been knocking off Thomas,' said Romilly.

'That's a bit thin,' said Barry. 'Why hasn't Avril blown up Gilly then? And Chloe? Or any of the others?'

'Yeah, point,' said Romilly. 'But then – misery loves company, yes? And they're a tight little clique. Means, though. If we could get a concrete link between her worker Timothy and some plastic . . . ?'

Rommily then turned to Bev: 'Opportunity?'

'Ah yes. Opportunity,' said Bev. 'That's where it all falls apart. Avril was not spotted anywhere near when Thomas died. Nor was she at Ruby Darke's place in Marlow before Kit Miller's car blew up. Nor was she seen in the crowds on the day or seen on the night before Ruby Darke's club went up. Neither – and I've checked and rechecked the various CCTV's – was her worker, Tim.'

'Okay.' Romilly blew out her cheeks. 'Gilly then. Wife number four.'

'She's as big a player as Thomas himself was,' said Bev. 'You've seen her, spoken to her. She's always on the scout-out for the next victim, that one.'

'Currently I believe she's fleecing a wealthy football manager.'

'Surely not just the one bloke though? She doesn't seem the type for fidelity.'

'Yeah, you wouldn't think so, would you.' Romilly stared at the glamorous redhead in the photo on the wall. Big hair, big shoulder pads. 'Has a serious cocaine habit going on, rotted the bottom part of her nose off with the stuff. So more money needed. Plastic surgeons don't come cheap. Can we get someone on stake-out near her flat? Tail her when she goes out, see who she's meeting?'

'We can,' said Barry. 'Bev, you got the quarry details there?' He pulled a pen and jotter toward him. 'I could get straight on that.'

Bev passed him the info and he snatched up his man bag.

'Wait up, Baz. We'll both go,' said Romilly.

'Okay. See you out front,' he said, and left the office.

'I'm going to cut the worker loose too. He stinks of innocence. I think his only crime – apart from a bit of thievery from his ex-employers – is that he's devoted to Avril, however unwisely. Probably fancies his chances there, the poor sap. And so we come to Chloe,' said Romilly to Bev Appleton, pointing out the final ex-wife of Thomas Knox.

Small, curvy, blonde Chloe. Big-titted and big-haired, all fake lashes and flashy crimson lipstick, wearing a sassy scarlet Miyake bandage dress to show off her perma-tanned curves.

'What do we think about her?' she asked.

'A tart,' Bev summed up neatly. 'She was a stripper and she met Thomas in a club. But he was closing in on sixty and she didn't fancy the idea of nursing him into old age – although she clearly loved his money – so she's been seen looking cosy with his son Declan. I'm guessing Thomas found out about that and – *ta da!* – back he went to the divorce courts. You'd think he'd get a season ticket.'

'So she's boffing Declan?' asked Romilly.

'Up until the past fortnight, she *was*. They haven't been seen together much since. She used to go over to Declan's place for a spot of afternoon delight. But now? That's stopped.'

Romilly sat down on her desktop and stared at the photo board. Cars in flames. Women, all in a row. Corpses, unrecognisable. A bombed-out building. And somewhere – surely? – the answer to the puzzle.

'You heard someone just went off the top floor of that multi-storey behind St James's?' asked Bev. 'Suicide, they reckon.'

'Yeah, well. In the midst of life we are in death and all that,' said Romilly distractedly. 'Find out who Gilly's seeing at the moment will you? Is it *still* the football manager? Or has she swapped him for someone more exciting? A politician? A high-profile journalist? A Formula One pit boss? If she's a player like Thomas, who's she's playing with? I'd like to keep the picture updated.'

'Got you.' Bev stood up. 'You okay?'

Romilly looked at her in surprise. 'Yes. Sure. Why d'you ask?'

'Detectives,' said Bev ruefully. 'We're a pain in the arse, aren't we. Always on the lookout. Asking awkward questions.'

'Meaning?'

'Meaning I saw you going into the Lamb and Flag with Kit Miller,' said Bev. 'And Romilly – ma'am – with all due respect, I hope that wasn't a social call?'

'It was business,' said Romilly stiffly.

'Only,' said Bev carefully, 'if it *was* social—'

'It wasn't. I told you. He knows the underbelly of the criminal world and that's useful. You know that.'

'Yeah. That makes sense, sort of. I guess it's a difficult line to tread though. From what you told me,' Bev said carefully, 'he probably saved my life, didn't he. When the car blew up in Marlow at his mum's place.'

'Yes. *Both* our lives. Probably.'

Bev hesitated. 'But that doesn't mean that I wouldn't take it further.'

Romilly let out a dry laugh. 'What? For my own good, you mean?'

'Yeah. That's what I mean.'

Romilly said nothing. She felt furious with Bev, which was unfair. But she was furious at *life* in general, utterly fucking furious at the hand it had dealt her. The career she'd craved. The man she wanted. One or the other, yes. Both? Impossible.

'If it was *not* business, well . . .' Bev stared at her boss, her friend, her mentor, and shook her head. 'Better make it the last one, yes?'

'It was business,' said Romilly, standing up. Talking to herself as much as to Bev. Yesterday had been the final farewell and it wasn't – *ever* – going to happen again. 'That's all,' she said, and left the room and went back to her own little office down the corridor, closing the door firmly behind her.

*Just once, and she'd already been spotted.*

*Oh Christ,* she thought, and gathered up her bag and went out to join Barry.

# 85

# DAY SIXTEEN

The two big metal gates at the entrance to the quarry were painted black and displayed an orange sign with Therex Mining Corporation Limited writ large on them. They were wide open and massive lorries laden with tons of rock, soil and general debris were thundering in and out when Romilly and Barry turned up. They showed their ID to the man on the gate, and he talked on a phone and then waved them through.

Dust swirled in the air, men in hard hats milled around the place. Barry parked up next to the Portakabin the gate man had directed them to, not far from the entrance. There was a dust-covered electric golf buggy parked outside it and a Porta-loo set some twenty feet away. Barry and Romilly got out and strolled over to the Portakabin. Romilly knocked on the door.

It opened, and a neat little grey-haired man in grey over-alls, a hard hat under his arm, looked out at them.

Romilly and Barry flashed their IDs.

The little man stuck out a hand. 'Ah yes. I'm James Birdsall. Site manager,' he said, his accent distinctly north of the border.

They shook his hand. He stepped back and they fol-lowed inside, into a comfortable little space. Sage green tough-wearing carpet on the floor; tea-and-coffee-making facilities on a long table; a desk with a telephone. On the walls were lots of pictures – a head-and-shoulders line-up of Therex board members and shots of various quarrying activities. Explosions. Loading lorries up with cranes. Men drilling holes in rocks. Setting explosives ready to blow.

Birdsall gave them each a hard hat and a small laminated sheet of paper.

Romilly put on her hat – it was tight and uncomfortable – and scanned the paper. Safety regs for visitors, under a banner headline of Therex Mining Corporation Limited, several addresses, a list of board members. She put it in her jacket pocket.

'We've been speaking to a bloke called Timothy Copnor. He used to work here. Got his hands on some black powder and he's been using it to blast out old trees,' Romilly told James Birdsall.

Birdsall stiffened as if at a personal insult. 'Not on my watch. When was this?'

She told him.

Birdsall looked satisfied. 'That was long before I came on the scene. Maybe things were looser then, but today we adhere very strictly to safety precautions with our stock. I assure you, explosives don't just *walk*.'

Seeing Romilly looking at the quarrying pictures, Birdsall said: 'The blasting with explosives reduces the rocks and hard soil. See that there?'

Romilly and Barry put on their hats and paid close attention to a picture of a man sporting a huge drill, applying it to a massive chunk of stone. The operative was drilling a neat line of holes.

'Once the holes are drilled, the detonator and charge are installed. Then the charge is detonated and the debris is removed.'

'Sounds simple,' said Romilly. 'I'm sure it's tightly regulated – for safety, I mean.'

'Regulations are scrupulously adhered to,' Birdsall assured her. 'For instance, if we're using dynamite, we mark all the drill holes – and that's a maximum of eight – with white paint so that there are no mistakes. Before we set the charge, red flags go up all around the site and all workers are counted and moved a minimum of two hundred metres clear of the blast site.'

A loud siren sounded suddenly.

'What's that?' asked Romilly.

'There'll be a succession of small blasts. Don't jump,' said Birdsall with a thin smile.

A pause.

Then – an explosion. Muffled. Not particularly loud. Another. Then another, fast upon the heels of the last. Eight blasts in total. But Romilly felt each one right up through her feet and she also felt a flicker of unease, thinking of that bomb going off on Ruby Darke's driveway. The one that could have killed her, and Bev, and Kit, just like it had killed Fats.

'What about nearby residents? Doesn't that bother them?' she asked, working some spit into her mouth, which was suddenly very dry.

'All that's been cleared a long time ago with the council. Government guidelines set limits for noise and vibration, concussion in the air. We aim to keep disturbance to a minimum, always. Follow me.'

They stepped outside the Portakabin and he herded them into the buggy and drove them down a long slope, past cranes shifting stones, past lorries thundering up to the entrance and away, past groups of men in overalls and hard hats, down to a big indentation in the earth, dust and smoke still swirling above it. Birdsall stopped the buggy right in front of what looked like a cave, blasted out of the earth. They got out.

'There are several types of blasting that we do,' Birdsall told them as they walked toward the site. There's line drill-ing and pre-splitting, smooth blasting and cushion blasting.'

'Right,' said Barry. 'Ever use Semtex?'

'Sometimes,' said Birdsall, and walked into the 'cave's' entrance and then on in, further. 'Not often.'

Dust eddied around them, chokingly, and they could see evidence of the fresh blasting – jagged split rocks, white paint marks. They went further still and it was getting dark, dark as a tomb – and cold. Romilly had never been claus-trophobic, but being in here under all this rock somehow gave her the shivers.

'Actually, can we get out of here?' Barry piped up, look-ing white and sweaty.

Birdsall said: 'Of course,' and smiled.

# 86

## DAY SIXTEEN

Boy Ankara phoned Kit.

'Anything?' asked Kit.

'Nah, not much really. I've asked around all over the damned place, but . . .'

'Yeah, what?'

'Someone mentioned the Therex outfit, they use a lot. That's all I can tell you.'

'Therex?'

'Aggregates concern. Building materials, you got to blast them out.'

'Right. Well, thanks.'

'How's your girl?'

'What?'

'The girl with you in the Lamb. I thought you were going to pass out cold when she hit the deck. I was married for fifty years, I know what it's like.'

'What?' Kit stared at the phone.

'Love, mate. *Love.* Catches you unawares, don't it, the strength of the feeling.'

Daisy phoned Brayfield House as usual at six o'clock, to speak with Matty and Luke. She was trying to settle herself down, but after all that had happened, she felt that she was slowly falling apart at the seams. However, for the boys she had to appear their mum, unchanged. Like she hadn't had that awful scare yesterday. Like Kit wasn't walking around glowering at her, having heard about the clash with the Danieri mob from Daniel. Like she wasn't trying to keep all this from Ruby, to act as if nothing whatsoever was the matter. Like she hadn't woken up in the dead of night and imagined Pizza-Face Donato looming over her in the semi-dark and had to stop herself from screaming.

'Oh, they're not here,' said Vanessa.

'Oh! Has Ivan taken them out?'

'No. Bradley called in, wanted to take them over to his house, show them the pygmy goats he's bought for them. You know how Luke was going on about that, getting a pet? He was driving us all mad with it, wasn't he.'

Daisy was silent. As usual, there was the usual faint pang at the mention of Sir Bradley's name. She knew that Vanessa and Lady Collins were acquaintances who attended the same golf club dinners and that they both fund-raised enthusiastically for various third-world charities. It was kind of Bradley to do all this for the twins, and as usual she felt that tiny twinge of guilt at the mention of the Collins name.

'Well . . . that's okay. I suppose,' said Daisy. 'I'm just a bit surprised, that's all. Has he had them before?'

'Only a couple of times, but I didn't think you'd object. He's such a nice man. And Susan's a doll, although I haven't seen her much lately. Didn't you find that Bradley was a sweetheart? And after all, they're the twins' grandparents too, aren't they?'

Of course they were. And Daisy knew she should have made more of an effort with them after they'd lost Simon.

But she'd never really liked them and had always had the feeling that it was mutual. She'd stumbled into marriage with Simon Collins when her own life had been a drug-induced mess. She couldn't say in all truthfulness that she had ever been in love with him. Her marriage to him had been miserable and memories of him and of his parents brought nothing except bad feelings – and horrible memories of Simon's tragic death at the hands of the Danieri gang.

'Of course I don't object,' said Daisy. 'Just so long as they're safe and happy, that's fine.'

'They are,' said Vanessa. 'Never worry, Daisy. I'll always look after them and I know – of course – that Bradley will too. How are you, darling? What's happening there at Ruby's?'

Daisy didn't know what to answer to that. Oh, all fine this end. Three explosions and no idea who's doing them, Kit combing through gangland and Ruby questioning the ex-wives of Thomas Knox; men waiting to gang-rape me in a multi-storey car park and the police crawling all over everything.

'Nothing much,' she managed to say.

Her mind went to Thomas's burial, to standing there all through that horribly elaborate and overlong funeral, his ex-wives bickering. Then laying flowers on Rob's and Simon's graves, Daniel right there beside her. The little metal tag on the grave next to Simon's. His grave number was H152, she knew that off by heart. But that fresh grave beside it, unknown. Another tag. H153.

Vanessa chattered on, distracting her. She lost her train of thought.

'It's best the twins are here with us, don't you think?' said Vanessa.

'I do. Definitely. They'll be back this evening?'

'Yes, they will. Phone about seven, will you, darling? They'll speak to you then. Luke was madly excited about these goats and no doubt he'll be pestering me to get some here too. Of course, Matt was acting cool, like he didn't care much either way.'

Daisy could hear the smile in Vanessa's voice. No matter how frosty and aristocratic Vanessa might be, there was never any doubt that she was the most devoted of grandmothers and it was a huge weight off Daisy's mind that the twins were there at Brayfield and not here in Marlow with her, much as she might wish it otherwise.

'I'll call back later,' said Daisy.

# 87

# DAY SIXTEEN

In the early evening Daisy sat alone at Ruby's place, watching TV. Intermittently, her eyes flickered shut and she dozed and there he was again. Pizza-Face Donato, leering down at her in her dreams.

*My turn* he whispered, and grinned, and she could *smell* him, how foul he was, how disgusting. She snapped awake. Once. Twice. Three times.

Each time she was sweating, gasping, her heart racing, her mouth dry. She sat up, flicked off the TV and found herself thinking about her talk to Vanessa and remembering the H153 grave tag beside Simon's last resting place.

Whose grave was that?

It was quite fresh. Newly dug.

*Whose?*

Daniel was lying fully clothed in bed watching TV in Ruby's spare room when there was a hammering at his bedroom door. He flicked off the TV, went to the door. Opened it. Daisy stood there.

'What?' he asked.

'We've got to go out,' she said.

*

They got to the graveyard at exactly the same time as the man was closing the gates, getting ready to lock them for the night.

'Can't go in there now,' said the man, a dour-faced and elderly stickler for rules and regulations.

'How much?' asked Daisy bluntly.

'You what?'

'How much to let us in there? A hundred?'

The man's eyes shifted. 'Look, I don't know what you want—'

'To look at a grave, that's all.'

'Two hundred—'

'Fuck . . .' said Daniel under his breath.

'Done. Come with us.'

'Money first,' said the man.

Daisy paid him.

The light was beginning to go. The man lit the way with a torch and they found the grave they were looking for. H153. There was the little metal tag, still there. There were a couple of bouquets of flowers there, wilting. Daisy fumbled among the cellophane-wrapped bunches. *In Loving Memory,* said one. And another. *RIP Susie.*

*Susie?*

'I don't know what you're looking for—' started the man.

'The church, is it locked?'

'Sure it is. Locked at five.'

'The vicarage?'

'Vicar's out.'

'Out? Out where? Would he know whose grave this is? When will he be back?'

'He's gone overnight. Theological convention. Why?'

*Overnight!*

Daisy's anxiety levels were ramping up to frantic. They *couldn't* wait until tomorrow. She had a bad, bad feeling about this, and it was getting worse with every moment that passed.

'Thanks for your help,' she said, and led the way back over to the gate.

# 88
# DAY SIXTEEN

Daisy was thinking of the disasters the family had been through. Rob's death. The medium, the letters spelling out on the Ouija board. *Daisy don't go there.*

She forced herself to think of Simon, Sir Bradley's long-lost son, her first husband. He'd been found dead years ago in the garage of his and Daisy's Berkshire home, the suicide note beside him, his dead body swinging from the rafters. She shivered. Maybe death and disaster *did* follow the Darkes around. Her father Cornelius, dead. Her first husband Simon, dead. And Rob; he was dead too.

*Don't go there.*

But where? *Where?* What the hell was Rob trying so hard to tell her?

Restless, she fished out her address book from her bag and thumbed through the contents. She found the address for Simon's parents, Sir Bradley and Lady Susan. Tythe Manor. And there was their phone number. On impulse, feeling that the presence of the twins being there should act as a salve, she yanked the phone toward her and tapped out the number. It rang. And rang.

No answer.

Daisy put the phone down.

What the hell had she meant to say to Bradley or Susan anyway? I'm sorry you lost your son but hey, at least I gave you two lovely grandkids?

All right, she might feel guilty for her part, but they had made no effort to get in touch with her either, had they? They had contacted *Vanessa* and asked permission to take the twins back to the Manor. Not her, not Daisy. And at the heart of it she knew there was a reason for that. She knew that they blamed her for Simon's death. They believed that he had been so unhappy in his marriage to her that he had taken his own life rather than go on with it.

But then – Simon's parents hadn't known the full story, had they. They hadn't known – as Daisy knew, as Ruby knew and Kit too – that the Danieri family had been involved. That Simon's death had in fact not been suicide, but cold-blooded murder. That they'd forced him to write the suicide note and then they'd strung him up: murdered him.

Daisy had never told Simon's parents the full truth of that.

How could she?

How, after all they had been through, could she have inflicted yet more pain on them? They'd lost their son, and she couldn't imagine the anguish of that. She thought – briefly, fleetingly – of losing Matt or Luke, and her innards shrivelled at the very thought. Unbearable. Cruel. No, she couldn't do that to them. She couldn't.

But she knew she wasn't without blame here. She *should* have kept in touch with Simon's parents. Made the effort. Taken the twins to see them, to cheer them, to try and compensate – somehow – for the awful loss they'd suffered.

But she hadn't. Because in all honesty, her marriage to Simon had been a sham, a deal done between Sir Bradley and Daisy's father Cornelius, and the only good thing to come out of it had been the twins. That was all. She couldn't act the grieving widow, not for Simon. She couldn't bring herself to be that false. So she'd stayed away, and his parents hadn't seemed unhappy about that. She'd always had the impression that Sir Bradley and his wife disapproved of the Darke family, of Ruby's shop-girl upbringing and her associations with crime lords, of Kit's rough childhood background and his strong connections to the underworld, to Daisy's wild-child behaviour before marriage to Simon had tied her – unhappily – down.

Over the years, the distance between Daisy and Simon's parents had grown and grown. Now it seemed – at last – that Simon's parents were reaching out tentatively, maybe coming at the thing sideways, through the twins, through Vanessa, but still; they were trying to reconnect, and she ought to at least meet them halfway.

Daisy pulled the phone back and dialled again, letting it ring and ring.

If they could make the effort, try to rebuild bridges, then surely she could too?

She let the phone ring on at the Manor. And she thought of Rob's other-worldly message to her. She stood there, staring without really seeing them at the China figurines in Ruby's display cabinet. Naff, she'd always thought them. *Don't go there . . .*

Hadn't Bradley given Ruby the first of those figurines years ago, produced with clay from one of his Cornish mines?

China clay and Bradley.

Now her brain was thundering along in time to her heart-beat and she was thinking: *aggregates.* You had to blast China clay out of the ground, wasn't that a fact? And aggregates for building work. You blasted. With explosives. *Fire in the hole.* They said that when the charge went in. Didn't they? China clay and aggregates – the twin foundations of Bradley's fortune.

Still, nobody answered the phone at the Manor.

# 89
# DAY SIXTEEN

It had been boring and exhausting, talking again to insurance men who didn't want to pay out and to demolition firms who were rabidly keen for new business. It looked as if the whole club building was going to have to be razed to the ground and rebuilt – if Ruby even *wanted* it rebuilt, which at the moment she was nowhere near sure about. She'd fielded phone calls from various burlesque acts who'd been due to appear at the club in the coming weeks, and batted away their enquiries as to when the club might reopen because the truth was, she didn't know; and she wasn't entirely sure that she would even bother. And then she got a phone call from Declan.

'Ms Darke. How are you?' he asked.

'Fine. You?'

'Oh, pining a bit,' he said.

'For what?'

'I think you already know the answer to that.'

Ruby found that she was having to suppress a smile.

'You're so smooth. Just like your dad,' she said. 'And this is extremely inappropriate.'

'What is? Talking to you?'

'You know exactly what I mean.'

'Okay, let's say I do. Where's the harm in it? Just dinner, how about that? Or lunch. Or a coffee. Or any of the above, yes?'

'No!' said Ruby, and still smiling she cut him off. She then phoned to check that Ursula was in and then drove over to her Olympia flat, with Alan at the wheel and Brennan in close attendance.

She wished she didn't feel so goddamned weary. Thomas's death had hit her very hard, much harder than she would have expected, and she was finding just functioning day-to-day to be an effort. What, after all, was the point? Thomas was dead and that part of her life, the part that she admitted had filled her with joy and excitement, was done with. Finished. Yes, Thomas had been a rascal. A womaniser. A crook. All of those things and more. But he'd made her laugh. Now all the fun seemed to have gone out of life. Sure, there was Declan. Ridiculous, really. A much younger man and Thomas's son. Would she go there? Could she bear to?

Ah, to hell with it.

She had promised Kit that she would visit and question each one of the 'gang' of ex-wives. And so here she was, being admitted to the sumptuously beautiful flat and thinking that it was absurd, really quite ridiculous, the way Ursula posed and pouted and tossed her gorgeous hair. No sign of daughter Evie.

'What can I help you with?' Ursula asked Ruby, without even offering her a seat or a cup of tea. She looked at Brennan, standing silently nearby. 'I'm in a bit of a hurry . . .'

'I was just curious. You know. About you and Thomas. How you got on,' said Ruby.

'*Got on?* Well . . . we didn't, really. Hence the divorce.' Ursula paused and gave a small, secret smug smile. 'He was obsessed with me, you know. Well, why wouldn't he be, after that dull horrible little thing Jean?'

'But your marriage to him didn't last long?'

'No. Three, four years? He liked to use me for arm candy. Strut about the place and play the villain with the prettiest woman in the room on his arm. He loved that. But I don't for one minute think that he loved *me*. And by the time I had Evie, the romance was over.'

'And you? Did you love him?'

'That's a very personal question.'

'It is. Did you?'

'Truthfully? For a while. He was quite fascinating. A real villain. Powerful. And there's a certain attraction in that, don't you find? I could see the same thing in your son. Kit, isn't it? Why's his surname Miller and not Darke, like yours?'

Ruby only shrugged. If Kit wanted to remain 'Miller', his adopted name that had been given to him in the orphanage where he'd been raised, then that was very much his business.

'I could see that same power in him. The attraction of the dominant alpha male,' said Ursula.

'So you've had no thoughts of remarriage?'

'No! God, why would I want to go through all that again? Look, can we wind this up? I can understand you being upset; God knows we *all* are. But I've got to go out I'm afraid. I have an appointment.'

'This won't take much longer,' said Ruby.

Brennan shifted restlessly and Ruby wondered what else she might ask this preening goddess. She already knew where the appointment was – Harley Street. There was a very effective and extremely expensive plastic surgeon there and she knew that Ursula was a regular customer. No wonder Ursula had been keen to get more money out of Thomas. And there was Jean, sitting on a gold mine, maybe teasing the exes with the slight possibility that she *might,* one day, sell up and shell out some more. Keeping her hold over them. So much bitterness, so much hatred. She thought of Avril, striking Thomas with the bottle. Then she had a sudden and quite shocking thought.

*Was* that Avril?

'Does . . . is there a garage with this flat?' Garage space was like gold dust around here.

Ursula looked at Ruby in surprise. 'Well yes. There is. Around the back, in the mews. I use it for storage.'

'You've got the key to hand?'

'Yes, but—'

'Show me.'

# 90

# DAY SIXTEEN

Brennan shifted closer to Ursula. She stepped smartly back. 'All right, all right! I'll show you. If we're quick,' she said, and went to a sideboard and plucked a key out of a dish there. Then she led the way out through the flat, around the end of the terrace, to a line of three garages. The very end one was hers. She inserted the key. At that moment, her daughter Evie rounded the corner and saw what was happening.

'What's going on?' she asked.

'Don't ask me! I've told her there's absolutely nothing in here, so I don't know why . . .' insisted Ursula.

The garage doors swung open.

Hogging the big central space inside the garage was a long, dark metallic grey Cabriolet car with tinted windows and no licence plates.

'What the . . . ?' asked Ursula, standing there staring in disbelief.

Ruby thought of the night outside the Dorchester with Thomas, the driver in the long dark car coming up onto the pavement and nearly – so nearly – crushing them. She thought of Kit and the Detective Inspector similarly attacked coming out of the Lamb and Flag two days ago.

Ursula turned to Evie, whose face was crimson.

'Evie?' she demanded. 'Do you . . . ? What the hell is this? Did you put this in here?'

Ruby turned to Brennan. 'Keep them both here, will you?' she asked, and not waiting for a reply she walked off just around the corner to a phone box and called the Marlow house, asking the man who answered if when Evie had arrived there last week anyone had noticed her car. One of the watchers on the gate had, apparently. A long grey Cabriolet. Darkly tinted windows. No, they hadn't caught the plates.

On the way back round to the mews she heard Brennan's car phone ringing. She opened the door with her spare key, reached in. It was Daisy. Daisy was babbling, making no sense at all. She was asking her to check out a grave number, of all things.

'At the church, where Thomas was buried. Can you do that?'

'What? How can I? Everyone's closed up for the night,' said Ruby.

'Look, just try. Can you?'

'There'll be nobody about. It'll have to wait until morning. I don't understand what you're asking, Daisy, or why. Is it important?'

'It is. The number's H153. You got that?'

'I have.'

'I've tried the vicarage. No good. Try the council offices, can you? They might still be open. They'll have records of the graves. Check whose it is and get back to me.'

'Okay. All right! This is mad, but I'll do it.'

Then Ruby phoned both Kit and the police.

# 91
## DAY SIXTEEN

Martin Crawshaw had oiled his way up the greasy pole to his current position as Town Clerk. He always came in early at the council offices and he always left late. This gave him the opportunity to look down his nose on staff when they sauntered in at a minute to nine, or to look pointedly at his watch if they – even worse – didn't show up until five past.

'What time d'you call this?' he'd asked one late-coming wit.

The cheeky sod had looked up at the reception clock, which had been stuck forever, unhelpfully, at ten to five. 'Ten to five, boss,' he'd said, and Martin had instantly fired his arse.

Anyone in the office who left before five was treated to a frosty glare, a blast of Crawshaw disapproval. Martin had two noisy projectile-vomiting kids at home and a nagging wife who never thought he was paid enough, so he was always very keen to get out of the house of a morning and never wanted to return there at night. So he sat sometimes at his desk until eight o'clock in the evening, not working but reading papers, books, smutty magazines, just killing time. He knew that by the time it got to nine, his raucous kids would be in bed and his wife would be too bloody tired to argue anymore.

Martin sat there and brooded over his misfortune. A chubby man of around forty years old with thinning straight brown hair and brown eyes hidden behind horn-rimmed glasses, he knew he was unpopular not only with his wife but also with his staff. Sometimes he stood around the back of the staging where all the files were kept and listened to what his 'workers' were saying. Then one of them spotted him doing that, told the rest, and their chatter dried up.

All staff were bastards. He hadn't even liked the cleaning lady – he hadn't hired her, the last Town Clerk had – so he fired her the minute he got his feet under the desk and got the rest of the staff to muck in with the cleaning, which they moaned about no end.

'Since when was a secretary supposed to do a fucking cleaning job as well as her own?' he'd heard one of the girls mutter angrily.

Martin wasn't too worried about all that. He was doing okay out of the new arrangement; he was still entering the cleaner's wage into the accounts and pocketing the cash himself, for beer money. So let the bastards moan. He didn't care.

*Nearly time to go home.*

There was a limit to how late he could push it before her indoors started kicking up merry hell and making the office phone ring off the hook. Well, let her. The cow. He was Town Clerk, an important man. She didn't seem to realise that. She'd even accused him of having an affair.

'*You* got me pregnant,' she'd roar at him. 'Now I'm off sex and it's your own bloody fault and you don't like that, do you? What, you found someone else to stick it to in that bloody office that you spend your entire ruddy life in?'

Truthfully, the only times he'd ever found his wife halfway bearable was when they'd had sex in the early days. Now, with another new baby forever attached to one or other of her ruined saggy tits, she wasn't interested and neither was he.

Maybe he *should* have an affair? But he wasn't really the type. And women didn't seem to like him very much, anyway.

Then there was a noise at the front of the building and he stiffened. Someone had just entered through the main door and was now coming through reception. One of his workers had forgotten something, shopping from the local Sainsbury's or a purchase from the High Street no doubt. He should have locked the outer door, but he'd forgotten the bloody thing. He fixed a false smile on his face as whoever it was came into the main office, thinking about the times when he came back from his solitary lunch and would surprise the staff lounging in the reception area. He'd make *rat-tat-tat* noises at them, as if he was brandishing a machine gun and mowing them all down. That always made him laugh.

'It's not funny,' one of the male clerks had complained.

'I think it is,' said Martin, shaking his head in exasperation. 'Talk about a sense of humour failure, you lot.'

'No. It isn't. Because you really mean it, don't you. You really wish you *could* gun us all down.'

Well, that much was true.

He sacked that same male clerk on a jumped-up charge a week later. Couldn't have the staff telling *him* what to do.

Now, much to his irritation, one of the workers was coming back into the office, and he was going to have to be all jokey and make some smart remark.

*Forget your head if it wasn't screwed on,* he'd say. *You avoiding the missus too?*

Something like that.

He opened his mouth in readiness, then shut it again with a snap.

It wasn't a member of staff coming toward him, it was a dusky-skinned looker of middle years – and a squat dark-haired bloke built like the side of a barn.

# 92
## DAY SIXTEEN

They came up to his desk. He sat up, looking nervously from one to the other. Outside it was getting darker, the night crowding against the windows, making him feel very alone here all of a sudden. Dammit, that was careless of him, not locking the door.

'You the Town Clerk?' asked the woman.

'I am. Yes. But these offices aren't open. You'll have to come back in the morning. We open at nine.'

'Do you?' she said. 'That's nice. But we need some information now.'

'Well as I say—' started Martin.

'A grave over at St Dunstan's, you know that church?'

'Well yes. I know it. What information?' asked Martin, looking with disapproval at Brennan as the man picked up his desk stapler and examined it closely.

'A grave. Number H153. Can you tell me who's buried there please?'

'Well that sort of information . . . I can't just pluck it out of thin air you know. I'd have to check the files. As I said, we're open at nine a.m. tomorrow, you'll have to come . . .' he paused, looked at Brennan. 'Can you put that down please? It's not a toy.'

Ruby nodded to Brennan. Brennan stepped around the desk.

'Now look,' said Martin sharply.

Brennan grabbed Martin's tie and stapled it smartly to the desk, banging Martin's chin on the woodwork.

'What the *fuck* . . . ?' demanded Martin, his arms flapping as he scrabbled to free himself.

'Grave H153,' repeated Ruby. 'I need that information. Who's buried in it? I've no objection to my assistant beating it out of you.'

'Now wait . . .'

'I'm done waiting,' said Ruby.

Brennan slapped Martin's face hard down into the desk. Martin let out a howl and blood started pouring from his nose. Brennan yanked the stapled tie free of the woodwork and, keeping hold of it, used it like a dog's lead to haul Martin to his feet and propel him around the desk to Ruby.

'Now,' said Brennan. 'Listen.'

Martin stood there on tiptoe and stared horrified into Brennan's baleful gaze. Blood was spattering all down Martin's shirtfront, and his nose hurt. His eyes watered. He gulped, trying to breathe. He only got a mouthful of blood. He spluttered and coughed. 'Now *wait* . . .' he pleaded.

'No waiting. You were just told that. No waiting,' said Brennan.

'Yes! All right. The grave. The number,' he coughed, choked, tried to breathe. 'What was the number?'

This was madness.

This could not be happening.

But it *was*.

They'd barged in here and now he could see that if he didn't tell them what they wanted to know, they'd hurt him. They'd hurt him *already*.

'H153,' said Ruby. 'Get the details. Get them *now!*'

Martin complied, Brennan at his heels. He wondered if anyone would ever believe this, if he told them about it. But no. He wasn't going to. He'd look bloody stupid, a laughing stock. More so than he already did. And also, if he did . . . these two might come back.

And he really, really didn't want that.

# 93
# DAY SIXTEEN

Daisy phoned Vanessa at seven on the dot; one ring, and Vanessa picked up.

'Hi Vanessa,' she started.

But Vanessa cut in. 'They're not back yet. Usually he has them back in time for tea at six, but he must have got held up.'

'I didn't realise this was a regular thing.'

'It isn't. He was just taking them to see the goats and I could see no harm in it. I feel badly about this, Daisy. I should have told you sooner that this was happening, shouldn't I.'

'It's okay,' said Daisy, although it wasn't.

'Phone again at eight, yes?'

'All right. I will.' All sorts of horrors arose in Daisy's mind. Road accidents. The twins lying hurt somewhere and her miles away. Unable to help.

She wished Ruby was here, but she was up in town and another car phone call from her had convinced Daisy that she wouldn't be coming back tonight. There'd been something about a car being found, and Ursula and her daughter being involved in something fishy.

'And the grave number? How'd that go? Did you find out who H153 belongs to?' Daisy asked Ruby.

'Yeah. It's a bit of a shocker, actually.'

'In what way?' Daisy didn't like the sound of this.

Ruby told her.

Daisy stared at the phone in astonishment. 'It *can't* be.'

'The Town Clerk gave me the details, with proof. It is.'

'But I didn't . . .' Daisy's head was spinning and she clutched at it in disbelief. 'I had no idea. Vanessa can't know this either. She'd have told me.'

'Well – it's a fact. Look, call Vanessa back, okay? I'm sure they'll be back by then.'

An hour crawled slowly by. Then, at eight, Daisy phoned. The boys were still not back at Brayfield House. Vanessa had phoned Bradley's home again: no answer.

'You're probably panicking over nothing,' Daisy heard Ivan say in the background. 'Try at nine, then we'll see.'

Never had an hour passed so slowly. At nine, Daisy's nerves were nearly shrieking as she picked up the phone and dialled.

'They're still not back,' said Vanessa. 'You'd think that if he'd been held up somehow, he would have at least had the decency to let us know.'

*Unless he couldn't. Unless there's been an accident and he can't.*

Daisy could feel her heart thumping hard in her chest, felt clammy cold sweat all over her body. This was no good, she couldn't go on like this. What, were they to wait for the small hours of the night? She couldn't. Anything could have happened to them. She had a *bad* feeling about all this. And . . .

'Vanessa?'

'Yes, darling?'

'When did you last actually *see* Susan Collins?'

'Oh! Well – months back, really. Maybe a year. Why?'

'Only I've heard . . .' Daisy hesitated, thinking of Ruby's earlier call, the shocking news she'd given her. 'Vanessa – there's a fresh grave, H153, right beside Simon's. It's hers. She's *dead!*'

# 94

## DAY SIXTEEN

A horror story was unfolding in Daisy's mind now. H153: the recently dug grave. And Bradley, maybe crazed with grief, demented with it, who could easily lay his hands on explosives because he was on the board of Therex Mining. He owned part of a big kaolin mine in Cornwall and also a massive local aggregates extraction business.

Bradley, blowing up the people he thought had somehow had a hand in his wife Susan's demise? But why Thomas Knox? What was the connection between Lady Susan and Thomas Knox? Daisy hadn't a clue. There was nothing, so far as she could see, except for the fact that Thomas had helped Kit that time when the Danieri mob had snatched Ruby: there was that. And Kit: someone had tried a hit on Kit. And on Mum's club – maybe they had even expected her to be in there at the time, who knew?

The phone was ringing. It *had* to be Vanessa, saying everything was okay and the twins were back at Brayfield.

It wasn't.

It was Ruby.

Daisy told her all her suspicions, all her fears.

'Is there anything else I can do?' asked Ruby.

'Tell Kit. Tell him everything,' she said, 'and pray that I'm wrong.'

# 95

# DAY SIXTEEN

Daisy hurried upstairs. She could hear the TV playing in the spare room. She knocked on the door. Presently, Daniel answered, wearing not his working clothes but a cream cotton shirt and faded blue jeans. The TV was chattering away in the background.

'Are you busy?' she asked.

'Why? What's up?'

'Bradley – you know Bradley?'

'What? Wasn't that Simon's dad? I know *of* him.'

'He's taken the boys out for the day. Said he had some pygmy goats at the Manor and he wanted to show them.'

'Right. And?'

'They were supposed to be back around six o'clock. Now it's nine. I'm worried.'

'Just a delay on the road, probably. And he hasn't phoned Vanessa?'

'No. He hasn't. She says that if he does, she'll contact me right away.'

'You want to go there? To his house? Tonight?'

'I have to.'

'We'll probably cross on the road.'

'Whether we do or not, I have to go. I'm . . .' Daisy paused, trying to grope for the right words, the ones that would properly explain why she felt so rattled by all this. 'Bradley's in aggregates isn't he. China clay and aggregates. Simon – you remember Simon my first husband?'

'I never met him. Rob always said he was a bolshy little bastard. Topped himself, didn't he?'

'No, he didn't! That's the point. Bradley believed that Simon's death was suicide, but *it was not*. I went to lay flowers outside the Berkshire house after I heard about it and I remember it like it was yesterday; I met the Danieri clan on the road. I thought they were going to kill me. And they as good as said that *they* had killed Simon, and made it look like he'd taken his own life.'

'Jesus.'

'Daisy nodded. 'Shocking, yes? And Rob was right about Simon being full of himself. He used to tell me all about the China clay mines in Cornwall, bored me to death. I can practically recite it, chapter and verse. For every one tonne of China clay mined and extracted, there's about nine times that amount of surplus rock waste. I know it all.'

'Fascinating,' said Daniel.

'Sir Bradley's been doing fantastically well, financially, from the mines. The pit at the top of the current Cornish site produces up to twelve thousand tonnes of kaolin – that's China clay – every month. And then there's the aggregates for construction, the brick clay and cement raw materials that's produced locally . . .'

Daniel's attention had sharpened. 'And that—' he started.

Daisy nodded her head vigorously. 'Yes! It would involve blasting. I've just found out from Ruby that Lady

Susan – Bradley's wife – has died. I think Kit and Ruby are barking up the wrong tree with Avril and her worker. *And* with Chloe's dead IRA dad and her brother. I know this sounds mad, but I think it could be Bradley we're after.'

Daniel blew out his cheeks in disbelief. 'Really?'

'Yes. And if he's got the twins . . .'

Daniel frowned. 'He's their grandfather. He wouldn't harm them, would he?'

'There's something else. Something I know you're going to sneer at.'

'Go ahead.' He sighed.

'The medium I went to see. Rob was saying *Daisy don't go there*.'

'Yeah, I know that. And it wasn't Rob saying it. Don't kid yourself.'

'You believe that if you want to. But I don't think he was saying *don't go there*. I think he was talking about Bradley's gravel extraction business. I think he was starting to say the name.'

'Which is?'

'It's Therex Mining Corporation Limited. He wasn't saying *there* at all. He was starting to say *Therex*.'

# 96

# DAY SIXTEEN

If you were laying a trap, what you needed was a lure. And he had that, didn't he. That silly cow Vanessa had handed it to him on a plate. Not one lure, actually, but two.

'Have you named them?' the bolder one was asking. Difficult to tell these boys apart, really. Blond hair, blue eyes. Very much like that aristocratic pig their other grandfather, Cornelius Bray. They would be big men, imposing – just like Cornelius had been before someone put an end to him.

Only . . . no, these handsome twins were never going to get that far, were they. A pity in a way, but the thing was, he wanted their family to suffer. To really suffer, just as he had. And there was only one way to achieve that, wasn't there?

'Named?' he asked vaguely.

'Yes! The goats, the little goats. Did you have to build a run for them?'

He was walking, crunching over gravel and loose shale at the Therex Mining site, and it was getting dark. He had a helmet on – he always carried one in the car, along with his power pack. He flicked the light on and a thin glimmer lit the way ahead. The helmet looked incongruous with his crumpled grey linen suit, but there was no one about at this late hour and he had the twins with him, each one holding on trustingly to his hand.

A shame, in a way.

Only, necessary. They were the lure, and she, the one who had caused Simon to die, the one who had by destroying Simon's life destroyed his beloved Susan's too, would know what it was to feel that pain.

The thought of what had happened to Simon tortured him. That cold merciless death, all alone in the garage at the Berkshire house, that big white building of which Simon had once been so proud. Bradley almost howled with anguish to think of his son, his precious boy, putting that rope over the rafters and in despair at the disintegration of his marriage to Daisy, the probable loss of his children – because of course she would snatch them away from him, women always did, the courts always sided with the mother, didn't they? – then Simon making out the suicide note and tying the noose around his neck and kicking the chair away, killing himself.

How long had he hung there, dangling, being strangled by slow degrees? Once, tormenting himself but somehow unable somehow to stop, Bradley had read the biography of Pierrepoint the last expert hangman in England. He'd learned that it took extreme skill to hang a man correctly, with the minimum of pain and distress and trauma. But Simon had been no expert. He would have suffered badly before death finally took him. Bradley knew it. Thought of it constantly. More and more, over the years, the thought of his son, his one child, hanging there in pain. It became unbearable, until his mind was swimming with it, with hideous images. He knew Susan had felt the same, only worse. He was the stronger of the two of them, he knew that.

He hadn't taken the pills, consulted the psychiatrists; he'd stood against the awfulness of it all, tried to support his darling wife even though day by day, week by week, he could see her slipping, leaving him, giving way to the madness that eventually took her and freed her from the extremity of her grief.

'A run?' He was barely listening to the twins' childish chatter. He had forgotten how tedious eight-year-olds could be with their endless demands of why, where, who. He could barely remember Simon at that age and it was painful to think of it now, to try to grope back over those years. Pale skin and copper-red hair and bright hazel eyes, he remembered. A cock-sure grin: endearing, sweet. Running into his arms and then he'd be twirling the boy around, sure of the future, sure of himself, not knowing what was coming, never suspecting the hell that would open up before them all. His son. His beloved boy. Gone forever, like Susan. And all because of Daisy Bray. Or Daisy Darke, as she now liked to call herself. Now her and her whole family was going to suffer loss upon loss, just like Bradley had. They would know the hell that he had lived.

They would *pay*.

# 97
# DAY SIXTEEN

'It's weird out here,' said Matt. 'In the dark.'

'I don't like it,' said Luke, ever the sensitive one.

'Weird? Weird in what way?' asked Bradley.

They were moving past huge yellow vehicles, crunching over shingle, the stuff he'd made a fortune from. Quarrying it out of the earth. From above, the extraction site looked like a giant hand had swept through, ploughing out huge furrows from the earth. *He* had done that and made a fortune. Bradley had looked at the quarry from the sky, he had taken a helicopter flight with his fellow board members and proudly seen the scars his work had inflicted on this green and pleasant land. Of course there'd been protests from villagers around the area, complaints about gigantic trucks thundering through the narrow roads, but he'd squared it with his MP, an old college friend, and he'd donated a huge stash of cash to the party, and all was smoothed over nicely. Back then, he'd been proud of his endeavours, full of enthusiasm, frankly uncaring of the little people who only ever tried to stop him achieving his goals. Of course, now those goals didn't matter to him. Now, nothing did. Except this revenge. The end game. The final, awful, *justified* revenge.

'It's like *Star Wars*, that planet,' observed Matt.

'Tatooine,' said Luke.

'That's it! Like it's all dead and desert.'

'This isn't dead,' said Bradley. 'This is the stuff of life, the stuff on which humankind builds.' He was saying it, but he didn't even believe it anymore. He'd ceased to care, long ago. And that ceasing had begun, sinking into him, taking over him like a cancer, at the time when his son had been so cruelly snatched away.

'So do the goats have a run?' asked Luke.

'Do we have to wear a helmet?' asked Matt.

'That's enough with the questions,' said Bradley. They were driving him mad. Or maybe, just maybe, he was mad already. Perhaps he was. 'There's a bit I particularly want to show you and then we'll go back to the Manor and you'll see the goats, all right?'

They followed him past vast wire cages on wheels, past even more of the huge inert machines that were flung about the scarred face of the quarry like so many gigantic Tonka toys.

'We're not going underground, are we?' asked Luke, nervous.

'Just a bit,' said Bradley. 'Not much. I told you. I've got something to show you.'

# 98

# DAY SIXTEEN

'I wonder if you realise just how much trouble you could be in?' Romilly asked Evie Grey.

It was evening. They were seated at the table in interview room A and the duty solicitor had been called to sit alongside Evie. She looked so young and yet she was eighteen: an adult. And when you were an adult, like it or not, ignorance of the law was no excuse. And the law said, quite clearly, that you didn't bowl about the roads in a big, powerful, plateless car trying to run people over.

Beside Romilly sat her DS, Bev Appleton. The tape was running.

'Where are the plates?' asked Romilly.

'No comment,' said Evie.

'It's illegal to drive on British roads without registration plates. I'm sure you know that.'

Silence.

'Is the car your mother's?' asked Romilly.

Evie's eyes flashed. 'Ma doesn't drive. Its mine. Actually, she didn't even know it was in the garage. I park it there. She never goes in there so I knew it would be okay.'

'You had the car long?'

'Since my eighteenth.'

'What, it was a gift? That's an expensive gift, Evie.'

'Olivia got a yacht for hers back in February. Daddy bought it. So I said to him, if Ollie can have a yacht, why can't I have a car? So he said go and pick one. Pass your driving test, and it's yours.'

'Obviously a rich man.'

'He was like that. Got a problem? Throw money at it. That was his answer to most things. Never *enough* money for the gang, though.'

'So you passed your driving test? I presume you *took* one?'

'Of course I took my driving test. It's the law, isn't it. I passed first time. Not that Dad cared or even gave me a single word of praise.'

'And so you got your birthday present. A very expensive and powerful car. Is your mother aware that you own it?'

'Ma doesn't take much notice of what I get up to,' said Evie. 'Hence the car, which I hid in the garage. She knows fuck all.'

'Did you try to run over your father and Ms Darke outside the Dorchester?' asked Romilly.

'No comment.'

'Oh come on Evie. I'd be interested to know why. Did you hate your father that much, despite all these lavish gifts? Or was that it? He was just "throwing money at it". Maybe he wasn't noticing *you*? So you thought you'd make him?'

'I wasn't trying to hit *him*,' snapped out Evie.

'Who then?'

'No comment.'

'What, Ms Darke?'

'Evie . . .' said the duty solicitor warningly.

'I didn't like it. Him and all these women. She was an old flame, wasn't she. She first got together with him when he was married to Ma. Then later on it looked like they were going to get together again, and I thought, for God's sake, is he *never* going to stop with all this?' Evie's face twisted in disgust. 'What is he, an animal or something?'

'Right. So you were trying to hit Ms Darke, yes?'

'Don't put words in my client's mouth,' said the duty solicitor.

'Yes,' said Evie forcefully. 'I was trying to hit her.'

'And what about the second time you tried to run someone over, Evie? How'd you justify *that*?'

Evie almost stifled a smirk.

'Evie . . .' said the duty solicitor again.

'I was walking out of the Lamb and Flag—' said Romilly.

'With Kit Miller,' Evie said. 'I like him.'

'If you like him, why were you trying to run him over?' asked Bev.

Evie ignored that. 'And that first time? I was only trying to hit the Darke woman. He was *my dad*. And he kept behaving like that, chasing after all these bits of skirt, and I couldn't stand it. I've spoken to Ollie about it; we're both disgusted by it all—'

'*Evie* . . .' interrupted the duty solicitor.

But Evie wasn't listening.

'I knew Dad and Chloe were getting divorced,' she burst out. 'I knew the Darke woman would be next and . . . he's never made a fuss of me, not like he has all these women, all these wives. He barely ever noticed me or Ollie. We were just a by-product of all these mad affairs and marriages. I wanted him for myself. For *me*. Never mind these affairs, he had children, he had me and he had Declan and he had Ollie, but not one of us seemed to matter very much to him.'

Evie was sobbing now, spluttering the words out, wiping her nose on her sleeve. Suddenly, she looked very, very young. 'And now he's dead and it'll never be right, there's no time left, is there? No time at all.'

'You're close to your stepsister? To Olivia?' Romilly was thinking about Timothy on the stud farm with access to explosives. Thinking about him and the young girl who lived there with her firecracker of a mother. Olivia. *Ollie.*

'Yeah. I suppose.'

'She knows Timothy Copnor? The one who works for her mother on the farm?'

'What? Oh, him. That weirdo. Yes. I suppose so.'

Then Romilly asked the question that was *really* bewildering her. She asked it even though she didn't want to, because Bev was sitting right there and this would all be on tape and she'd slept – again – with Kit Miller, and she shouldn't have, and any close contact with him was best kept away from the sharp eyes that watched her.

'Why me? Why Mr Miller? What have either of us ever done to you?'

'I asked him for a date,' said Evie, drying her eyes.

'What?'

'Kit Miller. I asked him. He took me out for a drink once. But then he turned me down. My dad never had time for me – and neither did he. I wanted to hurt him.'

Kit had taken this trainwreck of a girl out on a *date*? For God's sake!

'Interview paused at . . .' started Romilly, and left the room.

# 99
# DAY SIXTEEN

Outside in the main office, DS Bev Appleton said, 'It's pretty obvious that Kit Miller's catnip to the ladies, but I don't suppose he saw *that* coming. These young girls, they can get obsessional, particularly those with hangups over a bad father figure . . . you have to be very careful.'

'Thank you, Sigmund Freud,' said Romilly. 'Get Olivia Gulliver back in here. And her mother.'

She was still thinking about Evie, scarred by her parents' divorce, by her dad's abandonment. And Olivia, her too. Both of them marked by their parents' acrimonious love lives. Both scarred by a disordered childhood. She thought of that bottle, hitting Thomas's head.

She stalked back into interview room A, closing the door pointedly behind her. Went to the desk. Evie was still sitting there, the duty solicitor at her side. Romilly sat down.

'I heard you all spent Christmases together at Jean's place. Thomas's first wife.'

Evie made a face. 'Oh, you mean the hideous yearly torture. None of us ever wanted to go.'

'Then why did you?'

'Because all the exes had to. And so did me and Ollie.'

'Again – why?'

'Oh . . .' Evie fidgeted, folded her arms. 'Jean would issue the invitations in October, giving everyone plenty of warning. Then she'd start saying, "Well of course if you've made alternative arrangements I'd quite understand." And then when they agreed to go, she'd say, "Of course you'll change your mind, have something more important to do." She's a manipulative bitch. She *knew* they had to go, even if they hated it.'

'Why, Evie?'

'Because she had that place. That *house* and those massive grounds. She'd turned them down when they'd first asked her to sell up, downsize, share out the money. But she dangled the *possibility* of her selling it under their noses to keep them in line. She'd say, "Oh, the place is a bit too big for me now, maybe I'll sell, who knows?" And they're all strapped for cash. *Desperate* for it. My mum's modelling career's nearly over and she's only in her forties, that's not old really but in modelling terms it's ancient. Avril's stud farm's a wreck. And Gilly's battening on old rich men and her nose is disintegrating and she's so desperate she's climbing the walls. They *all* are. And then of course Jean had the Ollie thing too, to hold over Avril—'

'*Evie!*' warned the duty solicitor.

'What about the expensive presents? The car? The yachts?'

'None of that would be enough to keep them all in the style they wanted.'

'Tell me about the bottle of Bushmills Thomas got hit over the head with.'

Evie sat back in her seat. She was grinning, as if at some private joke.

'What, Evie?' prompted Romilly.

'All right. I don't see what difference it makes anyway.'

'*Evie*,' said the solicitor sharply.

'All the gang covered for her. Which of course gave Jean yet *more* dirt to hold over them all. So, big wow. It wasn't Avril who hit Dad with the bottle. It was *Ollie*.'

# 100

# DAY SIXTEEN

Ruby phoned Declan.

'This is good,' he said. 'You phoning me instead of playing so hard to get. I like it.'

'Shut up Declan. Just answer the questions I'm going to give you, okay?'

'I like this. Sort of dominatrix style. Go on then.'

'Gilly. I saw a grey-haired man coming down the stairs when I was in her Duplex.'

'Oh, the football manager? Yeah, she gets through them fast, our Gilly. She's onto the next one now. This one has a Citation jet of his very own, that's right up Gilly's street.'

'All right. Who is he?'

'Well . . .'

'Declan! I'm not playing twenty questions here. This is serious. Tell me who the fucker with the Citation jet is, *right now*!'

'Hmm. I like this rough approach. It's sexy.'

'Declan . . .'

'He's mega-rich of course.'

'I'm warning you . . .'

'Mega-rich and in aggregates. Owns a couple of mines. Therex, you know that name? That's one of his.'

'And . . . ?' The name was creepily familiar. Therex. Hadn't *Daisy* mentioned that name?

'It's Sir Bradley Collins.'

# 101

# DAY SIXTEEN

Daniel drove Daisy to Tythe Manor. The house was situated on the edge of a tiny rural hamlet in an area of outstanding natural beauty. The summer light was dying, displaying a spectacular peach-gold sunset that told of a fine bright day tomorrow.

For Daisy, tomorrow hardly mattered. The twins were missing, and they were missing with Bradley, and if everything Vanessa had said was true then Bradley was not himself. He'd been known to keep a dog or two, but farm animals? Pygmy goats? It didn't seem likely. Bradley was often in town or at his quarries, and that would mean that someone would have to be hired to care for any animals he kept at the house.

*Matt and Luke were with him.*

Her mind kept creeping toward the facts, then recoiling in horror. Fact: Thomas Knox, blown up in his car. Fact: Fats dying the same way, from an explosive device that had been intended for Kit. Fact: Ruby's club, destroyed.

And there was more. The graves. Simon's grave was H152. Now they knew that the grave right next to it, H153, was Lady Susan's, who was recently dead. And with her death, maybe something had flipped in Bradley's brain.

*And he had the twins.*

By the time Daniel parked the car outside the big electric gates of the Manor, Daisy felt like shrieking.

*Just let them be all right,* she thought in desperation. *I know I haven't been a great mother, but please, just this once, do me a favour, God, let them be all right. Let this all be a horrible misunderstanding. Let there be pygmy goats, let Matt and Luke be in there, playing with them, putting them to bed. Please let Bradley not be crazy.*

She was out of the car even before Daniel slammed on the handbrake. She ran to the solid wooden gates. Huge, tall, imposing. And closed. There was an intercom beside them, set to the left of the sign announcing Tythe Manor. She ran to it, pressed ON.

'Bradley? Are you there?'

No answer.

Daniel came up beside her. 'Nothing?' he asked.

'Bradley! It's Daisy! Are you there? Are the twins with you?' she shouted.

In the distance, a dog began to bark.

Daisy stepped back. 'No answer,' she said, looking up at the gates, looking left and right. Inch by inch, the light was fading. Soon it would be full dark. A summer night in England. Beautiful. Soft, not cold. But still, she shivered.

Daniel moved off along the wall to the left of the gates, looking up. It was six feet high, solid. He took a run at it, levered himself up onto the top; looked up at the manor house. Dropped back down.

'No lights on up there,' he told her.

'Where the hell is he? What's he done with them?'

'Nothing, I'm guessing. He's their grandad, right?' said Daniel. He said it, but he didn't believe it. He'd seen people lose it before; sense went out of the window. And very often – this was absolutely true – very often the victims of such catastrophic breakdowns were close family. That was something he could *never* tell Daisy.

'Come on,' he said, and went to the wall and cupped his hands.

Daisy didn't hesitate; dressed ready for action in jeans and a shirt and trainers, she put her foot up and Daniel boosted her onto the top of the wall. She twisted and fell down the other side, into scratchy shrubbery, but she barely felt it. She moved away. Presently, Daniel came over the wall after her.

A large expanse of lawn opened up in front of them. Up on a steadily sloping hill stood the house; eighteenth century in parts, sixteenth in others, its outline looming impressively against the evening sky. Up there, stars were winking on. Night was coming in.

Daniel took a Maglite torch out of his jeans pocket, flicked it on to light their way.

'Come on then,' he said and led the way up the lawn, toward the house.

Daisy followed. She felt breathless with fear. 'Do you think I'm a bad mother?' she asked him as they strode up to the house.

Daniel was silent.

'Hello?' Daisy demanded.

'You're not a bad mother. You've been through hell this past year and losing Rob made you a bit crazy. So Vanessa had to take over with the twins, didn't she. And Ruby. You sort of took your eye off the ball,' he told her.

'I *am* a bad mother,' she gasped out.

'Daise—'

'I told you before, *don't* call me that.'

'Because Rob did. I know.' Daniel stopped walking all of a sudden, sending Daisy careening into him. He grabbed her arm. 'Look. Daise. *Let him go.* You're doing yourself no good. He's gone. So let him rest for God's sake. Let him go and move on.'

*To what?* she wondered.

'Come on,' said Daniel, and was off again. Soon they were up against the house wall, peering into windows as blank as blind eyes. There was no movement, anywhere. They walked all around the place, hammered at the front door and then the back. They looked for pens in which these 'pygmy goats' might be kept. There were none. There was a workshop, a garage where a ride-on mower was stored, and some tools. No animal pens whatsoever.

They were back at the front of the house, looking down the driveway, wondering what the hell to do next.

'Let's go back to the car and I'll phone Kit and Ruby again. And the police,' Daisy was saying, and Daniel was thinking that each or all of those plans would be a damned good idea.

That was when they saw a wash of headlights from a car, spearing up into the navy-blue sky, down beyond the big wooden gates at the bottom of the drive – and then the gates started, very slowly, to open.

# 102

# DAY SIXTEEN

The car sped up the driveway and screeched to a stop. It *had* to be Bradley and the twins. She'd been stupid, letting her imagination run away with her . . .

But it wasn't. Instead, two men got out – one older, the other a man in his twenties who'd been driving. He looked pugnacious: ready for trouble. He'd left the headlights blaring, pinning the two interlopers there like convicts caught against a wall, escaping.

'What the hell are you doing?' asked the older one, a nervous tremble in his voice.

Daisy held up a hand. 'We're looking for Sir Bradley Collins.'

'You came in over the wall,' said the younger one accusingly. 'Chap from the village was walking his dog, he saw you and phoned.'

'We don't mean any harm. We're trying to get in touch with Sir Bradley. That's all,' said Daniel.

Both men eyed him up, the younger one clearly well up for a confrontation if it was called for. The older one looked less sure. Daniel, after all, was built on a frightening scale.

'Look,' said Daisy. 'I'm his daughter-in-law. I was married to his son, Simon. I'm concerned about him. He has my sons with him. They're twins. Matty and Luke. That's why we came over the wall when there was no answer from the house. We're worried.'

Something in her cut-glass accent settled the two men.

'Is there a housekeeper? Maybe she has a place on the grounds?' suggested Daniel.

Both men shook their heads. The older one said: 'He sacked Mary Porterville from the village months ago, she was very upset. She'd been cleaning the Manor and running the household for him ever since she was a girl. Always did a grand job. It hurt her feelings something awful.'

'Do you have a key to the house?' asked Daisy.

'I do,' he said. 'I never use it, though. I see to the gardens and all the outside. Never go indoors.'

'Do you have the key on you now? Is there an alarm system? Do you have the code?' asked Daisy desperately.

'Far as I know, I don't think there's an alarm.'

'You could be anybody,' said the younger one, not willing yet to let it go.

'No. I'm Daisy, and this is Daniel. All we are concerned about is finding Sir Bradley and my boys. That's all. We're not here to rob the place.'

The younger one didn't believe it. His mindset, they could see, would always veer toward the bad.

'Do I look like a house thief? Seriously?' demanded Daisy.

'Come on,' said the older one, seeming to make his mind up. He fished out a massive key and placed it in the lock of the big iron-studded door. It swung open and he reached inside and turned on the lights. A large many-branched chandelier lit up, illuminating a dusty wooden floor, big paintings of sailing vessels on pale green walls, a hall table littered with crumpled papers, bunches of keys, inches of dirt. No alarm system in evidence.

And clocks, many of them. A huge grandfather clock, and others, lined up on every available surface, all going *tick . . . tick . . . tick . . .*

It would drive you mad, that noise, thought Daisy.

Stuck in here all alone, had Bradley wound these clocks and listened to their endless ticking and slowly lost his mind?

The two men led the way further into the house, the older one clearly believing their story, the younger one still watching them with suspicion. Ignoring them both, Daisy set off along the hall and opened the first door she came to, flicking on the lights. It was a sitting room, and it looked as if a troupe of monkeys had passed through, ransacking it. Every surface was filthy. Untidy piles of old newspapers were stacked all over the place. Dirty plates with half-eaten food and half-full glasses were strewn over ever available space, even on the floor. Flies buzzed and batted themselves against the closed, smeared windows. Dead bees lay on the windowsills. It *stank* in here, of dirt and despair and neglect.

'Christ,' said the younger man.

Above the empty fireplace, set upon the grey and black Italian marble mantlepiece, were cards; some open and upright, others unopened, many of them black-edged; cards of condolence. Daisy moved closer. Picked up a card.

*In Deepest Sympathy,* she read.

She picked up another.

*Sincere Condolences on Your Loss . . .*

And another.

*Thinking of you in your Hour of Grief . . .*

She replaced the card, brushing dust from her hands with a shudder. He'd been here, all alone, and his wife had died and he had received these cards and not had the strength or will to even finish opening them all. He had just sat here, day after endless day, and his mind had wandered to thoughts of revenge. To thoughts of Daisy and her family, Daisy who had driven – so he thought – Simon to suicide, to a despair that had finally claimed not only Bradley's son but also his wife too.

'I don't think he's been well,' said Daisy faintly. Massive understatement. She looked around and admitted to herself that she saw a room representing the shallow shores of insanity. Whoever inhabited this place had ceased to care for themselves, utterly. She thought of the Bradley she'd known, the high-powered businessman, father of Simon, husband of Lady Susan, visibly proud of his many accomplishments, boastful of his achievements.

This wasn't the same man.

This was someone of the brink of madness.

*And he had the twins.*

There was a writing bureau placed up against the wall between two of the huge, deep sash windows. She imagined Bradley sitting there, sometimes gazing out over his considerable acreage, at other times penning notes; there was a large picture of an aggregate quarry set above the desk, a phone upon it. Notes, scraps of paper, what looked like a diary, an overflowing waste basket. A big burgundy leather blotter. Pens. Biros with Therex Mining Corporation Limited gold-blocked onto their sides.

She picked up the diary, opened it and saw not what she'd expected – comments, appointments, reminders – but scrawls, endless scribbles and, over and over again, jagged-edged circles. In two of the circles someone had written BOOM!

'Oh God,' she said faintly.

'What?' asked Daniel.

She handed him the diary. He thumbed through it. At the back, he found some intelligible pages. He read, then passed it back to Daisy to read.

*I love clocks. You set a clock correctly and what is supposed*
*to happen does happen, right on time. It isn't unpredictable,*
*time, not like people, not like those people who have*
*dragged my loved ones into the sewer alongside them.*
*But there is comfort in revenge. And it's almost here at last.*
*The time has arrived.*
*The clock ticks on. Soon it will tick no more.*
*Then . . . BOOM!*

# 103
## DAY SIXTEEN

Romilly Kane was just getting ready for an early night. She was tired and headachy; she'd just stepped out of the shower and her brain just *wouldn't stop*. The case. Operation Game. The quarry. All those bickering women who'd been married, one after the other, to Thomas Knox. The car blowing up on Ruby Darke's driveway . . .

She sat down on the bed and tapped her fingers on the mattress and looked over at the clothes she'd worn today, slung carelessly over an old Victorian nursing chair that Mum had foisted on her. Her jacket, thick with dust, was on top. Poking out of the pocket was the laminated sheet James Birdsall had given her.

She went over, picked the sheet up, looked at it. Something bothered her about it. She read through the safety instructions again.

*Blasting professionals must comply with a range of national and provincial laws . . .*
*Wind direction, temperature inversions, cloud cover and geologic conditions (such as soil type, bedrock, water table level, freeze/thaw conditions . . .*

It all meant very little to her. She sighed and looked at the heading. Therex Mining Corporation Limited. And the board of directors, all listed there, eight of them: Ian Carthew, Toby Smith, Kieran Stringfellow, Fabio Danieri, Colin Barton, Sir Bradley Collins . . .

She stopped reading.

Bradley Collins, on the board of Therex. Something about . . . she clutched at her head . . . something about a Citation jet. Kit phoning, telling her something about Gilly Taylor-Black who was – yes – moving on from the football manager and going on to someone who would appreciate her more. Who absolutely adored her. The man the police watchers had seen going in and out of her place – the man they had named as aggregates magnate Sir Bradley Collins.

Was that the same Bradley Collins whose son Simon had once been married to Daisy Bray, now Darke?

And now the damned phone was ringing. Irritably she went across to the bedside table, snatched it up.

'Yes?' she barked out.

'Romilly? It's Kit.'

'What do you . . . ?' Instantly she was annoyed, remembering what Evie had said. 'Is it true you took that little nut job Evie out for a drink? Are you mad? Or is that how you get your kicks, seducing stupid girls?'

'*What?*' asked Kit.

'You heard!'

'You're talking rubbish. I bought her a Coke one lunchtime at Maggie's behind Kensington Palace, that's all, and asked her a few questions.'

Romilly took a breath. 'Oh.'

'Yes, "oh". And we got more to worry about than all that shit.'

'Yeah we have. Sir Bradley Collins, who's on the board of Therex Mining Corporation Limited. Isn't he your sister's father-in-law from her first marriage?'

'Yes he is. Look, I think he killed Thomas Knox. Killed Fats. Blew up Mum's club. I think it's all to spite us. The Darkes.'

'What . . . ?'

Daisy's just been to his house and she called me. He's off his head. Left a diary there detailing what he's going to do.'

'Which is . . . ?'

'He's going to kill himself at the Therex quarry and he's taking Daisy's kids with him. Get your lot out there. I'm on my way now.'

The line went dead.

# 104

# DAY SIXTEEN

Luke didn't like this game. He didn't like being here in this blasted-out tunnel, it was spooky. It was cold. The shingle stuff slithered about under his feet so that several times, dragged along at Grandad's hectic pace, he almost fell. But Grandad Bradley had a tight hold of his hand and he couldn't break free. He was scared to break free, actually. If he ran off, what about Matt? Would Matt run too? Because if Luke ran alone, he could get lost. It was dark, as dark as anything he had ever seen, darker than night-time in his bedroom. The only light was on Grandad Bradley's helmet, flickering here and there, scudding over walls of pale twinkling rock. Beyond that little cone of light there was nothing but blackness and that scared Luke. He was afraid of the dark. In his room, his cosy little room, there was always a dinosaur night light, the door ajar so that the landing light could be seen. He knew it was babyish, but he was nervous in darkness. Matt was bolder and teased him about it.

And now Grandad Bradley had done something, primed something, he said, and Luke didn't know what he meant but there was a little box and a clock attached to the wall at a height of about three feet, and now, now Luke could hear it ticking and he knew it was not a good sound.

That was spooky too.

Tick . . . tick . . . tick . . .

He could see a face on the thing, could see a second hand moving. Yes, it was a clock, he was sure of it. What would they want a clock for, here, under the ground that seemed to almost press down, horribly, on their heads?

He asked Grandpa about it.

But Grandpa didn't answer. He just sat down in the dirt beside the thing and told them to sit too. They did.

'Is something going to explode?' asked Matt, who was always the first one to figure things out.

'Enough with the questions,' said Bradley, and leaned his head back tiredly against the wall of the cave. He closed his eyes.

'I don't like it here,' said Luke.

No answer.

Just . . .

tick . . . tick . . . tick . . .

# 105
# DAY SIXTEEN

As Daniel drove, Daisy flicked through the notes in Bradley's diary by the light of the Maglite torch. It made for hideous reading.

*It started with a phone call. I hate phones, they are bringers*
*of bad news. My son, Simon. My only son.*
*The call was from the police. And I would not,*
*could not, believe it.*
*'I'm sorry,' said the voice on the phone.*
*Sorry?*
*My son was dead. Not only dead but hanged.*
*He'd been found dangling from the rafters of the garage at*
*his Berkshire home. There was a note nearby,*
*a chair kicked aside. Simon had committed suicide.*
*And Susan, my beloved wife . . . she didn't take it well.*
*She was shattered, ruined by the news. So it fell to me to go*
*to the morgue and identify his body.*
*I've never wept in my life, but when I stood there looking*
*down at my boy's still, frozen face, tears poured out of me*
*like rain.*
*'Is this your son sir?' asked the detective.*
*'Yes. It is.'*

*It was a nightmare. My son dead on a slab. And the future? The future was finished. Everything was gone.*

Daisy looked up at Daniel.
'What?' he asked.
She couldn't answer. He drove on. She read some more.

# 106

# DAY SIXTEEN

*Susan was too upset to go to Simon's funeral. I stood alone*
*at the graveside, shivering with shock, stayed there as they*
*filled in the grave, placed a little metal tag upon it among*
*the flowers. H152. My boy, reduced to a number.*
*I drove home, went into the house. The clocks ticked on.*
*I went upstairs to find fresh horror. My darling Susan was*
*comatose, spread across the bed. She'd overdosed. I phoned*
*the ambulance, stayed with her. But although she lived,*
*I lost her that day. She never truly recovered.*

'Oh Christ,' said Daisy.
'Bad?' asked Daniel.
She could only nod and read on.

*Susan managed to try to kill herself three more times. Then*
*the doctor recommended a full-time nurse. But not even a*
*trained professional could cope when someone was deter-*
*mined to die. Simon had been Susan's everything. And*
*with him gone, she saw no reason to carry on living.*
*An institution, suggested the doctor. Seeing no other possible*
*solution, I agreed and had my wife, my Susan, committed.*
*I visited her every week, showed her pictures of work I was*

*involved in but all she ever gave me was that terrible vague stare.*

*I had to admit it to myself. The instant Simon was gone, Susan was too.*

# 107

## DAY SIXTEEN

*She was bright, Susan. Somehow she hoarded her meds.*
*She wanted out of the world. Couldn't take the pain of it.*
*And so, when the call came from the institute*
*I knew what was coming.*
*'I am so sorry,' said the voice on the other end of the phone.*
*I could have sued them. Negligence. But what would it prove,*
*what would I gain? My life is empty now. A wasteland.*

Daisy stared down at the words. Feeling the heartbreak in them. Shuddering at the pain they so clearly conveyed.

'What does he say in there?' asked Daniel.

Daisy could barely think, let alone speak. And oh God, he had the boys. She blinked as hot, panicky tears blinded her. The words blurred. Her hand trembled, but somehow she held the torch steady, and read on.

# 108

# DAY SIXTEEN

*The tag on Susan's grave is H153, right next to Simon's.*
*And this is horrible to say, but after her death I did feel a*
*kind of relief. No more suffering for her. And me? I went*
*out. Played golf. Had sex sometimes.*
*I was free, but for what? I couldn't seem to function – can't*
*seem to function or care about very much, except the enormity*
*of my loss and the need, growing stronger every single day,*
*that eats at me, chews into my soul. The need for revenge.*
*The clock is ticking down the hours, the minutes, the*
*seconds. Soon, for them, the time will run out. And I will*
*be glad. The Darkes caused this, the deaths of my wife, my*
*son. That mad bitch Daisy and her whore of a mother and*
*Thomas Knox who had assisted the Darkes in their fight*
*against the Danieris, who were my friends.*
*Fabio is my workmate, co-director on the board of Therex.*
*He has been so sweet, so sympathetic, over my awful losses.*
*'Oh my poor old fellow,' he says. 'Such a tragedy.*
*If there is anything at all that I can do to help,*
*you must tell me at once.'*
*Fabio is my dear friend. Fabio has a little island out in the*
*Indies and there sometimes I go to relax. I allow myself to*
*be comforted there and in London by that red-haired siren*

*Gilly, who reminds me somehow – just a little – of my own
dear Susan.
So yes, I have friends. Useful people. And a thirst for
vengeance. The Darkes will pay, the same way I paid – in
pain, in anguish, in desolation.
For me? The suffering is nearly over.
For them?
It's only just begun . . .*

'Anything?' asked Daniel.

'Just . . . for God's sake, hurry,' said Daisy, and flicked
off the torch.

# 109

# DAY SIXTEEN

Daisy and Daniel were the first ones to reach the entrance to the Therex Mining site. There were large side-lit black-painted metal gates barring their way. On one of the gates a four-by-four sign announced the company name, stark black on orange. Leaving the engine running, Daniel got out, had a look, shook the damned things. He peered beyond but could see very little except huge scars in the earth, massive lorries parked here and there; a dark outline of a car against paler soil, but was that just a cliff shadow, or his imagination? Apart from that, nothing; no movement, dead silence.

'Solid,' was his verdict when he got back in the car and strapped his seatbelt back on.

'What the hell do we do now?' asked Daisy, unable to keep the tremble out of her voice.

'What car does he drive?' asked Daniel.

'He used to drive a Merc. Got a new one every year.'

'Black?'

'Dark blue. I think. The last time I saw him, anyway. Years ago. But who knows now? I shouldn't have let this happen! I should have kept in touch with him, shouldn't I?'

But Daniel knew that Daisy had been going through her own type of hell, at least for this past year. Losing Rob.

Nearly losing her mind over it. He knew she'd been glad of Vanessa's unstinting support with the twins, taking a huge load off of her shoulders; and maybe Vanessa had found the whole thing too much on her own – or at least with no one to help but Ivan – and when Bradley had approached, she had been all too pleased to take whatever help he offered.

But help? Bradley? No. That hadn't been on offer at all. He'd wanted to punish Daisy and had sneaked in sideways to do it. *This* was the result.

'Then that could be his car down over there,' said Daniel. 'Not enough light to tell. There's a Portakabin, but that's all in darkness.'

'So what now?'

'So get out of the car, Daise. Hurry.'

'What are you going to do?'

Impatiently he flicked open the catch of her seatbelt. 'Get out, Daise.'

Something in his tone galvanised her into action. She scrambled out of the car, slammed the door closed. Immediately Daniel put it in reverse and slammed it back across the road. Then he threw it into first and gunned the engine to a roar. The car shot forward and with a crack like thunder slammed into the gates, sending them hurtling into the air. They bounced free of their hinges and flew back, scurrying end over end, thudding to the ground beyond the fence line.

Daisy ran and got back into the car. The bonnet was dented, the windscreen crazed. They were blind now; impossible to see a thing through it. Daniel reached under Daisy's seat and drew out a hammer and smashed the remains of the windscreen away, while Daisy covered her eyes and cowered back out of the way.

Then Daniel threw the hammer down and accelerated, the headlights' twin beams lighting the way hectically ahead as they bounced and crunched their way over acres of shale and shingle and sped down into the scarred land-scape and – yes, there was a car. It hadn't been a shadow. It was not a navy blue but a black Mercedes, parked up by the entrance to a large opening, formed by many previous blastings. Here and there were massive boulders, scored with lines of drill holes, remnants of other explosions. Daniel stopped the car, slapped on the handbrake and left the engine running so that the headlights were trained on the entrance itself.

'Come on,' he said, and got out.

Daisy followed.

'*Matt! Luke!*' Daniel shouted.

'Bradley!' yelled Daisy. 'Are you in there?'

But the engine was running, masking any noise. Daniel went back to it, grabbed a bigger torch from the boot, reached in, turned the engine off. The headlights died but at least they could hear if anyone replied.

'Matt! Luke!' shouted Daisy.

Nothing.

'Oh Christ,' moaned Daisy.

'Matt! Luke!' yelled Daniel, training the powerful torch on the entrance. Maybe Bradley and the twins *weren't* down here. There was the office, the Portakabin, further up near the entrance, was that it? Were they looking in the wrong place? But this must be Bradley's car and it was right here. This *had* to be it.

'Matt! Luke!' shrieked Daisy.

And then, so faint it was almost imaginary, so faint it could almost not be real . . .

'*Mum?*'

It was Matt's voice. Quivering with fright.

'I'll go in,' said Daniel.

'I'm coming too.'

'No you're not.'

'Yes I bloody am,' said Daisy, and started forward.

Daniel followed, all too aware of what could happen now. That they were all in the hands of a madman. Bradley could kill himself and the twins and – if he really did have explosives in there – Daniel and Daisy too.

But what choice was there?

One way or another, he was getting those kids *out* of there.

With his torch lighting the way, Daniel grabbed Daisy's hand and they started into the blasted-out earth.

# 110

# DAY SIXTEEN

'Matt? Luke?' shouted Daniel as they moved further in.

The tunnel was sloping downward. This was like entering a chilly subterranean hell. It grew colder with every step they took, as they left the outer world behind.

'Matt? Keep shouting so we know where you are!' yelled Daniel.

'*Daniel?*' Luke's voice this time.

Then a deeper voice, masculine. Shouting something.

The torch was lighting the way ahead, but it was just more of the same: the glittering walls, the grit underfoot. Daniel glanced back at the entrance, saw the faint half-light there. Somehow, he had to try to keep his bearings down here. But it was damned nigh impossible. He could feel his skin crawling and although he tried to keep his mind off it, he couldn't help but focus on the fact that Bradley was down here too and might blast them all to hell at any second.

Ahead, the torch's light struck a solid, glittering wall of minerals in golds and blues and oranges, as the roof became more steeply pitched and the walkway turned right.

'Keep shouting!' he tried again, but he had a feeling that Bradley had somehow shut the twins up. He didn't want to think about how.

'Matt! Luke!' yelled Daisy.

No answer.

Daniel hurried on, around the bend in the tunnel with Daisy following. When he glanced back, he could no longer see that comforting little circle of dark blue sky at the entrance.

'You ought to go back,' he told her. 'Kit and the police should be here soon. You can tell them what's happened.'

'I'm not going anywhere,' said Daisy through gritted teeth. Her eyes when the torchlight caught them were frantic, panicky. 'What's he done to them? Why aren't they answering?'

'They probably just can't hear us,' said Daniel, although he didn't believe that. They'd been answering before. Why not now?

Another sharp turn. They crunched onward, grit underfoot, slipping and sliding. The roof was lower here, brushing the top of Daniel's head. That remorseless downward slope increased and the chill in the air of this man-made, blasted-out cave deepened, getting more extreme with every minute that passed. Another turn, another, and then, quite suddenly, there was Bradley – and the boys.

# III

# DAY SIXTEEN

'Keep back!' yelled Bradley.

Daisy couldn't remember the last time she'd seen him. Shameful, really. Her first husband's father, and she'd lost touch. If she hadn't done that, maybe this awful situation could have been averted. But it was too late now. By the vivid light of Daniel's torch she could see Bradley there, but he was a changed man: gaunt, pale and dishevelled. He was sitting there on the floor of the cave, his clothes dust-covered, his helmet alight but askew, his back against the rock wall, one twin on either side of him. Both of them had a strip of tape over their mouths. Of course they hadn't been able to shout.

'It's all right, boys,' said Daisy with an attempt at calmness. Even so, her voice shook. 'Grandad Bradley's not very well. He's upset. But we're going to sort all this out, right now. Everything's going to be fine. Isn't it, Bradley?'

He said nothing. His face twisted into a grimace and then a chilling grin as he stared at Daisy.

'He died because of you. My boy. He *died*. Hanged himself. Because of *you*.'

Daisy shook her head. She was looking at the wall to one side of where Bradley and the boys were seated.

*A clock . . . ?*

'That isn't true, Bradley,' she said, trying harder to keep the tremor out of her voice. A *clock?* She was aware of Daniel moving to one side. Trying to surprise Bradley? Get in closer to him?

'It is. It's the truth.' He sighed wearily.

'*No!*' insisted Daisy. 'I was there next day. The Danieri mob caught me in the road outside the house and they told me they'd killed him, set it up as suicide. The note was a *fake,* Bradley. Simon didn't kill himself at all. *They* killed him. And it had nothing to do with me, nothing at all. And so, you see, this has nothing to do with my boys, either. Simon loved them. I love them. You . . . you aren't well or you would remember that you love them too. And you would know that whatever you're planning to do, you can't possibly do it.'

The clock was ticking, loudly.

Daisy tried not to look at it, but she couldn't help it. The red casing. Red for danger. And the clock face . . .

*Oh Christ* . . .

The hands on the face were ticking down.

*Two minutes.*

Two minutes left, and it was going to blow, exposing a new seam of aggregates.

And the blast was going to take them all with it.

Away in the distance, out there in the real world and not this deep dark subterranean hell, a police siren was sounding. Coming closer?

She couldn't tell.

Couldn't seem to *think.*

Could only wait. And listen to the remorseless *tick* . . . *tick . . . tick . . .*

# 112

# DAY SIXTEEN

Kit drew the car to a halt just inside the perimeter of the fence, where once there had been gates leading down into the vast Therex quarry. The gates, one with a sign on, one not, were now nothing but useless lumps of twisted metal, lying here and there like toys dumped by a giant ill-tempered child.

Ruby, sitting in the back of the car, pointed ahead. 'That's Daniel's car down there. Isn't it?'

It was too dark to be sure. Not even moonlight to see by. There were two parked cars down a slope away in the distance, they could see that much. But no more.

Brennan, in the front passenger seat, unclipped his seat-belt and said, 'I'll check out the Portakabins,' and was out of the car and streaking away into the distance toward the faintly lit buildings.

Kit gunned the engine and drove the car on down the slope, past huge earth movers and diggers. He pulled up not far from what they could now clearly see was Daniel's motor. And then there were more cars and the deafening shriek of sirens haring full speed through the entrance at the top of the hill, blue lights flashing.

'Shit,' said Kit. He and Ruby got out of the car as Brennan came running down the slope and shouted, 'Nobody up in the Portakabin.'

*So where were Daisy and the kids and Daniel and Sir Bradley, who had clearly lost what little remained of his mind?* Kit wondered.

The police cars pulled up around them in a huge phalanx and in the massive glare of twenty headlights Kit and Ruby and Brennan stood there blinking. Romilly Kane emerged from one of the cars and strode over to where the three of them stood, near the entrance to what looked like a blasted-out cave. A group of uniformed officers followed her.

'What's going on?' she asked.

'Daisy reckons the kids' grandad's gone mental,' said Kit succinctly. 'I think they're in there. I think he did Thomas, and Fats, and Mum's club.'

Romilly took a step forward. Kit grabbed her arm. 'No,' he said firmly. 'It's too bloody dangerous.'

'Your sister's in there,' Ruby reminded him, her eyes frantic.

'Daniel's with her. He'll figure something out.'

He was going to give it a minute; just that, and then, dangerous or not – he was going in.

# 113
## DAY SIXTEEN

Daniel was edging to the side.

'Bradley, this is madness,' said Daisy.

*Keep him looking at you,* Daniel's eyes told Daisy.

'It's time you paid,' said Bradley with a ghastly smile. On either side of him, the twins stirred. Luke moaned and Daisy felt a surge of pure maternal fury. What would this do to the twins, to her precious boys? What damage was Bradley inflicting on them today that would echo down the years, haunting them?

*Tick . . . tick . . . tick . . .*

*One minute left.*

Daniel leapt at the older man, dropping the torch, grabbed him by the throat. The twins, suddenly released from Bradley's grip, crawled away, stumbled, *scrabbled* over to Daisy. Matt, ever the clear thinker, snatched up the torch.

Daniel, wrestling the writhing Bradley to the gritty floor, shouted: 'Get out, Daise. Get them out! I'll be right behind you.'

*But if we take the torch then Daniel's in the dark,* she thought. But there was nothing else she could do. She *had* to save the twins. She grabbed the torch off Matt. 'Take your brother's hand,' she said to Matt, and he caught firmly hold of Luke and the three of them raced off, up the slope to the entrance.

God, how far was it?

How long had it taken her and Daniel to come down into this cold hell?

She couldn't think. All she could think about was that massive *boom* that would kill them, peel the skin from their backs, snatch the air from their lungs, shatter their brains and break their bodies. They would die. And Daniel! Daniel was closer to the thing, he was right on top of it . . .

She could hear the two men back there in the dark, struggling, cursing.

She couldn't let herself think of that. She ran, dragging the twins with her, and it seemed like forever but suddenly she could see blue lights, she could hear the crackle of radios, and she was stumbling, falling out of that horrible hole in the ground and into precious fresh air again. Ruby was there and she was catching hold of the twins, starting to take the tapes off them as gently as she could, ushering them further away.

'It's going to blow,' Daisy panted out, nearly collapsing into Kit's arms. 'There was a minute on it, we have to get clear . . .'

Everyone heard what she said. The police started getting back into their vehicles, reversing quickly. Romilly caught hold of Ruby and dragged her away.

*Tick . . . tick . . . tick . . .*

And then, the blast.

*BOOM!*

# 114

# DAY SIXTEEN

The explosion was so immense that Romilly, Ruby and Daisy all fell to the ground. Debris and a huge cloud of dust billowed out. For a long moment there was unearthly silence and then Daisy shrieked, '*Daniel!*'

She clambered to her feet and started back. Kit grabbed her, held her still.

'Daniel's still in there!' she shouted in his face.

The twins were crying. Daisy grabbed them, hugged them, and now she was crying too. Unable to believe it.

'Oh God, not Daniel,' she groaned. 'Please no. *No.*'

Kit was looking grimly at the dusty gaping hole she'd emerged from. *Nobody* could get out of that. He didn't know how to tell her so.

Then – suddenly – there was movement.

'What the fuck?' he asked.

# 115
## DAY SIXTEEN

Someone was coming out of the earth like a living statue, coated in white; he was stumbling, choking, dust cascading off him. They all stood around, astonished, staring. Whoever had been near that blast should be dead now. But this . . . this looked like a living being, emerging from the rubble.

It *was* a living being, it was . . .

'*Daniel?*' croaked Daisy, choking on tears.

'Daniel!' yelled Matt, and he and Luke charged forward and threw their arms around him.

'Come on, come on!' Ruby was pulling the twins back. 'Give him some air, you two. He's all right, you see? He's all right.'

Daisy couldn't believe it.

She had been convinced, from the moment she'd left Daniel in there with Bradley, that he was a dead man. Romilly was bending down, talking to the twins, reassuring them. Kit was patting Luke's arm, peeling the last remains of the sticky tape away from his mouth, hugging him.

'You all right, big man?' he asked.

'Yeah,' said Luke. 'I'm all right.'

'Good. You're tough, yeah? Tough as iron.'

While all that was going on, Daniel stood apart, coughing, running his hands through his hair, trying to get the dust off his head and his clothes. Daisy stood apart too, six paces away from him, not yet believing he could really be there.

'You said you'd be right behind me,' she said accusingly.

He stopped coughing and looked at her. 'I was. I fell over in the dark and had to get my bearings,' he said.

Suddenly filled with inexplicable fury, Daisy ran at him and punched him hard in the chest.

'What the *fuck*?' asked Daniel in surprise.

She punched him again, and again, and again, until Daniel caught her wrists and held her still.

'Don't you ever, *ever*, frighten me like that again!' she yelled.

'Daise! I'm okay, see? I'm all right.' He was grinning.

'*Never* do that again,' she said, more quietly.

'I won't.' He put his arms around her, pulled her in close. 'Shush, you silly mare. I'm all right. I won't do it again. Okay?'

Becoming aware that everyone was watching this spectacle, Daisy in confusion broke free of his hold and stepped back, away from him. 'Good,' she said flatly. 'Just make sure that you don't.'

# 116

## DAY SEVENTEEN

There was, of course, very little left of Sir Bradley Collins. Closed in with so powerful a blast, he was reduced to nothing but bits and pieces of flesh, blood and bone. The police were all over it, and the fire brigade. The pathologist Derek Potts arrived, dapper as ever despite the lateness of the hour. The twins and Daisy and Ruby were ferried off to hospital in an ambulance.

Kit and Daniel were escorted to the police station where they were interviewed intensively into the small hours of the morning – not by Romilly but by two other members of her team. Daisy had passed Sir Bradley's diary to Daniel, and the police had that now to refer to. All in all, it looked as if Bradley had lost his mind after being subjected to devastating personal losses, and it was lucky, the police told them, that the body count hadn't been larger than it was.

When they were finally allowed to leave the cop shop, Ashok drove them home to Ruby's. On the way, Kit called Ruby on the car phone and asked how everything was going at the hospital.

'We're fine,' she told him. 'They're keeping us in tonight. I feel like I could sleep for a week, to be honest.'

'That's just shock,' said Kit.

'Daisy's in bits. Can't stop hugging the twins. And the poor little sods keep asking when Grandpa Bradley is coming to the hospital. Can't seem to get their heads around the fact that he's dead.'

'That's good. Hopefully they'll be able to forget the whole thing ever happened, in time.'

'You're right.' She sighed. 'Daisy keeps on about what a hero Daniel was.' She paused. 'I can't believe how bad it got for Bradley. How crazy it all made him. Who the hell would kill two little kids to get even with their mother?'

'Bloody Daniel was a hero. That's true. No doubt about that. And Bradley? Whatever his troubles were, they're over now.'

'That was odd, DI Kane turning up so quickly at the quarry,' said Ruby.

'I told her to get over there.'

'Kit.'

'No. Don't go there.'

Ruby paused. 'Please don't tell me that's started up again.'

'Listen—'

'It would be madness. You do know that, don't you? It would be dangerous for you. And fucking impossible for her.'

He knew she was right. 'Look, try and get some rest. I'll come and get you in the morning.'

'Kit—'

'No. Drop it, will you?'

Kit put the phone down, his mind full of nightmare images. It could have been so much worse. Bradley bloody Collins. A total nut job, but who was behind him, pulling his strings? Kit thought that he knew, damned well. Who but his fellow Therex board member and dear old pal Fabio Danieri?

Everywhere Kit looked, he saw evidence of that bastard in the mix. Fabio turning up at Gabe's funeral, Fabio behind Bradley's attacks on Thomas, on Fats, on Ruby's club. Fabio pulling strings, laughing at the Darkes behind their backs, stirring up trouble, convincing a sorry deluded wreck of a man that Daisy had been responsible for his son's death, when she had not. *He* had. And he had relished the pain he caused. He'd intended to do the Darkes maximum harm.

Well, no more.

*This* time, the position was going to be reversed.

As daylight dawned, Kit phoned Romilly and told her what was going on. Romilly received the information quietly, and then said: 'Does this make you a grass?'

'Maybe it does. Can't seem to feel bad about it, though.'

'But you'll get some sort of trouble because of it?'

She was concerned for him; he could hear it in her voice. 'I've already *had* the trouble. This is the final piece. The last bit.'

'Right.'

'Romilly—'

'No. We'll talk later. Okay? Not now.'

# 117

# DAY SEVENTEEN

Operation Game was in the throes of being tied up and finished. Statements taken. Reports written. Sir Bradley Collins had lost his mind and committed two terrible crimes – killed Thomas Knox and Kevin Norton – and another one that could have proved equally deadly; the destruction of Ruby's Soho burlesque club.

The team assembled at the station and one by one the witnesses to yesterday's catastrophic explosion at the Therex extraction business were interviewed, processed, sent home.

By late afternoon DI Romilly Kane was alone in her office, feeling – as usual – that the case had stripped ten years off her life. But it was done, and she was satisfied.

There was a knock at her office door.

It was DS Bev Appleton.

She came in, shut the door. Sat down.

'What a fucking fiasco,' she said.

'Say that again.'

'So what happens now?'

'I go home. Heat up a dinner. Watch the TV and try to forget the past two weeks or so ever happened.'

'I don't mean the case,' said Bev.

'Then what do you mean?' asked Romilly, although she knew.

'It's started up again, hasn't it. The two of you.'

'Don't know what you're talking about.'

'Yeah you do.'

'Bev,' said Romilly, standing up, gathering up her bag. 'You better leave this. I'm too tired to go into this, all right?'

Bev shrugged. 'I'm concerned for you. That's all.'

'Don't be,' said Romilly, and swept out of the office and away.

# 118

# DAY EIGHTEEN

The following evening, Daisy was back at the Bermondsey flat. The twins were already down in Brayfield with Vanessa and Ivan and she hoped – prayed – that they could forget what had happened with Bradley. After tomorrow, Daisy was going to join them there.

Currently, there were the usual waves of disapproval coming from Daniel, of course, and he insisted, also as usual, on ruining the séance mood by being in the room while Mrs Chamberwell conducted her business.

It was the same process as usual. The closing of the curtains, everyone seated around the circular table. The hot-fingered fat man was on Daisy's left, the woman with the cold digits on her right. The board was there, the glass ready. They all placed a finger on the glass.

Nothing happened.

Dimly, Daisy could see Mrs Chamberwell seated across from her, and she could *feel* Daniel's looming presence at her back.

*What if it's not Rob who comes through?* she wondered. *What if it's Bradley?*

The thought made her shudder. But Bradley was gone. No threat remained from him. She gazed up at the ceiling and thought *Rob. Can I ask you this? Can I?*

She could. She *had* to. And only then could she go on with her life, the life that had stalled the day he left her.

'Can I . . . ?' she asked.

'Was there a Nora here?' asked Mrs Chamberwell.

No Nora.

'I want to talk to Rob,' said Daisy.

The glass jerked. There was a startled cry from the woman on her right.

*B.*

A pause.

Then *Y.*

Another pause.

*E.*

And then, slowly, letter after letter, *DAISE.*

*Bye Daise.*

'Rob?' said Daisy, dry-mouthed, staring up at the dark above her, thinking *Are you there? Are you really there? Because I have something really important to ask you.*

But could she ask this out loud? Really? With all these people listening, with Daniel standing solidly behind her?

*Bye Daise.*

Rob was leaving her at last; wasn't that what he was saying?

Desperately she said: 'Rob? Is it okay?'

The glass jerked and was off again, racing over the letters.

*O.*

*K.*

Daisy stared up into the dark. *Was* he there? Did he understand what she was asking?

She thought he did.

She *hoped* so.

It was time, at last, to say goodbye. Her eyes filled with tears, but her heart was lighter, easier. It was okay. And he really was gone. She shoved her chair back, broke the circle.

'Come on,' she said to Daniel, and left the room.

# 119

## DAY NINETEEN

It was the day of Fats's funeral. A bright and beautiful summer's day, which seemed all wrong for the occasion. But it was a magnificent funeral, the best that Kit's money could afford. Red roses everywhere. The most expensive coffin. And a church service that included a choir, a lavish ceremony, speeches, a touching eulogy from a Norton cousin; no expense spared anywhere.

Afterwards, there was the wake at an exclusive country house hotel and then slowly the mourners dispersed, went slowly homeward, got on with their lives.

'What's going on then? You and him?' Kit asked Ruby as they went out to his car, where Ashok awaited.

'Me and who?' asked Ruby.

'You *know* who,' said Kit, indicating with a nod of his head Declan Knox, who was standing some distance away, chatting to one of Fats's aunties, his eyes intermittently flickering over to where Ruby stood.

'What, Declan?'

'Yes, Declan.'

'Nothing. He's very sweet,' said Ruby.

'Sweet? Fuck's sake.'

'Do you think Daisy's been behaving strangely?' she asked him.

'What, stranger than usual?'

'I mean, around Daniel.'

'What?'

'Daniel went out the other morning and she seemed sort of *frantic*. Asked me where he was. I told her. Then she asked me if he was going to be long. I said no. Then when he came back, she literally ran out of the room when he came in it. Actually *blushed* when he spoke to her.' She saw Kit's blank face. 'Oh, never mind.' Ruby offered her cheek. Her son kissed it. She was smiling. 'G'night,' she said, and walked off toward Declan Knox.

Kit turned away. Of course she was going to move on with her life now that Thomas was gone. But *Declan* . . . ?

Ah, what the hell. If she was happy? Then he was happy too. And anyway – they were probably no more than friends, united in their grief over Thomas's loss. That was all. They had all come through a whirlwind of emotion, these last few weeks. Now, all he wanted was to get home, and sleep.

As everyone got back in their cars and the evening drew in, Daisy kissed Ruby goodbye, and Kit, and then Daniel drove her down to Brayfield to join her kids.

'Do you think Vanessa's sorted out what I asked?' Daisy said to him as he ushered her into the back seat of the car.

'Vanessa? Probably not. But Ivan, definitely.'

# 120

# DAY NINETEEN

You tended to forget how beautiful Brayfield House was after a long absence. It had been in the Bray family for five generations and was built of glowing rose-red brick with cream stone quoins at the corners. The Elizabethan manor house was a precious pink jewel set in dizzyingly vast acres of green, with two outer gables and a smaller central one, with a lake, a mausoleum, and a high clock tower.

It was nearly nine and still daylight by the time Daniel drew the car to a halt beside the big circular fountain of Neptune at the front of the house. The twins must have been waiting for the sound of the car, because the instant it stopped and Daniel switched off the engine they were out of the double doors of the house, hurtling down the steps.

Daisy just had time to get out of the car and then they were on her, hugging her, shouting some nonsense about goats. She was so pleased to see them. It had been an awkward journey down, she hadn't known what to say to Daniel and he wasn't a great speaker, so the silences between them had been painful. But even that was better than when he wasn't near. She was finding, more and more, that if he wasn't close by then she felt lost. Unsteady. Which was crazy. Wasn't it?

*Oh Christ,* she thought, getting flashbacks. Bradley. The damned goats. The lure he'd used to get her boys to the Therex site, to *kill* them. And Daniel, emerging, alive. She'd been *sure* he was dead.

Vanessa came down the steps.

'For goodness' sake, boys, come on. Let your mother at least get through the door. Hello darling, how are you?' Vanessa asked, hugging her.

Vanessa herded up the twins. 'Now inside, the pair of you. Shoo! Go and see Ivan, he's in the kitchen making the hot chocolate.'

They ran off. Daisy watched them out of sight.

'I was worried they weren't going to be all right,' said Daisy. 'After – you know – after Bradley.'

Vanessa linked an arm through Daisy's as they walked up the steps. 'They talked about it. For a while. And then they seemed to just let it go. Don't worry darling, I'll keep an eye on them.'

'It was horrific,' said Daisy, reliving in her mind the claustrophobic atmosphere in that enclosed place, the clock ticking, the fear, that *dreadful* fear, when Daniel hadn't come out of there, when she had believed him dead.

'It was, but darling, it's over. So sad, *tragic,* but it's done now and everything is all right.'

Daisy had to smile at that. Vanessa, ever the pragmatist. She admired this woman, the woman who had raised her for the early part of her life before she'd rediscovered her birth mother, Ruby.

'You're in your usual room, I've put Daniel in the Rose Room, all right?' she chatted on as they walked into the vast high-ceilinged hallway.

The Rose Room was right next door to the room she'd occupied when she was growing up at Brayfield. The Rose Room, the Garden Room, the Blue Room – there were twenty-odd bedrooms in the house, Daisy couldn't remember precisely how many, each with a chintzy name, each one with a strong colour theme. Daisy could hear yells and laughter coming from the downstairs kitchen while Ivan fixed the twins up with their hot chocolate. She loved it here. Felt safe here. Suddenly, she felt very tired. Felt the stresses of the past weeks fall away from her.

She thought of the séance. Of Rob's farewell.

*Bye Daise*

He was gone. And she was – at last – at peace.

There was only one thing left to do.

# 121

# DAY TWENTY

Daniel awoke to pitch blackness and with the awareness that someone had just come through the door of the Rose Room. Ridiculous room; all pink cabbage roses on the wallpaper, chintz furnishings, huge tasselled drapes. A woman's room, he thought, not a man's. He tensed, ready to move, ready to act, but he didn't sit up. No need to alert the intruder that he was aware of them. He could see the digital reading on the bedside clock blinking red: thirty-two minutes past midnight.

'Daniel?'

It was Daisy.

He sat up, reached over, flicked on the bedside light. A warm cosy glow drove back the shadows and there she was at the foot of the bed, wearing a purple satin dressing gown, her corn-blonde hair loose on her shoulders.

'Daisy? What's up?'

It had taken a lot of nerve to do this. To actually lay herself on the line and hope to God she wasn't going to be rejected, made a fool of. Now, seeing him sitting there, muscular, golden, so beautiful, his hair tousled just a little from sleep, she wondered at her own audacity. Did he sleep naked, like she did? She felt herself go limp with desire at the very idea.

*Do you know how much I adore you?* she wondered.

No. Of course he didn't.

She hadn't even known it *herself*, not until she'd thought he was dead and he had startled her by stumbling, very much alive, out of that hell-hole. Ever since then, she hadn't known how to act around him; she'd felt as giddy as a schoolgirl with her first crush.

*Daniel.*

For God's sake. This was mad. She had spent so long since Rob's death using Daniel as a whipping boy, sparring with him, arguing with him, giving him all kinds of trouble and it had taken *that*, the stark and hideous prospect of losing him, to bring her to her senses.

If this wasn't love, then she didn't know *what* the hell it was.

'I just wanted to say . . .' she stammered.

'Yes, what?'

'Just . . . thank you.'

'Thank you for what?'

'For saving me. For not losing patience with me. For just . . . being you.'

# 122

# DAY TWENTY

Daniel was staring at her, puzzled.

'Well . . . that's okay,' he said. Paused. 'Was that all? It's gone twelve.'

'No. It wasn't.'

'Well then . . . ?'

Daisy walked around the side of the bed. *Oh God,* she thought. He was going to reject her. Tell her she was crazy. But she had to do this. Couldn't possibly *live* without this.

She unknotted the sash on her robe. Paused. Then she eased it from her shoulders and let it fall to the floor. She stood there naked, exposed. He said nothing: did nothing. Just stared. Slowly, taking a deep breath, she lifted the covers, slipped under them, felt – shockingly – her skin touch his, which was cool, hard, so different to her own.

Yes – he was naked. She nearly groaned with sheer longing.

'Daise—' he said.

'I thought I told you not to call me that. And I know what you're going to say.'

'No you don't.'

'Say it then.'

'What the fuck are you doing?'

'Look, can you please not question this? It's just . . . God, I've been like a bitch on heat for days, ever since I saw you come out of there and I knew you weren't dead. It's mad. I *know* it's mad. You don't have to tell me.'

'I've thought about this,' said Daniel.

*God will you please stop talking? Will you please just touch me, you fool?*

'Oh. Really?'

'Dreamed of it. Ever since I was . . . oh, about fourteen I suppose.'

'Well, now it's happened.' She was getting annoyed. What was this? She was here, naked, in his bed, and all he could do was chat? This was a disaster! She scooted to the edge of the bed, stretched down to pick up her robe.

'Now where are you going?' He sounded almost amused.

'This was a mistake.' She was sitting on the edge of the bed, scrambling into the robe, standing up. 'I'm sorry to have disturbed you.'

# 123

# DAY TWENTY

'Daise,' said Daniel.

She was knotting the sash of the robe, looking anywhere but at him.

'What?' she snapped.

'Take the damned robe off, will you? And make it slowly this time. I want to see you.'

Daisy looked at him. He was smiling.

'This isn't funny,' she said.

'God, no,' he said on a shaky sigh. 'I know that. Take it off, will you? Before I rip the damned thing off you.'

'You wouldn't.'

Daniel caught hold of the sash of her robe and pulled. It came loose.

He leaned closer, opening the sides of the robe and taking a long, luxurious look at what he had revealed. 'Do you remember when you tried to drown yourself in Ruby's pool?'

'Of course I do.'

'And I pulled you out, stark naked.'

'I do.'

'I've never forgotten that.'

Daisy licked her lips. 'Daniel . . .'

'Hmm?'

'Touch me,' she said, and let the robe slither to the floor. 'Just shut up, will you? And touch me.'

# 124

# DAY TWENTY

She had intended, of course, to go back to her own room well before dawn, so that the boys would not find her in Daniel's bed. But they had made love well into the night and she'd discovered that Daniel was amazingly good at sex, astonishingly sensual, a real connoisseur, turning her this way and that, exhausting her, filling her.

He'd had to cover her mouth to stifle her cries when she'd come to orgasm; and in the aftermath of their lovemaking, Daisy, who was never a great sleeper, had fallen deeply, peacefully asleep – and now it was morning and Luke and Matty were crashing through the door of the Rose Room, waking them both up, and – *oh fuck* – she was in bed with Daniel and they were going to be horrified.

'Mum! Come on, breakfast is ready, what are you doing in here with Daniel?' demanded Matty.

'She was cold in the night,' said Daniel, trying not to laugh.

'Oh God,' winced Daisy, pulling the covers over her in desperation.

'Nanny Vanessa has blankets,' said Luke.

'Yes well your mum couldn't find them so she came in here with me,' said Daniel.

Then Vanessa appeared in the open doorway.

'Oh!' she said, her face eloquent.

'Oh God, is anyone else coming in here? Is Ivan going to arrive now?' demanded Daisy, squirming.

Vanessa was smiling, though. 'Come on boys! Your mother needs time to get dressed and washed up, and your breakfast is ready down in the kitchen, all right? Now come on.'

The boys hurtled out through the door and thundered off down the hallway, down the stairs, shouting for Ivan. Vanessa stood there and looked at Daisy and Daniel.

'Well?' said Daisy, making shooing motions. 'Do you think you can—?'

'May I just say something?' said Vanessa.

'Am I going to be able to stop you?'

'No. Just to say, I thought as much. Right from the first time Daniel came here, I could see a spark between the two of you.'

Vanessa went.

Daisy stared at the closed door in surprise.

'Time for round two?' suggested Daniel, stroking Daisy's back.

'No!' she said, laughing. She snatched up her robe.

'Is the shower in this room big enough for two?' he asked.

'No, but the shower in my room is.'

He grinned. 'Right.'

# 125

# DAY TWENTY

After breakfast, the boys led Daisy, Daniel, Ivan and Vanessa out into the grounds, right down the formal garden and there at the bottom, not too far from the trio of compost bins, there was a large high-sided pen, twenty feet by twelve. Inside were hay bales, water bowls, feeding troughs – and two adorable little pygmy goats, one grey, one chestnut, racing around their enclosure and calling loudly to each other.

'Whose is which?' Daisy asked the boys.

'Mine's the grey one,' said Matty.

'And mine's the gold one,' said Luke.

'Names?' asked Daisy.

'Goldie,' said Luke.

'Shadow,' said Matty, who had a taste for the dramatic.

'Aren't they beautiful. Are you pleased?' asked Daisy.

They nodded and Matty raced off into the pen and smoothed his new pet. Luke hung back, shyly taking Daniel's hand. 'Come on, I'll show you Goldie,' he said, and dragged Daniel off with him. Daniel sent Daisy a laughing glance as he went.

'He's so nice,' murmured Vanessa in her ear.

Yes. He was. 'I'm in love with him,' said Daisy. It was a simple, wonderful fact.

'That's good,' said Vanessa, smiling. 'I think he's been in love with you for years.'

Daisy looked at her in surprise. 'How did you know that?'

Vanessa shrugged. 'I just did. Intuition, I suppose. And I'm so pleased, darling. For both of you.'

# 126

# DAY TWENTY-ONE

'So,' said Kit. 'What's the deal?'

He and Romilly met up in a pub that evening, miles out from the centre of the London action, where there was no danger anyone could see them together and draw the right conclusion. Horse brasses on the walls, farming implements, wheelback chairs. A nice place, well off the beaten track. Separate cars. No Ashok. All very discreet.

Romilly took a sip of her orange juice.

'Well,' she said. 'Evie's in line for a custodial sentence.'

Big surprise. Kit felt a stab of sympathy for the poor little mixed-up cow, but really – running people over with a big motor, no matter what a screw-up you were because of all your family troubles? It just wasn't on.

'What about Fabio Danieri?'

'Oh now, that one's much more interesting. Your mate—'

'He's not my mate.'

She ignored that. 'Your mate Fabio is in very deep shit indeed.'

'Go on.'

'So – he finds a skeleton, the skeleton of his sister-in-law, and swears he's innocent of anything even when he's stood in the middle of Epping Forest burying the remains in three boxes? If you're innocent, why do that?'

'Because he thinks he'll be implicated?'

'He's implicated all right, up to his neck. Because there's more, much more, and much better.'

'Go on then.' Kit took a drink.

'He had a locket in his pocket – which he attempted to throw away but one of our guys stopped him in the act – which contains a lock of his hair. My guess?'

'The skeleton was wearing the locket?'

'You're no fun at all,' said Romilly, smiling. 'He's ranting and raving, saying that this Maria, his brother Vittore's wife, was obsessed with him, and he admits they did have an affair and of course that explains the romantic keepsake, but he didn't kill her, her husband did.'

'Is anyone in their right mind going to believe that?' asked Kit.

'Not on your life.' Romilly finished her juice with a satisfied smack of the lips.

'So he's going down?'

'For years! The CPS want to prosecute. They're certain of a hefty conviction.'

'What about the cousin he had sniffing around Daisy? That Luca character.'

'Vanished. Probably back in Italy by now, lying low.'

Kit drained his drink. 'Hungry?' he asked her.

'Curiously enough, no,' she smiled. There was a tinge of regret in that smile he didn't much like.

'I booked a room.'

'Thought you might.' She stood up. 'Shall we go up?'

'Romilly—'

'No. I don't want to discuss it, not tonight. Tomorrow maybe.'

# 127

# DAY TWENTY-TWO

Before nine next morning, she was up and driving away, back to her life. There was no time for discussion. They'd made love last night but there was a sadness in her that alarmed him. What he thought was this: Romilly Kane had just left him for the last time. And that was good, wasn't it?

Of course it was.

*Dangerous for you, madness for her.*

The echo of Ruby's words came back to him and of course she was right. Involvement with a copper? Watching every word, fearing every misstep that could take him down for a long, long time? Cause the loss of her career, the career she so loved and had fought for all her life?

No. She'd made her choice, he knew it. This business between them was putting his nerves on edge, and, worse, it was ripping her in half. It was *crazy*. So this was the end.

Back at the station, DS Bev Appleton was in, taking down the photos and facts and various scribbled bits of info from the board when her boss walked in.

'Operation Game, officially over,' said Bev. She gave Romilly a hard stare. 'Gawd, you look like I feel. Coffee?'

'Thanks,' said Romilly, and went along the corridor to her own little office, her kingdom, the place she always felt most at ease, closing the door firmly behind her.

She wasn't going to cry.

What good would that do?

She'd made her decision.

There was no more to be said.

Kit left the pub at eleven. He paid the bill, thanked the owner for a pleasant stay, went out to the car park and opened his car door. It was drizzling warm rain. The skies were dark, the atmosphere clammy, all of which reflected his mood. No Ashok, waiting patiently at the wheel, and for once he was glad of it. He didn't want to talk. Didn't even have the words.

*It was all for the best,* he thought.

Sooner or later, maybe he would believe that.

Then a voice behind him said: 'Hiya.'

He turned, thinking *Luca Romano*. The one that got away. Shit, there was a loose end that should have been tied up, tucked away.

But it wasn't Luca standing there.

# 128

# DAY TWENTY-TWO

Unexpectedly coming across Ashok in the kitchen of her Marlow home, busily spooning ground coffee beans into a cafetiere while he waited for the kettle to boil, Ruby did a double take.

'Ashok! Where's Kit?' she asked him.

Ashok shrugged. 'He said he had some business he wanted to do, and to come on down here.'

'Right.'

Ruby absorbed this. *Business? Or pleasure?* she wondered. She thought of that copper Romilly Kane but she didn't ask. Not her business. Not her concern. Her son was forever his own man, totally independent, and she had long since come to accept that. All their long years of separation might be over now, but they'd left their mark on him. He was as cool as Daisy was warm. Just a fact of life.

Nothing she could do about that now.

'He didn't say when he'd be back . . . ?' she asked.

'Nope.' Ashok filled the cafetiere. 'You want one of these?'

'Yeah, go on. Thanks.'

# 129

# DAY TWENTY-THREE

Welsh Joe's boys took Kit to the Bermondsey arches, dragged him inside, plonked him down in a chair, tied him to it so he couldn't move an inch, and then they left him there. The clock ticked on. Slowly, sensation returned after the beating they'd given him. His head ached. His ribs hurt. He urinated again and had to sit there in a pool of his own piss.

*Well, this is fucking annoying,* he thought.

His mouth was unbearably dry. Sitting for hours on end was painful. His muscles were cramping constantly, excruciatingly. He took in his surroundings. Metal pillars, concrete flooring. Leaks, here and there. Rust stains and tedious drips like Japanese water torture. The roar of traffic outside. The flutter of pigeons above. There was a long table at the side of the space, a baseball bat propped against it.

*Fuck.*

There was a big oblong window high up above the table. More pigeons fluttered and cooed outside there, high on a ledge. Free. He envied them. He saw the light start to fade and then darkness fell. It was sometime after midnight, he guessed – his hands were tied behind his back so he couldn't see his watch – when Joe and two of his boys came back, sliding back the metal doors, joking and laughing between them, triumphant when they flicked on the harsh blue-white fluorescent lights and he flinched, blinking in the sudden glare.

'Boyo! Had a comfortable wait then, have we?' boomed Joe, striding over to where Kit sat tethered like a sacrificial lamb.

'Fucking marvellous,' said Kit, having to cough to clear his throat.

'Thirsty I suppose?'

'Nah, had a drink yesterday morning.' He'd been in the situation before, after all. Remembered it vividly. Still had the scars. Tito Danieri standing over him with a red-hot poker. Beautiful golden-girl Gilda, lying dead. Michael Ward rescuing him, pulling his arse out of the fire.

There was no Gilda anymore. He'd lost her and now he'd lost Romilly.

Michael was long dead.

He was alone here.

He watched Joe walk over to the table, pick up the bat.

Fuck it. This was going to *hurt*.

# 130
# DAY TWENTY-THREE

'Thing is,' said Joe, coming over to Kit's chair with the baseball bat in his big meaty hand while his two boys lounged, grinning, over by the doors, 'the thing *is*, boyo, I was offended by your actions. *Belittled* by them, you know. Sort of played on my mind. I didn't like it.'

Kit looked up at him and smiled. 'Right,' he said.

'An apology would be nice,' said Joe.

'Go fuck yourself,' said Kit.

'There! You see, boys?' Joe spun around and addressed his two henchmen. 'That's the attitude I get when all I want is to be friends with the guy. You see? Dumb insolence.' He turned back to Kit. 'Well this is where all that ends. *This* is where you get down and kiss my boots, kiss my *arse* if I want you to, you got that, boyo?'

'Dream on,' said Kit.

Welsh Joe raised the bat, took aim at Kit's skull. 'You asked for this,' he pointed out.

*Sure did*, thought Kit, bracing himself.

Then there was a roar from outside and the doors caved in.

# 131
## DAY TWENTY-THREE

It was a grey souped-up Transit van, driven at speed, that pulverised the flimsy garage doors. Welsh Joe's two boys scattered, one of them limping, and as men piled out of the van the two of them very wisely scrambled out over the debris and legged it as fast as they could – leaving Joe standing there open-mouthed, the bat still in his hands, and Kit sitting there, tethered.

The men carried shotguns. Big beer-bellied men, some of them. Kit saw Pat Francis there, belligerent as a bulldog and twice as ugly in his vest and braces, and his two massive sons – and there was a skinny kid with big brown eyes with them, jumping down out of the van, a shotgun almost bigger than he was, held over his shoulder. Little Davey Francis, old ma Francis's youngest, her pride and joy. The one Kit had hauled out of here when Joe had been beating the crap out of the poor little fucker.

The two older Francis brothers grabbed Joe and ushered him into the back of the van, protesting loudly.

'Shut your *yap*,' said one of them, slamming the door hard on Joe's protestations of innocence. He kept yelling. One of the boys clouted the outside of the van, hard.

'You keep that up and I am going to get *very annoyed!*' he warned, and Joe subsided.

The young boy walked up to Kit's chair, took a good long look and said: 'You know you said I shouldn't tell Dad about Welsh Joe doing me?'

Kit nodded. Couldn't believe it. Little Davey Francis to the rescue! It was almost funny.

'Well, I told him,' said Davey. 'In the end I had to. After they done you in Soho, Dad was talking about having another go at you, so I *had* to tell him it wasn't you that done me over, it was *that* fat slob. Sorry about that. Dad's been keeping an eye on you – and Joe – ever since.'

One of the older Francis brothers produced a knife. He came over to Kit's chair and sawed through the ropes securing him there. Helped him, staggering, back to his feet.

Joe let out a holler.

'*Bastard,*' said Pat Francis, slamming a fist against the side of the van. Joe fell silent once again.

'You all right Mr Miller?' asked Davey.

'Yeah. I'm good.'

'We're taking over Joe's outfit,' said Davey, and there was something in those soft brown eyes of Davey's that told Kit the kid absolutely meant it and that he had seen the absolute last of big Joe Williams.

'Right. Good for you.' Kit was trying to get his joints working again. And Jesus, he stank. He needed a bath.

'You want a lift somewhere?' asked Davey.

'That would be great,' said Kit.

# 132

# DAY TWENTY-THREE

The case was solved and there was a party atmosphere in the office. Barry had brought in home-baked cakes. Bev had made coffee, they couldn't drink alcohol on duty. The DC's were sitting around, chatting – Fiona Batesy, Camille Porter and Tony Gutteridge – and DCI Barrow was congratulating the team on a job well done.

'He's in a good mood,' said Bev, as DCI Barrow left for lunch with the top brass.

''Course he is,' said Barry. 'He's about to be stroked big-time by the nobs. He loves that.'

They ate the cakes, drank the coffee. Romilly went back into her own little office and closed the door. She looked around at all the things she had accumulated over the years, commendations, praise; it all meant so much to her. Then she sat down at her desk and wrote.

An hour later, she slipped what she'd written into an envelope and took it along to DCI Barrow's office, which was still empty and would remain so, she knew, until late afternoon, when he would return, well-oiled and happy.

Then she left the building.

*

DCI Barrow was back and in a very good mood by a quarter to five. Everyone was pleased the explosives case had been put to bed. He was looking forward to an evening with his wife and his little girls. They were planning a picnic in the garden; he would fire up the barbeque and relax. It would be a nice evening. He picked up the letter on the desk. Neat writing. *DCI Barrow.*

He slit open the envelope and took out the letter inside. Looked at it.

The contented smile dropped from his face.

'*Fuck!*' he said out loud.

It was DC Romilly Kane's letter of resignation.

# 133
# DAY TWENTY-FOUR

Ashok opened the door at Kit's London house to Romilly Kane. He showed her into the sitting room, said he'd tell Kit she was here.

She sat down and waited, impatient. Wondered what the hell she was doing. DCI Barrow had read the letter now. He hadn't tried to contact her. Did that disappoint her? She thought yes, really. But also, the decision was made. She didn't want to chew it over again. She'd done enough of that over these past few weeks. The force would do just fine without her.

She heard movement on the stairs and Kit came into the room, closing the door carefully behind him.

'What are you doing here?' he asked.

'Charming.' She stood up.

'I didn't mean it like that. I meant is it wise? Coming here?'

'It doesn't matter anymore,' she said, and told him about the resignation letter.

Kit stared at her. Romilly stared right back, thinking that she had just made a fool of herself. Chucked away her career, the career she'd slaved for nearly all her life, and now the man she'd chucked it away for was looking at her

like this was unwelcome news. That she might want something more from him. That her ditching *that* was somehow
placing a weight on *him*.

'Look, it's okay,' she said quickly. 'I don't expect anything to change, I—'

'Shut up,' said Kit, and pulled her into his arms and
kissed her. Then he pushed her back, gazed at her face.
'Shut up, you silly cow. You shocked me, that's all.'

'You're sure?'

'I thought you were dumping me,' he said.

'What?'

'I knew you'd made up your mind about *something*. And
I thought it was me or the police, and the police had won.'

'Nah, they lost.'

'You're sure?'

'No! I'm not sure. I'm in turmoil here. Have I done
the right thing?' She was laughing but he could see she
meant it.

'What will your folks say?'

Romilly winced. 'Don't. I don't even want to *think* about
that, not yet. Can we just go somewhere, take a break or
something?'

'That would be good.'

Romilly cuddled in close to him. 'God, are we totally
mad? Am *I*?'

'Probably.' He thought back over these past few weeks.
Seeing her again. Getting that urge to *be* with her again.
Getting beaten up by the Francis mob, then rescued by
them. Three damned explosions! And what the hell had
happened to that bastard Welsh Joe?

Who knew?

Who cared!

420 *Jessie Keane*

He kissed her again. Romilly Kane. She was here, and so was he. This was good.

What else mattered?

# 134
## DAY THIRTY

It was perfectly clear to Ruby Darke that both her kids were crazy. Daisy was following Daniel around like a tame besotted puppy, actually *pining* when he wasn't there, and Kit had just taken off for the Maldives with DC Romilly Kane.

'She's resigned from the force,' he'd told her.

'She *lived* for that job,' Ruby pointed out.

'I know that. Now she don't.'

'Do you know what you're doing?'

'No. Probably not.'

Ruby herself was taking stock of the situation. A month ago to the day, Thomas had died and all this madness had begun. Now – somehow – they had come through it. Intact.

She thought of her club, gone.

Did she want it back, though?

She thought, on the whole, no.

The site would be cleared, but rebuilding? Restarting the business? She found she didn't have the will to do that.

She drifted. Shopped. Did nothing very much, really. Enjoyed leisure time, something she had rarely in her life ever had time for.

Life went on.

# 135

One late-summer day, when Mother Nature was taking her last graceful curtsey before succumbing to the ravages of autumn, Ruby got a call from Declan.

'Have dinner with me,' he said.

'That's a bad idea.'

'No, I think it's good. Have you considered the benefits of a younger lover, Ms Darke?'

'Declan, it's only been—'

'I know. I *know* that. But think of it. Far more tread on me, you know. More staying power.'

'For God's sake . . .'

'Too soon?'

'You're a callous brute.'

'Okay, too soon. Understood. I'll catch you later.'

He put down the phone.

And that, she thought, is *that*.

# 136

Ursula Grey was having a bad day. She walked into her bathroom one autumn morning – this room, like all the others, was all done out in tones of sapphire and emerald, all designed to flatter her own good looks – and she found *another wrinkle*, right there by her eyelid.

*Damn!*

She stared at her reflection in dismay, then patted face cream into the crease of this new – appalling – proof that she was growing older. She sighed. What Ursula wished was that she was more like Avril, who didn't give a shit what she looked like. She also wished that she was French: the French didn't care about a woman getting a little frayed around the edges.

But here she was, living in London. And who the hell – if she was honest – could afford London prices anymore?

Just yesterday she'd got another phone call from the agency. Another rejection. A cancellation of a long-standing contract. They wanted someone a bit 'fresher'. Which meant – yes – younger.

She showered, slathered herself head to toe in the too-expensive moisturiser she had always used but was going to have to *stop* using, of course. She was going to have to – she winced at the thought – trim her expenses. She went into the bedroom, opened the big, mirrored wardrobe doors and looked at the fabulous clothes inside. A few Vivienne Westwood pieces in there, exquisite, real works of art; she could sell them. She would *have* to.

She thought of all that had happened over this year. Her heart flinched. She *did* have a heart; people thought she didn't, but she did. And it was taking a battering. That one more wrinkle. That one more rejection. Bills, piles of them. Evie on remand and Ursula *knew* she wasn't blameless in her daughter's offences. She'd never really *done* kids, that was the problem. And Thomas hadn't either.

Thomas! Oh God. She didn't like to think of him, dead.

But she mustn't cry. Crease her face up even more. *Mustn't.*

She dressed meticulously, faultlessly, and looked all around at the dazzling photographs of herself. She stared at herself in the hall mirror. Ignored the bills piled up on the hall table.

Maybe when the courts were through with Evie and she had served whatever sentence they saw fit to throw down at her, maybe then they would take off together for Paris. Maybe life would be kinder there, rents cheaper.

*Maybe.*

The postman had been and with the usual shudder of misgiving, the usual clenching sickness in the stomach, she picked up the post from the mat. Circulars. Crap. More crap. And one very official-looking envelope.

She didn't want to open it.

She felt, in fact, that just one more slice of bad news would send her hurtling over the edge, that she might start to scream and never be able to stop.

*Ah what the hell.*

She opened it.

# 137

While Ursula fretted over funds and forced herself to confront the horrors contained in her post, Avril was getting a right royal bollocking off her accountant. She was so far in the red that she no longer quite knew what to do about any of it.

'Sell up,' said the accountant brutally. 'Liquidate your assets, clear your tax bills, problem solved.'

Hardly solved though. While the accountant droned on about her lack of financial acumen and the dangers of lurching from one crisis to the next, Avril found her eyes drifting to the window and to the view beyond. Mares and foals at foot. A long sweep of green, the low autumn sun peeping through, lighting it all up like a Stubbs painting.

*Beautiful.*

Truth was, she *loved* it here. Didn't want to leave it.

But she couldn't afford another stud stallion. Couldn't afford another load of winter feed. Couldn't afford, in fact, fuck all.

'The riding lesson idea's a no-go,' the accountant was telling her. 'Pays a pittance. And the insurance and the vet bills will cripple you.'

She gazed out at the view. *Her* view.

She didn't want any more brushes with officialdom, or the law. That idiot Tim had scared her badly with all that black powder nonsense. For a while she'd thought they would be implicated – seriously – in Thomas's death. The relief when she'd realised they were in the clear was enormous.

But now she was back staring her financial woes in the face, and – yes – she was going to have to sell up. Do something else.

But *what*?

She ushered the accountant out of the door at around eleven, snatching up the post from the mat as she did so.

Closed the door on him.

Pulled on her boots and crossed the yard, opening envelopes as she walked. Ollie was brushing down her placid little dapple-grey mare outside the stables and she looked up anxiously as her mother approached.

'How'd it go?' she asked, pausing her brushing.

'How d'you think? He wiped the floor with me. Not that there's much left of me to do that with.' Avril opened the thick official-looking envelope and stared at the letter it contained.

'Anything good?' asked Ollie.

'No, I . . .' Avril fell silent.

She read the letter.

She let out an ear-piercing shriek.

# 138

'It's a simple inflammatory reaction,' said the Harley Street surgeon while Gilly Taylor-black sat in his consulting rooms wondering how much this was all going to cost her.

Things were piling up on Gilly, one-time fourth wife of the late Thomas Knox. Debts, for sure. And other things. She sort of missed Bradley, who had – and this was crazy, unbelievable – apparently blown himself up at Therex and nearly taken a couple of Ruby Darke's grandkids with him.

Bradley had been nice to her. Sometimes, men were not very nice at all. And now her nose was . . .

'Mucosal bleeding, shortness of breath, nasal pain, crusting inside the nose . . . ?' The surgeon, the smooth bastard, was ticking these things off, one by one.

Gilly was nodding. *Oh yeah. All of the above.*

'Obviously the first thing is to stop using cocaine. Completely.'

It was like being in the headmaster's study at school. Gilly nodded dutifully. Well, she had to do that. *Had* to. Her nose was dissolving fast and the results were not pretty. So. No more nose candy.

'Do I have to point out how serious this can become? Vasculitis can develop. With extended cocaine use, a fistula can develop from the nose to the mouth . . .'

Oh God. She couldn't listen to any more of this.

Her nose was going to be rebuilt.

And the *cost*.

The cost would mean she would have to sell up everything she owned. Downsize. Economise. All those boring, horrible words she hated. She appealed to her father, but he cut off coldly. Then she'd tried tapping up a couple of her ex-lovers, but they hadn't been interested in bailing her out. If Bradley had still been alive, he might have reacted better. Been kinder. He had always been kind to her. But he was gone.

And Thomas was gone too.

Gilly didn't hear much more of what was said in this chic and expensive office. The plastic surgeon droned on, easily able to afford his high-end leather chairs, his Harley Street office – the rates must be frightening – and his Savile Row suits. When he'd finished, a chic receptionist booked her in for further appointments and smilingly handed her a card, but she took no notice of any of it.

She taxied over to The Ivy and had a drink. She needed one. Eyed up the prospects. Not many in today. And this was rather horrible, but she had noticed it, more and more – that male eyes passed her over these days, just skimmed right past her and fastened on the twenty-year-olds, the young honeys with thick glossy hair and intact, pert noses. The ones they could easily afford, the ones young enough to pique their jaded appetites.

She drank up and went home. Let herself in the front door and found the post on the mat.

One letter.

*Ah, what the hell. More bad news, no doubt.*

She picked it up.

She opened it.

# 139

Chloe Knox was leaving London, going back to Ireland. Her brother had invited her over to Dublin and she had accepted his invitation. Now she was sitting on the bottom stair and her suitcase was standing ready in the hall of Thomas Knox's Hampstead house. It had always been Thomas's house. She'd never thought of this place as hers. She wouldn't miss it.

All that had happened with Thomas – the explosion, the horror of that – was gone now. All the windows had been replaced, the driveway cleaned; it was as if he had never even existed.

Chloe had suggested to Nieve that she should come too, back to the auld country; but Nieve loved London too much to do that.

For Chloe, the gloss of London had long since worn off. Too many strip clubs, too many grabbing punters, until Thomas and a sort of safety – and then Ruby Darke, that bitch, stepping on her toes. And the bitter realisation that Thomas, with his gang of ex-wives and ongoing affairs, would never be completely hers and hers alone.

As she sat there, there was a clatter as the postman dumped a load of crap through the letterbox. She stood up, picked it all up. Holiday brochures. Care homes. The usual. And one thick envelope, official-looking.

She put the rest on the stairs but tucked that one envelope into her jacket pocket as the taxi tooted its horn
outside. She'd read it later.

Time to say goodbye.

She looked around the hall.

Nah, she wouldn't miss it.

*Bye Thomas.*

She went out of the door; went home. In the taxi, she
took out the envelope; read it. And then she started to
laugh – and cry.

# 140

'I didn't do it. I'm not guilty,' Fabio kept saying to anyone who would listen.

'That's what we all say,' said one of the other lags, smiling.

'But I'm *not*.'

Fabio was banged up for a very long stretch. He was appealing, of course. He would go on appealing, because this was a serious miscarriage of justice. He hadn't killed Maria. After a lifetime of lies, here he was, telling the absolute truth, over and over, while listening to metal gates and doors clanging shut, to lights out, to a nightmare.

'I didn't kill her,' he told his brief, the lags, the wardens, the governor, anyone.

'Of course not,' said his brief smoothly.

'Yeah, mate. We believe you,' said the lags, laughing.

'Oh do bloody shut up,' said the wardens.

'Keep yourself busy in here,' advised the governor. 'Don't annoy people.'

So here he was, in Parkhurst on the sunny Isle of Wight. Wearing shit clothes and eating shit food and cursing Maria every day and every night.

He *didn't* kill her.

But the trouble was nobody – *nobody* – believed that.

# 141

Mama Bella was wondering what on earth was going on. The police had come and hauled away . . . now which one was it?

'Fabio,' the nurse told her. 'They took Fabio away.'

'But he's coming back, yes?' asked Bella.

*Unlikely*, thought the nurse, not that she cared. She was helping herself to all Mama Bella's spare cash and spending it lavishly. Time passed. And then one day she stepped delicately over the dust sheets to answer the front door. Everything had been left since the cops had nabbed Fabio. The builders had scarpered, everything had ground to a halt. There'd been police tapes up in the hall, no one was allowed to go down into the cellar. Not that she wanted to. There'd been talk of something nasty being found down there, maybe a body. The place was a mess. And every day, without fail, Mama Bella asked when her boys were coming back home.

*Never*, thought the nurse.

But she was okay with that. She had the run of the place, threw wild parties whenever she fancied, had easy access to huge amounts of Mama's cash; she was happy.

She opened the front door. It would be somebody flogging some damned thing door-to-door. It always was. 'Yes?' she asked impatiently. 'What d'you want?'

A stunning woman of around thirty was standing there. She had close-cropped white-blonde hair and was wearing a short, white double-breasted coat and long, white leather boots. Slowly, she lifted her big Dolce and Gabbana shades and looked at the nurse.

'Who are you, *schifosa*?' she asked.

The nurse bristled at the woman's authoritative tone. And she had a feeling that she'd just been called something unpleasant.

'Who are *you*?' she shot back.

Mama came bustling up to the door. 'Maria?' she said anxiously. Then she stared hard at the woman in white, trawled the dim recesses of her mind and said, '*Bianca?*'

Bianca was her youngest child. Adopted. Much loved. She seemed to have been gone forever, but now she was back here, back home. Tears filled Mama Bella's eyes. 'Bianca!' she cried, and pushed the nurse roughly aside and grabbed the woman in white in a firm embrace.

'This is my daughter,' she gabbled at the nurse. 'She's come home!'

'I'm Bianca Danieri,' said the woman in white, staring at the nurse over her mother's shoulder. 'And you,' she said with a frosty smile, 'are fired.'

# 142

It had rather surprised Ruby, the gift Thomas Knox gave her in his will. The call from the solicitor, the visit to his office, had all passed in a disbelieving blur; but his pronouncement about the terms of the will was simple. Half of Thomas's entire estate – houses, businesses, savings, the lot – was to go to his son, Declan. And the other half to her – Ruby Darke.

'I've had a bit of a shock,' she told Kit over the phone.

Kit was down in St Kitts at the moment, with Romilly.

'What's that?' he asked.

'Thomas left me half his estate. The other half goes to Declan.'

'And what are you going to do with it all?' asked Kit, aware that they were talking millions.

'I've already done it,' she said, and told him about the letters that had gone out to the exes, the 'gang' – Ursula, Avril, Gilly and Chloe. 'So no more enforced Christmas dinners at Jean's place. No more emotional blackmail, dangling the carrot of a possible payout in front of them all. I think I've set each one of them free. I hope so, anyway.'

'Whoa, hold on. What about you?'

'I don't need Thomas's money. I've got plenty of my own.'

'The club?'

'I'm shutting it down.'

Kit paused. She could almost hear him thinking, considering the permutations of this event. 'And Declan? What's his take likely to be on this? Half what he thought he might inherit, coming to you instead? And then you passing it over to them?'

'Not his business. He can contest the damned thing if he wants to, but my guess is he won't. How are you down there? Having fun? How's the detective doing?'

'She's lying on a sunbed reading about a local murder and suggesting lines of inquiry.'

'Hard to switch off when you've been a rozzer for so long,' said Ruby.

'I suppose it is.'

'You're happy?'

'I am. How's Daise?'

Ruby laughed. 'Ecstatic. Completely obsessed with Daniel.'

'I never saw *that* coming. And what about you?' he asked.

'Oh – managing,' she said.

'You take care,' he said.

'You too,' said his mother, and rang off.

# EPILOGUE

'Buy me dinner,' said Ruby when Declan called on the phone. 'At the American bar at the Savoy. Eight o'clock, I'll see you there. You book it.'

Declan did.

She was waiting for him at the table, sipping chilled Bollinger, and she watched him come across the room. He was so like Thomas. The dirty-blond hair. The eyes. The tough-guy swagger he had about him. He sat down and the waiter poured him out a glass.

'I suppose,' said Declan, 'that I ought to congratulate you. And me too. The pair of us.'

'What, Thomas's estate? What are you going to do with your half?'

'Piss it up against a wall I expect,' he said with a grin. 'Invest some of it, maybe. Waste the rest on holidays,' he took a sip of champagne and his eyes played with hers, 'and hot women.'

Ruby clinked her glass against his and drank. 'Your mother's a monster,' she told him.

'I know that. Had all the gang dancing to her tune, didn't she. Christmas at home, with the Aga pumping out the heat until it feels like you're going to die of it, and her calling all the shots over the mince pies and the Yule log and the Queen's speech and all the rest of the shit she insisted on. Which will continue no doubt. They just keep waiting for the possible payout, the silly cows. It's not coming anytime soon.'

'Actually,' said Ruby, 'it already has.'

Declan stared at her. 'What? Explain.'

'What Thomas left me? I've passed it on to them. To Ursula, to Avril, to Gilly, to Chloe. They don't have to dance to Jean's tune anymore.'

Declan stared across the table at her. The waiter came.

'Give us a moment,' said Declan. The waiter withdrew.

Declan stared some more. 'Are you serious?'

'Deadly.'

'Why?'

'Because I understand what it is to be frightened, a woman, alone, coping without a man. I've done it all my life. Being tough; capable. But inside? Scared.'

He drank some more champagne.

'You and Chloe,' said Ruby.

'I told you about that. She came on to me and I was flattered. But almost straight away I could see it was shameful. A mistake. And I ended it.'

'So, have you booked a suite for tonight?' asked Ruby.

Declan choked on his drink.

'With a river view?' continued Ruby.

Declan recovered himself. 'Actually, Ms Darke,' he said, 'I have.'

'Good,' said Ruby. 'I warn you, I might cry. I said I would when all this sad business was finally over, and it is, so I might.'

'Okay,' he said.

Ruby smiled at him. A younger lover! How shocking and how absolutely *right*. The past was done and all that mattered, really, was *now*.

'And Declan?'

'Yes, Ms Darke?'

'I think it's time you called me Ruby.'

# ACKNOWLEDGEMENTS

To everyone who has helped in whatever way to get this book past the finishing post: bless you all.

Special thanks to the team at Hodder, to Judith Murdoch who spotted something in me all those years ago, to Wayne Brookes who just made me laugh and laugh, and to Jane Gregory.

More special thanks go to Emily Ould, Customer Services Assistant at Wheal Martyn, and to Steve Hawken, who answered my daft questions as best they could. Any factual or technical mistakes are entirely mine, not theirs.

Finally, to the friends I hideously neglect when I'm deep in the no-man's-land of writing a book. Sorry pals! All best to you & thank you for your patience.